A Fine
and
Private Place

A Fine and Private Place

Joanna Trevor

ROBERT HALE · LONDON

© Joanna Trevor 2002
First published in Great Britain 2002

ISBN 0 7090 7229 5

Robert Hale Limited
Clerkenwell House
Clerkenwell Green
London EC1R 0HT

2 4 6 8 10 9 7 5 3 1

To Liz again,
with love and thanks
for all the support and encouragement

Typeset by Derek Doyle & Associates, Liverpool.
Printed in Great Britain by
St Edmundsbury Press, Bury St Edmunds, Suffolk.
Bound by Woolnough Bookbinding Limited.

Unfriendly Flowers

Startled, the gardener learns to fear his art –
Seeing spring up, after long, loving hours
Of labour in the garden of his heart
The vivid, the metallic, the unfriendly flowers.

Martin Bell, *Complete Poems*, Bloodaxe Books, 1998

The grave's a fine and private place
But none, I think, do there embrace.

Andrew Marvell

CHAPTER 1

Red Catchfly – Youthful love

The scene was a quintessentially English one – the old Cotswold manor house, its golden stone glowing in the heat of a fine midsummer day, clipped topiary and bright herbaceous borders surrounded by emerald lawns neat as bowling-greens. And in their midst, incongruously, moved the tightly knit group of a television production team, backing slowly away from Helen Hartley as she moved twards them, speaking to the television camera and pausing regularly to fondle a rose and brush her hand over a bush of catmint.

Her voice was not a carrying one, and the intrusion into the scene from behind a nearby yew hedge of a squeaking wheelbarrow caused the whole team to switch their attention to the slight young woman who now came to a halt in embarrassment at the attention she had brought to herself. Looking too insubstantial to manage the weight of the barrow, and dressed in a skimpy black top and bright ethnic trousers, she was an attractive enough sight to hold the attention of the mainly male members of the television crew.

Helen, absorbed in her performance, was the last to notice the abrupt appearance of the intruder.

'I'm so sorry, Mrs Hartley,' the girl said. 'I forgot you were filming. I was going to ask you about changing the lavender plants in the urns at the front.' The wheelbarrow was indeed piled high with silvery-green shrubs showing early spikes of deep purple bloom.

'Couldn't it have waited?' Helen asked calmly, walking towards her.

'It was just that I've got a train to catch in Westwich at five. I'm going home for the weekend. And I knew you wanted this done. I just wasn't sure which plants.'

'The *Hidcotes* to replace the *Augustifolias*? Yes, that's right Mara.' She glanced over her shoulder to the front of the house. 'But it might be best if you keep out of camera range. Don't you think, Ros?' she added to a woman with spiky red hair holding a clipboard and standing to one side.

Ros nodded and waited patiently as Mara moved on again and then called after her, 'Get some oil on that wheel, though, if you're going to be around much longer.'

Mara looked over her shoulder and grinned in acknowledgement.

Helen took up her original position by the border and waited for the team to make ready again.

'So you finally made it into films, Helen,' a voice said.

Helen froze, then frowned. The cameraman sighed and once again lifted the camera from his shoulder as a man stepped forward.

'Alan?' Helen said faintly.

The man, average height, light-haired and dressed in a linen suit, held out his hand to her.

'You do pick your times, Alan. Couldn't you have waited till later?'

'After so many years, certainly not. Besides, I had no idea you were filming in your famous garden. You must let me know when it will be shown. I'll look out for it.' His voice had a faint mid-Atlantic twang which gave his words an edge of insincerity.

'It's her own programme – her own series,' Ros said. 'And it's not going too smoothly this afternoon.'

He stepped back in mock contrition. 'I do apologize. It's just that I was in the area and when I realized Helen lived just up the road I couldn't resist coming straight over to visit with her.'

'Visit her, Alan,' Helen corrected. 'You're in England now.'

He raised his hands theatrically and looked around. 'How could I possibly forget it?'

'I'm sorry about this, Ros,' Helen said. 'Shall we just carry on? After all this time, I'm sure you can wait, Alan.'

Ros squinted at the sky. 'The sun's come round a bit. We might as well finish for the day now.'

'Don't forget we're open here from Wednesday onwards,' Helen warned.

'Monday and Tuesday should finish it,' Ros said laconically. 'Don't worry, the forecast's holding for a fine spell. Besides, the evenings will be light enough after you've closed – if the weather stays fine.'

The group began to break up.

'I'll give you a ring over the weekend,' Ros said to Helen and, with a friendly enough glance at Helen's friend, strode off, followed by the rest of the team.

Helen turned in the direction of the house, Alan at her side.

'You've done very well for yourself, Helen,' he said. 'Clifford's Place is very beautiful and the garden, I understand, is all yours.'

'I've been working on it for twenty years. I suppose it ought to be good by now.'

'There's no call to be modest about it. And you're looking great, too. You've hardly changed since I saw you last.'

Helen glanced at him warily. He had changed, though not necessarily for the worse. He looked his age, which must be about forty-five by now, but the years had given some distinction to looks which had been good but bland in his youth.

'Can I offer you some tea?' she asked. 'And then you can tell me how you come to be in the area.'

'Don't you have anything stronger on offer?'

'Not at the moment.' She gestured to the right of the stone terrace, where Mara was up to her elbows in compost and lavender plants, and entered through a doorway in a recess of the house into a stone-flagged passageway. Helen led him through the dim light of a side-passage and thence into the main entrance hall of the old house.

'Very nice,' Alan said, looking round at the oil paintings and ceramics, but lingering at the lovely stained glass in the main door.

'We don't use that way in much these days – the glass isn't too secure. It's quite out of period anyway, done by a former owner who was keen on the arts and crafts movement.'

'I'm all for the eclectic myself. You are, too, judging by your garden.'

'You're a judge of that, too, are you?' Helen showed him into a bright sitting-room at the front of the house. A window was open, bringing in faint fragrances of lavender and roses. 'Make yourself comfortable.'

When she returned with a tray he was sitting on a linen sofa almost the same shade as his suit. She placed the tray on a low table and began to pour tea.

'So, how are you after all this time?' he asked.

'I'm very well. And you?' She handed him his tea and offered some biscuits, then sat in a chair at right-angles to her visitor, taking time to adjust some cushions.

He laughed. 'This is all very formal, Helen. Aren't you pleased to see me after all this time?' He raised his eyebrows and gave her the quizzical smile that she remembered well.

'Of course I am, Alan,' she said a little more warmly. 'It's just a bit of a surprise, that's all.'

'And a pleasant one, I hope?'

'Yes, I hope so, too. So what are you doing in this area?' she went on quickly, as if to distract from the cynical edge of her remark.

'I'm staying with Colin and Laura Wheatley in Chairford. You know them, I think?'

'Not well. But, yes I've met them. Are you with anyone?'

'I was. But my wife has just left me.'

'Oh!' Helen raised her eyebrows. 'I'm sorry.'

'Things have been a bit traumatic.'

There was a pause, and an opening for Helen to ask more. Instead, she added more tea to her cup and settled again in her chair.

'Everything seems fine with you, though,' he said. 'This is your second marriage, isn't it?'

She nodded. 'Gerald died five years ago.'

He reached for another biscuit. 'And your current husband is another wealthy city man, I hear?'

She took a small sip of tea and nodded, her eyes still avoiding his.

'Helen, you seem uncomfortable, seeing me again. There's no need. It's all a long time ago.' He leaned towards her.

She looked him full in the face and raised her chin.

10

'Don't be absurd, Alan. I'm just rather busy at the moment. I've got a lot on my mind.'

'Good. I mean I'm glad it's not me who's the cause of your uneasiness.'

'You always thought you were the centre of the universe, Alan,' she said coldly.

'Well, I was, for a while, wasn't I?'

'You thought so anyway.'

'And you soon disabused me of that.'

'And now someone else has, it seems.'

'Ouch. You have the talent to hit where it hurts.' But he didn't look as if the gibe had touched him, and he smiled at her rising colour.

'So what happened? Has she gone off with a younger man? Or perhaps a richer one?'

'As you did, you mean? No, though there is an echo of the past in it. We just lost our child. A cot death. Gina couldn't take it. Went to pieces. Didn't want me around. She seems to blame me because I was in the house when Patrick died.'

There was a moment's silence, then Helen said, 'I'm so sorry, Alan.'

'Yes, I don't seem destined for fatherhood, do I?'

Helen fiddled with her spoon. Small sounds seemed loud: birds singing in short bursts, the scrape of a trowel echoing the clinking of a teaspoon in a saucer.

'You have children, though?' he said after a moment.

'Two boys and a girl.'

'How old are they now?'

'Liam is nineteen and Benedict is eighteen. Vita is seventeen.'

'And ours would have been twenty-two.'

Helen made an abrupt movement and clattered her cup and saucer back on to the tray.

'Alan, I don't need this. If you've just come to stir up old memories and create trouble, you'd better go.'

'Hey, I'm sorry,' Alan said soothingly. 'That's not why I'm here.' He paused for a moment and placed his own cup and saucer carefully on the tray. 'It's just that, with all that's been happening lately, I've been thinking about my life a bit more than I've usually had time to. And then with the Wheatleys inviting me over, and finding I was staying quite close to you, it seemed right to come over and see you.'

'Right for you, perhaps.'

'Well, you don't seem like the one with problems right now, so why should you worry? I'm the one whose life seems to have taken a nosedive.'

Helen said, 'So what *have* you been doing with your life?'

'Well, I stayed in the States. Sunny California, or smoggy California, depending on where you're living. I've been there most of the time since. I was in a few films, though you probably wouldn't have noticed, and I've mainly been doing minor miniseries. Not the great acting career I hoped for – but I made a good living.'

'That's past tense?'

'Right. Work dried up a bit. Then a contact suggested work in England in a British series which required an American lead, so Gina and I came over, with the baby. The contract fell through and I thought I'd show Gina a bit of the UK before we headed back and before they forgot my existence over there. Which can happen fairly quickly.'

'You're quite American.' She smiled at him, seeming to relax.

He shrugged. 'I'm still paid to be British sometimes. Anyway, how about you? You've taken off in an unexpected way. I thought you were determined to make it in acting. And now you're the doyenne of glamour-gardening.' His expression changed. 'Why did you do it, Helen? We had such a lot going for us, together.'

'Alan, I don't want this.'

'Did I mean so very little to you that you just dropped me almost as soon as I got to the States? You knew I was coming back.'

She gave a short laugh. 'You make it all sound so idyllic, Alan. We couldn't find work, remember – that's why you went abroad. It was no fun scratching about trying to find voice-over jobs and living on next to no money.' She clasped her hands tightly and looked away.

'I should never have allowed you to let the baby go.'

'The baby was sick. And wasn't going to live.'

'And died in that home.'

'I couldn't cope. You know that I was ill myself.' Helen stood up, smoothing her skirt. 'I think you'd better go, Alan. There's no point in this.'

Alan remained seated. 'I just need to understand.' His voice lowered a little, reminding the listener that acting was his trade, that persuasion was a matter of technique. 'Maybe it's reaching my middle years or something, Helen. You look back and wonder what it was all about. . . .'

Helen moved impatiently. 'Alan, that sounds like a line from one of your miserable mini-series.'

'So it may. It doesn't make it any the less true. I still want to know. Did you really just stop loving me?'

'Oh please, Alan. This is just some kind of an ego-trip, wanting to know why you were rejected. Because it's happened again, and probably has in-between times. How long have you been married to – Gina, was it?'

'Three years – and that's got nothing to do with it. I just feel we have unfinished business, you and I. We never talked after it all happened.'

'There was nothing to talk about. I met Gerald. End of story.'

'Or beginning of it. You're a rich woman now. And famous, too.'

'Mildly. But I enjoy what I do. And I've been working at it for a long time.'

'You've had the money to indulge yourself. Thanks to Gerald. And your present husband. We've heard of Lewis Enright even in the States. You kept Gerald's surname, though.'

'It's the name I'm known by, in my work, my career.' Helen made another impatient gesture, as if warding off an importunate fly. She was still standing, facing him as if willing him to go.

He remained, leaning back, his arm along the arm of the sofa.

'I'd like to meet your children, and your husband. Why don't you invite me over one evening, with the Wheatleys if you like?'

'How long are you planning to stay in the area?' she asked.

'I'm not sure. It depends on how things work out with Gina.'

'I thought you said she'd left you.'

'She has. But I'm hoping it's not permanent. She's gone to stay with an old college-friend in London.'

'Shouldn't you perhaps follow her?'

He shook his head. 'Not yet. When she's ready. She wants some space at the moment.'

13

'Yes, you were always quick to give people space.'

Alan gave a narrow smile. 'You see, you do have things to say to me.'

Helen looked away from him towards the window. The garden was still brightly lit by sunshine, though the shadows were beginning subtly to lengthen.

'You'd better give me the Wheatleys home number. I'll see how Lewis is fixed for an evening sometime soon. Though I'm not promising anything.'

'I'd really like to meet your family,' Alan said, scribbling a telephone number and handing it to her. 'I've seen your books on sale in the States. And magazine articles about your garden designs for the rich and famous. It'll give me some kudos to say I've dined at Clifford's Place.'

'Can you assure me you'll not feel the need to drag up past times at this putative dinner party?'

'That's private, Helen. Of course I won't. This was just between you and me.' He stood, facing her. 'Did I tell you that you're looking wonderful? I think you've even improved with age.'

'How old is your wife?'

He smiled. 'Twenty-five.'

She smiled in return, without it reaching her eyes. 'I'll call you then, in a day or so. Perhaps you could all come over mid-week?'

CHAPTER 2

Everlasting Pea – An appointed meeting

Westwich station was busy with weekend travellers on this Friday evening in June. Detective Chief Inspector Christopher Simon, of Westwich police, looked around for a place to sit and wait for the train which was bringing his mother on a visit from Sussex. There was none vacant. He strolled over to examine the arrivals and departures screen and saw, without great surprise, that her train was running half an hour late. Unused to having time on his hands, he felt faintly irritated, as if such time wasted should, or could, have been spent in his office, clearing some of the paperwork piling up there. In fact, he realized, he had left nothing imperative unattended, since he was at the beginning of some leave due and timed to coincide with his mother's visit to himself and Jessie.

He was not feeling particularly comfortable about his mother's imminent arrival, fond though he was of her. She had become pressing of late in her encouragement of him and Jessie to formalize their rather loose cohabitation arrangements and consider her own increasingly urgent desire for a number of grandchildren. Since his sister Rose was showing no sign of settling into any relationship that could be considered stable, Christopher and Jessie were looking like her best hope at the moment. And Simon, though his own wishes were in fact perfectly in accord with his mother's, had somehow never found an appropriate occasion to broach the subject with Jessie.

He spent much of his spare time with her at her cottage – but they were both busy in their demanding jobs: Jessie in her new post as professor of psychology at the University of Westwich and he in his police work. Such spare time as they had was often spent in a sort of exhausted communion sprawled in Jessie's living-room or, of late in the fine weather, in her untidy and extensive garden – the which was ostensibly his mother's excuse for her visit. She and Jessie had been having increasingly lengthy and detailed discussions on the telephone about the garden's potential and Elizabeth, Simon's mother, was both an enthusiast and something of an expert on the subject.

It wasn't really lack of opportunity, though, that had kept him from broaching the question of marriage, and all that that involved. He was aware of his fear that Jessie might say no – that she might think he was yearning for a family and that she might have no such desire and so would decide – in her very decided way – that he should be released to pursue a more likely prospect. And he knew that being in Jessie's orbit was more important to him than any of the rest – so he was afraid of rocking their possibly fragile craft by broaching ticklish questions. Besides, she was enthusiastically involved in her job and he couldn't see that she would be keen to interrupt her career. But they were both in their mid-thirties and options were beginning to diminish. So he sighed at the thought of his mother's heavy hints and wondered how he was going to get through the next ten days or so.

If his parents had lived more orthodox lives themselves, he thought, he might find his mother's hints more tolerable, more easily dismissed as conventional granny-yearnings. But they had managed to raise two children while on the move for a good part of their lives, his father as a field naturalist at various sites over-seas and his mother as his partner in every sense of the word. It was only when his father had returned, near the age of sixty, to work in England with one of the University of London colleges that their lives had settled into a more routine pattern. And his mother, in her mid-fifties, and their work partnership dissolved, had taken what seemed a natural step for a trained botanist into horticultural interests.

Someone bumped into him, abruptly rousing him from thought.

'Oops! Sorry! Liam, look what you made me do. Stop fooling about.' The speaker was a slight young woman with dark hair, a small rucksack on her back. She smiled up at Simon, a narrow-eyed questioning smile, and repeated her apology. She was pretty, with small features, wearing bright ethnic cottons. Simon found it easy to smile back.

Liam, a tall youth, dark and with penetrating deep-set eyes, glanced at Simon and flung his arm around the girl's shoulders.

Another young man, fair-haired and squarer set, approached.

'Mara – we needn't have rushed. The train's fifteen minutes late.'

'We've got time for a drink, then,' the dark-haired one said.

'Never miss a chance, do you, Liam,' the girl said, giving him a shove. 'Make sure you let Ben drive back then.'

'Don't you want one? Come on.'

'Neither of us does,' the other young man, Ben, said.

'You don't speak for her, *brother*,' Liam said, frowning.

'Don't be a pain, Liam.' The girl put out a hand to him. 'I don't want to go inside. It's too hot and stuffy.'

He replaced his arm on her shoulder and leaned to kiss her on the cheek. 'I'm going to miss you, Mara.'

She shrugged him off, laughing. 'I'm only going for the week-end. I'll be back early on Monday. You'll survive all right without me until then.'

Benjamin hung back, watching the other two, his face expressionless. They didn't look like brothers, Simon thought, still watching them. But both had the same blue eyes and aquiline noses – and noses, Simon had often observed, were a feature which seemed to be a strong genetic trait in families. He wondered quite what their relationship with the girl was – other than one of rivalry.

A loud and incomprehensible string of utterances, identifiable as human only by the sing-song West Country cadence, emanated from the speaker above their heads. People looked about them, a similar look of blank confusion on their faces, as if hoping some-one nearby might have translated more successfully than themselves. Simon wandered over again to the arrivals screen and saw that his mother's train had made up five minutes and would be here very soon. He moved on down the platform, out of the

17

crowd, to the shade of a wooden-framed awning and spent the remainder of his wait gloomily examining Westwich station's contribution to the decline of the British railway industry.

When his mother's train arrived she was easy to spot at the carriage door, being preceded by what looked like most of a hedge. A large bag was flung out, his mother stepping gracefully behind.

'Christopher dear, you *are* here!' She leaned up only a little to kiss his cheek. She was almost as tall as he was himself.

He kissed her in return and relieved her of the heavy bag.

'You're looking well,' he said, which she did. She still carried herself well and only faint tracings of lines added to her face with inevitable age. Her hair was more grey though and, as usual, was escaping the ineffectual pins that held it in a loose bun high on her head.

'You're looking a bit wan.' She stood examining him for a moment. 'The break will obviously do you good.'

'Isn't it likely to be spent wrestling with stinging-nettles and brambles, though?' he asked as they made their way to the car park.

'A therapeutic change from wrestling with less attractive forms of life, I would imagine,' she said.

They passed the little group that Simon had observed earlier. The girl's train had pulled in and she was bestowing equal and affectionate farewell embraces on the two young men.

'So how is Jessie?' his mother asked as they drove out of the west side of town on to the dual carriageway.

'She was fine this morning when I left. Looking forward to seeing you and doing the garden. She's had a boy in from the village to start clearing some of the ground. He's rather keen on bonfires, though, so Jessie's had to give him a lecture about the environment.'

'Perhaps we should hire a shredder. You don't sound too keen to be involved.' This was more of a question than a statement.

Simon shrugged.

'Perhaps you don't relish having two women directing you to do what's necessary,' his mother said.

'I'm used to it these days. Though I don't think I should stand accused of being in anyway sexist.'

'No, of course not. You wouldn't have chosen a partner like

18

Jessie if you were afraid of women. And you've got a woman boss now, haven't you?'

'Yes. So between the two of them, I'm being dragged thoroughly into the twenty-first century.'

'Fascinating times we live in.' His mother sighed.

' "May you live in interesting times" is an ancient Chinese curse,' Simon remarked.

'Very astute of them. Life *is* so much more difficult these days. Partly because we have so much information thrown at us. The global village is just too much to feel responsible towards for a race that finds even a small village too demanding. But speaking of modern women, though I lived through unenlightened times myself, I don't remember feeling deprived in any way.'

'Perhaps the rules don't have to be changed for the few. It's the many who need the protection of changes in laws and procedures. There are always the few with the resources and courage to transcend the conventional.'

'I assume you are referring to laws regarding custom and social convention, rather than the sort you are involved in as a policeman. It seems that there it's the comparatively few who get the protection – the law-breakers.'

He had forgotten that it was unwise to make an idle remark in the presence of his mother. She was as rigorous as ever in requiring one to say what one meant and mean what one said. It occured to Simon with a sense of dismay that his mother and Jessie were alike, kindred spirits. He was amazed that he had never registered the fact before and drove thoughtfully for several miles without saying another word.

'You haven't gone to sleep, have you?' his mother's voice asked mildly from his side.

They were approaching the turning from the main road to Jessie's village and Simon slowed down and negotiated.

'How's Dad?' he asked, conscious that he had omitted to ask earlier.

'Robust. Still busy with his university work. He's only got a few students this year but he's still working on his book, so that suits him.'

'It's on some eco subject, isn't it?'

'It seems unavoidable, these days. They all seem to be to some extent if they're concerned with the natural world. Which is rapidly being made unnatural with the combined efforts of scientists and technologists aided by the government.'

Simon gave an inward sigh as he slowed down in his approach to the cottage. Acres of stinging and scratching undergrowth would be as nothing compared to the rigorous company of the two women in his life.

CHAPTER 3

Lesser Celandine – Joys to come

Simon, Jessie and Elizabeth were sitting at the back of the cottage enjoying a pre-prandial drink, a chilled bottle of white wine half-empty on the table between them. They were all observing with some satisfaction what had been achieved in the week since Elizabeth's arrival. The paved area they were sitting on had been laid, a vegetable parterre with paths made of reclaimed bricks set out and a sturdy trellis built to section it from more ornamental elements of the garden. Some planting had already been done – Jessie and Elizabeth having already indulged themselves in visits to obscure specialist nurseries in the area while Simon got on with the hard landscaping. It was not a large section of the two acres which Jessie owned that they had worked on but it was enough. He was ready for a break.

'What do I call this bit we're sitting on, Elizabeth?' Jessie said into the exhausted silence. 'I can't abide the word "patio". It's too foreign.'

'Yes, it always sounds a bit pretentious,' Elizabeth agreed. 'And "terrace" would be even more so, don't you think?'

'What about "backyard"?' Simon said, irritated by all the horticultural intensity he had experienced. 'Isn't this conversation a bit precious?'

'Too American,' Jessie said, ignoring the bite in his voice. 'Besides, in America it often refers to a few dozen acres of woodlot.'

21

'I suppose it is a sort of courtyard, the way you've designed it,' Elizabeth mused. 'Would that do?' She lifted the bottle of wine and replenished their glasses. 'This has gone to my head rather quickly.'

'It will probably be referred to as 'the sitting-out bit'. Jessie said.

'Mmmm,' Elizabeth concurred.

'Well, it's all pretty well done now,' Simon said optimistically. 'The lawn's laid, the hard landscaping's done, the woodwork's erected.'

'Apart from the summerhouse,' Jessie said.

'And the pond,' Elizabeth added.

'I didn't think we were attacking the wild area this time,' Simon said hollowly.

Jessie looked across at him and grinned. She had a smudge of dirt across one cheek and her long curly dark hair tied anyhow with a bandanna was wet with sweat around her face. Despite his irritation she looked eminently desirable.

'No, we can't disturb the wildlife at this time of year. We could get the pond dug in the rough grass, though.'

'Don't tease the poor boy,' Elizabeth said, stretching out her long legs luxuriously. 'No. I think that now all we have to do is the really pleasurable bits like visiting some gardens for inspiration and perhaps picking up a few of their choice plants at the same time. The rest can wait a while.'

'I hope I haven't made you overdo things, Elizabeth,' Jessie said without too much concern in her voice.

'You know perfectly well I've enjoyed it all immensely.'

'Well, she's made me overdo things,' Simon said. 'My back's killing me.'

'I'll give you a massage later,' Jessie said.

'Have a nice warm bath,' his mother added. 'With some lavender and rosemary in it.'

'Where do you fancy visiting, Elizabeth?' Jessie asked. 'Any particular gardens in mind?'

'We're spoilt for choice in this area.' Elizabeth reeled off a number of names. 'But one I'd really like to go to is Helen Hartley's garden at Clifford's Place.'

'The famous Helen Hartley? Yes, it's not far away – the other side of Westwich, in the Cotswolds.'

Simon actually knew who they were talking about. Jessie had a video of one of Helen Hartley's television series and he had watched it with her one wet Sunday afternoon recently.

'I went there years ago,' Elizabeth said. 'Fairly early on she was running gardening courses and I decided to go on one just after Chris left university and was off on his travels.'

'What's it like?'

'Well, it's so popular now and no doubt busy, but in those days it was lovely – a fine, private sort of place.'

' "The grave's a fine and private place, But none I think do there embrace",' Simon quoted softly.

Elizabeth shivered in the warm sun. 'Perhaps a bath will make you feel more cheerful, Christopher. Jessie and I will have some more wine before we have ours.'

'Are we going to this Clifford's Place tomorrow, then?' he asked, unwinding his long frame from an old basket-chair. It was a question he was to come to wish he had not asked. He might have offered to dig the pond instead.

'Why not?' Jessie said.

'Yes,' Elizabeth agreed with enthusiasm. 'It will be lovely to see Helen again after all this time, and see what she's done with the garden – if she's there, that is. Though I've bought some of her books, of course. I understand she's got a new television series coming out.'

'A sort of Delia Smith of horticulture, is she then?' Simon asked.

'I suppose you could say that.' Elizabeth took another sip of wine and leaned back with a comfortable sigh.

They left mid-morning the next day in Simon's car. While Simon drove, the two women conducted a conversation over the back of Jessie's passenger-seat on the subject of which roses to buy for the trellis. This lasted them well beyond Westwich, Elizabeth being an expert on proneness to black spot and other ills and Jessie having honed her knowledge on the best scents and colours. Simon let it all drift over him. He supposed he need not have come today, his sense of exclusion from the pair of them with their passionate interest in plants having been deeply intensified over the past week. But, in truth, he liked being in gardens. He liked the smells and the textures and the sounds, particularly where there was running water; he just wasn't too keen on working in them. Though secretly he had rather enjoyed the physical activity as a change from his usual fairly sedentary work. Even if he wasn't at his desk, he was usually in the seat of his car or standing or sitting, talking to witnesses, suspects, colleagues. He was very rarely engaged in any kind of Sweeney type of chase through the streets of Westwich these days.

Though he wasn't going to encourage her, he was beginning to see the appeal that gardening had for Jessie, hers being essentially a cerebral job, too. It was like so many things, he supposed, that one resisted because it was not one's own 'thing'. It made you a follower, if it wasn't your own idea in the first place. Though women tended to be more generous-spirited in such matters if the numbers of them rooting for husbands and boyfriends – and sons – from the edge of football pitches was anything to go by.

Besides, he suspected that Jessie would prefer him to remain in ignorance. She wouldn't want any arguments in her garden over whether a peony would be preferable to an penstemon in that particular spot. Not that she was really precious about gardening, it was more an extension of her keenness on environmental things. . . .

'Next turning left, Chris,' Jessie said, her finger marking a place on the map.

They drove out of a shady wooded road into the sunshine again and approached a crossroads with a sign attached for 'Clifford's Place: 1 mile'. Simon turned the car into a narrower road which began to fall at a slow gradient with a high grassy bank on its right topped by a dry-stone wall. A typical Cotswold valley view unfolded, the misty heads of oaks merging into small fields of already sere and harvested grass, bleached in the sun, and a stream, edged by groups of willows, reflecting a blue sky.

'There's Clifford's Place,' his mother said, pointing between him and Jessie in the front. Simon caught a brief glimpse of a stone-roofed manor house and twisted chimneys before they were into another tunnel of trees and shade again.

The large gravel car park, containing only a couple of cars so far, was in the shade of a row of trees. They all climbed out with relief into the comparative cool. Elizabeth remarked on the advantage of arriving early. 'Too many visitors always spoil the ambience of a garden.'

There was a small hut housing an elderly male who took their money and offered them a printed guide to the garden. Elizabeth immediately handed him some coins and studied it with interest.

'So much of this is new since I was here,' she said. 'The plants for sale are near the entrance. Do you want to go there first?'

Jessie glanced at Simon's expression of forbearance.

'Let's go there after we've had a look around.'

A path which wound through shrubberies led into sunshine at the front of the house, a broad paved area fronted by a wide knot garden. Beyond that a rill of water falling in shallow steps led the eye to an uninterrupted view of fields and stream and misted hills. Framing all this to right and left were profuse herbaceous borders backed by high clipped hedges. While the two women began their tour, Simon lingered and examined the front of the house.

He caught them up as they began to disappear behind a hedge which curved to the left and followed them into an enclosed garden with a circular pool at its centre. Jessie and his mother talked plants and Simon sat on the edge of the pool watching the fish. The heat of the day was already intense in this confined space and he moved on ahead of them through another garden 'room' profuse with roses, in the hope of something a bit more restful.

When he entered a pleached walk he saw, framed through the straight trunks, exactly what he was looking for – a total contrast with what had gone before. It was a wide open space edged by high clipped hedges on two sides, while beyond was open to the lovely view ahead. High banks were inset with rocks and small open-branched trees and, out of the bank, water pooled before cascading down to meander through lower banks and meadow-land. The planting was kept to a minimum and done as naturally as possible, common daisies and small purple flowers dotted the grass, a mown path leading through longer grasses with moon daisies, poppies and cornflowers. It was the simplicity that appealed. Simon felt suddenly inspired with ideas for some of the rest of Jessie's two acres.

Within the banks flat rocks provided seating in partial shade and Simon headed for them, planning to wait there for the others. It came as something of a surprise to find that someone was there before him, hidden by a large rock. A dark-haired young man looked up at Simon, a sandwich half-way to his mouth.

'I was afraid it wouldn't last,' he said.

'I'm sorry,' Simon said, backing away.

'No,' the young man gestured. 'You've got more right than I have. I only work here. I like to bring my lunch – it's nice and peaceful.'

Simon passed through the small grove of trees above the pool and seated himself on the rock shelf across the stream from his companion.

'Most people just look at this part of the garden and pass by – as if it's just another view.'

'Do they?' Simon said. 'I'm surprised. It's the part I've liked best so far.'

'Good. I designed it myself.' The young man took another bite from his sandwich and chewed vigorously.

Simon had seen him somewhere before, he thought, studying the strong-boned face, the deep-set eyes.

'I'm impressed,' he said.

'I've seen you somewhere before.' The young man narrowed his eyes, studying Simon's face.

Simon returned his regard. 'I remember. It was at Westwich railway station a week or so ago.'

'So it was. I'm Liam Hartley, by the way.' He put a finger in his mouth and rubbed at his gum.

'Chris Simon. So you must be Helen Hartley's son?'

Liam nodded.

'So she lets you have a hand in the design of the garden?'

'Only this bit,' Liam looked about him. 'It cost a lot because we had to buy in fairly mature trees, and they have to be kept carefully pruned to keep this effect of miniature landscape. The rocks were expensive too.' He took another bite from his sandwich.

'It feels very English,' Simon said.

'Do you think so?' Liam sounded disappointed. 'I was thinking more of those paintings of Greek shepherds.'

'Arcady,' Simon suggested.

'That's right. Anyway, this has been my lot as far as design here goes. I'm just a maintenance man really.'

Simon was conscious of the dissatisfaction in the young man's voice.

'I should think there's a lot more to it than that.'

Liam shrugged. 'I'm branching out on my own,' he said.

'Yes?' Simon closed his eyes and let the sun on to his face.

'I want to have my own design company. Something more modern.'

'Than Arcady?' Simon opened an eye.

'There's nothing new, is there?' Liam said grinning.

'Except technology, maybe?'

'Exactly.' Liam sat up. 'New materials, lighting, the whole bit. Gardens are outside living-spaces – there's so much going on.'

Jessie and Elizabeth appeared through the entrance way and walked towards them, unseen by Liam.

'Gardening's the new rock-'n'-roll,' he said.

'Isn't rock-'n'-roll slang for sex?' Elizabeth's voice came from behind him.

Liam turned and looked up over the bank.

'Too right,' he said with a smile.

Elizabeth smiled back. 'I confess I hadn't seen it in quite that light,' she said.

'Oh, I do like *this*,' Jessie said. She shook off her sandals and stepped into the stream.

'Yes, it's quite lovely,' Elizabeth agreed.

Simon was watching as Liam extracted another sandwich from his bag.

'We'd better get on. I'm getting hungry.'

'Have one of these if you like,' Liam offered. 'Dandelion and rocket with cream cheese.'

'We've brought some food with us in the car, thanks all the same,' Simon said.

Liam laughed. 'Just as well. These are a bit hot and bitter today.' He rubbed at his gums again. 'But bring your picnic back here, if you like. As I said, no one ever hangs about here and I shall be gone soon.'

'We might do that,' Simon agreed. 'This is Helen Hartley's son Liam, by the way,' he said to his mother.

'Really? I met you before when you were quite small,' Elizabeth said. 'How nice to see you again.' She asked after his brother and sister and Helen. 'Is your mother here today?'

'Yes, she's about. You'll run into her somewhere. She'll be pleased to see you, I'm sure.'

'Charming boy,' Elizabeth said as they moved on. Simon remembered his other meeting with Liam and recalled something other than surface charm.

'Their father died a few years ago,' Elizabeth said to Jessie. 'Then she married Lewis Enright the finance man. Married money both times so there's been no need to watch expenditure when it came to work on the gardens. Did you notice the new conservatory at the front? Beautifully done with those stone pillars, looked as if it had been there for ever. . . .'

Simon followed on behind, half-listening, pausing now and again to sniff a flower, touch a furry leaf.

CHAPTER 4

Aspen Tree – Lamentation

The pleached walk ended in a dramatic feature of water cascading noisily over a monolithic rock in a shady grotto, where they stood and cooled themselves. The route moved on past a small temple with a formal pond and then into a narrow hedged area, concealing down a side-path an attractive small cottage, glimpsed briefly. Back on the front terrace with its remote view, Simon noticed how the profusion of blue flowers planted at the ends of the borders allowed the immediate prospect to flow into the more distant one. He had come to realize that everything about this place was deliberate, and the fact interested him. Nothing was by chance, everything considered – a conscious decision. In his job it was in sorting the deliberate from the chance events and facts, in weighing one kind against the other, that he found most satisfaction. Perhaps this was part of the charm of a garden, he thought, that things were controlled into an understandable whole, an interpretation of the natural order.

'There's Helen!' his mother said.

A woman had emerged from the far end of the house, carrying a trug. Elizabeth put up her hand to her and the two women approached each other, Jessie and Simon following slowly in Elizabeth's wake.

Helen Hartley looked businesslike, dressed for work rather than for an elegant stroll around her domain in order to receive her visitors. She wore a loose pink cotton shirt over canvas trousers with a pair of stout and well-worn gardening-shoes. Her fine brown hair was tied up loosely and strands of it escaped to frame a face which was finely boned with beautiful lightly tanned skin. She was a lovely-looking woman, Simon thought. She pulled off a gardening-glove and held out her hand, and her smile, as she greeted Elizabeth, was warm and open.

They stood for a few minutes talking before Elizabeth introduced Jessie and Simon.

'We've met one of your sons,' Elizabeth said. 'Liam. Handsome boy. Children really mark the years, don't they?'

Helen laughed agreement. 'You'll probably run into Ben and Vita somewhere. Vita's usually in the greenhouses doing some propagating but today she's looking after the plant-sales area.'

'Look, I'll be somewhere about here, I'm only dead-heading roses.' She gestured to the trug. 'It's a nice easy job to be doing and it makes me available if people want to ask any questions about plants. So why don't you all come and have tea with me when you're finished?'

'We'll do that,' Elizabeth agreed, pleased.

They continued on for another forty-five minutes or so when Simon, who had had more than enough of perfected order, announced that he was going for the food.

'I'll meet you at the Arcadian plot,' he said, and returned to the car park.

On the way back he passed an elderly couple and a few other visitors, but the gardens were large enough to accommodate them without, as his mother put it, 'spoiling the ambience'. He spotted one gardener, a tall large-boned young man, clipping some overhanging branches.

It must be a pleasant life in its way, he thought, surrounded by beauty, assisting in its perfecting, attending nature like some vestal virgin in a temple. Yet there had been a worm of discontent in this little Eden: Liam.

Arcady was deserted. Jessie and Elizabeth had not yet arrived and thankfully no other group had decided to delay there. Simon entered again through the small glade of trees at the head of the stream and resumed his previous seat, placing the basket at his feet. It was only when he looked up that he saw that he was not, after all, alone.

Liam Hartley was lying partly on his back, one bare leg

immersed in the stream, his back twisted and his face half-buried in the grass. From the marks in the grass and at the edge of the stream where the gravel had been kicked by his feet, it appeared that the boy had writhed in pain before succumbing to the stillness of what looked like death. Beside his head was a pool of greenish vomit, into which his wide-open eyes stared as if with horrified intensity.

Simon crossed the stream, unheeding of soaked shoes, and leaned carefully, disturbing nothing, to feel for a pulse in the neck. There was none that he could sense, though he supposed that there might still be some faint trace of life. He willed Jessie and his mother to arrive. He didn't want to leave the body unattended. This looked like a poisoning and Liam Hartley had not appeared to be in a suicidal state an hour or so ago.

With relief he heard Jessie's voice. He stood and climbed the bank and quickly explained what he had found.

'Just wait here and don't touch anything. I'm going to the house to telephone for an ambulance.' Foolishly, deliberately, he had left his mobile phone behind in the car.

While Jessie was edging to peer over the bank, his mother said, 'I'll come too and find Helen. She must be told.'

It was half an hour before any ambulance could get there along the winding Cotswold roads, a period of time spent waiting near the body, for body only it was now, Simon was sure. Whatever had once animated the youthful good looks of Liam Hartley had departed with finality. While Elizabeth restrained a distraught Helen from a natural desire to touch and hold her son, Jessie and Simon stood at the entrance ready to deter visitors to this part of the garden. Someone at the house had been allotted to direct the paramedics.

They had not seen many visitors so far and perhaps those who had already been this way had done what Liam had said they did: merely looked and passed on, not feeling drawn into the scene as Simon himself had been. In which case Liam would have remained unnoticed where Simon had left him, after which he must have been quite quickly overwhelmed by whatever had poisoned him. A post mortem was inevitable and an inquest would follow at which he, Simon, would have to give evidence. It was possible, if this were no accident, that he would be put in charge of the case. While things were fresh in his mind he thought back over his brief time with Liam Hartley, remembering the way that he had rubbed absently at his gum with a finger, remembering with a shudder the young man's offer to him of a sandwich – filled with some unlikely combination of greenstuff. Dandelion was one, he remembered, and that bitter taste would probably mask a deadly bitter one.

Simon glanced around, the beauty and peace of the area undisturbed now that Helen's sobs had been stilled and she sat, her face in her hands, beside Elizabeth on one of the rocks. He thought it a sad irony that Liam's sole creation in this place, this idyllic spot, had been the place he had come to unwittingly to die.

CHAPTER 5

Pomegranate Flower – Mature elegance

Simon took Jessie and his mother as far as Westwich and put them in a taxi before seeking out Detective Superintendent Munro at headquarters. The family doctor, sent for by Barbara Meddick, Helen's friend and companion, had confirmed that Liam was dead. The emergency services' more sophisticated equipment had done the same.

'I shouldn't think there's any doubt he's been poisoned,' Dr Rafter said. 'There has to be the question of whether it was accidental, though. Or not,' he added meaningfully.

Simon mentioned the sandwiches Liam had been eating when he met him. 'I think he said they contained dandelions and some other herb, rocket perhaps.'

'Both strong-flavoured and the dandelion very bitter.' Rafter, middle-aged and overweight, was breathing heavily after the exertion of kneeling beside the body. 'The lad was a bit of a crank about health foods. Liked to eat as naturally as possible.'

'Do you think he might have made a mistake over the stuff he picked to go in these sandwiches?'

Irritably Rafter said, 'How should I know? I'd doubt it myself because the boy was no ignoramus when it came to plants.' He paused. 'If we're right and it is poisoning . . . Well, we'll have to wait on the post mortem now.'

So, here was a possible crime and he was informing Detective

Superintendent Munro about it because, whatever evolved, he, Simon, was going to have to give evidence at the inquest. He knocked on her door.

The room had improved noticeably since Bradley's day. The former detective superintendent, now retired on health grounds, had, despite the proportion of his time spent rooted to the chair at his desk from beyond which barrier he had maintained his hierarchical distance, never managed to imbue the room with anything else of his personality. It had been, always, a clinical statement of authority only.

Detective Superintendent Munro had introduced some easy-chairs, and a low table – making it possible to have rather more relaxed encounters with her – and several bright prints. There were also family photographs and, always, fresh flowers. It was altogether a less intimidating experience for the ranks to enter this transformed domain, though, ironically, in many ways more intimidating to meet its present incumbent.

'Chris! I thought you were on leave for a while yet.' She was seated at the low table on one of the comfortable chairs, looking through some paperwork. She gestured for him to join her. As always immaculately attired and considerably more impressive in every way than the room could ever reflect, today she was wearing a white sleeveless shirt and a knee-length skirt of emerald green linen. The jacket that went with it was laid on the seat beside her and she moved it so that he could sit down.

Simon was as little chauvinist as any man could be, he hoped, yet in the presence of this woman he could almost never forget that she was first of all a woman, rather than his senior officer who happened to be a woman. It was not that she played on her obvious attractions – far from it, she seemed largely unconscious of the way she looked. The way she dressed was in essence conservative – it was just that she could have hung a sack bag around her and risen above its humble provenance with a style that would have defeated almost any other woman. With her, he thought, it was more a matter of woman maketh the clothes than the other way around. Which could not be said for him, he realized regretfully. And he was dressed even more reprehensibly today, having come in from time on leave.

She was eyeing him now with that faint smile that lurked at the corners of her beautiful mouth whenever her eyes drifted over his sartorial unsplendour.

'So, what brings you back?'

He explained their trip to Clifford's Place today and its events.

'Do you know when the autopsy is?' she asked.

'Not yet. I'll give Havers a ring, shall I?'

She nodded, tapping perfectly manicured pale fingernails on the folder she held on her lap.

'Strictly speaking there's not much we can do until after that. But, if the young man was poisoned, and deliberately, we don't want to waste any time picking up anything that might be construed as evidence. We should seal off any area that might be relevant.' This Simon had already arranged. 'Did he live at Clifford's Place itself, with his mother?'

'He shares one of the former gardeners' cottages with his brother Benedict.'

'You'd better file an initial report and get back there. And find out as much as you can about the set-up. If it does turn out to be murder you'll want to get the facts as early on as you can.'

'As a witness . . .' Simon began.

'I don't think that need be a problem. You're not likely to be considered a suspect, are you?' She gave a wide smile and, as quickly, frowned. 'Are you saying that as you're on leave you'd prefer someone else to take this on?'

There was the faintest of warning notes in her voice that suggested that this would not be advisable. But that was not what was at issue. He had merely been conscious that his dual role might have made someone else preferable.

'No, not at all,' he said, knowing that further elaboration was unnecessary.

'I've visited Cliffords's Place,' she said. 'My daughter and I went there last summer.' Her daughter was a student at the University of Westwich, where Jessie was professor of psychology. 'It must be one of the best gardens in the country. It's horrible to think of something like this happening in such a place. On the other hand, from your point of view, it should be a relief from the mean city streets. A rather more salubrious place to ply your trade.'

Simon could only think that violence done in such an unlikely setting was perhaps more, rather than less, disturbing. But she did have a point, it would be a change from some of the cases he had been engaged on lately. And meaningless violence, which was much more the norm, was certainly less interesting than the meaningful kind, which he thought this was likely to turn out to be.

She stood up and Simon followed her to the door. He was well over six feet and she not much less, making no concessions by wearing flat-heeled shoes. Dark hair, dark skin, dark eyes compelled him.

'Let me know about the post mortem. See if Longman's available. He should be. We're short-staffed, though, so I won't be able to spare you many people for this.'

'Right.' Simon made for the door.

'Oh, and Chris . . .'

He turned.

'My daughter tells me that the new charity shop in West Walk has some really good things in it.' She looked him over. 'I accept that you have some allergy to menswear departments but do your best, would you, now that you're back in harness?'

'Super.' It was his usual acknowledgement.

CHAPTER 6

Aloe – Grief

This time Simon drove further along the lane and into the wide cobbled yard at the rear of Clifford's Place, Detective Constable Rhiannon Jones at his side, Longman being temporarily unavailable. The sun, in a still-clear sky, had moved into the west and dazzled him as he tried to park.

Rhiannon, unusually uncommunicative, got out of the passenger door and followed him along the side pathway towards the gardener's cottage that had been Liam Hartley's home and independent space.

A young policeman was standing on guard by the only door into the building. Simon nodded to him and entered the passageway, cluttered with mud-caked boots and gardening tools. He had not had time to examine the cottage earlier.

They surveyed the living-room: coke- and beer-cans on a stained old pine table in the centre of the room, throws over the sofa and chairs rumpled and not too clean. The computer system in the corner was in pristine contrast. Simon went on into the kitchen. It was larger than he had expected, looking as if at one time it had been extended. Another table standing in the centre of the room still bore witness to food preparation – a couple of smeared knives lay there and the surface was scattered with crumbs. Simon opened the door to the fridge-freezer. In the fridge section there were a few cartons of yoghurt and cans of beer and lager, some fruit juice, hummus, milk and a large carton of cream-cheese. Simon, wearing gloves, opened the last of these and looked inside. Half its contents had been used.

Rhiannon, who had been examining with distaste the sink and draining-board with its stacks of unwashed dishes, turned her attention to the bread-bin and opened its front.

'There's half a loaf of brown bread here,' she said. 'Is that what he was eating?'

Simon closed the door of the fridge. 'Yes,' he said, coming to look.

There was no sign of the green ingredients that Liam had claimed to be eating. Simon went over to a flip-top bin and peered inside.

'Look at this,' he said to Rhiannon, holding the lid open.

She wrinkled her nose and looked.

'Blow me!' she said, the Welsh valley accent pronounced. 'Four brown-bread sandwiches to go!'

Simon produced an evidence bag and placed the sandwiches within, then laid the bag on the table and lifted the corner of one to examine the contents.

'Looks like cream-cheese to me,' he said. 'Along with some unidentifiable greenstuff. Probably the dandelion and rocket that Liam referred to.'

'If someone did supply Liam Harvey with a poisoned lunch, replacing his own already prepared sandwiches,' Rhiannon said slowly, 'they've made no effort to hide the fact.'

'Interesting, isn't it?' Simon agreed.

Rhiannon took another look around, opening a few cupboard doors.

'And this might be relevant, too,' she said, holding open a door to the under-sink area. 'The compost bucket, by the look of it.'

Simon lifted it out into a better light.

'Those look like the bases of dandelion-leaves,' Rhiannon said.

'And these bits,' Simon delicately lifted some greenstuff with a gloved finger, 'look like the stalk-ends of rocket-leaves. But there's no sign of anything else Liam might have been eating unawares.' He added, 'Liam told me the contents, or rather, what he thought were the contents, of his sandwiches when I was talking to him. He even offered me one. All the same, we'd better get some samples.'

Rhiannon was wide-eyed. 'He offered you one? You could have been killed too.' She produced an evidence bag. 'What do you think it was that was put in his sandwiches, sir?'

'No idea. Though it's got to be something pretty fast-acting. And there's a number of plants in an English country garden that are dangerously poisonous.'

'I didn't know that.' Rhiannon sealed the bag. 'I know most of the wild ones we were always warned about as children, and I knew about laburnum seeds, but that's about it.'

'I suppose all garden plants derive from wild ones from somewhere in the world. Some are just poisonous enough to make you ill or cause some other allergic reaction, and others you'd be lucky to recover from. Especially if you take them into your system a good many miles from the nearest hospital.'

'And any poisoner would know that that would be the case here, wouldn't they?'

'So it makes for an efficient method for killing someone.'

'And we won't know what it was until after the autopsy.'

'The stomach contents will have to go to toxicology and it will take a while to get a clear identification of exactly what the poison was.' He gave a glance around. 'I think we'll leave the rest of this for now and go and speak to some of Liam's relations at the house. Scene of Crime should be arriving soon.'

He handed Rhiannon his own evidence bag. 'We'd better keep these in the fridge here until we leave. It'll be too hot in the car.'

As they re-entered the living-room Simon noticed, incongruous amid the squalor, a vase of violet-blue flower-spikes beside the empty fireplace. It had been obscured by the furniture when they entered the room from the other direction. It looked entirely out of place, a decorative domestic touch amid so much domestic disorder. He took a closer look. The flowers appeared very similar to those of a plant that Jessie and his mother had brought back from one of their forays to local nurseries – striking and somehow sinister. But perhaps that impression came from something he remembered his mother saying about how poisonous the plant was. Yes, because she had made some suggestive comment, which both he and Jessie had ignored, about it not being a plant to have in a garden if there were children in the house.

He took out his phone and called Jessie. She took a while to reply.

'Sorry,' he heard her say. 'We were in the garden.'

Where else? 'Jess, you bought a plant the other day, one with purple spikes of flowers, segmented leaves, that Mum said was poisonous. What's its name?'

'Let me think. We've bought so many plants. I remember. It was monkshood. *Aconitum*.'

'So the poison was aconite?'

'That's right. Why? Is that what killed Liam?'

'I don't know. I just found a vase of the cut flowers in his cottage.'

'Could be coincidence.'

'Could be. Thanks. See you later.' He rang off.

'Or no coincidence at all.' Rhiannon's eyes were fixed on the beautiful malevolent flowers.

Simon shook his head. 'No. He might have picked them and taken them into the kitchen and some of the leaves might have fallen on the table and he mistook them for rocket-leaves.'

'Well, you may be right.' Rhiannon's valley lilt somehow suggested that she thought otherwise. 'But it's a bit of a girly thing to do, isn't it: go out and pick flowers for a very neglected room at the start of the day? Besides, what about the sandwiches that had been thrown away?'

'You're right. I think we need to speak to Liam's brother Ben.'

Simon knocked briefly before opening the back door by which he had left earlier that day. A middle-aged woman appeared in the dimly lit passageway, emerging from a side door and wiping her hands on a tea towel.

'Police is it?' she asked. 'They're expecting you. Mrs Hartley is in the drawing-room with the others. I'll show you the way.'

'And you are?' he asked.

She looked over her shoulder, plump cheek folding into her neck.

'Mrs Taylor. I'm the cook-cum-housekeeper.' Abruptly she stopped, causing Rhiannon to come to a quick halt, her nose to Simon's shoulder. 'What's all the police involvement about?' she asked irritably. 'I mean, you don't think there's any crime involved, do you?' The woman was short and sturdy, her head not reaching Simon's chin, but she stared up at him unblinking and unintimidated.

'It's procedure in a case of sudden death, Mrs Taylor,' Simon reassured her.

She still made no move, still examined his face as if for some trace of disingenuousness.

'It's better for Mrs Hartley, don't you agree, that everything is done properly from the start?' he said, trying to make a move past her.

She turned away, saying, 'She's in no fit state to be questioned. The doctor's given her something and she's going to bed.'

They were led from the service area of the house into the central hall, where she held up a hand and knocked on a door, opening it just wide enough to announce them. 'Is that all right?' Simon heard her say in a sepulchral tone. Then she opened the door wider to admit them.

A small tableau of still figures sat close together on the sofa. Helen Hartley, her fine tanned skin drained of colour, was held on one side by a young woman with long blonde hair, who must be her daughter Vita, and on the other by her assistant Barbara Meddick, whom Simon had met briefly earlier. A young man rose from a nearby chair and came towards Simon. Simon recognized him by association as the one who had been with Liam and the girl at Westwich station.

'What is it you want?' he asked, his voice hoarse.

'You're Ben, are you?' Simon said.

'I'm Benedict Hartley, Liam's brother. Look, can't whatever it is wait? You can see my mother is in no state to be asked questions. And I can't see the need for it.'

'Is that true?' Simon asked quietly. 'You think your brother's death is not in need of some explanation?'

Benedict put a hand to his head and moved away, going to stand by one of the front windows.

Simon turned to the group of women on the sofa and introduced Rhiannon, who had remained standing by the door.

Three pairs of eyes stared up at him, reddened eyes, tearful eyes and eyes that were free of intense grief and were examining him as if he had just committed some social solecism and was in need of being made aware of it. Barbara Meddick was tall and slender with glossy black hair framing her face in a neat bob. She looked around the same age as Helen Hartley but there was little other similarity: her clothes were city rather than country and her skin city-pale. She shifted to the edge of the sofa, loosening her hold on Helen Hartley's shoulders.

'Could this not wait until tomorrow, Chief Inspector?' Her clear contralto was a relief after the knotted tension of Ben. 'Helen was just about to go to bed.'

'That's fine,' Simon agreed, 'But I need to have a few facts clear today.' He almost added – *before the post mortem* – but caught the words before they were uttered, knowing that the thought of the violations of an autopsy only added to the distress of people bereaved.

Helen Hartley had still not murmured. Probably the tablets the doctor had given her were well on their way to having an effect because the tears spilled now from her eyes and she made no attempt to check them. Her daughter Vita reached with a tissue and dabbed at her mother's cheeks.

'Come with me, Mum,' she said gently.

'Shall I come?' Barbara Meddick addressed Helen rather than the daughter.

Helen briefly shook her head but leaned on Barbara as she eased herself like an old woman from her seat.

Simon gestured to Rhiannon to open the door and go with them but, as she made to follow, Vita turned on her.

'We don't want you,' she said sharply. 'Leave us alone.' Rhiannon turned back impassively, hands folded in front of her as the door closed behind them.

'Haven't you lot got any sensitivity?' Ben said from his position by the window.

'We try, in difficult circumstances,' Simon said. 'I'm truly very sorry.'

'Well, I know I could do with a cup of tea,' Barbara Meddick said. 'Do you think your colleague could find Mrs Taylor and ask her to bring us some?'

Rhiannon left the room on Simon's nod and Benedict flung himself over to a drinks cabinet.

'I think a large brandy might be more the thing myself,' he said, amid much clinking of glass.

'Benedict! That's not going to help. Least of all your mother.

Now sit down and wait for some tea. I'm sure the Chief Inspector has some questions he needs to ask you and you'd best answer them sober.'

Surprisingly, though obviously unwillingly, Benedict abruptly dropped the crystal tumbler he was holding back on to the tray with a clatter and returned to where he had originally been sitting.

'Well?' he said to Simon. 'Let's get it over with, shall we? And I'd be glad to get back in to the cottage if you don't mind.'

More heavily built than his brother and broader-faced, he had the same strong bone structure. The eyes were less deep-set and the hair a lighter brown, closer to his mother's colouring, his eyes clear blue. He was a nice-looking boy, but an understatement to his brother's vibrant overstatement. Simon felt that in normal circumstances he probably had the easy going temperament he had displayed when he had observed him in Westwich. He decided to mention the occasion, some ordinary innocuous comment might calm the boy a little.

But Ben's eyes filled with tears. 'That's the last time Liam and I went anywhere together. We were seeing Mara off on the train to London.'

The memories of the bereaved were full of 'last things', Simon thought: this time last week, yesterday, he was alive; last birthday; last drink together – last meal together. It occurred to Simon for the first time that what had cost Liam's life might have endangered Benedict's.

'That was over a week ago. Did you not see much of Liam in the last week?'

Benedict brushed at his eyes. 'Plenty. We share the cottage. It's just that Liam's always out and about at something. And we're doing our own work in the gardens most of the time. But we met in the pub last night as a matter of fact. And had more than a few.'

So Liam's health consciousness was a selective thing, Simon thought.

'That attractive vase of flowers in the cottage, Ben, did you pick them?'

Ben gave Simon a look suggesting that he thought him mentally unhinged.

'What? What flowers and what the hell have flowers got to do with anything?'

43

'Bear with me. Would Liam have picked them?'

'I don't know what you're talking about. I'm not aware there *is* any bunch of flowers in the cottage. We neither of us liked cut flowers, we prefer to see them growing. Anyway, what's it got to do with anything?'

Simon left it. 'Ben, we want to establish clearly Liam's eating arrangements in the last twenty-four hours. He told me, for instance, that he was eating sandwiches with rocket and dandelion in them.'

'You met him?' Ben looked up at him, startled.

Simon pulled over an upright chair and sat down.

'Yes, earlier. And afterwards I was the one who found him.'

'Nobody told me.' Ben glanced accusingly at Barbara Meddick.

'We haven't had a chance, Ben,' she said soothingly. 'We couldn't find you at first.'

The door swung open and DC Jones entered, carrying a rattling tray.

Ben subsided again and watched while she poured them each a cup of tea.

'Did Liam make his own sandwiches?' Simon asked, handing Ben his cup.

'Yes, of course he did. It's one of the reasons we wanted to move into the cottage, so that we could eat the way we wanted. Neither of us could stand all the meat that gets eaten in this house.'

Barbara raised her eyes to the ceiling and sipped from her tea.

'When would he have made them?' Simon asked.

'This morning, before we started work. We each did our own. Only I didn't today because I left early. I was going to get some things from one of our suppliers and I'd decided to stop on the way back and get a ploughman's.'

'So, did he take his lunch-pack with him when he started work, or leave it prepared so that he could collect it later?'

'I don't know. Sometimes he did the one, sometimes the other. If it was hot like today he'd leave it at the cottage in the fridge, then take it to his usual place to eat. Where he was found.'

'Was it what he usually had for his sandwiches – cheese and salad-greens?'

'Or hummus or something else with salad. Yes. I suppose it

44

was. He had a thing about eating as naturally as possible and he was a bit of a fitness freak. He stuck to it more than I could, anyway.' Ben took a gulp of tea then placed the cup and saucer on the carpet by his feet.

'Do you think he could have made a mistake over what he put in those sandwiches?'

'Liam? Not a chance!' Ben stared in front of him for a moment then looked at Simon, his eyes wide. 'What are you saying? Are you saying Liam was deliberately poisoned?'

If the boy was so certain that Liam couldn't make such an error, surely the thought must already have occurred to him.

'I'm not saying anything, just asking questions at the moment,' Simon said quietly, watching the young man's face as the implications seemed to dawn.

Ben thrust himself from his seat and for a moment Simon thought the boy was going to grab hold of him. Instead he made for the door, protesting loudly:

'No way! It can't be and I don't believe it.' The door swung softly behind him, prevented from slamming by the sibilant sweep of the thick blue carpet.

'*Is* that what you think has happened?' Barbara Meddick said calmly. 'You think someone has *deliberately* poisoned Liam?'

CHAPTER 7

Yellow Balsam – Impatience

'What do *you* think, Mrs Meddick?' Simon asked.

'It's Miss Meddick,' she said.

'Not "Ms"?'

'Silly word. I used to be married some time ago but now I'm not and I've reverted to my maiden name because I am single. Though I concede that it is discriminatory and outmoded for men to have only one title, while women have two to distinguish their marital state. Does anyone care these days, with the convolutions of human relationships that go on?' She leaned back comfortably in her chair. 'I think we women should all be called Mistress, like Mistress Quickly. More egalitarian and much more fun.' Her sudden loquaciousness was accompanied by a glint in her eye that Simon could not quite read.

DC Jones had settled herself at a small table behind Barbara Meddick, her notebook open but with little written therein, Simon guessed. Not much had been gleaned so far. The older woman had paid her no attention, had focused solely on Simon, her eyes bright and fixed.

'It certainly sounds more colourful,' he said in reply to her remark. 'And Mistress Quickly's connubial status was a bit ambiguous. But, to go back to my question, what do *you* think about Liam's death?'

'I think I'm still too shocked to have any coherent opinion. But I admit I can't see Liam making a mistake over what he ate.' She picked up the teapot. 'Do you want some more tea? I think

I need some, strong and sweet.'

Simon declined and waited while she poured and stirred.

'Surely,' she said, 'if he has indeed died from poisoning, its source may have been something quite different. I mean there are so many botulism deaths these days, aren't there, and Liam and Ben hardly kept the cottage in the most hygienic state.'

'You're familiar with the cottage?'

She coloured slightly, her pale skin darkening along the cheekbones.

'I wouldn't say that. But I've been there now and again, if I've been trying to get hold of either of the boys for some reason.'

'Was the cottage left unlocked?'

'I'm afraid it was. They are both hopeless about keys, always losing them. And since Liam got his expensive computer kit in there they were supposed to be getting the lock changed on the door. The trouble is that in the winter when we're closed there never seems any need with only the family and employees about, so it's easy to get into bad habits.' She took a slow mouthful of tea and said, 'Which means, I suppose, that it would have been very easy for anyone to have access to the kitchen or any food, if what you imply is true.'

'He almost certainly died of poisoning and almost as certainly it was no accident, since everyone seems agreed that he wouldn't make a mistake over the plants he ate.'

She put down her cup, shuddering. 'God, what a horrible time its going to be. Poor Helen.'

'It may be inappropriate at this stage to speculate too much about who might have wished Liam ill, but is there anything you think I ought to know that might be relevant?'

She shook her head firmly. 'Nothing.' Then she added, 'Not at the moment, anyway,' and compressed her lips. She glanced at her watch. 'Lewis should be home soon. I couldn't get hold of him personally, but I left an urgent message with his secretary. He's going to be very shocked.'

'Were they close, he and Liam?'

'Lewis tried. He has no children of his own and I think he hoped that Helen's children would turn to him as some kind of substitute for their real father. But they were too old for that – at least the boys were. It's only five years since Gerald died.'

'Difficult for Lewis, then,' Simon murmured.

'Fortunately he's in London a lot of the time anyway.'

'How soon did Mrs Hartley marry her present husband after the death of her first?'

'About a year after Gerald died. But Lewis and Gerald were friends and colleagues, so Helen had known Lewis long before that. His first marriage ended several years ago.'

'And how long have you been with Mrs Hartley, Miss Meddick?'

'Oh, call me Barbara. Everyone else does.' She thought for a moment. 'It's a long time now. I used to be Gerald's personal assistant but after Helen and I became friends she asked me if I'd come and work with her here. Not that I knew anything about gardening, but I do her paperwork, help with her books and make sure the house runs smoothly.'

'It's certainly a pleasant place to work. And live,' Simon agreed, looking through the window at flowers lit by the western sun.

'I've been happy here,' she said simply.

'So Gerald Hartley didn't object too strongly to your leaving him?'

'Not in the least. His first consideration was always Helen.'

Simon wondered if there was an element of resentment in that last statement.

'Look, what are we talking about here, Chief Inspector? Surely this is all rather a waste of time?' She shifted and faced him more squarely.

Simon shrugged. 'It's helpful to have a clearer picture of Liam's background.'

'I'm not sure what *I've* got to do with it,' she said dismissively and stood up suddenly and gracefully.

'Not you personally, perhaps, but you may be the best person to talk to when it comes to some understanding of Clifford's Place and its inhabitants.'

She smiled down at him sardonically.

'Well you're not absolutely sure yet whether you have any need for such an understanding, are you, Chief Inspector?'

He was nettled, a feeling increased by her intimidating height as she towered over him. He had a rare insight into the power that his own considerable number of inches might have in unsettling other people and hoped that he used it cautiously.

'In so far as you have a sudden and unexplained death here, I do have grounds for asking questions, yes,' he said evenly.

She turned away from him and went to the window. 'I suppose Helen will want to close the gardens for the time being,' she said.

Simon was wondering if he had best leave it for today when the door swung softly open and a man entered the room. He crossed immediately to the drinks cabinet, dropping the jacket of his navy-blue suit over the back of a chair, and poured himself a whisky before turning abruptly to examine them both.

'I've just spoken to Mrs Taylor on the way in,' he announced. 'I always said that boy played around with too much funny food. I knew he'd cock it up some day.'

Lewis Enright, Simon assumed. Not very tall but sinewy and radiating energy. His hair was almost black, some grey at the temples, and worn quite long, curling at the collar of his immaculate white shirt. He had deep-set eyes, not unlike Liam's, and a straight firm mouth. A hard chin jutted in Simon's direction, proclaimed to anyone who had not already got the message from his dynamic movements that he was not to be messed with.

Simon found himself getting to his feet, an exercise he seldom managed with any semblance of grace.

'You must be the police presence,' Enright said in a sharp staccato.

Simon showed his ID and introduced himself and Rhiannon.

'We couldn't get you on your mobile, Lewis,' Barbara Meddick said.

'It was switched off. I was in a meeting,' Lewis said. He turned to Simon. 'So, Chief Inspector, why exactly are you here?'

'It's customary with an unexplained, unexpected death, for enquiries to be made. There will necessarily be an inquest,' Simon said.

'As I said, I wouldn't say it was unexpected – not with the way that boy played around with health-food fads. So how, in that case, can it be termed unexplained?'

'An investigation is required to make clear whether there may be a case likely to follow on from the inquest as well as supply information for that inquest.' Simon was aware that he had a tendency to sententiousness when he was under pressure.

Enright grunted and took a mouthful of whisky. 'Shouldn't that wait on the results of the post mortem? When's that going to be?'

'Tomorrow morning.'

'It *was* poisoning from some meal he'd concocted for himself, was it? Mrs Taylor's account of things was a bit garbled to say the least.'

'We can't be sure that it was until after the post mortem. But it seems very likely,' Simon said.

'Well, there you are then.' Enright, apparently responding only to the first part of Simon's reply, flung himself into a chair.

'Others don't seem to share your opinion that Liam was ignorant of the properties of the food he ate, Mr Enright.'

'Nonsense! I've heard Helen herself warn him. Isn't that right, Barbara?'

She said carefully, 'Helen brought up the children to a good knowledge of the plants in the garden and in the wild. I can't say I remember her saying anything specifically to Liam about what food he was eating. She knew he was very knowledgeable.'

'Where is Helen, anyway?' Enright asked the room in general.

'Vita's taken her up to her room. The doctor gave her some sort of tranquillizer,' Barbara said.

'I'd better go up and see her.' Enright placed his empty glass, on a table at his side and sprang from his chair. He gave Simon curt nod. 'No doubt I'll see you again, Chief Inspector.'

'No doubt,' Simon said after him. The door swished to a close.

'He doesn't seem too upset by his stepson's death,' he commented to Barbara Meddick.

She sighed. 'He's not the sort to exhibit his feelings.'

Simon thought that even if the man had no love for Liam, he might have shown more concern for Helen. At his expression Barbara Meddick added:

'As I said, they weren't close, he and Liam. Lewis's early efforts were rejected and Ben followed his brother's lead as usual. I've no idea if Lewis felt the rejection in any way, but he's a busy man and I imagine his efforts came from a sense of duty to Helen more than any particular interest in the children.'

'How does the daughter, Vita, get on with him?'

'Is all this relevant to the issue, Chief Inspector, or just idle curiosity?'

'*Is* there such a thing in a case of possible murder?' Simon countered.

She took a sharp intake of breath. 'You are sounding increasingly confident that that is what happened. Is there some evidence you haven't mentioned?'

Simon preferred for the moment not to go into details of his findings in the cottage. He said merely, 'It just seems increasingly likely, given Liam's knowledge of plants.'

'I suppose there's always the chance that he had a hangover and made the error. For a first and fatal time.'

'He was a heavy drinker?'

She pulled a wry face. 'No more than most of youth these days. But Ben did say they were in the pub last night.'

Simon supposed that it might be possible, too, that alcohol in the bloodstream might hasten the effects of any poison taken afterwards.

'Is that the pub in the village?'

'It's their usual place: the Clifford Arms in Chairford.'

'Miss Meddick – Barbara – how many people had access to Liam's cottage? You say it was left unlocked.'

'Are we back on the murder hypothesis?' she asked, raising an eyebrow.

'There's always the possibility of an accident, but I'd like to be clear about who lives and works here and could have gone there yesterday morning.'

'Anyone could – even members of the public, which means the world in general.'

'But the gates don't open to the public until ten in the morning, so let's keep to residents and workers, if you would.'

She said after a moment's pause, 'In the house itself, Helen, Lewis and myself, though Lewis wasn't here. Mrs Taylor lives in the flat over the stables and comes in at about seven. Linda Carver, the daily, lives in Chairford and she's in from seven thirty till one usually.' She paused and Rhiannon scribbled rapidly.

'Then we have Ben and Vita whom you know about, and the garden staff: Gavin Taylor is June Taylor's son, lives with his mother and has worked here since leaving school – and gone to college in the meantime; Clive Ashby lives in Banwick, a village which you probably came through on the way here – he does

general maintenance; Mara Kennedy is another gardener, quali-
fied before she came here, and finally there's Stephen Orchard,
ditto.'

'Where do the last two live?'

'They both have cottages that go with the job. Mara has the
south-east one, Stephen the north-west. All four cottages are at
the corners of the inner gardens.'

'Convenient,' Simon commented.

'There were a lot more gardeners in the old days. The ones
within the main gardens were for the head gardener and his assis-
tants. They'd all fallen into disrepair before Helen took over and
restored them.'

'Thank you.' Simon said. 'Perhaps you could let Liam's parents
know I'll be back tomorrow after we have some post mortem
results.'

'There'll be further tests presumably? If it's poison?'

Simon nodded. 'I'm afraid the cottage will have to remain off-
limits for the time being.'

'There's plenty of space in this house. Ben can use his old
room. The place has seemed terribly empty since the children
moved out.'

'Vita is still living here, is she?'

'No. She has one of the other cottages. Said she didn't see why
she couldn't when the boys had theirs. They call it independence.
And much good has it done them,' she said with a change of
expression.

Simon and DC Jones saw themselves out through the rear
entrance unaccosted by Mrs Taylor or anyone else.

After retrieving the evidence bags from the cottage they
returned to the car, which had become stiflingly hot.

'Any comments, Rhiannon?' Simon asked as they rapidly
lowered their windows. Since the onlooker saw most of the
game, and Rhiannon's role had been a boringly passive one,
Simon wondered what she might have picked up on that he had
missed.

'Not really,' she said. 'I mean, as yet officially, you've made out
no crime to answer for, but you still have to behave as if there
might be one in case evidence is damaged or destroyed. And you
risk upsetting people and putting up their backs at a time that's

difficult enough for them without our presence.'

'But it's a presence they'd call for soon enough if a crime were proved to be committed.'

'Not necessarily,' Rhiannon said. 'Especially if one of their own is responsible.'

'True enough,' Simon said, guiding the car into the lane.

'That Lewis Enright seemed determined to make out it couldn't have been anything else but an accident.'

'Understandable rather than suspicious, though, as you say.'

'Maybe,' Rhiannon said dubiously. 'But why didn't you mention the evidence we found at the cottage, sir? Surely that would have supported your reasons for asking questions at this stage?'

'Because, unlikely as it may be, there is always the faint possibility that Liam died from some other cause and was merely sick in the process. And if that proved to be the case at the PM, we'd look pretty silly talking about discarded sandwiches.'

'But you saw him. He showed all the signs of being poisoned, didn't he? I mean, he didn't look as if he was having a heart attack instead, did he?'

'No. He looked as if he had died of poisoning, and the doctor thought so too. If the PM supports what we think then our other evidence is completely relevant and the whole thing becomes more straightforward.'

'I see what you mean. I expect we'll be back here with the team tomorrow, then.'

They drove out from a tunnel of trees into a golden Cotswold evening and Simon's spirits lifted.

CHAPTER 8

Allspice – Compassion

Before Simon left the following morning for his unwished-for engagement with the pathologist his mother asked after Helen Hartley.

'You will be seeing her today, I suppose? Do let her know that if there is anything at all I can do . . . well, that I'll be glad to come over.'

Simon said that he would, and knew that he wouldn't. His mother seemed quite unable to acknowledge that Liam's death could have been anything other than an accident, preferring, it seemed, to consider that her son was being alarmist and policemanlike.

He collected Sergeant Longman and filled him in on the case on the way to the post mortem.

'It looks as if whoever did it doesn't want there to be any doubts about the fact that it *was* murder, then,' Longman commented.

'Interesting, isn't it?' Simon agreed.

'Unless, of course,' Longman added, 'Liam Hartley wanted to make what was really suicide look like murder.'

Simon thought that one could always rely on Longman to look for a perverse interpretation of events.

'And cleverly chose a policeman in whose presence to commit the deed,' he said drily. Longman enjoyed post mortems about as much as he did himself and Simon was aware that this was a part of his effort to keep his mind off the ordeal ahead.

Longman waved to a uniformed policeman in the street and turned again to Simon.

'You've had your leave cancelled, then. Is that a great disappointment?'

'It wasn't so bad that I was hoping someone would kill a fellow human being to get me out of it.'

'Bad enough then,' Longman said sympathetically. 'Hard work, was it?'

'Fortunately the brute force required has already been expended.'

'By you presumably. Funny it should all lead to you getting yourself involved in a likely murder case.'

'Very funny.' Simon pulled into the car park and stepped out on to tarmac that was already steaming, sweating and smelling in the early heat of the day. He drew lungfuls of the tarry odour into himself, hoping to numb his olfactory sensibilities to the odiferous assaults ahead.

Havers, the pathologist, short, rotund and unfailingly cheerful, was waiting for them with his assistant, the tools of his trade gleaming mercilessly in the bright lights.

'Nice change from knife-wounds and blunt instruments,' he greeted them.

'Always glad to oblige,' Longman said, moving into the room by some mysterious process of peripheral vision, never allowing his eyes to alight on anything that might alarm his stomach. He furtively stuck some Vick up his nose.

Havers made a few preliminary remarks into a small tape recorder and switched on a high-speed saw, as always in a hurry to begin.

Simon held up his hand and the ghastly whine ceased.

'We think the cause of death may possibly be poisoning with monkshood. Can you make sure the toxicologist knows this? It should speed things up.'

'Aconite, eh? It would fit very well, I would think.'

'Are you up on poisons?' Simon asked, hopefully. Some early advice would be a help.

'Not really.' Havers shook his head and gazed almost affectionately at Liam Hartley's corpse. 'Let's say I know enough to know how much I don't know.' He glanced at Simon. 'But the evidence seems consistent with what you say.' The high-pitched whine started again and the attack on Liam Hartley's earthly remains began.

Simon, though his attention was officially required, stared at the ceiling until his eyes ached from the glare of the lights and he closed them. He concentrated on the case and what he needed to do next. He thought he knew what had killed Liam because the murderer had made every effort to make sure that he knew. The unexplained vase of monkshood at the cottage pointed a mocking finger at the cause of death, as did the blatant leaving of Liam's original pack of sandwiches – to be discovered by the most casual inspection. Unless the clues so carefully laid were meant to obscure, rather than reveal. He sighed and shifted his weight to his other leg. Havers's voice continued its commentary, assisted by the usual sounds of pieces of anatomy being dismembered, slopped on to weighing-instruments and disposed of into various receptacles.

The question was, *why* had the murderer wanted it to be clearly a case of murder? Why had he, or she, not taken advantage of the possibility that the death might have been put down to accident, misadventure, or whatever? Was it meant as a warning to others, or another, perhaps? He shrugged mentally: those questions would not be answered until he had asked a lot of other questions of a number of people, because it seemed that virtually anybody could have had access to Liam's cottage that morning.

He needed to get an incident room set up. Would Helen Hartley agree to finding space for it somewhere at Clifford's Place, or would resistance to the idea of her son having been murdered get in the way of the investigation? He would have to see how things stood with her today, if she were recovered sufficiently from the tablets she had been given and the shock of the death of her eldest child.

'I think I've done all that must be done for the moment,' Havers said. He was prodding at something in a stainless steel dish. 'There seems to be more than one colour amongst the bits of leaves in the stomach contents. What did the boy think he was eating?'

'Dandelion and rocket with cream-cheese sandwiches.'

'So the murderer would have added the monkshood to that. Well there's no need to prolong this. The cause of death seems entirely consistent with what you have told me, so he can be kept on ice for any further investigation. But I can go on all day, if you prefer.'

Simon cleared his throat which had gone dry. 'No, that's fine,' he said, and hoped that this was a right decision. The fear that he was somehow being led, or misled, was still with him.

'You won't be pestering me for time of death calculations this time, then. I understand you were more or less a witness to what happened.' Havers cocked his head, robinlike, at Simon.

'Yes.'

'Very efficient of you.'

Simon supposed he would be getting more of that sort of comment.

'I'll get the stomach contents off to toxicology straight away. Along with the request you've made with regard to aconite. They should be able to answer the direct question without too much delay.'

'Fine.' Simon was, as usual, anxious to be gone from this soulless place. Longman was already at the door, his eyes fixed on an anatomy chart.

Outside, Longman leaned against the car, his eyes closed, breathing deeply.

'Normally I can't stand the smell of tar,' he said. 'I suppose everything's relative, isn't it?'

Inside the car it was oven hot and they both immediately lowered the windows.

'Clifford's Place?' Longman asked.

'Clifford's Place.'

The house and garden simmered in the misty heat, everything, including the birds, driven to shady places and silenced by the oppressive atmosphere. Or perhaps that was just his imagination, Simon thought, as he once again announced his unwanted presence. He told Mrs Taylor that he was going to the cottage but would be glad of a word with Mr or Mrs Hartley in about half an hour.

'Well, she's up,' Mrs Taylor said grudgingly. 'Though she shouldn't be, I'm sure. I'll tell her.' She closed the door abruptly.

The scene-of-crime personnel were all over the cottage. It was routine and necessary but Simon doubted the value of their efforts. Anyone associated with Liam must have been in this cottage and left evidence of being there. Only the prints of Liam himself had been found on the discarded pack of non-lethal sand-wiches that he and Rhiannon had found.

'It's such a secluded place,' Longman said, looking from Liam's bedroom window. 'I mean, you can see out fairly well from up here, but anyone approaching the cottage would be invisible from elsewhere in the garden.'

'And in a close community like this, there would probably be nothing remarkable in seeing someone coming here if it were one of themselves.'

'They might not even notice consciously something that was commonplace,' Longman agreed.

'I've got a feeling this is going to be a long haul.' Simon turned to the door. 'We'd better go and see if we can get things set up properly.'

Helen Hartley and Lewis Enright were waiting in the room Simon had seen them in separately the previous day, seated at the table as if ready for a conference, his hand on her shoulder. Her skin had lost its vitality and even her hair had flattened and looked lank. Enright looked as dapper as before and outwardly unaffected by events.

He gestured to the other chairs at the table. 'Come in, Chief Inspector, and sit down.'

Simon did as he was asked, introducing Longman as he did so.

'Anything new to report to us?' Enright asked.

Simon knew that post mortem violation was an image best kept firmly at the back of the minds of the bereaved so he made no direct mention of it.

'We can only confirm at this stage that the evidence is consis-tent with poisoning and that we have to treat Liam's death as suspicious. Which means an investigation, I'm afraid.'

Enright frowned. 'Even though I consider that it's likely to have been an accident?'

Simon felt that he was being accorded the treatment of a lowly clerk by the chairman of the board.

'There is certain evidence which points to a different conclu-sion,' he said, aware that formality of language might actually help here rather than be taken amiss.

Helen leaned forward in her seat and Enright's hand was removed from her shoulder.

'What evidence?' he asked, eyebrows raised.

Simon gave an account of what he had found in the cottage.

'So you think someone substituted the sandwiches Liam had made for different, and lethal, ones?' Enright said. Helen lowered her face into her hands.

'There's a vase of monkshood in the sitting-room at the cottage which appears to have been left by the intruder since Ben had no explanation for it. It's possible that this might be the poison used.'

Helen spoke for the first time, turning to her husband. 'You see, I told you Liam could never make a mistake like that.' She looked at Simon. 'The only possible way that it might be feasible that Liam got it wrong would have been if he had picked leaves growing close to a deadly plant. That just isn't possible. You said yesterday that he told you he was eating rocket and dandelion with cream-cheese. They are growing in the vegetable parterre. The monkshood is in the herbaceous borders.'

Simon realized with relief that she was no longer in denial of what had happened.

'Perhaps you could show me some time today, Mrs Hartley?'

Enright bristled. 'Surely you can get one of the others to do that for you, Chief Inspector?'

Helen said quietly, 'It's all right.'

'I suppose we're going to get a lot of this sort of thing, so we'd better get used to it,' her husband said resentfully.

'We'll need to speak to everyone here,' Simon agreed. 'In fact, I'd like to set up an incident room here if that's possible.'

'Yes, of course, Chief Inspector.' Helen Hartley laid her hands flat on the table and looked at Simon with a brittle brightness. 'The children's old games-room would do, I think,' she said sidelong to her husband. Her eyes widened as she tried to blink away the tears that suddenly sprang to them.

'Shall I show them the way?' Enright said, more subdued.

'If you would.' She wiped discreetly at her face with a tangled mansize handkerchief. 'I'll wait here for you, Chief Inspector.'

Enright held the door wide for Simon and Longman and directed them to follow him towards the western wing of the house. Over his shoulder he said:

'I realize your job is not an easy one, Chief Inspector, but I would appreciate it if you would tread gently. My wife is in a fragile state and there are others of us here who are feeling almost equally devastated by Liam's death.'

Except, it appeared, for at least one of them, Simon thought.

He said, 'I'll do my best, Mr Enright. I'm aware that any questioning at such a time is distressing to those involved.'

'Still can't really believe that Liam's death was murder,' Enright said, flinging wide a broad oak door and ushering them into a huge dusty room. 'A Victorian addition to the house,' he announced, 'designed as a ballroom but used, as Helen said, for the children's games on wet days. It's been used very little for some time now.'

A table-tennis table had been sited end-up against a wall and a collection of old and broken games' kit was scattered in corners and about the room. The floor itself was marked as a badminton court. Along the wall opposite the windows were huge mirrors, tarnished but adding greatly to the light in the room.

'They've used it occasionally to play loud music in and have a bit of a rave,' Enright said, looking around tolerantly at the disorder. 'I'll speak to Mrs Taylor. She can have Mrs Carver give it a quick once-over with her vacuum cleaner and I imagine that will do, will it?'

'Very well. Thank you,' Simon said.

'I'll leave you to it,' Enright said abruptly and disappeared through the door.

'This room is about twice the size of the area of our house,' Longman said. 'It's a bit warm though, with these south-facing windows.' He went over to one of them where dead flies lay in cobwebbed piles and tried to open it. After a couple of grunts he succeeded and garden-scented air wafted over them. 'It's going get even hotter when the sun gets round on to these windows properly.'

'Get the team out here to set up around noon and we'll all meet at three,' Simon said. 'Have a quick wander to orientate yourself meanwhile, Geoff.'

Simon found Helen Hartley still sitting at the table. Her husband had not returned. She stood as Simon entered.

'I'll show you where the plants are now, shall I?'

He was led through a recessed door at the front of the house and out into the unrelenting sunlight. The mist had been burned off the distant view. In the foreground the orderly beauty of the surrounding gardens made the ugly anarchy of murder seem ever more incongruous.

Simon glanced down at Helen Hartley's set features. She had wrapped her arms around herself as if she felt a metaphysical chill in the burning heat. He sensed she was a woman unused to the harsher realities, a woman who had lived a largely protected existence and who had no hard-won reserves of resilience with which to face unbearable sorrow. She looked so forlorn that his instinct was to put a protective arm around her. She must feel very alone in this crisis – with Liam's father already dead and her present husband hardly seeming to exude tender compassion.

She paused mid-way along the herbaceous border on their left and pointed.

'Monkshood,' she said, indicating the tall misty purple spires in the centre of the bed. 'Steel Blue. It's an early flowering variety.'

Simon looked automatically for traces of footprints, realizing as he did so that any such marks made innocently or otherwise would routinely be covered over tidily with soil. There was nothing to indicate that anyone had been near them.

'The same in the opposite border,' she said and they crossed over to stare pointlessly at a matching group of plants. Again the soil was undisturbed.

'There is some in the pool garden as well. I'll show you.' She set off walking stiffly, puppet-like. They neared the garden where Liam had died and Simon expected Helen to move quickly on, but she stopped and walked slowly over to the place where her son had choked out his life, staring down at the stream as if in a trance.

'You saw him,' she said, looking over her shoulder at Simon. 'Did he suffer very much? I had no chance to ask you anything before.'

Simon hated to think how much agony Liam Hartley must have been in. He could only lie.

'It was very quick, Mrs Hartley. So I don't think so.'

'I still can't take it in, not really. He was so much of a presence. Everything will be different now.' He could hardly distinguish her words above the sound of water falling over rocks.

'And I find it even more difficult to believe that anyone did this to him deliberately,' she said in a firmer voice, turning to face him. 'It makes it harder to bear.'

He said gently, 'You are so sure that Liam had not perhaps angered someone too much, done something to provoke?' He remembered the assertive, even arrogant, young man he had observed at Westwich station, the confident Liam he had spoken to even as he had begun to die.

She swallowed, as if trying to swallow invisible tears.

'Perhaps it's just that the whole idea of murder is unthinkable when it happens to someone you love. Death itself is that. This is so much, much worse.'

She had not denied that motive might have been there, somewhere, but Simon was unable to press the point.

She turned away, saying, 'He called this his Arcadian grove.'

'They were a savage lot, the Arcadians,' Simon said.

'Were they? I don't think Liam knew that.' She added, 'I think I may have him buried here.' She had a beautiful voice, Simon noticed, soft and low, suggestive of innate gentleness and kindness.

They went on in silence until they reached the pool garden, the blank eye of the pool reflecting a cloudless blue sky. A man was working there, repointing the walls of the raised pond. He stood up as Helen approached and bent his head to her, speaking in a low voice. She stepped back after a few moments, quickly dabbing at her eyes with the crumpled handkerchief.

'Thank you, Clive,' she said. 'Chief Inspector Simon, this is Clive Ashby, who is the man who manages to do all the maintenance at Clifford's Place.'

He was a tall sinewy man with rough sandy hair and a tanned lined face with bright dark eyes. He glanced at Simon, his eyes quickly assessing, and nodded his head.

'I'll get on, shall I, Mrs Hartley?' he said.

'Please do, Clive,' she said, managing a smile for him.

She turned to Simon. Again she pointed at a group of the sinister hooded flowers.

'They're beautiful, aren't they?' she said. 'Though I shall not be able to grow them in my garden any more.'

But Simon had learned enough by a process of osmosis from

his mother to know that there were other equally deadly plants in any plant enthusiast's garden, many of them as seductively beautiful as the one now shadowing the lower stems of a pink climbing rose. And it was likely that the murderer was more aware of them than he or even Helen Hartley was, and had chosen carefully.

'Do the people who work here know which plants have poisonous properties?' he asked Helen.

As if forgetting for a moment she said, 'Oh yes. They mostly know anyway from their training but I always make sure to tell the staff and we make a point of labelling any such plants that we sell accordingly.' More haltingly she added, 'But whoever did this to Liam would have researched the difference between poisonous and deadly poisonous – I wasn't that detailed in what I told them. Many plants are poisonous, but comparatively few would kill as quickly as monkshood, if that's what it was, killed Liam.'

'This is where they must have been picked from,' she said quietly. She pointed to the clump again. 'They've been cut, not broken off, mainly from the left side of the group.'

Again there were no footprints. Too much to have asked, Simon thought. But the ground beside the plants looked recently scratched over, fresher than the baked-looking earth around. It was unlikely that any prints would have shown in the soil, but perhaps in the morning dew that would have seemed less obvious to the killer.

Beside him, Helen Hartley shuddered. 'I suppose you want to see where we grow the rocket?' she said.

There was no real necessity. Whoever had made up Liam's sandwiches could have picked the salad leaves at any time and stored them in their fridge if need be. It was only the monkshood that was likely to have been fresh-cut. But he agreed and followed as she led him down a slope. This joined a path beside the ha-ha that allowed the unbroken view of the fields and hills to the south, and led into the western section of the garden – a part that he, Jessie and Elizabeth had not managed to explore before the discovery of Liam had ended their expedition. More gardens within gardens followed, and open grass with specimen trees, before they reached a walled area entered through an old oak door.

Within was an ornamental parterre divided into squares and triangles edged by lavender, catmint and box and given added form by well-pruned fruit-trees, already showing tight clusters of small red apples and miniature pears. The heat there was intensified and the scent from herbs soporific.

'This is very lovely,' he said, unable not to comment. He supposed it was the effect Jessie was aiming for on a less grand scale and without the impossibly expensive high old red-brick walls.

'They're the original kitchen gardens,' she said, again holding her arms tightly around her. 'The rocket's here.' She led him further into the garden beyond some small trees. A sturdy dark-haired young man was weeding in one of the vegetable sections.

He looked up, an expression of embarrassment and alarm on his face.

'Mrs Hartley,' he acknowledged, the colour intensifying in his already ruddy cheeks. He swallowed visibly, apparently uncertain whether he should say more. He had none of the comparative ease of the older man, Clive Ashby, when faced with someone recently, and shockingly, bereaved.

'It's all right, Gavin,' Helen assured him. 'We're just here for a few moments. You just carry on.' She managed a smile for him, too, before leading Simon to a small bed with neat rows of a green plant with leaves the shape of elongated oak-leaves. It was clear they had already been well picked.

'Rocket is always used as a salad green, isn't it?' he asked.

'Yes, that's right. We use it a lot. Liam was very fond of it.'

'He would presumably have come out and picked this early in the morning before he started work?'

'He always liked his food to be as fresh as possible. He had strong opinions on the goodness being lost as it got staler. He said the life force would be too long gone.' She leaned and picked a leaf. 'Ironical, isn't it?'

The whereabouts of the rocket plants was largely irrelevant to the investigation. It was where the monkshood was and how easily accessible to a poisoner that was of interest. And the plants in the pool garden, hidden from view by the enclosing hedges, would have been available to just about anyone who wanted their actions to be kept secret. Everyone who worked here was going to have to be closely questioned about their whereabouts early on the day Liam died. Though the monkshood might have been picked hours earlier, during the night.

'Where would Liam have taken the dandelion leaves from?' he asked Helen, wondering where in these immaculately tended gardens such a weed would be likely to grow.

'As I said, we grow them here,' she pointed to a neighbouring bed where the vigorous weed sprouted its sunny yellow flowers. She knelt and pulled off their heads. 'We can't let them set seed. A pity really.' She scrunched the bright petals in her hand and Simon felt a sudden frisson, as if something significant had been said or done. He shook it away; if anyone must be held innocent in this affair, surely it had to be Helen Hartley.

'I wanted the dandelion plants to be blanched by covering the leaves,' Helen said. 'But Liam insisted that they would lose a lot of their vitamin and mineral content if we did that. Blanching reduces the bitterness of the leaves.' She looked up at Simon, a hurt expression on her face. 'It would not have been so easy to fool him if the leaves he thought he was eating had not been bitter.' She moved away. 'Whoever did this picked off the leaves from the monkshood for his sandwiches and then considerately arranged a vase of the flowers to look their best. A deliberate taunt,' she said bitterly. 'It's unbearable to think it might be some-one from here.'

'Unlikely that it's not.' He spoke gently.

'I suppose that must be so.'

Aware that she had seemed to evade the question before, he asked her again, 'Do you have any thoughts about who it could be, Mrs Hartley?'

She turned away from him and began walking slowly back towards the oak door.

'It's hard to think the unthinkable,' she said over her shoulder. As she closed the door behind them she murmured, 'If you don't mind, Chief Inspector, I'm going back to the house for a rest. Mrs Taylor should be able to help you with any practical matters.'

She disappeared swiftly along a turn in the path, leaving him again with only an enigmatic reply.

CHAPTER 9

Acacia – Friendship

Simon took a path to his right in an effort to orientate himself to the gardens and where the secluded staff cottages were. One of the buildings appeared quickly, built close to the western external wall of the vegetable parterre. This one, like Liam and Ben's, was discreetly placed behind high hedges. The cottages would all have been screened, in the best Victorian manner, from sensibilities too delicate for the less aesthetic realities behind the cultivation of a pleasure garden and the growing of food for the house. It differed from theirs in having a larger garden to itself, contained by low box-hedges and filled with scented flowers.

Behind it, backing against the west wall of the parterre, were some traditional wooden greenhouses and polytunnels. He remembered Helen making some remark about Vita and green-houses and thought that this must be where the daughter of the house had decided to live. Did the decision of Helen's offspring to move into semi-independent quarters signify anything about their relationship with Helen's second husband Enright, or was it just the usual youthful desire for independent space?

He could see no sign of Vita or anyone else and retreated back along the path to take a different turning, which led him along the western fringes of the garden opening into wide lawns with fine ornamental trees. Near the south-western boundary, again hidden away, he saw the eaves of a third cottage. As he turned yet another corner he bumped into a slight dark girl in a pink T-shirt, accompanied by a young man.

'Oh!' she said. 'You startled me.' She put a hand over her heart and smiled. 'Are you the police?'

Simon introduced himself.

'I'm Mara Kennedy. I work here.'

He remembered her from Westwich station, with Liam and Ben, but it was obvious that she had no recollection of him.

'Were you coming to see me?' She sounded surprised.

'Just getting my bearings,' Simon said.

'I could show you around sometime, if you like. We were just going to the cottage for a cup of tea. This is Stephen Orchard who also works here,' she said, turning to introduce him.

He was a good-looking young man in his mid-twenties, with longish brown hair and clear blue eyes. He gave a faint smile of acknowledgement to Simon but said nothing.

Mara hesitated. 'Would you like to join us?'

He would, quite. He would have to speak to both of them sooner or later. He hesitated too, and she smiled up at him, showing small white teeth. It could wait, he decided. He wanted to speak to Barbara Meddick again first – someone more mature with perhaps a dispassionate overview of everyone at Clifford's Place. He asked if Mara knew where Barbara was.

'I was just talking to her. I've been tying in roses on the arbour. She's hiding there.'

'Does she feel the need to hide, then?'

'Oh, not from you, I'm sure.'

'From whom then?' he asked, smiling.

Mara's expression changed. 'I forgot for a moment that I was talking to a policeman.'

Simon thought that highly unlikely.

She went on rapidly, 'I just meant, well, it's all a bit heavy and Barbara is always at the centre of a crisis. You know, a bit of a rock for everyone. Do you want me to show you where she is?'

'Just point me in the general direction.'

'Go on in and put the kettle on, Steve, would you?' she said and without waiting for a response led Simon along another blissfully shaded path to a wider one. 'You'll be wanting to speak to all of us, I suppose, at some point?' she said as he came to walk beside her.

'Yes, we will. Is there anything you think I ought to know sooner?'

'I'll have to watch my words, won't I?' she said, her small brow knitted anxiously. 'I don't think I know anything that will help you. Is it true that Liam ate sandwiches that had monkshood in them?'

'So it seems.' That piece of information had filtered out quickly.

'He would never have made a mistake,' she said.

'So I gather.'

'Someone did it to him deliberately,' she stated.

'No idea who?' he asked looking down at her nut-brown shoulders, her tawny neck with tendrils of sweat-wet hair clinging to it.

She raised green eyes to him and shrugged. 'I can't even imagine it,' she said. 'It all seems unbelievable. I know Liam could get people's backs up but I can't think who'd want to kill him.' She sighed, lifting her brown shoulders. 'And now the gardens are closed and we're all over the place. I just keep working. It seems best.'

'I'm sure it is,' he said banally.

She came to a halt and pointed through an archway to an arbour smothered with white roses.

'She's still there.' The seated figure of Barbara Meddick could just be made out through the foliage.

He thanked Mara.

'I'll see you again, then,' she said, looking up at him through dark lashes. She turned quickly and was gone like some species of bright elf disappearing into the greenery.

Barbara Meddick was gazing at the view down the valley where sheep lay soporifically chewing grass in the shade of oak trees. She nodded at him, seemingly unsurprised by his arrival.

'Those are what the Cotswolds are all about – sheep,' she said, her gaze once more on the lovely and peaceful view. 'Without them, this privileged corner of England would not be as it is.'

'Churches, manor houses, "and all that beauty, all that wealth e'er gave",' Simon agreed.

She rubbed her arms, as if suddenly cold.

'Doesn't that verse end with: "the paths of glory lead but to the grave"?'

'Thomas Gray was a melancholy fellow.'

'But not inappropriate at this moment.'

'I suppose not. Did Liam have a glorious path cut short?' Simon asked, sitting beside her on the curved stone seat.

'He could have done very well, I'm sure, with or without his mother's help,' Barbara said.

'He spoke about his ambitions to me just before he died.'

'Makes it all the more sad, doesn't it?'

'Had there been any talk of his going it alone?' Simon asked, half-turning to face her.

She paused a moment before replying. 'I think he would have liked to. He was beginning to get bored. Said he was mostly just a maintenance man. He did make some input into the designs his mother drew up for her clients, but it didn't satisfy.'

A bee nosed dozily around them before landing on a white rose by Barbara's cheek. She continued to stare, eyes half-closed, into the far distance. The scents and the heat combined to make Simon's job seem even more alien than usual. He struggled to focus as he knew he should, but Barbara Meddick was soothing company and he had the illusion at the moment that he had all time in the world.

'Liam did have some commissions of his own and his clients were pleased, but I think he always felt that in his situation he was somehow taking work away from his mother. It made for awkwardness, I think,' Barbara added.

Simon supposed that such compunction in Liam had been possible, but the young man had not seemed to him the type to show such concern where his own ambition was concerned. In a modified form he suggested this to Barbara.

She smiled. 'Well, perhaps I was gilding the lily a little. I suppose one tends to try to say the best of people when they're dead.'

'And yet, that's the last thing that helps the police in their enquiries. They need to know the quite unvarnished truth,' Simon said.

There was a slight pause. 'It's very hard to give you that. All sorts of things go on in families that don't mean anything serious but might not look that way to an outsider. Particularly in the context of a murder. I spoke to Helen when Lewis was showing you the games room and she told me what you'd found at Liam's cottage.' She turned her head to Simon, her eyes now wide open. 'You must be aware of all kinds of conflicting loyalties that make it difficult for people to be entirely frank with you.'

Simon knew exactly what she meant. A murder in a community had a devastating effect on the individuals within it, causing divisions, tensions and suspicion. He understood that Barbara Meddick might feel it disloyal to Helen Hartley to speak too frankly about her son or anyone else in the family.

'If it's not too fanciful,' he said, 'try thinking about the investigation as a form of drastic surgery, painful but necessary to survival.'

'But not Liam's survival. Too late for that,' she replied.

He waited, waving another drunken bee from his head.

He heard her sigh beside him and shift slightly.

'You will be asking everyone about Liam,' she said. 'You will want everyone's ideas on who might have done this to him, so I suppose I may as well give you my image of him, to add to all those others.' She clasped her hands tightly in her lap and breathed deeply.

She was wearing a green linen dress, its arms elbow-length and its neckline scooped fairly low. It was elegant but not a form of clothing designed to disguise her obvious merits. He thought that she was not a woman who would readily dissemble. And yet he recognized that there was something in her that was innately very private, so that, though she might not lie to him she might, as they say, be economical with the truth.

'I should say, first of all,' she said, rubbing a glossy fingernail, 'that I have no idea who might have done this to Liam. And that I still find it hard to believe,' she added firmly. 'But he was a difficult sort of person. By that I mean that he didn't mind offending people and even liked to stir people up. He was spoilt, of course. Helen was always overindulgent with him.'

'Was there anyone in particular whom he offended, do you know?'

'He'd have to do a bit more than merely offend them to produce this effect, wouldn't you say?' she said sharply. 'No, not that I'm aware of, anyway.'

'As you told me, you've known them all a long time, haven't you, Miss Meddick?'

70

'Do call me Barbara. I imagine you're going to be around for a little while yet, Chief Inspector. Yes, as I said before, since Helen poached me from her first husband.'

'What's Lewis Enright like?'

'You've met him. In computer parlance, what you see is what you get.'

'Meaning?'

Barbara's tone suggested she was not wholly in favour of Helen's more recent husband. 'Just that. He's energetic, abrasive and good at what he does.'

'Some kind of financial expert, I understand.'

'Something like that.'

'How did he and Mrs Hartley meet?'

'He was a friend of Gerald's, as I told you. He'd been for weekends and to dinner on various occasions. After Gerald died he took on a protective role with the bereaved widow and the rest followed.'

'How did the children accept him – Liam, Ben and Vita?'

Barbara pulled down a white rose and held it to her nose. 'Not easily to begin with. Liam was at that sort of age to resent anyone trying to usurp his father. Ben was a bit harder to read, though he always tended to follow his big brother. When Liam did a couple of years at college things were peaceful enough. But when he came back and Ben went away things got a bit disrupted at times. He didn't like Lewis exerting his authority over anything that happened here.'

'And Vita?'

'Oh, Vita's never much trouble,' Barbara said easily. She lifted her face in the dappled sunlight.

'There was no signficance, then, in the fact that the children of the house have all moved out into former gardeners' cottages?'

She said nothing for a moment and then gave a short laugh.

'It began with Liam's fads over food. Mrs Taylor complained about him making his *concoctions* as she put it, in *her* kitchen. So Liam demanded that one of the cottages be made available to him. It had been empty for a while, anyway. Ben joined him.'

'And Vita followed suit?'

Barbara smiled at the view. 'Said she didn't see why she couldn't too, especially as she was spending so much time in the greenhouses over there. Lewis had it done up for her. It had been renovated but it was fairly basic.' She made as if to move.

Simon said, 'I wonder if you would give us a list of the employees here, with some information on their backgrounds, what they do here exactly, etcetera. As soon as possible, if you wouldn't mind. With any details such as how long they've worked here, their ages and so on.'

She agreed, getting to her feet and smoothing her dress. She stood for a moment staring out across the fields as if, Simon thought, she longed for escape. 'The gardens are closed for goodness knows how long. But at least Helen managed to finish filming her latest series last week. I'm glad that wasn't wrecked as well,' she added, as if to herself. Then she straightened and turned to Simon.

'I should be getting back now. I don't like leaving Helen for so long. I just came here for a little peace and quiet, rather selfishly, I'm afraid.'

'And I disturbed you,' Simon said.

'I'm sure you're going to be doing more of that,' she replied, looking down at him unsmilingly.

CHAPTER 10

Woodbine – Fraternal love

Simon dropped Jessie at Westwich station the following morning. She had had a telephone call from her sister Jane the evening before, asking Jessie to come and give some support in a crisis with her daughter Amanda. Amanda of the ferocious spiky red hair, currently doing her A-levels, had got herself pregnant and was intending to have and keep the baby – and Jane was totally opposed to the idea.

'I don't know what Jane expects me to do about it,' Jessie confided to Simon and Elizabeth. 'It has to be Amanda's decision. But I suppose if it helps Amanda to have an independent ear listening to her . . .'

'What about the father?' Elizabeth had demanded robustly.

But the student father had his own career prospects in sight and there was no question of marriage and not much hope of financial support.

'The trouble today,' Elizabeth had intoned, 'is that people don't take enough responsibility for their actions – and action for their responsibilities.'

'Good luck.' Simon grinned sympathetically as he kissed Jessie goodbye.

'I'll be back tomorrow evening. Let me know who's picking me up,' Jessie said as the early train began pulling out of the station.

Simon collected Detective Superintendent Longman and drove out to Clifford's Place through a misty haze signalling yet another hot day. The small team was already assembled in a corner of the large games room, leaning on tables and drinking coffee apparently provided by Mrs Taylor. Rhiannon Jones pointed to an ancient filter machine and offered some to Simon and Longman.

'We've got all the gear,' she said to Simon, indicating filters and a packet of ground coffee. 'And there's water in the cloakroom next door.'

Simon took a brimming mug from her. 'I'm glad the essentials have been attended to.'

The whiteboards had been set up, with a photograph of Liam Hartley and the minimum of facts so far known outlined beside it. Simon called them to order and began with the news from pathology that there had been a high level of alcohol in Liam's body.

'Which may have hastened the effects of other, much more lethal toxins.' He turned to the board. 'These are the names of people resident and working at Clifford's Place, all of whom need to be interviewed. I want you to find out if anyone has anything to suggest about possible motives for Liam's death and I want to know where they were, when they were there and whom they saw and when they saw them from the start of Saturday. Also any background you can glean about themselves and others connected with Clifford's Place. Miss Meddick has promised to supply us with additional information on employees soon.'

He assigned names to each of them. 'I'll speak to Benedict, the brother, first. Any other names that you think may be relevant to the inquiry can be added here, along with their relationship to the victim.'

'We're still waiting on the official toxicology report, but there doesn't seem any doubt that it was aconite that killed Liam Hartley. Any questions?'

There weren't any. They took it as a dismissal and began slowly filing from the room.

'Ben Hartley's staying here at the big house, is he, while we're still looking at the cottage?' Longman said. 'What do we do? Wander around the bedrooms? I mean, it's not like going and knocking on someone's door in an ordinary house when you want to interview someone, is it?'

'I shouldn't worry too much about the etiquette, Geoff. We'll ask Mrs Taylor. I imagine she knows most of what goes on around here.'

In fact they found Ben seated at the kitchen table, sharing a pot of tea with her. For a moment they looked like conspirators, leaning forward, elbows on the table, their hands grasping their cups: Mrs Taylor upholstered in a cream-coloured pinafore, dark frizzy hair framing her highly coloured face, Ben pale, his face set. He coloured as he looked up at them.

'Have you finished with the cottage yet?' he asked.

'It will take a little while, I'm afraid. A day or so,' Longman said.

Mrs Taylor raised the teapot. 'Would you like a cup?'

'We've just had coffee, thanks,' Simon said.

'I don't understand what you need the cottage for, all this time,' Ben said sullenly. ' I mean, what are you looking for?'

'Just procedure,' Simon said. 'If there's anything you want from there you must say and I'll see what I can do.'

'Thanks very much,' Ben said insincerely. 'But if you're looking for incriminating fingerprints, mine are all over the place. And everybody else's here. We had a party there a few weeks ago.'

'That should keep them busy, then,' Longman said, eyeing the teapot.

'Is there somewhere we can talk privately, Ben?' Simon asked.

'Don't mind me, I'm sure,' Mrs Taylor said, her back to them at the large Belfast sink.

'We'd like to talk to you as well, Mrs Taylor. Later on if that would be convenient,' Longman said.

She turned and gave them a level stare for a moment. 'Oh, I shall be here, or hereabouts. Though I don't know what I'm supposed to tell you.'

Ben Hartley stood up abruptly. 'We could try Lewis's study. I'm sure he won't mind.' His expression suggested otherwise.

The room was somewhere to the rear of the house where the sun had not yet penetrated so that it was cool, even chilly. A large desk stood near the window which looked out to the west and the high brick wall that contained the vegetable garden. The room was lined with books and a table near the centre of the room held a drinks tray and glasses. With the club chairs near the fireplace it

all added up to a comfortably masculine retreat. The only feminine touch was the charming portrait of a young Dutch girl staring serenely at them from above the mantelpiece. Ben Hartley
took one of the easy-chairs near the empty fireplace and Simon
and Longman lodged by the desk.

'You've had some time to think about things since I saw you
last,' Simon said to Ben. 'Have you had any thoughts about who
might have done this to your brother?'

'I'm afraid not.' The young man stared into the dead fireplace.

Simon let the silence linger for a little before saying: 'I'm told
that Liam was not averse to, shall we say, annoying people. That
he spoke his mind and may have made enemies.'

'Enemies! You make it sound so dramatic.'

'It seems to me that it is rather dramatic, being murdered,'
Simon said mildly.

'I suppose so.' It was said grudgingly.

'So Liam had had no rows with anyone lately?'

'I didn't say that.' Ben looked across at Simon. 'But we're a
close-knit community here and you're seriously expecting me to
tell tales about them?'

'Did you love your brother, Mr Hartley?'

Ben looked embarrassed. He said quietly, 'Of course I did.'

'But you're not interested in helping us find his murderer?'

'It's not like that! I just can't believe that anyone here would
have done it.'

'You think some stranger did it, then?'

There was a pause. 'I don't suppose that's likely either,' the
young man said reluctantly.

'Anything you say will be in the strictest confidence, you
know.'

Ben looked disbelieving.

This was going nowhere, Simon thought. Perhaps facts rather
than speculation might get him talking.

'Mr Hartley—'

'You called me Ben before, like everyone else. It always sounds
ominous when the police call you Mr.' Ben shifted uncomfortably
in his chair and kept his eyes averted from Simon and Longman.

'All right, Ben, tell me about when you met Liam for a drink the
evening before he died. I understand he had a fair bit to drink.'

'How do you know that?' Ben looked up from lowered brows.

Simon said. 'You said so and the post mortem showed a level of alcohol still in his body. We're assuming, unless you can tell us he started the day with a few doses of alcohol, that he had been drinking the night before in fairly large quantities.'

'We went to the Clifford Arms in Chairford.'

Simon had noticed the signpost to Chairford, a turning north from the road into Clifford's Place.

'That's the next village, just up the valley?'

Ben nodded.

'You went with him then. Who else was there? You may as well tell us, Ben, because we'll be talking to the landlord.'

'Gavin Taylor was there with Jenny Shipman, his girlfriend, and Mara came in just after me and Ben.'

'No one else?'

'No one we knew particularly. Except Alan Fairburn. He came in with his friend a bit later.'

'Who is Alan Fairburn?'

Ben shrugged. 'An old friend of my mother's.'

It was like extracting teeth. 'Does he live locally?'

'He's been staying with the friend who was with him – Colin Wheatley, who lives in Chairford.'

'So he's visited Clifford's Place since he came to stay in the village?'

'They all came too dinner last week.' Ben supplied this doggedly extracted information in a dull monotone, as if detaching himself from any substance that might be there.

'Did anything in particular happen that night at the Clifford Arms?'

The young man looked quickly across at Simon; his carefully impassive expression changed to something much more intent.

'So who's already been talking to you?'

'We haven't spoken to anyone in detail yet, Ben. What happened?'

Ben tightened his lips, as if he had said all he was going to say.

Simon flipped his notebook shut. 'If you'd prefer us to hear other people's versions of events rather than your own, we can do it that way.'

'All right, I'll tell you. It's nothing important but no doubt you lot will try and make something of it. Liam and Gavin had a row.'

'This is Gavin Taylor, Mrs Taylor's son?'

Ben nodded.

Simon waited, conscious that this intrusiveness must be painful to a young man who had just lost his brother, and one who had apparently been very close to him. He understood Ben's distaste for what he, Simon, was putting him through, but there was nothing he could do to make the process any easier.

The silence grew and Longman stood up and began looking through the volumes on the shelves – his not particularly subtle statement that they weren't going anywhere just yet.

'It was over Jenny,' Ben said in a small voice.

'Yes?'

'Jenny is Gavin's girlfriend and she's pregnant.' Ben let out a breath. 'Liam said something stupid about the paternity.'

'He suggested that Gavin wasn't the father?'

Ben nodded. 'And implied that he might be himself.'

Likely to earn Liam a knock on the nose at the very least, Simon thought.

'Was that possible, do you think? That Liam was the father?'

Ben shifted impatiently. 'How should I know? I shouldn't think so, but Liam always fancied himself with women.'

'What happened then?'

'Gavin let fly at Liam and knocked him down. Jenny started crying and Mara went over to her. Then Liam got up and thumped Gavin. A few tables got knocked over and the landlord rushed in from the other bar. Then Alan and his friend came in and broke it up. Liam went off after that and we all tried to calm down Jenny and Gavin.'

'How long had you been there before all this started? Had Liam just had too much to drink?'

'He'd had a few. But he and Gavin didn't get on and Liam knew how to wind him up.'

'Why should he want to? Was Liam upset about anything when he went there that evening?'

A pause. 'No, I don't think so. It just happened.'

'Did Gavin go after Liam? When Liam left?'

'No. He was too busy making a fuss of Jenny. She was even more upset because by then the whole pub and everybody knew

Jenny was pregnant and it wasn't common knowledge until then. And Alan's friend Colin is Jenny's boss, which made it even worse.'

'I can imagine. What is Jenny's job with Colin?'

'She's nanny to his children.'

Which made everyone whose name he had come across so far interlinked in one way or another with Clifford's Place and its occupants.

'Gavin lives with his mother in a flat over the stables, doesn't he?'

Ben nodded.

'Does Jenny live in?'

'With the Wheatleys, yes.'

'Has anything else of a similar nature happened recently? Any rows or fights involving Liam?'

Ben hunched in his chair. He looked very young and vulnerable. 'No,' he said into his chest.

Simon came to sit in one of the chairs nearer to Ben.

'Ben, can you give me any details of how Liam normally prepared his food.'

Ben glanced nervously at Simon and tensed even more.

'You asked me that the other day.'

'You may have been told what I reported to your parents – that we found the sandwiches that Liam had prepared for himself thrown into the waste-bin in the kitchen at your cottage. Which means that the killer discarded them and replaced them with some lethal ones that he or she had made up. So Liam must have made his sandwiches earlier, then come back to the cottage to collect them – or the ones that he thought were his – and taken them to eat in the garden. He presumably ate his breakfast first and then prepared his lunch?'

'Yes,' Ben said impatiently.

'What sort of time would he leave the cottage to work in the gardens?'

'Eight at the latest, I suppose.'

'So the person who made the second batch must have come into the cottage after that and made up a fresh set, using the bread that was already there, or a matching loaf?'

'What are you getting at?'

79

'I want to know how premeditated this was. So was there sufficient bread already in the cottage to make a second batch? When did he, or you, buy the loaf?'

'I think Barbara got it for him from Bilton the day before. It's where we usually got bread from because there's a really good bakery there. I didn't have any of it. It probably wasn't used until Liam made his sandwiches up.'

'So the half-loaf left in the bread-bin would account for the sandwiches Liam made and the ones that were made afterwards,' Simon said.

So the murderer, who must have planned this method of killing Liam, would have had to know that enough bread was in the cottage to make the substitute sandwiches or would have had to supply it himself, or herself. And anyone living or working here might have been aware that Barbara had bought bread for Liam.

'Would you say it was an easy thing to do, slip into the cottage, make up the sandwiches and leave them in place of the others?' Simon asked.

'If you mean would anyone expect to be able to do it without being noticed, then the answer's yes. Anyone might have known I'd gone to the wholesalers – I often did on Saturday mornings. And the cottage isn't exactly exposed to all eyes, is it?'

'You don't lock the cottage, I understand. Are you all used to walking into each other's homes as a matter of course?'

'I suppose so. It's a bit like an extension to the house. We haven't really regarded it as separate. Except Vita, I suppose. She's not so keen on people just barging in.'

'So, if you *had* come in and found someone making up sandwiches in your kitchen, would it have surprised you particularly? If they said they'd run out of bread, for instance. In other words, was the person who did it taking any particular risk if discovered?'

'I'd have been pretty surprised to find Lewis there making up chunky sandwiches.'

'Or Barbara, perhaps?'

Ben looked derisive. 'Or Barbara, as you say.'

'But none of the younger people would have risked much?'

'They would with a bunch of monkshood in their hand. But as I've already said, anyone could have gone into the cottage with-

80

out it being likely they'd be seen. Expecially with me out of the way.'

'Exactly where did you go, Ben, and at what time?'

'I need an alibi, do I?'

'We just need to know where everyone was.'

Ben folded his arms, hugging them to his chest.

'I left at seven-thirty in the pick-up and drove to Bilton, which as you probably know is twenty miles away, to the wholesalers on the outskirts of town. I was there about an hour, so I must have left at around half past nine. I stopped on the way back at Monk's Herbarium near Winchampton and had a look around. Then I called in at the Tamvale Garden Centre, where there's good cafeteria, and had some brunch. I got back here at just after twelve.'

'Did you go back to the cottage?'

'No. I unloaded the compost bags and then went into the kitchen and had a cup of tea with Mrs Taylor and Mrs Carver. I was there when we heard about Liam.'

'Ben, did you see Liam when you got back from the Clifford Arms the night before?'

'No. He'd gone to bed.' His mouth and the muscles in his cheeks were working as if the emotional impact of his brother's death was threatening to overwhelm him again. 'I never saw him again after he left the pub,' he said, blinking rapidly.

Simon said quietly: 'Just one last question, Ben. Did you see anyone before you left in the pick-up? Was anyone hanging around near the cottage, working close by?'

Ben looked at him blankly. 'No. I shouldn't think anyone would make themselves that obvious would they?'

Simon had had to ask the question though he was sure Ben was right. He could hardly hope that Ben had seen someone emerge from the shrubbery clutching a fistful of monkshood and muttering imprecations on the head of the ill-fated Liam.

'Thanks for your help, Ben,' he said. 'I realize it's all very painful for you but we must ask a lot of questions of everyone which probably seem irrelevant.'

Ben stood up. 'Can I go now?'

As the door closed behind him Longman went to stand with his back to the empty hearth.

'Well, at least there's one with a probably foolproof alibi.'

81

'Unless he made his brother's sandwiches before he left.'

Longman's eyebrows, in desperate need of a trimming, shot up.

'Is that what you think?'

Simon pulled a face. 'No. But it's possible.'

'You mean he might have offered to make them for Liam? But if that was the case, there'd be no second lot in the bin, would there?'

'Liam might have made them the night before, perhaps. And Ben simply put some others in their place. We've only got Ben's word that he always made them after breakfast.'

Longman frowned and pulled at the hairs of an eyebrow.

'Not very likely if he'd got a lot on board. More likely he just fell into bed. And why would Ben leave the original sandwiches so that it was obvious it was no accident?'

'The same question applies to whoever did it. Murder being seen to be done was as important as the murder itself. And that,' said Simon, standing up, 'no doubt lies at the root of the whole mystery.' He wandered over to look through the window. 'And the other question is, as usual, "why now"?' What has happened at Clifford's Place recently, in the life of Liam Hartley, that's provoked this murder right now?'

'There's the fight with Gavin Taylor for a start.'

' I wonder. There might be more behind that but this doesn't seem to me the kind of killing that comes as a result of an impulse, a sudden anger. I think it took planning and I think it came from something more like a slow-burning rage.'

CHAPTER 11

Great Bindweed –
Insinuations

In the kitchen Mrs Taylor was stabbing with a spoon at something in a large pot on the huge green Aga. She looked over her shoulder at them as Simon and Longman entered.

'There's no point in talking to me,' she said, her back firmly towards them. 'I've got nothing to tell you.'

It seemed likely that Ben must have called in on her after their talk in the library.

Simon jerked his head at Longman and his sergeant silently retreated.

'I was hoping that the offer of tea was still available,' he said, pulling out a chair and seating himself at the table. She stopped stirring and turned her flushed face to him, examining him expressionlessly.

'I'm due for a break,' he said.

Without comment, she shifted the huge kettle on the cooker and retrieved the teapot from the draining board.

'Thirsty work talking people to death, I suppose,' she said, plonking a couple of mugs on the table and staring down at him, sharp-eyed.

'I can't think of any other way of finding out what happened to Liam,' Simon said, undaunted. 'What would you suggest, Mrs Taylor?'

'That you get all your facts right before you start jumping to any conclusions, to begin with.' She shook some loose tea into the pot and sloshed on the now boiling water. 'The police have got a bad record of jumping to conclusions, just so they can get a nice tidy arrest. But the chickens are beginning to come home to roost a bit more often, aren't they?' Teapot, milk and sugar were slapped down beside a pair of mugs, then she took a seat at right-angles to Simon, shifting her plump body in a sideways shuffle.

There was no point in telling her that he agreed with her, nor that certain pressures on the police to push up their arrest rates were not always the best route to justice being done, nor the best measure of good policing, so he kept silent.

She slid a mug of tea across the shiny surface of the table towards him.

'Thank you,' he said.

They sat quietly for a few moments while she busily stirred sugar into her tea.

'Mrs Hartley's badly upset by all this,' she said accusingly.

'I'm sure. She seems like an extremely nice woman,' Simon replied, his eyes on his tea.

'She is.' It was said defiantly, as if there might have been any doubt in the matter.

'Well, you must know. You've been here quite a while, I suppose.'

'Ten years. Since before *he* came here.'

It was immediately evident that Mrs Taylor did not care for Mr Enright.

'When Gerald Hartley was still alive, then?'

'A nice man, he was. Kindly, and knew how to treat people.' Mrs Taylor punctuated her remark with a large mouthful of tea.

'I suppose his death must have been something of a shock?'

She nodded, pursing her lips. 'Complete shock. Never a sign there was a thing wrong with him, as far as I knew. Then he gets a heart attack and he's gone, just like that. Turned everything upside down.'

'How did the children cope? It must have been very hard for them.'

Mrs Taylor shifted more comfortably on her chair.

'Well, they did know Enright from before because he was a friend of their father's and of Miss Meddick in those days. Liam seemed to manage all right. And Ben always took his brother's lead, so whatever he felt, he didn't seem to let it show. It was Vita felt it the most. She was very close to her father.'

'I suppose Mr Enright must have helped to fill the gap a little,' Simon said, gazing idly at the steam rising from the saucepan. It was an appetizing smell, intermingled with the fragrance of newly baked bread also emerging from the Aga.

Mrs Taylor darted a sharp look at him. She seemed for a moment lost for words.

'Do the children of the house not like him much, then?' Simon asked, glancing at her. It was at times like this that he missed smoking, having something to focus on, play with, while seeming to be making conversation rather than asking questions.

'Liam didn't, for sure,' she said bluntly. 'And Liam was never the type to hide his feelings if he didn't like someone. He and Ben have mostly kept out of his way. Upset Mrs Hartley, I think.'

'What about Vita?' he asked. 'I haven't really met Vita yet.'

'Oh, I think young Vita likes him well enough.' It was said with enough meaning to leave Simon in no doubt of what Mrs Taylor was hinting.

'Enough to be a problem to him?' Simon felt on safe enough ground speaking of Enright, Mrs Taylor having obviously so little liking for the man.

'Well, let's just say, shall we, that Mr Enright never finds a bit of unhealthy admiration any problem at all.' Her face settled into self-satisfied folds.

'You mean, he encourages her?'

She nodded, her lips compressed.

'Vita is only seventeen, isn't she?'

She gave a short laugh. 'It's not long since she was fifteen,' she said cryptically.

Simon realized that Mrs Taylor had not allowed herself to say anything truly overt about the relationship she so clearly suspected and disapproved of.

'Does Mrs Hartley know about this?' he asked. 'Is she aware of what's going on?'

'Not she,' she said, beginning to gather together the empty mugs and teapot. 'A nice woman, as I said. And dotes on her children.'

Simon hesitated, not wanting to alienate her by a tactless word.

'How is it then, that you know about it and Mrs Hartley doesn't?'

She put a finger to her pink nose and tapped it.

'I keep my eyes open around here. Mrs Hartley is a very busy woman.' She pushed back her chair. 'Not that I'm not, you understand, but in a job like this, housekeeping and all, I get about inside and out, seeing the staff and the family. There's times *I* know of when Mr Enright was about this place and Mrs Hartley thinking he was in London.'

Simon looked suitably impressed. 'You surprise me, Mrs Taylor.'

'I *hope* I shock you,' she said, standing up and placing her hands, knuckles down, on the table.

'Indeed you do,' Simon said, thinking that she did in more ways than one.

Satisfied, she went over to the oven and pulled out a huge brown loaf of bread, steaming and smelling of all good things. Simon supposed a cook such as this might be forgiven much.

'Well,' she said, pushing the oven door to with her foot, 'I must get on and take Mrs Hartley her lunch. Thought I might be able to tempt her with some chicken soup and fresh bread today.'

'You could certainly tempt me,' Simon said, unfolding his long frame from the chair.

She chuckled, making him warm to her a little.

'You look as if you could do with something a bit more substantial than soup, my boy, great lanky thing like you.'

He smiled and thanked her for the tea.

'Would you mind, Mrs Taylor, if I came to talk to you again? It's obvious that you know probably more than anyone else about this place and the people in it.'

It was blatant flattery but she showed no consciousness of its accepting it as the mere truth in her eyes.

'I suppose so. No doubt you'll have to be talking to everyone. I understand that that's your job.' She turned the loaf on to a grid and gave the soup a stir as Simon made for the door.

'But,' she said, as she tapped the spoon and waved it in his direction, 'don't you go picking on my Gavin, just because he and Liam didn't always get along.'

He had considered asking her about her son's relationship with Liam but had rejected it: Ben had probably been here before him and warned her of his conversation with the detectives – no doubt pointing out that the story had come better from him than from some other witness. And to have questioned her on the subject would almost certainly have alienated her. Instead he had from her at least the interesting accusation of Lewis Enright, whether or not distorted or exaggerated through dislike.

'I promise to try not to pick on anyone, Mrs Taylor,' Simon assured her.

As he opened the door to leave he found a woman about to enter the room. She was younger than Mrs Taylor but looked worn and dejected, her otherwise pleasant features blurred by tiredness. She stepped back timidly to allow Simon through.

'No, please,' he said, retreating into the kitchen and holding the door for her.

'Oh it's you, Linda,' Mrs Taylor said, already pouring the bowl of soup. 'You're a bit late for your cup of tea, aren't you?'

Linda, her hands crossed in front of her, sidled past Simon with a murmur of thanks.

'This is Linda Carver who does most of the hard work around here, Chief Inspector Simon,' Mrs Taylor said.

'The cleaner,' Linda said in an undertone as she took a seat at the table.

'What kept you, dear?' Mrs Taylor was now pouring her friend a cup of tea. Simon hoped she liked it strong – it must be a bit stewed by now.

'The police,' Linda Carver said, her cheeks colouring up.

'They haven't upset you, have they?' Mrs Taylor, concerned, put a hand on her shoulder. 'They couldn't possibly think you had anything to do with it, could they, Chief Inspector?' she raised her eyes to Simon.

Simon shrugged. 'Who spoke to you, Mrs Carver?' he asked quietly.

She glanced up, her eyes not quite meeting his. 'I can't remember his name. A very dark man.'

'Detective Inspector Monkton.' With his black oiled hair and the black leather coat that always accompanied him, it could be no one else.

Linda Carver nodded and sipped her tea.

'He didn't upset you, I hope?' Monkton always upset people.

'No, not really. He was just a bit . . .'

'Intimidating?' June Taylor said intimidatingly.

'He was a bit.' Linda looked apologetically at Simon.

'I'm sorry. I don't think he means to be,' Simon apologized. The poor woman did look as if she had had a shocking time. But he'd lied about Monkton; Monkton loved being intimidating, especially to the timid. 'I'll speak to him,' he assured her.

'Oh please don't do that. It was all right, really it was. It's just that we're all upset anyway about what's happened to Liam and . . .' She broke off again, burying her face in her cup.

Simon smiled in an effort to reassure her.

'Thank you for the tea, Mrs Taylor,' he said, opening the door again.

'Don't forget what I said, will you?' she replied.

CHAPTER 12

Rocket – Rivalry

Rhiannon had made arrangements for food to be supplied from the village shop to the team. Rural cases were not popular with the pizza-and-burger brigade and a daytime diet of sandwiches and pasties was the most they could hope for. Simon decided to walk to the Clifford Arms with Longman and see what might, apart fron what he hoped would be a decent meal, be gleaned from the landlord on the events of the previous Friday night.

Their path was for the most part shaded by overhanging trees leaning from the high banks of an ancient lane. It was quiet and soothingly cool. Simon repeated to Longman what June Taylor had had to say on the subject of Lewis Enright and Vita.

'Maybe that was why young Vita wanted to move out to her own cottage. She might have needed a bit of privacy as well as independence,' Longman said. 'But it may be just gossip. I can't think what it's got to do with Liam Hartley's death. Perhaps Mrs Taylor was just trying to distract you from her son and his row with Liam.'

'Quite likely she was. She's obviously concerned about that. But you never know what's going to be relevant in a case. We haven't got much of a picture yet.'

'She said Helen Hartley had no idea what was going on with Vita and Enright?'

'She did. But that's not necessarily so. Others might be aware of it, too. It's a close-knit community.'

'Tends to make it harder to winkle out the facts. They stick together.'

'Until someone is threatened. Either themselves or someone particularly close – as with Mrs Taylor and her son.'

'Good point. So we need to set some cats among the pigeons.'

Simon glanced down at the stocky sergeant with a faint smile.

'We'd have to be sure we weren't just setting pigeons among the cats.'

'Eh?' Longman paused to slip off his jacket. Even in this relative cool the exercise was raising a sweat.

'I mean, be cautious. When you don't know what you are dealing with, it's wise to tread carefully before changing the equations – if you'll forgive the mixed metaphors.'

Longman shrugged. 'Well we'll have to do something to shift 'em. As far as I can see any one of them could have got to those sandwiches while Liam was out and about in the garden.'

'We haven't had the reports yet on where they were all supposed to be. It was a Saturday morning but I gather that most of them were all there on duty as it was a busy open day. Enright, though, had a meeting in town.'

'Leaving early, I suppose?'

'Apparently. But given the geography of the place, it would be easy enough to slip back unseen. The job of changing the sandwiches wouldn't take long.'

'It took some nerve, though. Anyone could have seen whoever did it.'

'But if they did, it would have been possible to explain at least some of it away.'

'I can't see Lewis Enright being able to explain away tiptoeing through the monkshood.'

Simon smiled. 'True. But if he had been seen he could just have aborted that particular plan. As could anyone else.'

'And,' Longman said thoughtfully, 'we can't know for sure that whoever did it *wasn't* seen. It's always possible someone's keeping quiet about it.'

'That could be dangerous,' Simon said soberly.

'And complicate matters,' Longman agreed.

They emerged, blinking, into the bright sunlit village. The Clifford Arms was immediately on their left, set back from the road behind a neatly kept sward of green. Glorious hanging baskets, wilting in the heat, hung over the windows, contrasting in their vivid colours with the mellow Cotswold stone of which the pub and the rest of the village was built. The road widened here, and the houses and few shops were also set back behind grassy banks, presenting a discreet closed appearance. There was no one about and no vehicle had passed them on the road.

'It's a bit like a time warp,' Longman said. 'Doesn't seem quite real, does it?'

'That's because it isn't,' Simon said. He had mixed feelings about these perfect Cotswold villages. They were, indeed, a sham in some respects. Since you had to be probably more than a thousand times richer to live in them now than their original inhabitants had been, and since their purpose had changed to that of retreat for wealthy city-workers, the whole concept and meaning of a village had changed drastically and, in his view, very much for the worse.

Two bicycles were propped against the front wall of the Clifford Arms and wooden tables and chairs were set out on the green in front, unoccupied in this intense heat. Simon pushed open the swing door to the interior where they met once again with blessed cool. To the right, through an open door, could be glimpsed a comfortably upholstered and carpeted room, apparently empty. From the left came a murmur of voices through a doorway into a stoneflagged bar. Simon chose the latter and Longman followed.

There were only three people in the room. Mara Kennedy and Stephen Orchard sat at a table near the bar, a man leaning on the counter apparently in quiet conversation with them. Mara Kennedy looked up with a feline smile.

'Chief Inspector! Are you investigating the case, or the chance of a decent meal?'

The question jarred and Stephen Orchard looked away as if dissociating himself.

'What can I get you, sirs?' the man said, pushing himself to a standing position.

They ordered cold beers and there was an uncomfortable silence while they waited.

'I'm Ken Jenson, the landlord.' He pushed two beaded glasses of beer across the highly polished bar.

'Perhaps we could speak to you later?' Simon said.

'Will you come and sit with us?' Mara Kennedy said, a little more subdued. 'Steve says the police haven't spoken to him yet.' Steve studied his beer and said nothing.

Simon nodded a brief acknowledgement and ordered his food. Suddenly he couldn't stomach anything more substantial than some bland sandwiches. The table that the two were sitting at was spacious enough; he and Longman placed themselves at a distance, towards the end away from the bar.

'How's it going?' Stephen Orchard said gruffly with a glance in their direction. His long well-built frame was draped uncomfortably around the chair on which he was sitting. He had an attractive face, tanned to a healthy-looking shade like all of those working in the gardens. The features were angular in a long bony face with a wide straight mouth that curved at the corners and looked as if it might smile readily – in the right circumstances.

'Not going yet, really,' Longman answered, taking a long mouthful of the cool beer.

Simon realized that Longman had not met either of them before and introduced them. He felt uncomfortable. It was not a scenario he would have sought.

'It's all a bit weird,' Stephen ventured. 'What happened to Liam? I mean.' He looked, embarrassed, into his glass.

'Yes, it seems unreal,' Mara sighed and ran her hand back through her short crop of hair.

'It's not, though,' Longman said uncompromisingly, and Simon regarded his sergeant with something akin to affection. Longman cleared his throat. 'This is where Liam was on Friday night, is it? When there was a bit of a row, we understand.'

'I wasn't here,' Stephen said, straightening in his seat.

'I was, of course,' Mara added reluctantly.

The landlord returned with their sandwiches, tastefully presented with side-salad.

'So was I,' he said grimly, placing the plates in front of Simon and Longman with cutlery wrapped in red napkins. He stood back waiting, as if willing to be drawn into any ensuing discussion.

When no one spoke, he said, 'I can't say it surprises me that someone finished off that young man. He always seemed to be asking for trouble one way or another. Though I'm surprisd by the way he was killed. A knock over the head on a dark night would have been more like it.'

Ken Jenson was a stocky man with short bristly grey hair and showing a decided paunch. He was dressed smartly in a white open-necked shirt with a navy-blue sleeveless sweater and grey pressed trousers. His face, lined deeply from nose to mouth, expressed a weary air of profound cynicism, and his eyes, a watery blue, betrayed a likely love-affair with the bottle.

The last thing that Simon wanted was a cosy gossip about the case in the local bar, but Longman seemed to differ.

'Friday night wasn't the first time he's caused trouble, then?' He cocked a bushy eyebrow at the landlord.

'Not the first time, no. In fact I was going to ban him after last Friday anyway. The only reason I put up with him for so long was Mrs Hartley. She's a nice lady.' His eyes settled on their half-empty glasses. 'Any more? No? Enjoy your meal, then.' He quickly disappeared into the depths behind the bar.

Stephen Orchard scraped the legs of his chair on the flagged floor and stood up, draining the last of his beer.

'I'd better be getting back. I spoke to two of your men this morning,' he said to Simon.

'We're speaking to everyone at Clifford's Place, naturally,' Simon agreed.

'Naturally,' Stephen echoed, and with a quick nod to Mara, turned and left, his boots loud on the stone floor.

Mara gave Simon a quick smile. 'He's very shy, Stephen.'

'Do you usually come here to lunch?' Simon asked, from politeness rather than interest.

'Stephen and I? No, not usually. We met accidentally, both cycled over.' She was wearing pink again, a sleeveless shirt with knee-length canvas shorts, her legs brown and smooth. 'I think we were both looking for a break from the tensions at work. Things are a bit all over the place without Helen doing her daily rounds.'

'It must be very difficult,' Simon agreed and began on his sand-wiches, noticing that Longman had already consumed most of his own insubstantial pile.

'Have any of you talked together, at work, about what happened to Liam?' Longman asked, wiping his mouth with a scarlet napkin.

'Well, yes, of course we have, in a way. Everyone seems stunned by it all.' Mara finished her drink and toyed with the glass, clinking the ice cubes.

'Can I get you another?' Longman asked, half-rising.

'Thanks. I'll have a lager. With ice.' Longman went over to the bar and rang the bell.

'And has anyone come up with any thoughts or explanations?' Simon asked.

She shook her head. 'We all know that Liam could be a pain at times. But he was all right really. It was just his way. I think he wanted to get away from Clifford's Place and start up on his own and he got a bit frustrated about it so he tended to take it out on other people.'

'Anyone in particular?'

She didn't answer for a moment, apparently thinking about his question.

'It's not so much that, is it?' I mean, it depends on the person. What one person might shrug off, even if it's a real insult, someone else might feel deeply. You just can't tell.'

It was an intelligent reply. But it occurred to Simon that the idea might not have arisen from any abstract thought.

'And who feels things deeply?'

She gave him a quick smile. 'Not me, anyway. I could handle Liam.'

It had certainly appeared that way when Simon had seen them at Westwich station. She had handled the rivalry between the two young men with tact and good humour.

'Mrs Hartley has quite a young staff at Clifford's Place,' Simon remarked. 'Does she prefer it that way?'

'I think it's just more or less happened that way. The person whom I replaced was older, and Clive of course is a different age group. Gavin works there mostly on account of his mother already being there.'

'How did Liam and Ben get on?' Simon asked.

Longman placed her glass in front of her and two more halves for himself and Simon.

'All right. They were different, but they got along. Ben looked up to Liam in lots of ways. Liam had more drive.'

'There was no jealousy?' Simon asked, thinking again of the scene at the station.

Mara raised her eyebrows. 'You can't think that Ben did this! He wouldn't hurt anyone.'

'I'm just asking questions. One thing can influence another. We need the broad picture.' Impossible to explain to the layman, impossible to justify the millions of words that made up an investigation, all to be condensed at some future point into the concise questionings of a trial.

'Ben heard Liam having a row with someone at the cottage,' she said suddenly. She swallowed a large mouthful of lager.

'Who?'

'I don't know. He didn't say.'

'When was this?'

She shrugged, raised a bronzed shoulder to rub her cheek. 'Recently. I don't know exactly.'

Simon and Longman quietly sipped their beer.

'I really don't know. You'll have to ask Ben.' She pushed her glass away. 'Perhaps I shouldn't have said anything. Don't tell Ben I told you. It's just that I don't want you thinking anything bad about Ben. You should look elsewhere.' She made as if to get up and said quietly, 'That's the only reason I told you.'

Ken the landlord was just about to join them again when two men came through the door. Mara sat back in her chair.

'Hello Alan, Colin,' she said, smiling at them. She ruffled her hair at the back and Simon noticed that, in a reversal of the usual pattern, she had light-coloured roots. Inconsequentially he thought that she would have seemed less vivid, less defined, with her natural colour.

Ken the landlord drifted back behind the bar, welcoming the men with more warmth than Simon had yet seen in him. He offered to bring them their drinks and immediately Mara invited them to join the table at which she, Simon and Longman were sitting.

'These are policemen who are investigating Liam's death,' she said. Simon felt somehow subverted and annoyed. He nodded as Mara introduced them as Alan Fairburn and Colin Wheatley. Fairburn had well-cut wavy hair, almost the colour of corn. He was assured and sleek, even in his casual clothes. Wheatley was altogether more comfortable-looking – untidy reddish hair, a mild expression, creased chinos and blue polo shirt.

Mara said, 'It was Alan who sorted Liam last Friday when he got out of order.'

Fairburn didn't look much of a match for Liam Hartley, Simon thought. He was not as tall, and considerably older. He also looked soft, compared with the spare leanness of Liam.

Fairburn made a deprecating gesture with his hand.

'As much Colin as myself,' he said, glancing at his friend.

They both pulled out chairs and sat at the table. Colin said gruffly:

'Just concerned about how upset Jenny was.'

'Not a pleasant situation,' Alan agreed.

Colin looked across at Mara and said: 'Though Jenny seemed more concerned about you, Mara, than herself.'

'Me?' Mara's colour heightened.

'After we got her home she said, "Poor Mara" a couple of times and asked if we thought you were all right.'

Mara's smile was embarrassed. 'I can't think why.'

The landlord placed a beer in front of Wheatley and a short for Fairburn, pulled up a chair and sat down. The situation felt increasingly bizarre to Simon and entirely inappropriate. Yet he had no desire to move, just at the moment.

'I think she thought that it might have upset you, Liam suggesting that he had some sort of relationship with her,' Alan said baldly, his mid-Atlantic twang giving the statement a mocking edge.

'That's silly,' Mara said defensively. 'What does Jenny know, anyway? Liam and I weren't an item.'

'Ah,' Alan said, taking a mouthful of scotch on the rocks, 'She must be mistaken, then.'

'How is Jenny, anyway?' Mara asked, a bit sharply, Simon thought, watching on.

'Seems OK. No lasting damage.' Colin drank some beer and looked around the bar, letting the subject drop.

'So, how is the investigation going?' Alan Fairburn asked Simon, disregarding Longman who had sat silent and bright-eyed throughout.

'Only at the beginning,' Simon murmured, entirely at a loss as to an alternative response other than a pompous or cutting one.

'Alan is an old friend of Helen's,' Mara said.

'Yes,' Alan said easily. 'Knew her many years ago and as I've been staying in the area with another old friend, Colin here, I looked her up. We had dinner at Clifford's Place only last week, didn't we?' He glanced at his friend who nodded into his beer. 'It's a dreadful blow for poor Helen, what's happened. I could tell she was really proud of Liam.'

'So you met all the family?' Simon asked.

'Yes, indeed. I remember thinking what a perfect life she had, now.' He smiled ruefully into his whisky. 'Ironical, isn't it? And then this terrible thing happened.'

'You knew Mrs Hartley before she was married?'

'Before she was married to her first husband, even. You knew Helen used to be an actor?'

'No, I didn't.'

'We both were back then. I still am but I've been working in the States mostly ever since.'

'Explains the accent then, sir,' Longman said, making Simon smile involuntarily.

'Oh, I can still do upper-class English,' Fairburn said, demonstrating the fact. 'It's how I get a lot of my work over there.'

Simon wondered if Fairburn had entirely forgotten his authentic voice. There was a element of sham in Fairburn, but perhaps that could be an occupational hazard. He found it difficult to imagine Helen Hartley on stage, though she still had looks and presence enough. But unlike Fairburn she gave the impression of lacking ready camouflage for her emotions, of having difficulty in dissimulating.

'Yes, she was good, Helen,' Fairburn mused. 'But she's done very nicely for herself all the same.'

'Very nice lady, Mrs Hartley,' Ken the landlord interposed from the edge of the group.

Fairburn turned to him in surprise. 'Would I say otherwise?' he said, a mite ambiguously.

'I really must go,' Mara got to her feet. She glanced quickly around the table at them. 'Can't be letting her down at a time like this.' She went swiftly through the door and all heads turned to watch her leave. Simon watched her push her bike past the window, her small features set.

CHAPTER 13

Marigold – Uneasiness

'So Ben overheard someone having a row with Liam at the cottage,' Longman said as they walked back along the narrow road beneath the trees.

'So Mara says.'

'She's protective of Ben.'

'Yes, she seems fond of him.'

Simon and Longman had left soon after Mara. An awkward silence had fallen and, though Simon had been planning to have a word with the landlord as someone with a detached, though no doubt jaundiced, view of his customers from Clifford's Place, he had no desire to conduct such an interview with interested onlookers. It could wait, he supposed, as could any further word with Colin Wheatley and Alan Fairburn, should need arise.

'Interesting what Wheatley said about young Jenny,' Longman ventured again.

'You mean her concern over Mara? Seems to suggest that Mara was more involved with Liam than she's letting on.'

'And what about Jenny's involvement with Liam? I mean why feel bothered about Mara unless she felt guilty towards her – as if she'd betrayed her in some way?'

Simon shook his head in irritation, or at a fly, Longman wasn't sure. 'Such a lot of hearsay in all this.'

'And a lot of denials. Mara wasn't having any of it.'

'Did she convince you?' Simon asked.

'Not sure,' Longman said thoughtfully, waving off another

flying insect. 'Could be she's just trying to distance herself from it all.'

'If it's true, that Liam was sexually involved with both Jenny and Mara, that gives her a motive for murder based on jealousy, you mean?'

Longman nodded. 'Well, it would.'

'As well as Jenny herself and Gavin Taylor.'

'Well, I don't find it impossible to believe it of Mara, but we haven't talked to either of the others yet.'

'Too soon, too much speculation,' Simon said.

'Too hot,' Longman added, as they emerged from the trees into an unshaded patch of roadway.

'That too,' Simon smiled and rolled up his sleeves. He had made an effort sartorially, as Superintendent Munro had demanded, but the heat was defeating him. He was crumpled, sweating, and too inherently shambolic for elegance, he told himself.

'We'll need to speak to Ben again – ask who it was having a row with Liam,' Longman said, dragging his tie a lot further from his neck and perspiring freely.

'And Jenny and Gavin and Mara and a lot of other people no doubt,' Simon said sharply. The heat was definitely getting to him.

He added, to compensate for his brusqueness with the amiable Longman: 'But what always interests me is "Why now?". What provoked the murder of Liam Hartley just at this time? What happened that meant it had to be now, rather than any other time?'

'Or not at all?'

'Or not at all.'

'There was the row at the pub, for a start. And Jenny finding she was pregnant.'

'And a row between Liam and some person unknown – or so Mara says.'

'And the appearance of an old boyfriend of Mrs Hartley's, Alan Fairburn.'

'What's that got to do with anything?'

Longman wiped his brow with his forearm. 'I don't know,' he said shrugging. 'It's just something that happened recently.'

'And there may be other things that we know nothing about. Something else Liam had done, apart from start a fight in the Clifford Arms.'

'We just have to keep on digging.' Longman put on speed as Simon suddenly increased his stride to reach the next patch of shade.

'What did you make of Alan Fairburn?' he asked as he caught up.

'I didn't exactly warm to him.' Simon shrugged. 'He struck me as a bit fake.'

'Smoothie. A bit insinuating, I thought.'

'Let's keep to the point, shall we? I've got enough potential suspects to worry about without adding half the local population, itinerant or otherwise.'

Undaunted, Longman said, 'It's an interest in human nature that makes a good policeman, or woman.'

'All women have an interest in human nature. I confess I have a struggle with it sometimes.'

Longman gave up. He was looking forward to another drink. Water would be nice.

They were approaching the main gates to Clifford's Place and some further welcome shade. They ran the gauntlet of the press and slipped through without uttering a word. As they reached the stables Rhiannon appeared from the back door.

'I tried phoning you at the pub but you'd left. And your mobile must be switched off.' Simon reached guiltily into his pocket. 'And yours too,' she said to Longman.

'Why? What's up?' Simon asked.

'Vita's disappeared. Her mother's frantic.'

'Is her car gone?' was the first thing Simon wanted to know.

'It's still in the garage.' She nodded in the direction of the old stables behind them.

'When was she last seen?'

'Not since last night. She came over for a meal at the house then went back to the cottage – or so they assumed. Mrs Hartley went over to call on her this morning and couldn't find her anywhere. She looked all round the cottage and grounds with no luck, so she called us in. After what happened to Liam she's terrified something similar has happened to Vita.'

'Understandable,' Simon said. Something clutched at his gut at the image of Vita also poisoned and wandering off only to collapse in some obscure place in the extensive grounds and shrubberies. 'I'll get the others in and we'll do a proper search.'

'They're all in there now,' Rhiannon said, looking anxiously at Simon. 'I got them together as soon as Mrs Hartley told me. I hope I did the right thing, only I—'

'Yes, that's fine,' he gave her a quick smile. 'You did do the right thing, thank you, Rhiannon.' Rhiannon coloured with pleasure. 'Mrs Hartley has looked in all the obvious places, has she?' Simon added.

'Yes, sir. She's quite sure something terrible's happened.'

'Where's Mrs Hartley now?'

'That big room at the front of the house where we were before. She wanted to go on looking for her daughter, but she's plainly exhausted what with everything, so I persuaded her to go and sit down while we did the search. Barbara Meddick's with her.'

As the three of them went into the passageway at the back of the house Mrs Taylor emerged from the kitchen door.

'All this fuss about young Vita?' she asked, hands on hips. 'She'll be about somewhere, little madam. Not been getting enough attention lately, that's her problem.'

Simon thought that, even if true, such a remark redounded somewhat on the speaker.

'You're sure of that, are you, Mrs Taylor?'

'Sure enough,' she said with a sniff. 'Vita shouldn't be worrying her mother at a time like this.' She retreated into the kitchen, closing the door behind her.

The old games room was stifling, the sun in the south shining relentlessly on the windows. They had all been opened, some of them propped with whatever was to hand, including an old hockey stick. Detective Inspector Monkton and Detective Constables Savage and Tremaine were drinking bottled water and looking uncomfortably hot. He sent them and Rhiannon to search the four sectors of the gardens individually, including outhouses and potting-sheds, and Longman to check with the employees whether anyone had seen Vita since last night.

'Report to me immediately by phone if you find out anything.'

They moved off lethargically. 'And get a move on,' he said. 'If she's been poisoned as well, time could be vital.'

In the drawing-room the two women were sitting as before on the large sofa, Helen looking as if she had been crying, Barbara Meddick immaculate, composed.

'Have you found her?' Helen asked as soon as she saw Simon.

'Not yet, but I'm sure we soon will.' Simon expressed the platitude without really thinking of what he was saying. The turn of events had surprised him as much as it had the girl's mother and left him with a distinct unease that he had not properly anticipated danger where it might exist. 'The whole team is out looking now. You searched her cottage thoroughly?' he asked.

Barbara Meddick spoke. 'We both have, Chief Inspector.'

'Were there any signs of when she disappeared?' he asked. 'Had she had breakfast, for instance? Had her bed been slept in?'

'Vita is meticulous,' her mother said. 'She would have washed up and put away her breakfast things. And made her bed. She was always very tidy. Unlike the boys,' she added with a watery smile.

'So there's no way of telling when she went. No one's seen her since the meal here last night, I, understand?'

'That's right, Chief Inspector,' Barbara Meddick said calmly.

'And how was she when you saw her at the evening meal?'

The two women glanced at each other. It was Barbara Meddick who replied.

'Vita is obviously still very troubled and upset about what happened to Liam, like the rest of us. She was quiet, didn't say much.'

It would be difficult, in the current circumstances, Simon thought, to distinguish any new anguish or trouble from that original one: Liam's death. 'Can either of you think of any reason why she might deliberately take herself off?'

They looked at him blankly. 'Perhaps people are a little too absorbed in their own cares to notice others' problems at the moment,' Barbara Meddick observed.

'And nothing you know of has happened to upset her? Beyond the obvious grief over Liam.'

Both women made slight movements of their heads in the negative. Helen Hartley seemed dazed.

'Were they close, she and Liam?'

There was a pause, perhaps each woman waiting for the other

to answer. It was again Barbara Meddick who answered.

'Normally close, Chief Inspector.'

Meaning that sometimes they weren't, at all? Or, as close as such siblings might usually be? Helen Hartley made a sudden impatient movement.

'Is Mr Enright here?' he asked.

'He's gone up to town,' Barbara Meddick said. There was a faint note of disapproval.

'To London?' Simon deliberately clarified, recognizing the county-speak.

Both women nodded their heads in agreement.

'Could Vita have gone with him?'

'Why ever would she do that?' Helen said irritably. If she had any suspicion of an improper relationship there, her reaction to the suggestion seemed genuine enough.

'It's always possible,' Barbara Meddick said quietly. 'In the unusual circumstances. She may have felt the need to get away.' She put a protective hand on Helen's bronzed arm.

Helen frowned. 'But surely Lewis would have let me know,' she said.

Barbara rose gracefully to her feet. 'I'll telephone and check anyway,' she said.

While she made the call Simon went over to the window and looked out. He saw nothing moving apart from a blackbird pulling a worm from the lawn. He heard the murmur of Barbara's voice, a pause as she waited, presumably to be put through, and then an urgent exchange in which she seemed both to be explaining and reassuring at the same time. He heard her replace the phone-piece and turned.

'No,' she said.

'He was upset, I could tell,' Helen said. She looked at Simon. 'He's very fond of Vita. She's the one that accepted him best, after Gerald. She needs a father-figure.' Her voice was free of irony.

Would a mother, a wife, remain unaware of such a relationship as Mrs Taylor had described? It happened, he reminded himself. There were a few cases of genuine incest he knew of where the mother had been totally unaware. But Helen Hartley had been an actor. How good an actor? A bad one, he hoped at the moment.

'Have you checked with anyone else whether they have seen her this morning?' he asked.

'Everyone we could find,' Barbara answered. 'Nobody has seen her today.'

'Mara Kennedy and Stephen Orchard were at the Clifford Arms at lunch-time,' he said.

'I spoke to Stephen when he got back,' Barbara said. 'I'll go and find Mara. If she hasn't heard, she can help us look. I haven't seen Ben.'

Helen gazed uncertainly after her as she left. 'I should go, too.'

'There's no real need. A lot of people are searching,' Simon reassured her again. 'Her car hasn't gone. Perhaps she took herself off for a long walk, wanting to be on her own for a while.'

'If she wanted that, I would have thought that she would have taken her car,' Helen said. 'That's what worries me. Surely it makes it more likely that something has happened to her.' She got to her feet, suddenly and awkwardly, so that Simon had to reach to steady her. 'I can't just sit about. I'll be better if I'm out looking for her,' she exclaimed. 'You should be looking, too.'

She shrugged off his steadying hand and made for the door, Simon following.

He stayed with her but she searched aimlessly and mostly in the full heat of the sun so that her hair grew wet and clung to her neck. They met Gavin Taylor who, from the look of his sweaty and dust-streaked face, had also been searching for Vita.

'No luck?' he asked Helen, sympathetic concern on his young face.

'Not yet,' she replied. 'But don't stop looking, will you, Gavin?' She gave him a tremulous smile.

''Course not, Mrs Hartley.' Gavin ambled away with a glance over his shoulder at them both.

Simon insisted that Helen should rest for a moment, leading her unprotesting into the shade of a tree where she sank on to a garden seat. He had a couple of calls from the team, each saying they had completed their search and found nothing. 'Keep on looking,' he said.

Helen had her face in her hands. 'I just couldn't bear it if anything's happened to her,' she said.

Simon couldn't allow himself to believe that anything serious had occurred. If it had, surely Vita would have been found by now. Mrs Taylor's bracing words suddenly held an attraction.

'Vita's lived here all her life, hasn't she?'

'Yes, of course. Apart from time at school.' Helen lifted her face to him. 'Why?'

'When she was younger, did she have a favourite place she would go to, as children sometimes do, to nurse a grievance, or heal a hurt. A refuge of some sort?'

Helen sat up straight, her eyes widened.

'She did. She used to climb the huge old oak by the fields. It has a hollowed area quite high up that she used to hide in. We always looked for her there first if she did a disappearing act. But that's not been for years and years now.' Despite the doubt she expressed Helen looked hopeful, some colour returning to her cheeks. She stood up. 'We'll go and look, now.'

As Simon followed her he hoped intensely that he, or Mrs Taylor, was right.

It was a fair distance, involving the negotiation of winding walkways and Helen's short cut through some bruising shrubbery. He estimated they were some distance south of Vita's cottage and way beyond and behind Mara Kennedy's when they emerged into open parkland that ended in a row of mature trees edging the bleached fields beyond. Helen almost ran to the largest oak tree, its girth showing it to be centuries old. A sheep and her two fat lambs enjoying the shade of the tree inside the field leapt to their feet and ran away protesting loudly at Helen's sudden approach.

'Vita!' Helen cried. 'Vita, are you there?'

No sound but that of the leaves in the light breeze.

Helen turned to look at Simon. She looked devastated. He wished he hadn't suggested the idea. Braced again by the wraith of Mrs Taylor, he added his own voice to Helen's.

'Vita, it's Chief Inspector Simon. If you don't come down, I shall have to come up. I'm no mean climber you know.' It wasn't true, but his height gave him an advantage, and the lowest bough was in easy reach. The sheep had returned to stare at them, all yellow-eyed astonishment, and he thought, not for the first time, how ridiculous humans must frequently look to animals.

A rustling sound came from overhead, distinct sounds of movement. About twenty feet above, a pale-blonde fall of hair appeared, then a leg, the foot in faded blue canvas. Vita pulled herself into a sitting position and looked down on them.

'What's all the fuss? Has something happened?'

Helen closed her eyes in exasperation and glanced apologetically at Simon.

'Darling, for goodness sake! We've been worried sick about you.' The anger in her voice was typical of the parent with errant child safely restored.

'If you're going to take that attitude, I'll stay up here, thank you.' Vita made to withdraw her legs.

'No, Vita. I'm not angry. I've just been so worried.' Helen's strained face peered upwards.

'Whatever for? I just wanted a bit of quiet and privacy, for God's sake!'

'With what happened to Liam, I was afraid for you.' Helen was almost in tears now.

The sheep continued to stare. Simon wasn't surprised.

'Oh, I see. Sorry. I didn't think.' Vita began a quick and agile descent from the tree. The sheep backed away as she landed, hard, from about six feet.

She straightened and faced them. There were twigs in her flaxen hair and her face was drained, streaked with tree-dust or tears, or both: Simon couldn't tell. Helen put her arm around Vita's narrow shoulders. In her sleeveless blue shirt and denim shorts she looked about twelve years old.

Simon put out the call to end the search.

'You've all been looking for me?' Vita asked. There was a small smile at the corners of her mouth.

'Everyone,' he said flatly.

CHAPTER 14

Sweetbriar – I wound to heal

Simon followed the two women and relayed the news to the team. Helen kept her arm around her daughter, their heads close. Simon could hear a low-voiced exchange of words, but was unable to distinguish what they were saying. Vita soon broke away from her mother, exclaiming loudly:

'For Heaven's sake mother, I'm not a child, you know.'

'You're my child, Vita,' Helen said.

Vita folded her arms and walked alone, head down. Simon caught up with her.

'I'd like to speak to you, Vita. Your cottage or the house?'

She glanced up at him, her expression still mutinous, then looked away without answering.

'I should be with her,' Helen said.

'DC Rhiannon Jones will do,' Simon said firmly. 'Your cottage or the house?' he repeated.

'I'm sure she should have me with her if you're questioning her,' Helen protested. 'She's very stressed.'

Vita made an exasperated sound. Simon thought that a day spent mooning about in a tree was considerably less stressful than the day that her mother had gone through. He said so, more or less.

'The cottage, then,' Vita said, impatiently. 'Go home, Mum, and have a cup of tea or something. I'm fine.'

'It doesn't seem like it, going off the way you did today,' Helen said, showing more assertiveness with her daughter than she had before.

Simon contacted Rhiannon. By this time they had reached a dividing of their ways. Vita, arms still folded, marched off along the path to her cottage, Helen stood at the fork in the path watching her stiff retreating back.

'Will you speak to me later?' she appealed to Simon. 'If there's any explanation for all this?'

'I'll see,' he said, not unsympathetically. 'It is for Vita herself to confide in you if she chooses.'

Helen looked as if she wanted to say more but instead turned without speaking and walked away.

Simon lingered a moment then slowly followed the path to Vita's cottage. He waited in the garden for the few minutes it took for Rhiannon to appear.

She arrived a bit breathless, smoothing her dark hair. Her clothes, a grey linen suit and white top, showed evidence of her searches for Vita; a cobweb clung to her shoulder. Simon removed it as she rubbed crossly at the marks on her clothes.

'Well? Did she give any explanation for causing all this fuss?' she said irritably.

'She sees it from a different perpective,' Simon said drily.

'Yes, from up a tree, she would!'

'It's a difficult time for all of them, Rhiannon. I'd like us to take this gently, if you don't mind.'

'Sorry, sir.'

Vita was slow in answering to their knock and showed them wordlessly from the narrow hall into the sitting-room. She had evidently washed her face and combed her hair, and changed into a clean T-shirt and jeans.

The contrast with the boys' cottage could hardly have been greater, though the building seemed identical in size and layout. All was feminine prettiness – chintz curtains at the window, pastel walls, an expensive-looking pale patterned rug on the polished wood floor and antique tapestry-covered chairs. It made Simon think of a doll's house: everything was scaled to suit the dimensions of the small cottage.

'Would you like a cup of tea?' Vita asked, her equilibrium apparently restored. 'I'm having one.'

'Thank you,' they both said. Vita, much in command, gestured for them to sit down.

'Meticulous,' Helen had said of Vita. And it appeared to be true. There was no muddle or dust anywhere, and no sign that its tenant worked in a job that called for wrestling with soil and greenery. Perhaps she just stuck with propagating plants Simon thought, in an orderly and controlled environment.

There was little that was personal in the room, no books, or evidence of other interests, just some photographs in silver frames on a small oak chest and on the mantelpiece. Simon looked at these more closely while Rhiannon rubbed surreptitiously at her clothes with a handkerchief. One was a charming photograph of the three children, their ages probably between ten and eight, Vita in the centre, taken in what looked like the arbour in which Simon had talked to Barbara Meddick. Liam's smile was the broadest of the three, Ben's a little less certain, while Vita looked coolly at the camera with only a ceremonious curl to her lips. They were a handsome trio even then.

Another photograph was of the children at a slightly younger age with Helen and probably Gerald, their father. They were lazing outside what appeared to be a Mediterranean villa. All looked fit and happy. Several pictures showed Vita herself at various ages. Simon always wondered about people who kept pictures of themselves on display. He must ask Jessie for a psychologist's view. One photograph showed Vita with Lewis Enright, his arm lying casually along her shoulders. It had been taken outside an unidentifiable building. As if to balance this, another picture was of Vita and her mother taken at the front of Clifford's Place.

Vita came into the room and placed a tray on a small side table.

'Oh dear,' she said to Rhiannon, observing her efforts with the handkerchief. 'Is that my fault? Can I help?'

Rhiannon shoved the handkerchief into her pocket.

'I'll see to it later, thanks.' She smoothed down her clothes.

Vita handed them their tea, served in fine-china cups, and offered them sugar which they both refused. Simon found it almost painful to see the studied way in which this almost-child played grown up with them after the débâcle of the day.

They all sat down, Rhiannon at a highly polished table by the window, Simon on one of the antique chairs which was surprisingly comfortable. Vita sat on a similar one, the three of them making a triangle.

Rhiannon lifted her face, sniffing. 'What's the wonderful scent I can smell?'

Vita pointed a small hand at the windowsill behind Rhiannon. 'The lily of the valley.' A group of them were growing in a large terracotta pot, their spires of small white bells standing proud of broad-bladed leaves.

'They're out of season by now. But they're Mum's favourite flower so I found out how to keep them growing over a longer period so that she can have pots of them in her room for a few months of the year,' Vita said proudly.

'How do you do that?' Rhiannon asked. 'Keep them going so long, I mean.'

'You have to chill them to delay flowering. It's the way flower-shows manage to have so many plants flowering out of season. We've all got a bit of a thing about cutting flowers. We like to see them growing.'

'One of the tricks of the trade, then,' Rhiannon said admiringly and turned to sniff the plants more closely.

Her confidence re-established, Vita asked, 'What was it you wanted to talk to me about?' Her enunciation was perfect, her voice quiet but high and girlish. She looked at Simon, her blue eyes wide over the rim of her cup.

'Much the same things as we're asking others,' Simon said.

She appeared to relax, lowering her cup and saucer to her lap.

'I don't know anything that will help you,' she said. 'I have no idea why that happened to Liam.'

'Why did you feel the need to disappear today?' Simon asked.

She shrugged. 'I told you. I just wanted to get away from everyone for a bit.'

'Nothing had happened that made you want to do that today, rather than yesterday, say?'

Her transparent skin reddened slightly. 'No.'

'No one had upset you?'

'Well, yes actually. The person who murdered my brother has rather upset me.' She looked at Simon defiantly.

'And have you no idea who that person might be?'

'If I thought I knew, I promise I would have told you,' she said pettishly.

'Were you close to Liam?'

111

'Of course.'

'So you would be aware if anyone had been threatening him. He would tell you?'

She looked unsure. 'Perhaps not that close. After all, I was his little sister – he'd hardly be likely to tell me if he was scared of someone. Anyway, it was usually the other way around. I think it was other people who found Liam a bit threatening.'

'Can you think of any instances?'

'Not off hand.' She buried her face in her cup.

'We know about the argument that took place at the Clifford Arms on Friday night, but we understand that Liam was also having a row with someone at his cottage sometime last week. Did he tell you anything about that?'

Her colour deepened. 'No he didn't,' she said quickly.

'Did anyone else, perhaps, mention it to you?'

'I don't know what you're talking about,' she said, her voice faltering.

Simon glanced at Rhiannon. She said gently:

'Vita, please don't be upset by our questions. Their only purpose is to find out who harmed your brother Liam. I'm sure you are even more anxious than we are to have this cleared up.'

Vita nodded silently, her eyes on her cup.

'Well, Vita? Is there anything you know that might help us? Has anything happened or been said which might offer some clue to who might have harmed Liam?' Rhiannon persisted.

'I don't know,' the girl said helplessly. She wiped at an eye with her fingers.

'Fine,' Simon said. 'In that case we'll just ask you the same as we're asking everyone. What were you doing on Saturday morning?'

'You surely can't think I poisoned Liam?' she said tearfully.

'Of course we don't think that,' Rhiannon hastened to assure. 'But when we have the big picture of where everyone was, it helps us to sort things out better. Did you see anyone that morning?'

Vita was silent, appearing to think.

'I saw Stephen. He was collecting some compost from the service area. That's near the greenhouses.'

'What time was this?' Simon asked.

'About half past eight, I suppose. He was doing some planting in the pool garden, he said.'

Where the monkshood grew, Simon thought.

'And I saw Liam.'

'Where?'

'I went over to the house. I'd run out of milk and needed some for breakfast. Liam was just coming from the back of the house as I was going to the kitchen.'

'The time?'

'Earlier. It was probably nearer half past seven.'

'Did he say anything?'

'Just "Hello, sis", or something like that.'

'How did he seem?'

'Cheerful,' she said biting her lip. 'That was the last time I ever saw him.'

'Was he coming from the house itself?'

'I don't know.'

'You mean he could have come from the old stables where the cars are kept?'

'I don't know. He was at the corner of the house where the path leads back to his cottage. Anyway he doesn't keep his Land-Rover there, he keeps it in the public car park. It's closer to his cottage. There's a wicket gate nearby.'

'Was there anyone about when you went into the kitchen?'

'Barbara was there, making a cup of tea.'

'She didn't mention seeing Liam?'

'No.'

'What about the rest of your morning? What were you doing?'

'I spent some time in the greenhouses and the nursery getting some plants ready for the sales area. Mara turned up to help move them over around half past nine.'

Simon remembered that the plant-sales area was close to the entrance gate that he, Jessie and his mother had come through that Saturday morning, fairly close to the path that led to Liam and Ben's cottage.

'Did you see anyone else that morning?'

She shrugged slightly. 'Just visitors.'

He finished his tea and got up to place his cup and saucer on the tray.

'Do you want some more?' Vita asked politely. The sun had moved off the south-facing window some time ago but the room was still very warm.

Thirst and even a degree of compassion overcame his momentary hesitation. He was aware that Vita had seized on the chance of some practical activity to have time to collect herself. She was entirely too guarded for him to have any faith that she was not holding something back.

'Thank you,' he said. Rhiannon held out her cup.

'D'you mind if I open the window?' Rhiannon called to Vita in the kitchen.

Vita appeared at the doorway. 'Go ahead. But you might find some wasps come in. There's a nest nearby. Stephen thought they ought to be killed, but wasps are useful in gardens. They kill insect pests.' She coloured self-consciously and disappeared again.

Simon got up and wandered after her, while Rhiannon flung wide the window and some welcome air moved in. The kitchen was neat and bright, the sun having moved well into the west and shining on the glossy surfaces. It was expensively fitted with custom-made wood units and a marble work-surface. Simon remembered Barbara saying that Enright had had the cottage decorated for Vita. It seemed it had involved a little more than mere decoration.

Vita edged past him with the tray, glancing warily up at him through a curtain of white-blonde hair. Rhiannon had slipped off her jacket and was doodling in her notebook.

When they were settled again and civilly sipping tea, Simon asked:

'As his sister you'd probably be more aware than most, Vita. Did Liam have any special girlfriend?'

'Girls, yes.' Vita made an odd sound, almost a snigger. 'He saw girls.'

'Anyone he was involved with?'

'I've seen Mara coming from the cottage several times.'

'At night?'

'I'm not about much at night, Chief Inspector. And besides, you can't see a lot after dark in the gardens. No, at different times of the day.'

'On Saturday last?'

There was a perceptible pause. 'No,' she said.

He felt distinctly that Vita was acutely aware of all the nuances of her answers. He was sure that she was hiding something, and also that she placed a subtle emphasis here and there in an attempt to manipulate in some small or greater way. He let his gaze rest on her for a moment. Despite its almost perfect features her face was unformed, apart from that occasional curl at the corner of her lips. It would be attractive to a certain type of man, that combination of youthful innocence with its hint of know-ingness.

She fidgeted under his gaze and leaned to top up her tea.

'Was Liam keen on Mara, do you think?'

'He seemed to like her company,' she said, a primness return-ing. 'But I don't think he exactly ever lost his head over anyone.'

'Jenny?'

'Gavin's girlfriend?' Vita transferred her gaze from Simon to the window. 'I did see her coming from Liam's cottage once.'

'When was that?'

'Oh, it was some time ago. Not long after the party we had there.'

Simon waited.

'Two, three months ago, I suppose. I'd joined them at the house for an evening meal and was walking back when I bumped into her. It was quite late.'

'Were you surprised? Or could she have been visiting Ben?'

Vita turned innocent blue eyes on Simon.

'Surprised? Not really. And no. Ben was with us at the house that evening.'

'Are you in a relationship, Vita?'

She blinked. 'No.' Her colour heightening, she said, 'Though I don't see what that has to do with you.'

Simon got up and went over to the mantelpiece. 'I was looking at your photographs. They are all taken here at Clifford's Place, except this one of you and Lewis Enright, your stepfather.'

She swallowed. 'It was taken at the golf club at Winchampton. Lewis is teaching me to play golf.'

'Did your mother take it?'

'A friend of Lewis's.' Vita bit her lip, her colour still high.

'You obviously get on well with your stepfather. What did you think of his relationship with Liam?'

Vita suddenly stood up and backed away.

'Why are you asking me all these stupid questions?' she said angrily, tears pooling in her eyes. 'Trying to trap me into saying things about people I know – my family.' She burst into tears.

Rhiannon pushed back her chair and started to get up. Simon held up a hand to her.

'Who, Vita?' he asked. 'Who do you think you're going to get into trouble?'

The door opened and Lewis Enright burst in. He never seemed to enter a room normally, Simon thought resentfully.

'Just what is going on? Have you no respect, no feelings? This poor girl has just suffered a bereavement and you think it's acceptable to harass and upset her!' He went over to Vita, who collapsed sobbing on his shoulder.

'Really, sir, it was only a few questions—' Rhiannon protested.

'Besides, you shouldn't be talking to her at all like this. She's under age.' Enright stroked Vita's hair, patting and calming her.

'I'm sure you are perfectly aware that she is now of age, Mr Enright,' Simon said coldly.

'And what is that supposed to mean?'

'Exactly what it says, Mr Enright. What else?'

CHAPTER 15

Monkshood – A deadly foe is near

'Were you implying what I thought you were?' Rhiannon asked as they walked back to the house.

'That Vita was old enough to be questioned without a parent or other adult present?'

Rhiannon gave him an old-fashioned look.

'That she was old enough "now" to be questioned, as well as old enough for other things.' She gave a shrug. 'P'raps it's just me, but there's something not quite right there.'

'Where?'

Rhiannon said with studied patience:

'I think you know what I'm saying, sir.'

Simon relented and told her of Mrs Taylor's innuendo about Vita and Lewis Enright.

'And she implied it's been going on for years – since Vita was underage?'

'She reckons.'

'And apparently Helen Hartley doesn't know.' Rhiannon halted as they reached the edge of the lawns fronting the house. 'I mean, if she was underage when it began, it could ruin him. Keeping that quiet might make a motive for murder.'

'It might,' Simon said over his shoulder as she caught up. 'And so might other things.' He looked at his watch. 'The meeting's due. Let's see what the others have come up with.'

'Not much, after having half the day lost looking for Miss Hartley,' Rhiannon grumbled.

The other four were already present, but hardly present and correct, Simon noted. They bore signs of their searches in shrubberies and sheds and looked hot and bothered, except perhaps Detective Inspector Monkton, who looked his usual unhealthily pale self, his black shirt still knotted at the neck with a red-patterned tie. Longman, his plump features pink, was pouring himself some water from a bottle. Simon went over to him.

'Geoff, SOC are still at the cottage, but get over there, would you, and have a look at Liam's computer. See what you can find.'

Longman nodded, drank off the water in one gulp and left while Simon called the meeting to order. He began with a report on his own day and the rather meagre pickings thereof.

'What I hope you've got for me is some detail of where people were from early Saturday morning, and whom they saw, when and where. You take note, Detective Inspector Monkton, because I want you to draw up a co-ordinate from the facts we are given.'

Monkton straightened up. 'Supposed facts,' he said.

' "Supposed" might possibly be distinguished from "actual" when you've done the co-ordinations.' Simon was, almost, inured to Monkton's habitual hostility.

Monkton ostentatiously moved to a chair next to a table and drew out his notebook.

Rhiannon (bless her) offered to begin.

'I began by speaking to Mrs Hartley, asking her how the work in the gardens is organized how they all know what they are supposed to be doing.' She flicked open her notebook. 'I understand that she, Mrs Hartley, has a meeting with them, usually on a Monday morning, and they discuss the jobs that need doing that week, and anything else that's going to be happening – such as Mrs Hartley filming, or whatever.' She looked up. 'So they all know more or less where the others are likely to be and what they were supposed to be doing.

'Broadly speaking, they're not that regimented but they have certain areas of specialism. Vita, for instance, spends most of her time in the greenhouses and polytunnels, propagating plants, potting them on and so on, some for the garden itself, the rest for the plant-sales area which she looks after on open days. But she's often about the garden getting cuttings and collecting seed.'

The others began to shift restlessly. It had been a long hot day and the room was still overwarm. Rhiannon speeded up.

'Yes, well, Mara mostly cares for the herbaceous borders and Stephen Orchard does the lawns, pruning, and topiary, as well as the hedges. Gavin does varied duties and works in the vegetable area. Clive Ashby does general maintenance, stonework, construction and so on. Ben and Liam did a variety of things and were usually involved in any new developments in the garden.'

'So where exactly were they all on Saturday morning, Rhiannon?' Tremaine asked with a laugh.

Rhiannon reddened. 'After that I only spoke to Gavin Taylor.' She glanced at her notebook again. 'He says he came in to work on Saturday, just before half past eight. His job was to check the paths and see there were no obstructions or problems. He was cutting back greenery and raking paths most of the morning. He saw Mara at about half past nine, wheeling plants to the plant-sales area and he ran into Liam near his cottage around eleven.'

'Did they have any words together?' Monkton asked from the sidelines.

'I asked that. Gavin said he just passed him by without speaking.'

'Thanks, Rhiannon,' Simon said. 'Did you ask Mrs Hartley abou her own movements earlier that morning, whom she saw?'

'She said she didn't come out into the garden until later on in the morning and stayed near the front of the house dead-heading roses. She went briefly to the plant-sales area and saw Vita and Mara there at about eleven.'

'Let's speed things along a bit, then.' Simon gave them a brief breakdown of his own day and its meagre highlights, ending with Vita and Enright.

'You've got a motive right there,' Monkton said. He never seemed to be able to speak without sneering, Simon thought. 'Have you spoken to Benedict about what he supposedly over-heard at the cottage?'

'Not yet. I've been otherwise occupied.' Simon said sharply.

'And did Miss Vita Hartley have any explanation or apology for wasting our time today?'

'A rather feeble need to be alone, I'm afraid.' Simon turned to face the others. 'The fight in the pub on Friday night raises the possibility of motives, too. Gavin Taylor was obviously very angry at Liam for the insult to Jenny.'

'Even more so if Liam really had been messing around with his girlfriend,' Monkton suggested loudly. He sniggered. 'Especially when he's just found out she's pregnant. He must be wondering if he's really the father.'

'Jenny would be pretty angry too, I should think,' Rhiannon said seriously.

'She was here that morning,' DC Tremaine said. 'Mara Kennedy saw her coming from Liam's cottage at about half past nine.'

'I'll follow that up,' Simon said. No doubt Jenny had had something to say to Liam after the night before. But she could have had something more lethal in mind.

'Alan Fairburn, Mrs Hartley's friend, was here too,' Monkton added. 'Barbara Meddick saw him from the office window at around nine. You'll be able to kill two birds with one stone.'

'Did she say why he was here?'

'She said she assumed he was here to see Mrs Hartley, but she didn't know if he had. With all that happened after, it slipped her mind.'

'Anything else to report?' Simon asked him.

'I spoke to the house staff,' Monkton said, leaning back and putting his feet on the table in front of him. 'Linda Carver and June Taylor were in the kitchen together all morning, preparing food for the teas that day. One interesting fact that emerged was that Linda Carver saw Lewis Enright and Liam Hartley talking together near the stables early on at half past seven, when she arrived.'

'Did she hear anything that was said?' Simon asked.

'Just saw them as she drove past to park, she said.'

And if she had seen or heard more, given her reaction to the interview with Monkton, Linda Carver was unlikely to have confided it to the Inspector, Simon thought.

'Thanks,' said Simon. 'So just about everyone connected to Clifford's Place was here during that morning, except Ben, whose story we still have to check, and Lewis Enright, who was at a meeting in London.'

'We spoke to Stephen Orchard and Clive Ashby as well,'

120

Tremaine went on. 'Clive Ashby wasn't in that day. What Stephen said seems to tie up with what the others said.'

Simon, remembering his own formal entry to the place on Saturday morning, asked:

'Is there any other entrance on that side of the gardens apart from the main gates?'

'The wicket gate,' Monkton said. 'It's just south of Liam Hartley's cottage. Comes from the far end of the public car park – where Liam and Ben kept their Land-Rovers.'

Simon recalled Vita's mentioning it.

'Well we seem to have a situation where most people connected with Liam Hartley had the likely opportunity of doctoring his midday meal.

'Everybody get your reports ready for DI Monkton first thing. It's possible,' he said to Monkton, 'that you might find some discrepancies when you have people's full reports but I don't think it's an avenue that's likely to yield anything much more than we've got already.'

'Thanks,' Monkton said sarcastically.

'It's still important that it's done.'

'I reckon time would be better spent checking on Lewis Enright.' Monkton dropped his pen noisily.

'We'll be doing that. He's a bit elusive,' Simon said to Savage and Tremaine, 'so you'd better speak to him tonight before you leave. Get a clear picture of his movements on Saturday morning and check on it tomorrow. And ask him what he was talking to Liam about early that day. And check out Ben's story, too. I'll leave copies of my own report here.'

He said to Rhiannon, 'See what more you can find out about the people here. Barbara Meddick was a bit economical with the details in the list she gave us. And run the usual check for any criminal background on them.

'I'll be speaking to Ben, asking about the argument he heard Liam having. I'll go on to see Alan Fairburn and Jenny Shipman.'

He turned to Monkton. 'Perhaps you could contact toxicology and see if you can hurry them along after you've done the report.'

'They'll be a while yet.' Monkton made his habitual, or ritual, objection.

'All the more reason,' Simon said. 'Check with SOC as well.

They began packing up and filing out as Simon settled to a computer screen and started his report for Detective Superintendent Munro. He had just completed it, in its unsatisfactory entirety, when Longman came in.

'Anything, Geoff?'

Longman had a few sheets of paper in his hand. 'Only this,' he said. 'He seems to have used his PC mostly for doing garden designs but this was something different.' He pulled over a chair and sat down beside Simon. 'It's a business plan. A plan for his own garden design firm.' He pointed and Simon looked. 'Most of the outlay goes on a showplace base and setting up some model gardens. Then there's a projection of likely earnings, costs and so on.'

'So where was he going to get this outlay?' Simon said.

'His mother?' Longman cocked a bushy eyebrow.

'It's a lot of money. Would Helen be prepared to let him go? He was still young to be setting up on his own. And she seems to have involved him in her own garden design work as well as working at Clifford's Place itself.'

'Maybe there are things we don't know about.'

'I'm sure there are an awful lot of those.' Simon stretched his arms and eased his back, yawning. 'Still, interesting nonetheless. Shows he wasn't just all talk.'

'Maybe there's some money to come from his father's will,' Longman said.

'Something we should ask about I suppose. Though this doesn't really tell us anything new.' Simon stretched again. 'Let's knock off. It's been a long hot day.'

'We'd better get the windows secure,' Longman said, going over to unwedge the hockey stick. 'Not that there's much on the board for anyone to see.'

Simon draped some sheets from the large sheet pad over the photograph of Liam Hartley and the accompanying list of names. He locked the door on their way out. Rhiannon had a copy of the key and she was unfailingly early at work.

As they made their way through the house to the back door they met Lewis Enright and Helen Hartley crossing the main hallway.

'I've just had two of your men questioning me,' Enright said.

Simon paused, waiting for the expected protest, but Enright

seemed comparatively subdued. 'I suppose it has to be done. Though it's hard to take, I must say.'

'We understand, sir,' Longman said sincerely.

'There will be still more questions to come, I'm afraid,' Simon said, less agreeably. He felt unable to summon up the energy to dissemble.

'Such as?' Enright asked, bristling again, his studied equanimity already spent.

Helen Hartley linked her hands through her husband's arm and looked at the floor.

'We wondered whether Liam had any inheritance to come from his father's estate,' Simon said to her. 'He seems to have had real plans for setting up independently.'

'You were wondering, were you?' Enright said. 'Spend a lot of time wondering and thinking up trouble, do you?'

Simon disregarded him. 'Mrs Hartley?'

'Yes, there was money,' she said calmly. 'But it wouldn't have been available until he was twenty-five.' She frowned. 'Why do you say he was making plans? He never said anything to me about it.'

'Just a fantasy on Liam's part, I'm sure,' Enright said, putting an arm around his wife.

Simon explained what Longman had found on Liam's computer.

'Fantasy,' Enright said again. 'He was only nineteen.'

'They're in a hurry, kids these days,' Longman said. 'Dotcom millionaires in their teens.'

Enright said, 'Anything else you want of us, Chief Inspector?'

'Just one thing. Mrs Hartley, we're clarifying everyone's whereabouts on Saturday morning. Alan Fairburn was seen in the gardens at around nine a.m. Was he coming to see you?'

She looked startled. 'Alan? Was he? No, I didn't see him that morning. How odd.' She paused. 'Though I did tell them when they came to dinner last week that they were welcome to visit, without regard to official opening times. He was probably having an early morning walk and decided to call in.'

'Strange he didn't make himself known,' Enright said, frowning at his wife.

'Not really,' she said lightly. 'Not if he was just taking a walk.

He probably called in on impulse. Anyway,' Helen shrugged, 'I can't think that Alan is of any importance to you,' she said to Simon.

'It was mentioned when we were discussing who saw whom that morning, Mrs Hartley.'

'Is that all?' Enright asked.

'It can wait until tomorrow. I want to speak to Ben again and DC Jones will see you again briefly, if that's all right,' Simon said to Helen.

'Has anything emerged today?' Enright asked, putting a sarcastic emphasis on the penultimate word.

'Nothing I need concern you with at the moment, sir,' Simon said amiably and made to move on.

Helen stopped him with her hand. 'Did Vita have anything to say about her disappearance?'

Simon was aware of Enright staring balefully at him.

'She said she had just needed a little time alone, Mrs Hartley.'

'Sad,' she said. 'A time like this should draw people closer.'

Simon started to move on but she put out her hand again. 'Have you heard anything of the toxicology report yet?'

'It's a bit soon yet, Mrs Hartley. But we'll keep you informed.'

She let him go, but he was aware that they remained standing watching after him and Longman as they made their way out.

CHAPTER 16

Amaranthus – Affectation

Ben Hartley was not at the house the following morning. No one seemed to have any idea where he might be. Simon left a message with Mrs Taylor for him to be at the incident room at two o'clock, then he and Longman drove on into Chairford. The place was busier than before. People stood about talking outside the post office in the middle of the village, others walked their dogs. The cooler air must have brought them out, Simon thought. There had been a violent thunderstorm the night before which he and his mother watched companionably from Jessie's sitting-room window. A brief call had come from Jessie to tell them the (expected) time of arrival of her train this evening, and nothing had been said between his mother and himself to jar the tranquillity of an evening spent viewing some spectacular lightning flashing around them.

Now, the sun shone again in clearer air as they drove slowly looking for the turning to Colin Wheatley's house. At a short distance down a narrow lane they found The Forge. It was a long, low building with a pantiled roof and stone-mullioned windows, backing on to fields and a hill, with an overgrown but colourful country garden. They parked in front of the garage beside a blue four-track, a silver Ford and a red mini. Simon looked around with interest, imagining how different it must once have been if the name of the place was true to its origins.

The excited cries of two small children broke the peace. They raced across the lawn from behind the garage pursued by a young woman with long light-brown hair. She came to an abrupt halt as she sighted Simon and Longman. The children subsided giggling against the trunk of an old apple-tree.

'Can I help you?' she asked.

Simon explained who they were. 'We're looking for Mr Fairburn.'

'Oh!' She seemed puzzled. 'Is this about Liam? I don't think he'll be able to help you much.'

She was probably in her early twenties, Simon thought. Tanned from the hot summer and wearing a short shift-dress in a flattering shade of blue which showed off her brown limbs and light-blue eyes. She had a strong face with a wide firm mouth, striking rather than pretty, and she stared at him steadily expecting a response. He realized how readily he had imagined her different, weaker, because he had heard of her only as a sort of victim.

'You must be Jenny Shipman,' he said.

One of the children let out a shriek and she turned instantly and ran over to them. One was sitting on top of the other and apparently stuffing grass in its mouth. It was impossible to tell what sex they were from their clothes or even from their hair.

'Jack, stop it!' they heard her say firmly as she hauled the slightly larger of the two to his feet. The other seemed to have survived the ordeal with equanimity: he, or she, scrambled to its feet saying:

'What are we going to play now Jenny?'

Jenny glanced back at Simon and he strolled over to her. 'Can we speak to you a little later?'

'If you like,' she said impassively, turning back to her charges.

'Dinosaurs!' said Jack fiercely, peering up at Simon from under a fringe of hair and grinning.

'Nicest insult we'll get today,' Longman said as Simon joined him.

A young woman answered their knock at the front door, blonde hair tousled, dressed in jeans and a white cotton shirt. Simon showed her his ID and asked for Alan Fairburn. She opened the door wide.

'If it's about poor Liam Hartley I can't think what use Alan's going to be.'

Simon was becoming wearied by the varying forms in which

this sort of comment had been made to him since the case began.

'I'm Laura Wheatley, by the way,' she said as she led them through a stone-flagged hallway, stepping over children's bikes and toys scattered there.

'Coffee, tea?' she asked brightly as they arrived in the large farmhouse kitchen. On closer inspection she looked around her mid-thirties, considerably younger than her husband.

'Coffee would be lovely,' Longman said, and Simon thanked her.

'Good! I'll just put the kettle on and go and find them. We're all running a bit late this morning. You don't mind instant?' Without waiting for a response she splashed water in the kettle and made a dash for the door.

They looked around them at a scene of chaos. A bundle of clothes in a washing-basket stood on one of the kitchen counters, dirty dishes were stacked on another, various items of children's clutter lay on the floor, chairs and even the table they were sitting at. Beneath it all appeared what might otherwise be an attractive, comfortable room.

'Scatty.' Longman said.

The kettle came to a boil and still they waited. Just as Simon was deciding to make a move – somewhere – Laura Wheatley, breathless, appeared.

'They'd gone for a walk up the hill,' she said. 'Sorry. They'll be with you now.'

It was not until she had made the coffee and placed their mugs in front of Simon and Longman that her husband and Alan Fairburn strolled into the kitchen. Colin Wheatley removed a stuffed toy from a chair and joined them. Alan Fairburn asked Laura if they could have coffee too and leaned on the kitchen counter watching while she poured water into their mugs.

'Sorry Alan,' she said, 'I know you like proper coffee but I'm run off my feet this morning.'

At last, Alan Fairburn came to the table and sat down.

'Do you want to speak to Alan alone, Chief Inspector?' Wheatley asked diffidently.

'Not necessarily,' Simon said.

Laura Wheatley thrust a plate of biscuits on to the table.

'We only want to ask Mr Fairburn a question or two,' Simon

added. 'But we'd like to speak to Jenny afterwards.'

'Fine,' Wheatley agreed, taking a biscuit and biting on it, scattering crumbs on the table and down his shirt front. 'So you don't need me here?'

'Stay, by all means.' Alan Fairburn placed a hand on his friend's arm. 'I've never been questioned by the police before.'

'You've led a sheltered life then, sir,' Longman said. 'I thought the police in America were always arresting people even for minor traffic offences. Bristling with guns as well.'

'Now you mention it,' Fairburn smiled, 'I did get into trouble for changing lanes a bit too often when I first moved over there.'

'When was that?' Simon asked.

'Over twenty years ago.'

'Is this the first time you've been back?'

'No, I've been over a few times. But only briefly.'

'You two are friends from your time in England?'

'Oddly enough, we met in California,' Wheatley said. 'I'm a scriptwriter and was working on a British book being filmed in Hollywood a couple of years ago. It was actually Jenny who introduced us. She came across Alan's wife on the beach one day – she's around Jenny's age – they got talking and Gina thought we might enjoy meeting up.'

'Is your wife over here?' Simon asked.

'She's in London visiting friends,' Alan said.

'So it was quite a coincidence that Mr and Mrs Wheatley lived so close to an old acquaintance of yours, Mrs Hartley?'

'Oh, everyone lives in the Cotswolds these days,' Colin said expansively. His tone implied that anyone who was anyone did. 'But actually we've only been here about a year. We wanted to move out of London because of the children beginning to run around. Jenny found it for us when she was having a holiday down here.' He looked across at his wife who was stacking the dishwasher. 'We've been delighted with her choice, haven't we, love?'

'Delighted,' she echoed, pausing only briefly in what she doing.

'She sounds a very resourceful young woman,' Longman said.

'Jenny?' Wheatley glanced at him. 'She's a treasure. I don't know how we'll manage without her when she . . .'

'Has the baby?' Simon asked.

Wheatley looked pained.

'Has she discussed it with you?'

'Not really,' Laura called across. 'We want her to take her time to make up her mind without any pressure from us.'

'How long has she been with you?' Simon asked, taking a sip from the bland coffee.

'About two and a half years, since Alice was just under a year old.' Colin Wheatley said.

His wife added, 'It was the year in California that attracted Jenny. Lucky for us. I wanted to have the chance to get about with Colin while we were over there and then we found we couldn't do without her, didn't we?'

Her husband nodded his agreement, picking up another biscuit brushing crumbs from his chest.

'So what was it you wanted to speak to me about, Chief Inspector?' Alan Fairburn said. He wrapped long fine fingers around his coffee mug and lifted it to his mouth.

'You were at Clifford's Place around nine last Saturday morning. I wondered what you were doing there.'

A slight flicker of surprise, or annoyance, crossed Fairburn's face, though Simon might only have imagined it. It did appear to be news to Wheatley though, who looked at his friend with interest.

'I was poisoning Liam Hartley's sandwiches, what else?' Fairburn said with a grin that showed the benefit of American orthodontics.

'Alan!' Laura remonstrated from across the room where she now stood watching them.

'Perhaps we could have that in writing, sir,' Longman said.

'Sorry. That was in poor taste,' Fairburn replied, the smile still lingering.

'Well?' Simon raised his eyebrows.

Fairburn shrugged his shoulders. 'I went out for a walk on my own, if you remember,' he said to Wheatley. 'You and Laura were busy with the children as it was Jenny's day off.' He turned to Simon. 'It was such a lovely morning I just carried on through the village, thought I'd go to Clifford's Place and see what it was like early on before the visitors arrived. Helen had said we were welcome to go over outside visiting times if we wished.' He made a brief impatient gesture. 'I can assure you I had no sinister purpose, Chief Inspector. Anyway, I hardly knew the boy.'

Simon wondered why he had bothered to add that last defensive note.

'We weren't suggesting you were guilty of anything, Mr Fairburn. We're merely clarifying what was happening at Clifford's Place that morning, who was where and so on. Did you meet anyone when you were there?'

'I thought of calling on Helen, but it was a bit early so I just wandered around a bit. The gardens are a lot more extensive than I had realized. I saw one or two people doing jobs about place, though I can't be sure they saw me as they were busy in what they were doing. I saw Mara from a distance at one point, but as I'm not familiar with the gardens I'm afraid I can't be much help in giving you map references.'

'You knew Mara of course from meeting her at the Clifford Arms on Friday night,' Simon said.

'We met her before that,' Wheatley interposed. 'As well as Gavin and Stephen Orchard, and of course the boys, Liam and Ben. It's the only local around here. Everyone goes there.'

'So you'd recognize the others you saw that morning?' Simon asked Fairburn.

'That big chap, what's his name?' Fairburn said to his friend.

'Stephen Orchard.'

'That's the one. He was doing some digging at one point. Actually, I can't remember seeing anyone else. I wasn't there long. It was already getting too hot for me.'

'I'd have thought you'd be used to it after California, Mr Fairburn,' Longman said. 'Did you see Jenny? She was there too that morning.'

'Was she?' Fairburn glanced at Wheatley. 'No, I didn't see her.'

'It's a dreadful thing,' Colin Wheatley said, 'what's happened to young Liam. Poor Helen must be devastated. Is she holding up all right?'

'About as well as can be expected, I suppose,' Simon said neutrally. 'You all had dinner at Clifford's Place recently, I understand. Did everything seem as it should be?'

'I wouldn't know,' Fairburn drawled. 'Not having been with the family before I had nothing to compare it with.'

'Oh, come on Alan!' Laura Wheatley protested, coming over to the table. 'Personally, I thought there was a bit of an atmosphere.'

'I bow to your feminine intuition, Laura,' Fairburn said, smiling again.

'Didn't you think so, Colin? In fact I remember we talked about it on the way back. I felt quite sorry for Helen.' She pulled up a chair and joined them, her expression concerned. 'I mean, I've always thought of her as the woman who's got it all – lovely looks, perfect family, rich husband and beautiful home – not to mention the garden she's created and her very successful career.' She looked from her husband to his friend. 'Surely you remember?'

'I can recall something of the sort,' Colin said with a doubtful pursing of the lips. 'I mean, I remember you talking about it, Laura. But I can't say I noticed anything much at the time.'

Laura made an exasperated sound and turned to Alan. 'Didn't you notice? Perhaps men are just blind to these things.'

'There was a bit of inhibited bickering going on, I suppose,' he said slowly, after a theatrical pause. 'Mostly between Liam and his stepfather.'

'Which Helen kept trying to smooth over,' Laura agreed.

'Vita was very quiet, I noticed,' Alan added.

'And Barbara, Helen's friend, seemed so watchful. She hardly said a word. It didn't seem quite normal to me, anyway. But perhaps I'm not normal,' Laura ended cheerfully.

'Never that!' her husband agreed.

She looked at him.

He laughed. 'Wouldn't want you to be. Anyway, what's normal?' Laura put her hands flat on the table and stood up, her eyes on Simon.

'It was an odd way to kill anyone,' she said. 'I mean, I could see that Liam was a pretty forceful character: he practically dominated the evening, almost as if he was orchestrating things, in a way. But I'd have thought someone might hit him over the head rather than poison him.' She pushed her chair back. 'Is it still the woman's weapon, poison?'

'By no means, I'm afraid,' Simon said. 'It would make our job simpler if it were. There've been enough male poisoners even in recent years.'

'But it's still an easier choice for a woman than physical violence.'

'I suppose so.'

'Is it true that the murderer left a vase of monkshood in Liam's cottage?'

Simon assumed that the local grapevine worked efficiently via the Clifford Arms.

'Someone did.'

'That's what killed him, then. How awful for Helen, that it was one of her plants from her own garden.' Running her hands through her hair Laura turned and looked around the room. 'What a tip! I'd better get on, the children will be in for their elevenses soon.'

Simon hadn't heard that quaint expression for many years.

'Perhaps we could have a word with Jenny while they do?' he said.

Laura looked dismayed for a moment then smiled agreement.

'Of course you must. I'm sure Jenny knows more about them at Clifford's Place than we do. I wonder what she was doing there on Saturday, she never said . . .' She wandered over to the laundry basket and heaved it on to her hip. 'I'll just go and peg these out.'

'You've finished with me?' Alan Fairburn said quietly.

Simon had the familiar feeling that there was something he'd forgotten to ask.

'Yes, I think so.'

'Where would you like to speak to Jenny now?' Wheatley got his feet along with Fairburn. 'You won't want to be in the kitchen with the children. I'll go and take them off Jenny's hands.'

'Where would you suggest?'

'The sitting-room? I'll show you the way.'

CHAPTER 17

Rue – Disdain

'Does anyone ever have a good word to say about Liam Hartley?' Longman asked after Colin Wheatley had deposited them in the comparatively serene sitting-room.

'His mother?' Simon said. 'And Barbara Meddick did her best. Otherwise all you hear is the same old thing about troublemaking, domineering and getting his own way.'

'Enough to make someone want to get rid of him.' Longman threw himself down on a huge soft sofa. 'Well we've got a few possibilities in mind. What's bothering me is that the chances of finding evidence are not looking hopeful. I mean, as far as opportunity goes any one of them could have done it – unless Ben's and Enright's alibis hold out. And even those might be a bit tricky, depending on what time Liam left the cottage free for the poisoner.'

'So we do what we usually do for the time being and wait for the information to build up.'

Longman began to speak again but Jenny Shipman confidently entered the room. She brought a scent of the outdoors with her.

'Shall I sit down?' she asked, and without waiting for a reply chose a deep armchair with its back to the window. She leaned back displaying long brown legs and gave Simon a look of amused enquiry.

This was no Amanda in need of an aunt's counselling. This young woman seemed entirely in command of her life. And yet she had been in tears, apparently, on that evening at the Clifford Arms, distressed and in need of comfort.

Simon sat beside Longman, leaning forward and facing her.

'We're checking with everyone who was at Clifford's Place on Saturday morning,' he said. 'You were there, we understand.'

'Yes,' she said.

'Why?'

'I went to see Liam.'

'And did you see him?'

'Yes, I did.' She crossed her hands calmly in her lap.

Simon paused and gave her a level look. 'Could you perhaps be a little more expansive about your trip to Clifford's Place the morning that Liam Hartley was murdered?'

The smile on her face tightened. 'Well, I saw him and said what I had to say and then I left.'

'And what was it that you had to say, Miss Shipman?'

'Is that really any of your business?' she said evenly.

'I'm afraid it is. People's privacy tends to get invaded in a murder inquiry,' Simon said. The young woman's pretended naïvety was instructive rather than annoying.

'But I could lie to you and you wouldn't know any different. Just as other people you have spoken to may well have lied to you.'

'It's a point of view,' Longman agreed, crossing his short legs and laying his arm along the back of the sofa.

'You could, of course, lie,' Simon replied in the same tone as before. 'But that would be a crime in itself and so rather unwise, unless you have something you need to hide. So, if you haven't, and even if you have, I should still be obliged if you would be a bit more forthcoming. Wasting police time is in itself an offence.'

She sat up straighter, silky hair sliding from brown shoulders, with a wry expression.

'Fair enough. Though I don't think I can help you.' She took a breath. 'You want it all, do you?'

Simon waited.

'I left here around nine and walked over to Clifford's Place, arriving there around twenty past, twenty-five past? I didn't hurry, anyway. I went in through the wicket gate near Liam's place and called at the cottage itself. The door was open so I went in and called him. There was no reply so I came out again and went looking for him. I remember I tripped over a wheelbarrow parked nearby.' She lifted a slim brown leg, showing more of her thighs, and rubbed at a point near her knee.

'How far into the cottage did you go?'

'The sitting-room. Then I went back into the hall and called upstairs from there.'

'You didn't go as far as the kitchen?'

'No. And I didn't make up a new batch of sandwiches, either.'

'Did you happen to notice a vase of flowers by the fireplace?'

She frowned. 'I can't say I did. Is it important?' Her expression cleared. 'You mean the monkshood that was found there, do you?'

Simon remembered that the flowers had not been visible to him until he was returning from the kitchen. 'Go on.'

'I wandered around a bit and found Liam down by the lower path, by the ha-ha. He was cutting back some brambles that were coming in from the field.'

'And what did you have to say to him?'

She looked down for the first time. 'I was still angry about what had happened the night before at the pub. I told him to stop putting about suggestions and rumours about me and him.'

'What did he say?'

'He said something like, "Take it easy, I was only winding Gavin up".'

'Was he at all apologetic?'

'Liam? I didn't really expect him to be. He still thought it was funny.'

'So if you didn't expect an apology, did you think he would take any notice of what you said?'

She shrugged. 'I just didn't want him to think he could get away with it.'

'But he did, all the same. Or did you threaten him in some way?'

'No! How could I threaten Liam?' She seemed unconscious of the fact that someone had threatened Liam, terminally. Her head on one side, she said, 'He did say something else, though. He said not to worry because he didn't plan on being around much longer.'

'Prophetic,' Simon said drily. 'Did you ask him what he meant?'

'Of course I did. He told me he was getting out and was setting up his own business. I said it was the first I'd heard of it and he laughed and said I was only the second to know. I left after that and came straight back here.' She smoothed down her dress, tightening its hem across her thighs.

'You didn't ask who the other person was who knew he was leaving?'

'No.' She shook her head. 'I assumed at first that he meant his mother. But the way he laughed about it made me think that whoever it was, he was putting pressure on them in some way. That would have been typical of Liam.' Tossing her hair, she said, twisting her lips, 'It was probably poor old Lewis.'

'Why do you say that?'

'Who else? He had some control over the funds, I understand. At least, Liam was known to complain about not getting his hands on his own money and muttering about what Lewis was up to with it.'

'You seem to know the family quite well, Jenny. Have you had a lot to do with them?'

'Not really.' She began playing with the ends of her hair. 'I probably just feel that I know them, what with my involvement with Gavin and the general gossip at the Clifford Arms.'

Simon got up and wandered over to the window, so that he stood behind her.

'Did you see anyone else, apart from Liam, when you were at Clifford's Place that morning?'

'I saw Steve Orchard while I was looking for Liam but he had his back to me, wheeling a barrow along one of the paths.'

'Where was that?'

'Along the lower half of the gardens somewhere. He was heading for the other side from Liam's cottage, if that's what you mean.'

'Did you see Alan Fairburn while you were there?'

'No.' She twisted in her seat to face Simon, so that the sun shone fully on her face for the first time. She blinked. 'Was Alan there? That's interesting.' She smiled, showing strong white teeth.

'Why interesting?'

'He's an old friend of Helen's, isn't he? Maybe he's trying to renew the relationship.' Perhaps she caught the look of distaste that crossed Simon's face because she turned away.

'Funny time to do it,' Longman said, 'early morning.'

'Unless he was just leaving.' She put a hand over her mouth stifling another smile.

Simon sat opposite her again. 'Is that merely innuendo, or do you have grounds for saying that?' There was a hint of reprimand in his voice and he regretted it. She was the first person he had spoken to who was prepared to open up about the inhabitants of Clifford's Place, even if it were with a salacious and possibly malicious edge.

Her face under the tan went a dull red and she crossed her legs. 'It's just that Alan's talked about her a lot since he's been here.'

'I see,' Simon said, infusing his voice with more interest. 'He's still fond of her, you think?'

'I suppose so,' she said, evidently still put out.

After all his years of police work, Simon hadn't lost his discomfort with what he felt were its prying aspects – particularly those which encouraged the tendency in others. He tried to smile encouragingly.

'Were they very close then, all those years ago?'

'From what I gather,' she said grudgingly. 'About as close as it gets.'

'Mr Fairburn's wife is in London, I understand. Has she been here to stay?'

'No. It's all very sad. Soon after they arrived in England with their baby son, he died. A cot death I think. Gina was out at the time and Alan was at the hotel, with the baby in the next room. I think she blamed him to some extent. Anyway, after the funeral she went off to stay with some friends somewhere in London and Alan came down here.' She pulled down her shift dress and bit her lip. 'Perhaps that's what got him reminiscing about the old days with Helen. People do look back, don't they, when times get painful?'

It was a so far uncharacteristically sensitive remark.

'I suppose they do,' Simon said. The room dimmed slightly as the sun moved on and he was conscious of time passing. 'Jenny, we've heard from others about the argument in the Clifford Arms last Friday night. Can we hear your version of events?'

She sighed. 'I wish I could forget all about it.'

'I'm sorry to have to drag it up again.'

She gave him a disbelieving look, then focused on her hands in her lap.

'In a way it was Gavin's fault. We were in the bar on our own. I thought it was as good a time as any to tell him I was pregnant. I didn't know how he'd react. I wasn't sure how I felt about it for that matter. But he was really pleased, assuming we'd get married soon and so on. Then Mara and Ben came in and he told them, without even asking me. She asked me how many months and Ben went to get us a drink to celebrate and then Liam arrived and asked what all the fuss was about.

'I was feeling embarrassed enough already. I mean I didn't want it being talked about like that in the pub. I hadn't had a chance to speak to Gavin about it properly and in private. And then Mara piped up and told Liam that I was two months pregnant. He looked sly and said "Two months, eh?" very suggestively.' Jenny was picking at the skin at the edge of one of her fingernails, concentrating fiercely.

'Of course, like he always does with Liam, Gavin rose to the bait and asked him what he was insinuating. Liam said he wasn't insinuating anything, just remembering what a great time he and I had had at his party a couple of months ago.'

She looked at Simon, pale eyes wide. 'It wasn't true. I mean I did go to the party. Gavin was away on a course at the time. Nothing happened between me and Liam.' She clasped her hands, gripping them tightly. 'So Gavin went for Liam, without waiting for me to say anything.'

'He hit him?'

She nodded. 'Knocked him over, and the chair he was sitting on.'

'What did the others do?'

She hesitated. 'I remember catching sight of Mara. She looked really stunned and was giving me this accusing look. I always understood that she and Liam were a bit of an item and I felt terrible. I said something like, "You know it's not true". But she turned away. I don't think she believed me.

'Anyway, Ben came over from the bar and tried to separate them but they both pushed him off and were facing up to each other again when the landlord came in. Liam told him to keep out of it. I think they both hit each other again but Alan and Colin came in and grabbed hold of one each.' She paused, rubbing at her forehead. 'Colin hadn't even known about the baby. I felt really shaky. It was so upsetting, all the violence, and I burst into tears. It had turned something private and important into a sordid row. It was horrible.'

She glanced at Simon. 'That was why I had to speak to Liam next day. I wanted him to make clear to everyone that he had been lying.' She shrugged again. 'I might have known it would be a waste of time.'

'Gavin didn't believe him? Or did he?' Simon asked.

'He said that of course he didn't. But it was damaging what Liam did. It hurt people.'

It seemed to be Liam's epitaph.

'Do you know what you're going to do now, Jenny? Will you keep the baby?'

Her response startled him. 'Do you think I'm going to have an abortion, or give it up for adoption?' she said indignantly.

Simon, appalled at the insensitivity of his question, could only think that Jane's recent agonizing over Amanda had led him into the error of assuming that these options occurred to all young unmarried women.

'Of course not, he said, apologizing. 'I'm sorry.'

'I hope so,' she said, glaring at him.

He was about to ask how she would manage, if she would marry Gavin, but realized she would, no doubt rightly, tell him to mind his own business.

Longman, out of the line of fire, said the more appropriate thing.

'The children here will miss you. And their parents, no doubt.'

'Not necessarily. We haven't decided yet what we'll do. I may be able to manage their children along with my own child after a short break.' She said this with a proud lift to her head. 'I love children.'

She would need to, Simon thought, if that was the plan.

'Is that all?' she asked, eyes on Longman rather than Simon's unforgiven self. 'I'd like to get back to the children. Mrs Wheatley has to go shopping.'

They let her go, her lean athletic body moving quickly to the door and away.

Longman blew out his cheeks.

'A bit of a force of nature, that one,' he said.

CHAPTER 18

Rhododendron – Danger, beware

After a brief meal at the Clifford Arms, where Simon and Longman had several words with, and gained little insight from, the landlord, they drove on slowly to Clifford's Place.

'I suppose there's one thing you can say for Liam Hartley,' Longman said. 'He was nothing if not consistent.'

'Usually, an individual is one thing to one person and something else to another. As you say, Liam showed an untypical conformability.' Simon uttered a rare expletive. 'You know, people are a complete mystery to me a lot of the time.'

Longman folded his arms over his rotund form. 'I'm a complete mystery to myself. Aren't you?'

Simon gave a wry smile. 'I think I'm so busy trying to fathom other people I've hardly noticed. I'm sure it's true, though.'

Spending a few years with Jessie, a professional psychologist, had inevitably increased his self-awareness but Simon thought, as he had on other subjects, that it became a matter of 'the more you know, the more you know you don't know'.

Longman stared out at the passing trees, the sun coming through them creating a dazzling flickering effect.

'When you think about it, everything's about motivation. It's what makes people say and do the things they do. There's an agenda for everything, all the time. And with some people they can hardly open their mouths without signalling some kind of subtext. Haven't you noticed?'

Simon was surprised by this harsh assessment of others coming from the good-natured Longman.

'I register it some of the time,' he agreed, 'usually with people I've been closer to – as most of us do, I suppose.' He was thinking at the moment of his mother's heavily weighted words. He glanced at Longman who was gazing ahead with a serene expression on his face. 'I hadn't thought about motivation in quite such a universal way, though.'

'It's probably what gives this sometimes wholly unrewarding job some interest. I mean, we spend a lot of time looking at people's motives.'

'But it seems a pretty cynical point of view of people in general.' Simon braked quickly to avoid a squirrel which had decided to halt suddenly in the middle of the road, staring at the car bright-eyed with alarm.

'Not absolutely everyone is like it,' Longman said, settling back in his seat. 'It just seems to me that the general run of people are manipulative – and that comes from motive, the desire to make others conform to what they want of them. Or what they want them to think of them.'

'The control freak being an extreme example.'

'Liam Hartley was one, I'd say.'

'I think most people would agree with that. How did Jenny Shipman fit into your scheme of things?'

'I'd say she was pretty manipulative.'

'Why d'you say that?' Simon instinctively went along with Longman's assessment, but that was all it was at the moment – instinct. In the midst of all the questions he asked he was constantly assailed by fleeting hints of deeper significance. But he rarely assimilated them quickly enough at the time to make his questioning more astute.

'The whole way she answered your questions. She's very intelligent, don't you think? I mean, most people are fairly nervous when they're interviewed by police – the usual thing about feeling guilty even if they haven't done anything wrong. But she tried to take control when you began questioning her.'

'Yes, I did notice,' Simon said. He turned the car right towards the entrance to Clifford's Place and slowed down.

'I thought she was very conscious of everything she said to you.

A lot of people say more than they mean to say, because they're nervous, but she was aware of the implications of what she said – even when she made that remark about Alan Fairburn and Helen Hartley. She coloured up, but it wasn't because she was embarrassed that you made her feel she'd said something malicious. It was just that she was angry with you for, in a way, trying to control her.'

'Is that what I did?' Simon drove the car into their parking space beside the stables. He turned and faced Longman quizzically.

'Challenging people is a form of control, maybe. Questioning their behaviour.'

'But an acceptable form of control, surely? Anyway, do go on.'

'Oh, I could think of a number of things.' Longman opened the door to let in some air. 'The way she reacted to what happened at the pub that night. It was all out of her control – that's what really got to her.'

'Normal enough reaction, I'd have thought.'

'She's not the sort to get easily upset, though. But getting upset got her out of the situation. They all rallied round and took her home, we're told. Now, I'd have thought she'd be more the sort to slap Liam Hartley's face for what he said. She's not a victim type.'

Simon remembered thinking exactly that.

'Well, this is all very interesting, but I'm not sure where it gets us.' He opened the driver's door. It was far too hot to stay in the car.

'Well, let's say I wouldn't put it past her to poison Liam's sandwiches,' Longman said with a grin.

Simon paused in getting out of the car. 'Surely, as you said, the slap on the face is more her style. You know, I was thinking that she was the first person who seemed to open up a bit, give us a bit more information about other people. You've put a different slant on it.'

Longman got out of the car red-faced and sweating and leaned on the roof.

'Well, she's more of an outsider than the others you've spoken to. I'm not saying she didn't say a few interesting things, and they were probably true. It just seemed to me that she was calculating in what she did say.'

Simon wiped his brow and leaned opposite him. 'I did notice some of what you're saying. For instance, when I was asking about the fracas at the pub, the first thing she remarked on was how upset Mara Kennedy was. In the natural course of things she'd have stuck with describing the fight.'

'Exactly. She got that one in first.'

'And why?'

'Well it drags Mara into the frame, doesn't it? Motive: revenge?'

'She did a job on Lewis Enright then, as well.'

'I think what she said about that was probably right, don't you? It was astute, anyway. As I said, she's not stupid.'

Simon walked over to the shade at the back of the house. He said as Longman joined him:

'Not stupid enough to risk her freedom over a thoughtless insult, certainly.'

'No,' Longman agreed smiling broadly. 'She was just a useful illustration of my cynical view of the generality of mankind. Whenever we interview anyone, they're trying to put a fix on it, a slant. They want you to see it the way they want it seen. I could go on,' he offered, as they made their way towards the rear entrance.

'And I could go on listening.' Simon rested his hand on the sergeant's shoulder as they approached the back door. 'I suggest you do the questions with Ben Hartley, and this time I'll sit back and have the luxury of interesting thoughts.'

June Taylor emerged from the kitchen as they were passing. She held out a key.

'Mr Enright left a note asking me to give this to you. It's the key to the door at the end of the corridor from you. It opens on to the path that leads around the back of the house where you all park. He thought it might be more convenient for you all than coming through the house.' She was obviously torn between her hostility to Lewis Enright and her suspicion of the police, for she wavered between a conciliatory smile and stiff formality.

Simon thanked her and took the key.

'You can get some cut at the post office in Chairford,' she said helpfully. 'Her husband does it as a sideline.' She gave a little sniff. 'We've been very glad of him around here.' She ducked back behind the door.

'Understandable, I suppose,' Longman commented. 'Can't be very comfortable having us lot wandering through the house.'

'Loss of privacy's inevitable anyway,' Simon said, pushing open the door to the corridor and expecting to see Ben Hartley waiting for them. He wasn't there.

Simon looked into the incident room where a solitary Detective Inspector Monkton, being Monkton, sweated only metaphorically over a computer.

'Has Ben Hartley been here?'

Monkton looked over his shoulder. 'No.'

Simon walked over to him. 'Nobody else around?'

Monkton did a swivel of his chair, theatrically looking at him. 'Don't think so.'

'Anything on the toxicology results?'

'Yep. They tested specifically. It was aconite all right.'

Simon felt relief, despite his inner certainty that the monkshood must have been the cause of Liam's death. There had always been the faint chance that there had been some other unsuspected, even natural cause.

'Do you fancy a break from the desk-work? I'm afraid it's something menial.'

'Something else menial, you mean?' Monkton looked up with a satanic grin.

'Nothing useful emerging?' Simon asked, perching on the edge of the desk.

'It's all too vague.' Monkton flung a pen across the desk. 'I mean, you'd need to have people mark maps of the garden with where they were at particular times to be sure of anything showing up.'

'I take your point,' Simon said agreeably. 'I've got a bit more input for you from this morning, but it's, as you say, too vague to be of much use. People aren't that conscious of time, particularly within a limited time span. And, as you say, they're not too clear in describing exactly where they or other people were.'

'So what's the point?' Monkton leaned back, his arms behind his head.

'Something might stand out. It's just something that has to be done.' Simon stood up. 'Have you had a lunch break?'

'No. Wasn't hungry in this heat.'

Simon proffered the key June Taylor had given him. 'Have a beer at the pub in Chairford while you're waiting for half a dozen of these to be cut at the village post office.'

'Menial, but congenial,' Monkton agreed, showing a rare hint of humour and taking the key.

'I'll leave you some notes to be included in your report.'

'Great!' Monkton sloped out of the room, his trademark black leather jacket slung over his shoulder. Longman, unacknowledged, moved out of his way.

'Now there's an example of someone whose every word is loaded,' he said when Monkton was out of earshot.

'He's a master of it,' Simon agreed, pulling out a chair to do his report. 'Go and see if you can get hold of Ben Hartley, will you, Geoff? I'd be interested to know if the row Liam was having at the cottage was with his stepfather.'

By the time Simon had finished Longman was back.

'No one seems to have seen him since breakfast and they don't seem to know where he is.'

'Who did you ask?'

'Mrs Taylor in the kitchen. She called Mrs Hartley and Barbara Meddick on the house phone and they didn't know either.'

'Is his vehicle here?'

'I nipped over to check. His and Liam's Land-Rovers are in the usual place.'

'To try the most obvious, unless he's gone to live in a tree for the day, has anyone looked in his room?'

'I don't know. I'll go and see, shall I?' Longman turned away.

'I'll come with you.' Simon picked up his jacket and followed. 'Do we know where his room is?'

'I'll ask Mrs Taylor.'

Directed by the long-suffering cook, they went up the main staircase and turned left into a wide hallway carpeted in pale blue. Light poured in from a large window at the head of the stairs and another at the end of the hallway. All the doors were closed but as they reached what they had been told was Ben's room, a door somewhere behind them opened and they heard Helen Hartley call out, a note of alarm in her voice.

'What are you doing? Can't you find Ben?'

Barbara Meddick, looking equally concerned, appeared behind her. 'When Mrs Taylor called us we started to get concerned,' she said.

'There's nothing to be worried about, I'm sure,' Simon said calmly. 'It's just that Ben didn't turn up to speak to us as we asked. We thought we'd check whether he was in his room.'

'I see.' Barbara Meddick put an arm around Helen's shoulders. 'You gave us a bit of a fright. He's probably in the grounds somewhere. Have you looked?'

'Does he usually just not bother to turn up for appointments?' Simon countered. He was conscious that with this conversation going on outside the door Ben would, if he were in his room, probably have come out by now. He tapped on the door.

All of them waited, their eyes on that single point.

When no movement or response was heard Simon turned the knob and went in, speaking Ben's name. The room appeared to be empty, the bed unmade. It was still the room of a boy, with posters of pop stars clinging to expensive wallpaper. But the lack of clutter made it look unlived in, as indeed it had been for some time until the last few days: most of Ben's belongings were still at the cottage. The fitted bookshelves on either side of the fireplace were free of books and papers and there was not much furniture, a Georgian chest to the right of the door, a pembroke table in front of a window, a chair beside it. The head of the bed was against the left-hand wall, facing the tall windows which must look over the cobbled yard and the place where they parked their cars.

'Does the cleaner make the beds?' he asked Helen who had come with Barbara to stand at the door.

'Mrs Carver couldn't come in today. She had to take her husband to the doctor.' Helen stared around the room as if she had never seen it before. 'I meant to get this redecorated, and Liam's room, after they moved out. I wish I had got around to it.'

The room, being on the north side of the house, was relatively cool. Longman moved over to the window and peered out.

Barbara was saying, rather sharply: 'Well as he's obviously not here . . .' when they all caught sight of Longman's face as he turned back from the window.

Simon immediately started forward, following Longman's gaze.

Helen cried: 'What is it? Oh, what is it?'

What it was, was Ben's body, lying on the floor on the far side of his bed, a trail of vomit across his cheek and beneath it. Simon felt for a pulse and could find none. He looked up to find Barbara Meddick trying to restrain Helen.

'It's Ben, isn't it? What's wrong?' Helen cried out, pulling herself free of her friend. Simon held her as she fell on her knees beside her son's body. 'He's not dead? He can't be dead!' She reached out and Simon held her back.

Ben's face was white with death, the eyes half-closed. One hand was at his throat and he lay on his back, his legs at an awkward angle. The bed-cover was dragged beneath him, as if he had half-fallen from the bed.

'I'm so sorry, Mrs Hartley. So sorry.' She struggled against him but he held her firmly. 'I can't let you nearer. We all have to get out of the room.'

Barbara Meddick stepped forward to take Helen from Simon, staring down at the same time at Ben lying twisted at Simon's feet.

'Not poison again?' she whispered. Helen let out a howl of anguish and broke down sobbing.

'Make the necessary calls, Geoff,' Simon said.

Longman walked over to the window again and did so.

CHAPTER 19

Tamarisk – Crime

It was only later, after all the ritual attending violent death was under way, after he had contacted Detective Superintendent Munro, that Simon truly felt the sickening impact of Ben's death.

'It's poison again, all right,' he said to Longman. 'I should have realized, should have warned them more thoroughly. Even after Vita disappeared, when I was having visions of her lying dead somewhere, I still didn't think to say anything more.'

'Why should you?' Longman said stoutly. They had gone outside away from the now crowded bedroom, for a brief break of fresh air. 'No point in blaming yourself. Besides, guilt addles the brain.'

Simon managed a brief smile, then his face settled into a frown again. 'Poisoners often don't stop at one,' he said. 'They get a taste for it.'

'One way of putting it, I suppose,' Longman murmured.

'Was he killed so that we couldn't question him, do you suppose?' Simon sank down on to a wooden seat near the west side of the house. 'To stop him telling us something that might have implicated the person who murdered Liam?'

'Like who Liam was having a shouting match with that day at the cottage? It's possible.' Longman sat beside him. 'In which case it wasn't just a random serial poisoning, was it?'

'But how could it happen? He's been living and eating at the house. Nobody else there has been poisoned.'

They stared unseeing at the lovely scene in front of them,

unconscious of scent and heat and the excited buzzing of bees in the lavender.

Simon suddenly got to his feet.

'I want to speak to Mrs Taylor.'

She was sitting at the kitchen table, a mug of tea in front of her.

'Police inside this very house! Fine protection you lot turned out to be,' she said, red-faced, red-eyed. Simon was too conscious of the truth of what she said to make a protest.

Longman felt differently.

'Where did Ben have his last meal, Mrs Taylor?' he asked uncompromisingly.

'He didn't come in for his lunch,' she said defiantly.

Simon said gently, 'He wouldn't have been able to, Mrs Taylor. Ben looked as if he had been dead some little while.'

She produced a crumpled handkerchief and scrubbed at her eyes and cheeks. 'I was very fond of Ben,' she said. 'He was a nice lad.'

A better epitaph than any afforded to Liam, Simon thought.

'Did he have any breakfast this morning?'

She swallowed and picked up her mug of tea. 'He'd been having his breakfast in here with me.' She drank some tea, making little slurping sounds. 'Since he moved back. He used to come over to me even when he moved to the cottage with Liam, said he couldn't do himself a good breakfast like I could.'

She wiped her eyes again. 'He wasn't really what you'd call a committed vegetarian like Liam was. He liked his bacon and eggs too much.'

'Is that what he had this morning, Mrs Taylor?' Longman asked.

Realization seemed to dawn. 'Are you saying I poisoned him?' she said, her voice rising.

'No, Mrs Taylor,' Simon said firmly. 'We're not for a moment suggesting that. But we do need to know what Ben has eaten in the last twenty-four hours or so.' He was thinking as he spoke. If the poison had been a fast-acting one, then breakfast was the obvious source. If it were a slower-acting substance, then they would need to look at a longer period of time. But if it were the latter, surely Ben would have shown symptoms that would have been noticed, might have been treated.

'Sit down, both of you, why don't you?' Mrs Taylor said, getting to her feet more heavily than usual. 'I'll make another pot of tea.'

As she filled the kettle she looked over her shoulder at them. 'He had the same as the others for breakfast, except for Mrs Hartley. She always has that muesli that I can't abide. Tastes like straw to me.' She plonked the kettle heavily on the Aga and came and sat down again.

'He had the usual bacon and eggs with mushrooms and tomato. Same as Mr Enright had and Miss Meddick. Though Mr Enright did his own because he left for work before I came in.' She rubbed her hands over her face, pulling the skin tight over her cheekbones. 'Poor Mrs Hartley. How ever is she going to bear it? I've only got the one son, Gavin, but I know it would finish me if anything were to happen to him.'

Simon waited a moment. However urgent his desire for information right now, as usual he was inhibited by the presence of genuine grief.

'So all the food you used for Ben and Miss Meddick came from the same source?'

She nodded, clutching her handkerchief. 'Same packet of bacon, same batch of eggs. I used tinned tomatoes this morning because I'd forgotten to go out and get some from the green-houses yesterday. And the mushrooms came out of the same bag as I bought in the village yesterday.' She frowned. 'So it couldn't have been anything he had here.'

'What about previous meals?'

'Same again. He ate with the family last night and they all had the same thing. I did watercress soup and a nice quiche because Ben's not that keen on meat in general, just the bacon. There was french beans and new potatoes to go with it.'

'Any dessert?'

'Just fruit salad and cream which they all ate, I think.' The kettle began a wavering whistle and she got up and lifted it from the heat.

'Did you see Ben after he had his breakfast, Mrs Taylor?'

She paused in pouring the water into the big brown teapot.

'No I didn't. He said he'd just take his vitamins up to his room and then he was going to do some work or other in the garden.

He was trying to keep busy.' She looked across at Simon, kettle still poised. 'When you left your message that you wanted to see him, of course I assumed he'd be in during the morning so I could tell him. He usually popped in for a cup of tea with me around eleven.' She dropped the kettle heavily back on to the Aga. 'Now if I'd gone and looked for him to tell him you wanted to see him . . .'

Ben might possibly have been saved, Simon added mentally. But Mrs Taylor had been too ambivalent about the police in their midst to be that accommodating.

She finished making the tea, moving awkwardly, spilling things. Their mugs she brought to them individually, making a separate trip for each. Finally she lowered herself into her chair.

'The vitamins, Mrs Taylor? Did Ben take them every day?' Longman asked.

She sniffed indulgently. 'After he'd eaten. I used to tell him off about it. Told him I made good healthy meals and there would be no need for vitamins and supplements if he ate my food and got some meat into him occasionally.' She sipped her tea. 'But he got in the way of it, living with Liam. His brother was a great one for supplements of one kind and another.'

'He brought them with him, did he, when he moved back from cottage?' Simon asked.

She had been gazing at the mug in her hands but now looked up suddenly, her eyes going from Simon's face to Longman's.

'That'll be it, then,' she said slowly. 'Maybe someone poisoned his vitamins.'

'You say he kept them in his room?' Simon asked.

'He did. He took them twice a day, most of them, after the evening meal as well as after breakfast.' She clapped a hand over her mouth. 'Oh my Lord.'

'We can't be sure it's that, Mrs Taylor,' Simon said. After his own initial surge of interest he was having doubts. Jessie took a couple of vitamin supplements – Vitamins E and C, he thought. One was a sealed capsule, the other a large tablet. Not things that could be interfered with.

'He used to bring them down to have with his breakfast but he didn't take them into the dining-room at night because Mr Enright had been scoffing at him about them.' She blew her nose.

'He told me that when I was teasing him about them. Said, "Don't you start June, I've had enough from old Lewis." Then he said he'd keep them out of Lewis's way in future, keep them in his room.'

'So he took them after his breakfast this morning as usual?' Simon asked.

'He didn't even look at them while he was taking them,' she said, her voice rising again. 'Used to read my newspaper while he was eating and then just carry on unscrewing tops of jars and so on and popping the things in his mouth. Always had a glass of water ready.'

'Worth checking, sir,' Longman said in a low voice.

Simon took a mouthful of his largely untouched tea. 'We'll take a look,' he said, standing. 'Thank you Mrs Taylor.' He paused at the door. 'Did Ben go upstairs straight after he'd taken the supplements?'

'Oh no. We had a cup of tea together and a chat. He was feeling low. Couldn't come to terms with his brother's death, you understand. He said it was hard to get motivated, but he was determined to keep working because he knew he'd probably feel worse if he stopped.'

'So how long, would you say?'

She puckered her brow, thinking.

'It must have been at least an half hour. He went up about a quarter to nine. I know I should have been getting on with things, but I thought it was more important to give Ben the benefit of some sympathetic company.' She sniffed and reached for her handkerchief again. 'I'm glad I did now.'

'Did he confide in you at all, in these talks you had? Did he say anything that might help us find out who did this?'

'Not really.' She picked up her mug and Simon noticed with quick sympathy that her hands were trembling. 'I know he was bothered. He did say that the worst thing about a police investigation was how it could cause trouble even for innocent people, because of the way the police turn everything over.'

'I'm afraid he was right there,' Simon said, not pressing her. She would think about Ben and what he had said to her in their little chats together and he believed that now she might be more prepared to confide anything that might be of help.

'You can't be blamed,' she said looking up at him with tired eyes. 'If it was his supplements that were tampered with, how could you possibly have stopped it?'

The pathologist had only just arrived. She was struggling into white overalls outside Ben's bedroom.

'Another one?' she said, raising finely plucked eyebrows at Simon. 'Poisoned right under your nose, I gather.'

Dr Starkey was a homely-looking middle-aged woman, lacking the relentless cheerfulness of Havers, but with a quiet good-humoured serenity. Simon had always felt that should his own body ever require the services of a Home Office pathologist he would be, as it were, content in the respectful hands of this pleasant woman.

They zipped up and followed her into the room watching as she directed the photographer. SOC had come over from the cottage and were already at work. Simon joined Richards. 'I suppose I'd have heard by now if anything of interest had turned up at Liam's place?'

Richards paused in his work and looked up. 'We've more or less finished there. With no blood or other bodily fluids to be examined it's been mostly fingerprinting. And there are a lot of different fingerprints, probably from that party they had a bit back. The lads weren't too houseproud, which made things easier in some ways. But in the relevant place, the kitchen, it's mostly two sets, Liam's and Ben's.'

'On the fridge?'

'Same thing. A bit of smudging, but you'd get that anyway.'

'And I suppose in a place where it's normal to wear gloves for garden jobs it wouldn't look suspicious to walk in there with that sort of protection on your hands.'

Richards nodded. 'Bits of earth everywhere. Would have come from boots, gloves, clothing.'

'You kept a note, didn't you, of what Ben Hartley was allowed to take from the cottage when he moved out?'

'It wasn't much. A few items of clothing, his toiletries. Oh, and his box of vitamins. He was most insistent he should have those.' At Simon's expression Richards said, 'I didn't do the wrong thing there, did I?'

'Not your responsibility.' He should have overseen things more closely, Simon told himself. But he had been completely certain that no food would have been allowed to be taken away. Vitamins and supplements had not occurred to him.

'They were in a box, you say. Is it here in this room now?'

'I checked inside it,' Richards said, getting to his feet. 'There was nothing but a few bottles and small drums.' He looked around the room from the shelving to the table by the window. Glancing with a worried expression at Simon he turned to the bed. 'That's it, I think,' he pointed.

Simon looked. It was actually an old biscuit tin, dented and battered, its original pattern obscured by the usage of many years.

'Get it for me, will you?'

The tin was on the bedside table on the side where the body lay and Richards had to climb across the bed to get hold of it. He handed it to Simon.

'Where was it kept in the cottage, do you remember?'

'In one of the kitchen cupboards.' Richards eyed the tin. 'You think someone tampered with what's in there?' He uttered a short Anglo-Saxon expletive.

Simon opened the hinged lid. There were half a dozen containers inside.

Richards said anxiously: 'Someone could have tampered with them after he brought them over here, couldn't they?'

'Certainly,' Simon said. 'We don't know yet if this is the source of the poison anyway. It's just a guess at the moment.' Richards was still hovering uncertainly. Simon took pity on him. 'Whatever, don't worry about it. As I said, it's not ultimately your responsibility. And we may never know either way, if anyone did interfere with the contents of this box, whether they did it here or there. Just carry on with what you're doing.'

Simon took the tin over to the table by the window, Longman joining him. With gloves on, Simon took out the containers and placed them on the table. He carefully shook a few tablets and capsules from each on to separate evidence bags. Three were gelatine capsules: fish-oil, vitamin E and garlic; one was a large tablet, Vitamin C, another tablet a multivitamin compound; the last was a bee-pollen extract in a clear capsule in a form that pulled apart, presumably allowing the consumer to sprinkle it on food if they chose. He returned the first five lots to their containers and poured out all of the bee-pollen capsules.

Longman pointed. 'A couple there are a different colour. They're a bit darker than the others.'

They looked more closely 'They look a different texture, too,' Simon said. 'Less powdery.'

'Crushed dried leaves, perhaps?'

'Another herbal gift from the garden?' Simon looked around the room. 'No tantalizing clue this time in the form of a vase of flowers?'

'I've already checked,' Longman said. 'Just wondered if they might have done the same thing. There're no flowers or plants in the room.'

'They wouldn't know,' Simon said thoughtfully.

'How do you mean?'

'With a container like this,' Simon held it up, 'it's wide enough to have four or five capsules on the top layer, so they couldn't be certain exactly when Ben would take a poisoned one.'

'Or,' Longman said, 'they planted them lower down in the bottle so it would be a few days before he'd be likely to take one.'

'Why not put poison in them all?'

'Too much time and effort, perhaps, and no need if they just wanted Ben to die sometime soon, rather than on a specific date.' Longman held out his hand. 'What's the recommended dose?'

Simon gave him the container, a white plastic drum with a printed label. Longman held it to the light then reached inside his zipsuit for his glasses.

'The print's minuscule. "One or two capsules daily after meals", he read out. 'What's this stuff for, anyway?'

'I'm finished for now,' Dr Starkey appeared at Simon's elbow.

'Any opinion on time of death?' Simon asked her.

'A few hours. Sometime this morning is all I can venture at present.'

'Definitely poison?' Simon asked.

'Signs are,' she said briefly. 'And given the context I suppose it seems even more likely. What have you got there?' she asked, peering around Simon at the bottles on the table.

'Possible source of the poison.' Simon nodded at the container in Longman's hands. 'It seems that Ben had the same food as the others this morning. His supplements were the only things he had that no one else did.'

'Do you know what this stuff is for?' Longman asked, handing it to her.

She read the label. 'Yes, I do. My daughter takes it. It supposedly gives some protection to heart and lungs and it has some antihistamine qualities. It's anti-infectious. My daughter suffers from asthma and it was recommended by her consultant.'

'But it is an over-the-counter treatment?' Simon asked.

'Oh yes, any health-food shop would sell it. It seems to have helped Naomi anyway.' She gave the container a gentle shake. 'It's empty.'

Simon pointed to the capsules on the table. 'They're there. A few are a different colour from the others. It's likely they've been refilled with something else.'

'Something pretty lethal.' She held out a hand. 'I'll take charge of those. And you'd better let me have the others as well just in case.'

'Do you mind if I keep the container and the tin itself for forensics?' Simon said. She handed back the container good-humouredly. Longman poured the capsules into an evidence bag, labelled it and passed it to her. She quickly filled in a form and handed it to Simon.

'When was Ben last seen by anyone?' she asked.

'At breakfast as far as we know. He came up here about half an hour after taking these things.'

'So if he had one or two after his food as recommended on the bottle, then came up here to his room and wasn't seen afterwards it would have to be a pretty fast-acting poison. The capsule itself would take a little time to dissolve in the stomach acids but he must have been overcome before he could leave his room.' She looked from Simon to Longman. 'Was there no one around he might have called out to?'

'We haven't found that out yet. His mother's office is along the hallway up here but we've no idea if she was there this morning,' Simon answered.

'And everyone else would have been out and about, one supposes, rather than in their bedrooms?' She picked up her things. 'I'll make sure his stomach contents are checked for very fast-acting plant poisons for starters and ditto for what's in the capsules. There's a limited number of things it could be. That is, if the poisoner has used a plant poison again. It will be a start, though one shouldn't make assumptions.'

She moved towards the door and looked back again. 'It's possible it's monkshood again. Very efficient stuff.'

'Is it likely to take as long this time?' Simon asked, without much hope.

'As long?' She arched fine eyebrows. 'That was a quick result you got.'

Since the issue of murder seemed in no doubt this time around, Simon supposed that the exact nature of the poison might not be too vital to the investigation. As Dr Starkey had said, though, one should not make assumptions. It might be some obscure poison available only to those who had travelled to the South American jungle, thus pointing the finger where it firmly belonged. He thought, glumly, that that was most unlikely. It would be an innocuous-looking plant from the garden here, available to one and all.

'You know, there's one thing this might suggest,' Longman said at his elbow. 'If we're right about the capsules . . .'

'Mmm?'

'What you were worrying about, that Ben might have been killed now to stop him telling us something. If that was the case, using capsules, where the killer couldn't be certain whether Ben would take them in time, makes that less likely.'

CHAPTER 20

Milk Vetch – Your presence softens my pain

As Simon drove through the golden Cotswold evening to pick up Jessie at Westwich station he was aware that he had a lot of thinking – rethinking – to do. He couldn't be sure that Longman's assessment was right, that the more random method of poisoned capsules made it less likely that Ben's death was dependent in some way on Liam's. It was true that the exact time of Ben's death would be less controlled if, indeed, that had been the source of poison, but it still offered a limited period in which the poison had had the chance to do its stuff.

He wound the window further down and let the warm hay-scented air blow vigorously around him. The scenery he drove through was too peacefully seductive to be conducive to incisive thought. A sudden blast of horn as he rounded a bend brought him sharply back to himself.

If Ben was not killed because of his possible knowledge of Liam's murderer, then he was killed for some other reason that Ben himself had provoked independently. Or something that involved the two brothers together. The second seemed unlikely, given what he had learned of Ben so far, the third changed the picture. Until now they had only had to consider motives for the killing of Liam. In this case they would have to look at what the two boys together might have done to give cause for their deaths.

But it didn't feel right. To him, it still seemed most likely that Ben died because he knew something about Liam's death. Which meant that they would not change direction in their investigation: the second killing was dependent on the first.

It still made the method of killing Ben – and surely it had to be the capsules? – a dangerously uncertain one timewise. Or did it? It would have been easier to doctor the capsules while they were still at the cottage. But at that point Liam was not yet dead and the killer, if Simon's theory was right, would therefore have no motive yet for murdering Ben. So, if Ben died because the killer realized afterwards that Ben knew something dangerous to himself, then the poison had to have been added to the capsules after Ben moved back to the house – a more hazardous procedure.

And why use poison again anyway? There were other methods of disposing of someone. Yes, he remembered Laura Wheatley's question, it was considered the woman's weapon, presumably because it required no physical strength. But neither really did a carefully aimed knife to the heart. Or damaged brakes on a vehicle perhaps. But poison, administered at a distance, must feel safer because there need be little danger, if you were careful, of being caught in the act, with the weapon in hand as it were.

There was still the puzzle of the placing of the vase of monkshood flowers in the cottage. It had signalled a significance – certainly an invitation, along with the discarded sandwiches, to treat the case as murder rather than misadventure.

No, he would have to continue the investigation along the same lines. The two murders must be connected. This meant that the poison was added to the capsules after Ben had moved back to the house. So the investigation would look at who had access to Ben's bedroom where he had kept his supply of supplements. The answer, he thought with an inward groan, must be just about anyone provided they had the nerve. It wouldn't take long to do the substitution, especially if a separate supply of capsules was bought, a few refilled with a deadly alternative. If the poisoner ensured that Ben was out of the way and ostensibly went looking for him, would anyone question them being in his room? And if they had, some other means could be thought of to dispose of

Ben. It was the same risk as the one taken at the cottage when the sandwiches were exchanged, though surely needing more nerve, given the location of Ben's room in the house as compared with the cottage.

After he and Longman had left Ben's room, after the body had been removed, he had done little other than call in the rest of the team to the incident room and let them know what had happened. Rhiannon had been volubly shocked, the rest showed an uneasy consciousness of the implications. Then Lewis Enright had arrived and, with a quick blast from the doorway, let them all know exactly what he thought of them. By then it was getting late and, Enright's hostility or not, it was not a time to be continuing with questions; the family needed a break, if only a short one. Helen was in a state of collapse and Barbara was with her. The employees seemed to have all gathered in Mrs Taylor's kitchen. Meanwhile the team could do some succinct reports for him before they met tomorrow and he would finalize his own for Detective Superintendent Munro.

Now, as he slowed down for the speed limit on entering Westwich, he looked with some relief to seeing Jessie again and the chance of thinking and talking about some other subject than sudden death and all its ramifications. He wondered how she had got on with Amanda and Jane, whether her habitually objective insights had soothed or ruffled the feathers in that particular nest. He suspected they had done both, severally: Amanda had always appreciated her aunt's unsentimental approach to matters personal, Jane, Jessie's sister, had a more ambivalent attitude. While she might request a balanced view, in practice she most often really wanted only sympathy and a listening ear. Jessie had been known to fail her in that respect, being a little too bracing intellectually, too pragmatic and unwilling to be emotionally indulgent. Simon raised a smile of anticipation as he found a space in the station car park.

The train was, predictably, late. But only by ten minutes. Simon hung about the main concourse, reading posters and glancing occasionally at the arrivals screen to see if the train had made up any time. Inevitably, and unhappily, he was reminded of the last time he had waited here for a train, of seeing Liam and Ben full of life and youth. He decided to get some needed exercise and fill time by walking to the far end of the platform.

Neglected containers with their suffering dying plants did nothing to cheer him. The whole place reeked of neglect, a bored lack of interest. Station awnings carried cracked and peeled paint, rubbish defiled both the platform and the track. He believed it mirrored the more dangerous neglect that had infiltrated safety standards on the railways. He was old enough to have some memory as a child of stations which lingered on from the days of steam, when station gardens flourished and train livery gleamed. It was a distant memory though, and perhaps only a dream, though a few pretty stations remained, some perhaps inevitably in the Cotwolds themselves.

Money was at the root of it, profit being the main consideration. But it was also because the relationship between people and their work had changed. Where there had once been pride in the work a person did, now there was cynicism, disenchantment. And it was the same for him, the same in the police force. The shiny-faced village bobby on his bicycle belonged to the age of cheerful grimy engine-drivers, comfortable waiting-rooms with fires on winter evenings. Most people worked now reluctantly, only because they had to, for the income alone. And perhaps in the end it was down to people individually to do their work willingly and with conviction, ignoring as far as possible the corrupting winds of change that came from on high.

He found his thoughts chastening. He was as guilty as anyone of unhappiness in his work, a yearning for something more satisfying and less dogged by political expediency, a recurrent envy of Jessie's commitment to and interest in what she did, and the invidious comparisons that dogged him. It was like a war within. Time to commit, he thought. Time to accept and just do his best. It was a necessary job, a job worth the doing, whatever ignorant fools were running the country. Particularly if ignorant fools were running the country.

He had returned to the central platform and was leaning on the end of one of the station buildings when Jessie's train pulled in. He stayed where he was, watching the stream of humanity disembark. Some diverted from the flow, pausing to embrace a lover, a friend. Others moved steadily onward carrying briefcases, haversacks and suitcases, their minds grimly intent on their ultimate destination. He caught sight of Jessie, taller than most, her long, dark, curly hair tossed by the sudden draughts of air, and stayed to enjoy the luxury of watching her unseen as she looked for him. He felt a sudden lift of the heart, an immense pride that it was he whom she searched for.

He emerged into the flow just as she was drawing level with him. Instead of giving him her familiar cheery grin of acknowledgement and keeping on moving as she usually did on such occasions, she stopped and waited for him, dropping her overnight bag to the platform. When he reached her she flung her arms around him and held him tight without speaking. He returned the embrace, feeling oddly close to tears. Finally she leaned back in his arms and studied his face.

'I'm so glad to see you,' she said simply.

He swallowed. 'And me, you.' He picked up her bag and they walked out to the car, their arms around each other, unspeaking.

It was not until they were crossing the old West Bridge into the countryside beyond the city that he asked her how things had gone at her sister's.

Jessie made no immediate reply so he glanced at her set face.

'Not well,' she said.

To leave it at that would seem to display lack of interest, but he waited anyway, hoping she might say more. After a minute or so she shifted in her seat and looked away from him, away from the glare of the setting sun spreading its glow over the low hills ahead.

'I didn't go there to dispense advice,' she said, her voice low.

He hesitated. 'Is that what Jane wanted?'

'It's what she wanted me to give to Amanda. Or preferably some rather clear directions.' Her voice had sharpened.

'And what did you do?' he asked, giving the question as little weight as possible. He was dismayed that their recent accord might be fragile, that merely by asking about her visit he was risking being subtly embroiled in the cross-currents of whatever emotional upheavals had taken place, that her anger with her sister would transfer to him as she spoke.

'I listened. To Amanda, that is. I also did a lot of listening to Jane,' she said. Her voice was weary rather than fierce, then it quickened. 'You just cannot tell people what to do with their lives.

It's a waste of time and it's wrong. All you can do is help them to see what the options involve, help them in understanding them, so that they can make a decision that they feel is right for them. Jane is so determined that the right thing for Amanda is for her to have an abortion. All she keeps saying is that having a baby now will ruin Amanda's life.'

'What did you say to that?'

'I said that the decision had to be Amanda's own, made without pressure. And that if Jane persuaded her against her will she might end up hating her mother.'

Simon attempted a lighter note. 'So you did manage a bit of advice?'

'That's not advice, it's information.' He caught her wry smile and was relieved.

'And what information did you give to Amanda?'

He felt her shrug. 'I just went through the options and their implications – their pros and cons. They're all pretty obvious. The fact is, she just doesn't know what's the right thing. But her instinct is against abortion.'

'But if she delays her choice, the number of options diminish,' Simon added.

Jessie spread her hands. 'Not, however, as Amanda so succinctly put it, the options for the baby itself. So that's the way I think it will have to be. She may not know what she wants until after she's given birth.'

'So was that how it was left? Take it a step at a time?'

'As far as Amanda is concerned, yes. The baby is due in December. If she feels up to it she'll go on and take her A levels. If not, she'll take them the following year and go on for her degree. If she decides to keep the baby she expects to take up her degree course at a later date. She feels she can't make any further decision until she knows what's right. Jane is another matter. She won't accept her plans, I'm sure, and she'll put pressure on Amanda even more now.'

Jessie sighed. 'I do understand something of how Jane feels. She's afraid of her own involvement if Amanda has the baby. And she just doesn't want a young baby in the house again. She's already saying things like: "And who's going to feed and look after you while you're pregnant and after you have the baby?

Who's going to keep you when the baby's born?" And Amanda shouts back that the state will support her if her parents won't, which drives Jane into an absolute frenzy.' Jessie tipped her head back and gave a deep sigh. 'God, families can be a pain! I'm never getting drawn in again. That sort of thing needs the professionals.'

He raised his eyebrows at her. 'I thought that's what you were.'

She looked scornful. 'You're never that to your family. There are so many currents eddying about you, so much old baggage emotionally, that just about everything you say is heard through a filter of prejudice and,' she raised her hands and dropped them helplessly in her lap, 'bias.'

This was in a sense the reverse side of the coin of what Longman had been saying that morning, Simon thought: while we might weary of the hidden agendas in what people said to us, we had also to be conscious of the slant we ourselves put on their words – the 'listening ear' with all its distortions developed over a lifetime of individual experience.

'Jane asked me to go there,' Jessie said in exasperation, 'but she can't listen to me without everything I say being coloured by her resentment of me – the little sister who got herself a career and no encumbrances. And,' Jessie's voice rose, 'that's of course how I'm disqualified, because I don't have children myself, so how can I presume to know what's best!'

'The onlooker sees most of the game?' Simon ventured.

'Huh! She wouldn't wear that one,' Jessie said disgustedly. 'Do you know she ended up by implying that it suited me to sabotage her perfect little family because I was jealous that I didn't have one myself. As if I got the girl pregnant!'

Simon gave a hoot of laughter, he couldn't help himself. It was partly the absurdity of Jessie's words, partly a reaction to finding the usually equable Jessie in such a state of incandescence.

To his relief she laughed too and it was a joyous rather than scornful explosion.

'I am so glad to be back,' she said, leaning her head on his shoulder and putting a hand through his arm.

He squeezed it and changed gear, turning left into a wooded road and away from the sun's glare.

'How's your mother?' she asked.

He told her about their enjoyment of the thunderstorm the night before.

'We had that, too,' she said, stretching her legs. 'It was like living through the *Götterdämmerung* with Jane and Aamanda screaming at each other.'

Simon could picture it clearly.

'What did Tom have to say in all this?' He had liked Tom, Jane's husband, on the one occasion they had met. A successful barrister, he had not conformed to Simon's expectations of urbane sophistication. He was a big man with overlong grey hair, long through lack of personal vanity rather than the reverse, and a similarly casual approach to sartorial matters, thus making him and Simon kindred spirits from the start. He gave a significant portion of his time to less well-off clients, particularly when his sense of justice was engaged.

'Tom kept out of the way,' Jessie said. 'Like most men he's a bit of an emotional coward.'

'If I made a similar remark about women you would be morally outraged,' Simon said, provoked.

'You couldn't make a similar remark about women,' she replied. 'It wouldn't be true.'

He was forced to acknowledge the accuracy of her answer, while deploring the spirit of it. He said so.

'Oh, come on, Chris! You have to admit that most men run a mile when intense emotional things are at issue.'

He was surprised at the force of his anger. But chauvinism, whether male, female or otherwise, was prejudice and a failure of intelligence – something that Jessie was not lacking in and had therefore betrayed. But he realized his reaction was stronger than perceived disappointment in Jessie's momentary loss of integrity: she had touched a nerve – he feared that he himself suffered from emotional cowardice. That was what had kept him so long from confronting Jessie over the long-term implications of their relationship. He wanted to marry her, have children with her, and he feared the consequences if he said so, feared she might feel she had to release him from a relationship from which each wanted different things. And he was too scared to find out whether that was actually the case. Even so, he defended himself.

'That may be true for some men. But it's the intense emotional bit that's the female thing, isn't it? I mean, women build up everything into such a frenzy of feeling, instead of approaching things calmly, with detachment.'

'I didn't get into a frenzy!,' Jessie exclaimed. 'And if I said such a thing about men you would be morally outraged,' she parodied.

He smiled in spite of himself. 'You couldn't because it wouldn't be true. But I can imagine Tom wouldn't have been given a look-in when it came to discussing Amanda's future.'

There was silence for a mile or more while Simon negotiated the narrow twisting lanes that led to Jessie's village. Out of the sun with dusk falling, the tree-hung lanes were dark enough for Simon to have to switch on his lights.

Eventually Jessie responded. 'You're quite right, of course. We have gone from the Victorian extreme of the heavy father to a place where women occupy the moral high ground when it comes to feelings so that men are affectively emasculated. Which does nothing for either sex.'

'No doubt the pendulum will swing back at some time to a point of equilibrium,' he said neutrally.

Another silence followed as Simon drove out of the woodland roads and back into the light of the setting sun. Jessie pulled down her sun visor and asked, 'How is the case going?'

'Badly. Ben Hartley was found dead today. Probably poisoned like his brother.'

Jessie never issued platitudes. Her silence on this occasion was more eloquent. After another half-mile she asked, 'Has that changed everything? I mean, has it changed the way the case was shaping?'

'I don't know,' was all he could say. They were now driving into the village and there was little time left for private conversation, if she wanted such a topic.

She gave his arm a squeeze. 'We'll talk later, if you like.'

He thought he did like. It was some time now since he had overcome his discomfort at discussing cases with Jessie. Her insights had often been very helpful, but it was just as beneficial to him to have a listener while he told his tale, heard his own words and searched them for meaning.

Elizabeth had heard them drive up and had come to the front

porch where she waited for them. She was characteristically putting the stems of a climbing rose into place.

'Dinner's ready,' she called as they got out of the car. 'But have a glass of wine first, Jessie, and come and see what I've done in the garden.'

CHAPTER 21

Hydrangea – A boaster, heart-lessness

The thunderstorms had done nothing to change the pattern of the weather; it continued blazingly hot, even at 8.30 in the morning as Simon drove direct from Oxton to Clifford's Place. His mother had been deeply concerned about the effects of the hot dry weather on the new planting in Jessie's garden: much of today was to be spent using the hosepipe to soak the new flower beds.

Jessie and he had managed some time together the evening before. Elizabeth, on learning of the fate of Ben, had been very distressed and after the meal had taken herself off for a lengthy walk, arriving back some time after dark. Simon, to his chagrin, had hardly noticed her absence, absorbed as he was in unburdening himself to Jessie. She had not said a lot, recognizing the exercise was helpful to him as a simple process of evaluation. She had, though, repeated her comment that there was perhaps an element of symbolism in the manner of the deaths of Liam and Ben.

'How do you mean?'

'I'm not sure,' she said slowly. 'Only that there seems a measure of ritual about it. There is nothing opportunistic about these murders. It's all planned very carefully, it seems to me. Were there flowers left again?'

He repeated his idea that, if the capsules had caused Ben's death, then its timing would not have been predictable enough for the killer to display the tell-tale flowers.

'I think you may find that they will turn up,' Jessie had said consideringly.

At this point Elizabeth had entered the room and asked with customary forthrightness what they were referring to.

When Jessie explained, Elizabeth said, 'There can't be that many plant poisons which are that fast-acting.'

'If it is a plant poison,' Simon reminded them.

'But didn't Jessie just say that you discovered capsules which were evidently different and apparently filled with dried plant material?'

'Yes, that's true,' Simon agreed.

'Then why are you saying "if" like that? Really, Christopher, I understand that policemen need to be cautious. Heaven knows they do because look what happens when they are not. But are you seriously suggesting that someone, either the killer or someone else, introduced some alien capsules into Ben's bottle of supplements just for the fun of it?' Elizabeth had not yet sat down and her height seemed to increase with her indignation.

'When you put it like that—' Simon began.

'How else is one to put it?'

'We should never make assumptions, we should work on evidence,' Simon protested.

Both women snorted rudely in disbelief. Jessie said:

'But you must make assumptions all the time in your work. If you waited for proof every step of the way it would take for ever to finish a case.'

'That's not what I meant. You have to keep an open mind about things. If you place too much emphasis on an assumption that's in the end wrong you can waste a lot of time.'

'But,' Elizabeth said drily, 'if you don't place emphasis on something that turns out to be right, you probably waste an awful lot more time, as Jessie says.'

'And in this particular instance, what harm can following the logical assumption do anyway?' Jessie asked, folding her arms at close of argument.

'None at all,' Elizabeth briskly agreed. 'I'm going to telephone your father and ask him to check for me in one of my books: *Medicinal and Poisonous Plants of Britain and Europe* I think it's called.' She sailed out of the room.

'She's angry and upset,' Jessie said.

'I noticed.'

'It's not being able to do anything about it as well. She has fond memories of Helen and the children.'

'I understand,' Simon said, but their conversation was at an end.

Elizabeth returned. 'He's going to ring me back,' she announced, 'when he's looked it up.'

Jessie offered to make some tea and they were drinking it when the phone rang. They heard the murmur of Elizabeth's voice, raised slightly in questioning, go on for a few minutes and a pause before she returned.

'There are a few likely possibilities,' she announced. She sat down suddenly and picked up her tea cup. 'But he hasn't looked through the whole book.'

'Yes?' Simon ventured.

Elizabeth replaced the cup and turned her face to Simon. 'The first, and most readily available, is digitalis.'

'Foxglove?' Simon and Jessie spoke together.

His mother nodded. 'All parts are poisonous, but the leaves are deadly dried or fresh. The symptoms include nausea and blurred vision, but death comes from the poison forcing the strength of contractions of the heart.' She nodded, 'The foxgloves were beginning to flower in Helen's garden, but the leaves are abundant long before the flower spikes emerge.'

'Other possibilities?' Jessie asked.

'Monkshood of course, which you already know about. And a plant that is usually grown in a conservatory in this country.' Elizabeth was tight-lipped.

Simon remembered that she and Jessie had delayed some time in the impressive restored conservatory at Clifford's Place.

'Was it there?' he asked.

'It was there. Nerium Oleander. Do you remember,' she said to Jessie, 'the beautiful yellow scented flower in a pot near the door?'

'Yes I do.'

'It's a yellow form of the usual pink oleander. And all of it is deadly, even the nectar and the seeds. If seeds were ground up with the leaves,' she said to Simon, 'it would have been a very potent poison indeed. It causes sweating, vomiting and respiratory paralysis.'

Jessie had fetched her plant encyclopaedia and found a photograph of the pink form of the plant. They were all silent for a moment, contemplating the translation of a beguiling flower into an instrument of horror.

'You've got to catch this person, Christopher,' Elizabeth said. 'He's very wicked indeed.'

'Or she,' Jessie corrected.

'As you say, Jessie. Anyway, I'm going to my bed – and in hope of having no nightmares.'

Simon and Jessie had retired soon after. His mother's solemnity had put an end to their discussions. She seemed to construe them as mere intellectual gymnastics uninformed by righteous indignation.

Now he slowed the car as he turned on to the Westwich bypass. There was no Longman to pick up today; the Detective Sergeant was returning to Clifford's Place as he had left, with Rhiannon Jones. There would be things to do all over again now that Ben was dead. His mind went back to what Jessie had said about there being a ritual quality to the murders. She had said it implied careful planning. Did that apply to Ben's death as well, truly? If so, it didn't sit well with his theory that Ben's death was in some way dependent on Liam's. And what was it he himself had said about making assumptions? He let out a sigh. Keep plugging away at the evidence, he told himself, still things in a turning world.

Having no real theory of what was going on was disorientating. If he was honest with himself, he reluctantly agreed with Monkton that Lewis Enright offered a plausible suspect. Wasn't that the way after all that most police investigations proceeded, with suspect after suspect pursued and discarded, or not? Perhaps it was the nature of the case itself, a group of people living and working together, immured as it were in an idyllic country place with all the interdependence physically, mentally and emotionally, that made him hold back from the resolution of pursuit of a particular person such as Enright. All murder investigations caused damage, on top of that brought by the killer him- or herself, and in a community such as Clifford's Place the clumsy trampling of police questionings could cause distress to those who were quite innocent of any wrong. They brought suspicion and fear amongst the group but they also could produce a fierce drawing together in the face of police inquiries. So far, he felt the latter had been true in this case. He wondered whether Ben's death might change things.

As he was pulling into the parking space at Clifford's Place he realized he had forgotten to ask Monkton to distribute the newly cut keys. The others' cars were already there: they must have gone through the house as usual.

As he was passing the kitchen the door opened a crack and June Taylor's face peered out at him.

'Oh, it is you. I've been looking out for you.'

Simon paused, conscious of the others waiting for him.

'Will you come in a moment?' She opened the door wider and he stepped forward.

She looked exhausted and dishevelled, her habitual pinafore tied on awkwardly, rucked up at one side.

'What is it, Mrs Taylor?' he asked.

'That.' She pointed to the table behind her and moved aside. A vase of flowers stood there, beautiful pale-yellow flowers with stiff grey-green leaves. Nerium Oleander. Jessie had been right in her prediction. The killer had again left flowers.

'It was there this morning when I came in to work.' Mrs Taylor sat down suddenly. Even the customary pot of tea was absent. 'Is that what it was?' she asked. 'Is that what killed Ben? Has the murderer left flowers like the last time with Liam?'

'Have you touched it?' he asked.

'Not me,' she shuddered. 'It's horrible. To think of someone coming into my kitchen and putting that in it. It is a poisonous plant, is it? I didn't know. I've seen it in the conservatoy and always thought how pretty it was. It looks different now.'

'It is a poisonous plant. Very poisonous. Don't touch it, Mrs Taylor. I'll be back in a minute, and I'll get SOC to deal with it.'

He left by the back door and skirted the side of the house to the conservatory at the front. The pot of flowers was, as his mother had said, near the door on the floor. It was a large and resplendent plant, the flowers held in groups of furled pale yellow, bent with the weight of flowers at the top but on straight rigid stalks. He looked more closely and could see that stems had been cut from it, some freshly, but others older and sealed dark brown. Some of the flower-heads had faded. No doubt the plant had been dead-headed in the course of everyday maintenance. It was an easy and accessible place for a killer to collect from.

He went indoors again and up to Ben's room to inform Richards, then back to Mrs Taylor.

'What time did you come in this morning, Mrs Taylor?'

She was sitting at the table staring with morbid fascination at the pale flowers.

'Half past seven as usual,' she said without looking up.

'Had anyone been in before you?' he asked, thinking of Barbara Meddick's appearance there on Saturday morning.

She stared at him. 'Well of course someone had been in here before me. How else did those get here?'

'It's possible they were placed there last night,' Simon said.

She gave a grudging shrug. 'No, I didn't see any signs of anyone being about before me. Miss Meddick sometimes comes in to make an early cuppa but the teapot wasn't warm.'

'So you made breakfast this morning, as usual?'

'Couldn't be as usual, could it?' she said, and sniffed. 'Not without Ben. And Mrs Hartley isn't up yet and didn't want any. Mr Enright, lo and behold, is staying at home today but he just wanted some toast and coffee along with Miss Meddick at eight o'clock.'

'Did you mention the vase of flowers to them?'

'No. I thought I'd best wait and tell you.' Her shoulders slumped and she put her head in her hands. 'This place will never be the same,' she mourned.

At that point Richards came in, carrying his kit, and set to work brushing powder on to the surface of the vase.

'I doubt if the killer left any trace,' Simon observed.

'I'll do the table as well,' Richards said. 'Whether it's any use or not it still has to be done.'

'Mrs Taylor,' Simon said, turning as he approached the door, 'I know Ben talked to you a lot, probably confided in you. Did he ever mention an argument that he heard going on in the cottage between Liam and someone else? Fairly recently, I think.'

She frowned in concentration. 'He did say something, yes. It was a little while ago, though. I remember it because he came into the kitchen and explained that he wasn't able to go home, as he put it, because of this row that was going on.'

'Did he say who it was with Liam?'

'No. And as he didn't volunteer it, I didn't ask.'

'Can you remember when it was?'

'Well,' she squinted her eyes as if looking back in time, 'I remember it was around time for the evening meal because I was busy with that. It was a Friday, because, it's tradition, I suppose, we always have fish on Fridays and I was doing some nice sole.' She looked up. 'That would have been the week before young Liam died, not the day before.'

'Thank you, Mrs Taylor.' He was turning again to leave when someone tapped lightly on the half-open door.

Linda Carver stood on the threshold, nervously clutching her hands, a look of pained anxiety on her face.

'Did you want Mrs Taylor?' Simon asked gently, opening the door wider.

She backed away. 'Oh no, it was you I was wanting to speak to,' she said in a low voice.

'Come with me then.' He stepped outside and put out an arm to guide her in the direction of the incident room.

'Oh no,' she said again, shrinking away from him. 'Not with all them other police officers there.'

He paused, keen to hear what she had to say but frustrated that he had already kept the others waiting longer than he ought.

'Will it keep for half an hour, Mrs Carver?' he asked.

She looked, if it were possible, even more deflated.

'I do apologize,' he said. 'But I have already kept my team waiting overlong and they will be wondering what's become of me. Would you be kind enough to wait until I've spoken to them and they've gone their several ways? That is, if you don't want to come with me now?'

His measured courtesy had a positive effect. She smiled more confidently.

'I expect I can find a few things to do while I'm waiting. Though God knows we're all at sixes and sevens with what's been happening here.' She looked over her shoulder towards the now

175

closed kitchen door and said in an even lower voice, 'That's what I've been wanting to talk to you about. I should have said something before only . . .' she broke off uneasily.

'I understand, Mrs Carver. Make it half an hour and I'll see you in the games room.'

She nodded and scurried off, Simon following in her wake.

They were drinking coffee, talking to each other in a low murmur when he entered the room. Rhiannon immediately offered him a mug too, which he declined. He called for their attention and told them about the discovery in the kitchen.

'Very cheeky,' was Monkton's verdict. There were murmurs of agreement.

'Very confident and very arrogant,' Simon agreed, telling them about the location and properties of the plant.

'So now we need a report on who's been near the kitchen, I suppose,' Monkton said with a smirk.

'And the conservatory. We'll include the question in the rest of our interviews – most people will need to be spoken with again.' He had a few more words to say on the implications of Ben's death.

'We don't know for sure that Ben was killed because he knew something about Liam's killer,' he said, 'but the questioning continues in the same vein and a lot of it will have to be gone over again, finding out if anyone saw someone in the house who wouldn't normally be there – someone who took an opportunity to doctor Ben's supplemments.'

'Are we sure about that, then?' Monkton objected.

'Not absolutely, until we get confirmation, but it might be wise to carry on with that assumption.'

'And you think the capsules weren't got at until after Ben moved back to the house?' Monkton said. 'Surely they could have been fixed when he was at the cottage? In which case, of course, we made a serious slip-up.'

Monkton could have been depended on to point that out, Simon thought, as he always pointed to a perceived failure in his senior officer.

'We can't know, either way,' Simon said evenly. 'But if what we think may be the case is true, that Ben was killed because of knowing something of Liam's death, then it must follow that the poisoned capsules were introduced after he moved back into the house.'

'But we don't know that, do we? I mean that Ben was killed for that reason.' Monkton was not letting go of this opportunity. 'And,' he continued, 'It's not a very exact way of timing someone's death, is it. The capsules could have been shaken down in the container and not been used for a few days by which time you could have got around to questioning him again.'

Monkton was being excessively obstructive and Simon was strongly tempted to throw him out of the team, except that to do so would look abject. Into the silence that followed Monkton's words Rhiannon spoke hesitantly.

'Actually, it is more exact than you would think,' she said, earnestness intensifying her valley accent. All eyes turned on her. 'I tried it out,' she coloured slightly, 'with some of the capsules I take. What I did was, I marked a couple of capsules with a silver marker-pen and put them on top of the others. Then I moved the container about a bit, not tipping it upside down, you understand,' she said to Simon. 'They didn't shift to speak of. So he would have been sure to take them within a limited period of time.'

'Thank you Rhiannon, that helps. It does suggest that the killer could expect Ben to die within a limited period of time after introducing the poison.' Simon's smile made Rhiannon's colour deepen.

Monkton's nasal voice broke in like a Greek chorus.

'*If* it was poison, *if* it was in the capsules, *if* the killer didn't want Ben dead anyway, regardless of what he knew about Liam's killer, *if* the poison, if it *was* poison, wasn't added when he was in the cottage.' He leaned back in his chair in the manner of an amused onlooker.

Simon's bile was increased rather than diminished by the fact that Monkton was to some extent here being the voice of his own conscience. Remembering in time that the greatest revenge is to be happy, Simon turned his smile on Monkton.

'Thank you for that. Despite the little floral gift in the kitchen, despite the previous one advertising the source of that poison, it is a caution I was about to pronounce and DI Monkton here has put it so succinctly: in other words we don't take anything for granted. We have to follow certain avenues, but that is all they are.' His eyes returned to Monkton. 'And how did you get on in your own avenue? Did you get the keys cut?'

There was an appreciative snort of laughter from somewhere and Monkton's normally dark complexion deepened.

'They're over there.' He pointed to a side table.

Simon explained their purpose, something forgotten in the aftermath of Ben's death, and turned again to the Detective Inspector.

'Thank you. Were you as successful with the collating of people's movements on Saturday morning?'

'Waste of time,' Monkton announced to the room in general. 'People's reports were too vague to be any use.'

'That's because what we were told was vague,' Tremaine said.

'And how did you and DC Savage get on?' Simon asked.

Enright had told them that his talk with Liam early on Saturday morning had been on the subject of Liam's demand for a more top-of-the-range Land-Rover.

'Mr Enright seems to have some control over their money through a trust fund set up for the children by their father,' Savage said. They had also checked out Ben's alibi, now almost certainly redundant, and found that he had been where he said he had been on Saturday morning at the times he had said. 'Shall we continue today with looking into Mr Enright's story for Saturday morning? We'll have to go into London.'

Nothing had changed its relevance. Simon told them to go ahead.

Monkton said, 'Didn't anyone hear Ben when he was taken ill? Isn't his mother's office close by?'

'We'll be asking about that, obviously,' Simon said, turning to Rhiannon again. 'Anything else?'

She got out her notebook. 'You asked me to get a bit more background on the employees. What she gave me is all pretty factual: Stephen Orchard, aged twenty-six, has been here for five years, trained in horticulture before coming; Mara Kennedy is twenty-three, also trained before arriving and has been here only a year. Mrs Hartley took on Gavin Taylor as a trainee when he reached school-leaving age. He's been doing release courses at college, he's twenty-four. These all live in accommodation that goes with the job. Clive Ashby has worked here about six years and isn't trained specifically in horticulture but, as you know, does maintenance and construction on the house as well as the garden.'

'Nothing more colourful to add?' Simon asked 'What about Linda Carver?'

Rhiannon turned over another page. 'Sorry. She lives in Chairford, she's thirty-seven, married with a couple of teenage kids that her mother has looked after for some time and has worked here more or less since she got married, about twelve years ago. Her husband's unemployed most of the time.'

'And that's it? No anecdotes or comments?'

'I'm afraid not, sir. Miss Meddick doesn't seem the sort and she's not easy to get information from when she doesn't want to give it.'

'Why didn't Ben use his mobile phone when he became ill?' Savage suddenly asked. 'And why didn't Liam for that matter?' Savage was a confident young DC who had joined the team at the same time as DC Tremaine. Simon eyed him with respect.

'That's a good question, one we can include in our interviews today.' It was something he should of course have thought of himself but, perhaps given his allergy to cellphones, had unconsciously repressed. He was surprised though that none of the family had raised the issue.

Conscious of Mrs Carver's appointment he wound down the session. He himself would speak to her and Barbara Meddick, along with Lewis Enright and perhaps Helen. Monkton and Rhiannon were to question members of staff while Tremaine and Savage were in London. He put through a call to Dr Starkey informing her of the killer's latest calling-card, found in the kitchen.

CHAPTER 22

Ice Plant – Your looks freeze me

Linda Carver entered the room timidly, looking cautiously around her and pushing thin strands of mousy hair into her elastic hairband. Simon offered her a chair and pulled up another to sit opposite her. She lowered herself to her seat as if fearing it was red-hot and glanced at the placid figure of Longman sitting unobtrusively near one of the windows, apparently involved in paperwork.

'What was it you wanted to speak to me about, Mrs Carver?' Simon asked quietly.

She twisted her hands in her lap. 'I suppose I should have said something before,' she said, her voice barely above a whisper. 'But it's difficult. I mean, working here you don't like to say anything that might get someone into trouble.'

'I understand,' Simon said, 'but there is no need for anyone to know that you have spoken to me. Not unless it's needed in evidence in a court of law.'

She looked at him for the first time, alarm in her eyes. 'Oh, I hadn't thought of that,' she said.

Simon hastened to reassure her. 'Even if that was the case and you knew something about a guilty person, your evidence wouldn't necessarily be needed, you know.'

She still looked doubtful and afraid.

'I expect you decided to speak to me because of what has

happened to young Ben,' Simon encouraged her.

Her back straightened slightly. 'Yes, it was that. He was such a nice young boy, always polite and pleasant. I mean, I've known him since he was a little lad. Liam was a different kettle of fish, never had any time for the servants as he called us, made trouble and lost people their jobs. But what's happened to Ben has upset me a lot.' Pink spots appeared in her pale cheeks.

'So you want to help us find out who did this to him,' Simon said firmly.

'Well, that's just it, I don't know if it will help where Ben is concerned. It was after what happened to Liam that I thought I ought to tell you. But it might be nothing, and jobs aren't that easy to get in country areas. And I've got a lot of respect for Mrs Hartley.'

'I expect no one saw you come in here,' Simon reassured her. He could understand the reticence of this worn woman, her fear of losing a job she had evidently been comfortable in, judging by the number of years she had worked here.

'I was careful,' she admitted.

'Was it perhaps something you overheard, or saw, that you thought you should tell me about?'

She seemed, at last, to make up her mind.

'Yes.' She twisted her hands in her faded floral skirt. 'It was Liam and Mr Enright, the morning that Liam died. I did hear something of what they said, even though I didn't tell your officers that.' She winced, as if expecting a rebuke.

'I can understand that you would be reluctant to say anything,' Simon reassured her again. Especially as it was Monkton she had been talking to.

'My husband said I shouldn't. You know, not risk my job. He said it was none of my business.'

'But you've done the right thing,' Simon said. 'I don't think you could live with yourself if you thought you hadn't helped in any way you could. Isn't that right?' It was like talking to a child, a repressed and timid child.

Her eyes on her hands, still knotting the cloth of her skirt, she started talking.

'They didn't notice me, they were so busy arguing with one another. I don't think they even saw me drive by. Then when I got out of the car, in the space just beyond the stables, I didn't like to walk past them while they were going on like that, it would have been embarrassing. So I waited a bit, hoping they'd get on.' She glanced up at Simon.

'Liam was threatening Mr Enright, saying he wanted some money he'd promised him. It was him mostly who was doing the talking. He said he'd tell his mother what Mr Enright had been up to if he didn't do what Liam said. It was all a bit more jumbled than this, you understand,' she said anxiously.

'Yes, of course. But it was what you gathered it was about. Go on.'

She nodded her head. 'Well, Mr Enright didn't say much, because he was mostly swearing at Liam but he did say quite loudly at one point to keep Vita out of it. That Liam would get nothing if she was upset by any of this.' She finished breathlessly and compressed her thin lips tightly.

'Anything else you heard?'

'There wasn't really anything more. Mr Enright's car started up and Liam said quite loudly something like, "Don't forget the money, Enright", and the car drove off. I waited a few minutes for Liam to go and then I went on into the house.'

'Thank you, Mrs Carver. I'm very grateful you told me.'

'I feel terrible about this,' she said. 'I mean, I can't believe Mr Enright would really have hurt Liam. And especially now that it must be the same person who killed Ben,' she finished uncertainly. 'I mean, why would he kill Ben as well?'

'Not really your worry, Mrs Carver. As you say, it may well have nothing to do with what has happened to the boys, but you were right to tell us all the same.'

'Can I go now?' She got to her feet and half-turned towards the door. Simon walked over with her and she peered out before scurrying off into the depths of the house.

'More of the same?' Longman stood up stretching his back. 'Isn't it time we questioned Mr Enright more closely?'

'I'd prefer to do it after Tremaine and Savage have checked his alibi for the morning of Liam's death,' Simon said thoughtfully.

'Living in the house, of course, Lewis Enright wouldn't have had any difficulty getting into Ben's room.'

'That goes for other people too,' Simon said.

Longman shrugged. 'Who are we speaking to next?'

'Richards. I wonder if they found Liam's mobile in the cottage. And maybe SOC didn't hand over Ben's to him if it was left there.'

Richards was back with the team in Ben's room. 'No prints on the vase of flowers,' he said, looking up as Simon and Longman entered. 'Plenty on the table.'

There would be, Simon thought, remembering the gathering of people in the kitchen the evening before. He asked Richards about the cellphones.

'We found one in their cottage,' Richards said. 'Funny place to keep it, though. It was in one of the kitchen drawers, under some tea towels.'

'Was one found here in Ben's room?'

Richards pursed his lips. 'We've looked through pretty thoroughly. No phone.'

Simon and Longman were leaving the room just as Barbara Meddick emerged from the office.

'May I have a word with you?' Simon asked her. In an aside he asked Longman to fetch the phone from the cottage.

Barbara Meddick stood, an elegant vision in black and white, with her back to the open office door as she gestured for him to enter. The room was light and airy, well lit by two windows facing south and cooled by a large white desk-fan. It was furnished comfortably, with low easy-chairs to the right and an oak coffee table near a fine Adam fireplace, filled now with a vase of white lilies. In the alcoves Simon noticed copies of Helen Hartley's own gardening books alongside a considerable horticultural reference section. There were several videos of her television programmes on a shelf of their own.

'Have a seat, Chief Inspector,' Barbara Meddick said coolly, directing Simon to the work area of the room and a seat by one of the large tables. He declined her offer of coffee from the machine and she seated herself on one of the armchairs.

The alarms and upset of the previous day seemed to have left no discernible mark on this composed woman. Simon wondered what it would take really to ruffle her. Or perhaps she was just a good actress, as her friend and employer Helen was supposed to be.

'How is Mrs Hartley?' Simon asked.

'Very unwell, as you might expect. I've just come from her. Lewis is with her now, but she is heavily sedated.'

There were no words of horror at what had happened, no expressions of sympathy for her friend. Simon was unsure whether to admire her for her measured restraint, or deplore what might be unusual coldness. Judgement was for judges, he reminded himself.

'And Vita?' he asked.

'She spent the night here, very distressed, as you might imagine. But she insisted on going back to her cottage this morning.' She crossed her legs, smoothing her skirt as she did so. 'It is kind of you to ask, Chief Inspector, but I am sure this isn't just a social call.'

Previously he had felt some rapport with this woman, even admiration of what he had perceived in her as strength. This had changed subtly, her manner was deliberately distant. Perhaps it was unsurprising, given the demise of yet another loved son right under police noses as it were. Confidence, had it existed at all, was bound to be shaken.

He said, 'I wondered why no one heard Ben, in what must have been great distress, yesterday morning. Why nobody heard him if he called out.'

'There was no one here,' she said. 'Helen and I didn't come into the office until after lunch, at about two. Lewis was not here and, as you know, Mrs Carver didn't come in at all yesterday. No one else would have had cause to be upstairs and hear him. Unfortunately.'

'So where were you and Mrs Hartley during that time?'

'We had run out of ink-cartridges for the printer.' She wafted a hand in the general direction of the machine. 'I went into Westwich to buy a new supply. Helen said she was going to spend some time in the garden. I thought it would do her good, be healing perhaps. She has been trying to throw herself into a writing project she has planned in the hope it would distract her from Liam's death.' She stood and went over to the coffee machine. 'Are you sure you won't join me?'

He declined again. 'We also wondered why Ben didn't try to call someone on his cellphone when he was taken ill, but it seems it was not in his room.'

She finished filling her cup and placed it carefully on its saucer.

'He asked if anyone had seen it when we were having dinner the evening before he died.'

'Did he say when he had last had it?'

Seated again, she sipped black coffee from a white cup.

'No, he didn't. Do you think that whoever killed him took it deliberately?'

'It's quite possible. Having a phone might have been a lifeline for both of them,' Simon said. 'Liam's also was not on his person, and was found hidden away in a drawer at the cottage.'

'How utterly cold-blooded,' she said, a look of distaste crossing her face. 'Though it has to be said that Ben was very forgetful of his possessions. His mother was forever mourning the number of times he left things like secateurs out in the rain.'

'Has Ben's phone been found since?'

'Not that I'm aware.' She placed her cup and saucer carefully on the low table. 'It is poison again, is it?'

'It's not confirmed by the lab yet, but it looks like it.'

'But you don't know the source of the poison this time, if that's what it was?'

Simon told her of Mrs Taylor's discovery in the kitchen that morning.

'Did you go into the kitchen this morning, earlier, as you sometimes do, Miss Meddick?'

'Not this morning, no. So I can't help you there. Unless you are wondering if I was the one who placed the yellow oleander in the kitchen.' She looked at him questioningly.

'Did you, Miss Meddick?'

'Don't be absurd.' She leaned forward to pick up her cup, her black hair swinging in a smooth curtain over her face. 'Though how on earth it happened I can't think. He ate with us the evening before, had the same food. And then I assume he had breakfast with Mrs Taylor as usual. I really think we should all be taking great precautions over what we eat, though. Ben's death from the same method seems unforgivably lax, don't you think?'

The plain implication was police incompetence.

'We believe that it was Ben's supplements that were poisoned, not his food.' Simon explained what they had found.

'Not much you could do about that, I suppose,' she allowed.

'Nor really about anything else he ate.'

There was a light tap at the door and Longman entered, giving Simon a brief nod and taking a chair behind one of the desks.

'I'm sure Mrs Taylor will be very vigilant,' Simon added.

Barbara Meddick gave him a sceptical look. He remembered that she and Enright had had only relatively innocuous toast for breakfast – though that could be put down to understandable lack of appetite in the circumstances.

Simon got up and walked over to one of the windows. It gave an excellent view over the gardens, the symmetry of the lawns and borders serenely orderly amid the mess of murder. As they were designed to be, the boys' cottage and Mara Kennedy's were obscured by the high hedges around them. Vita's and Stephen Orchard's were out of view. Sprinklers were on in several places creating rainbow arcs of startling brilliance. Symbols of hope and redemption, Simon thought. How incongruous. He half-turned to speak to Barbara Meddick.

'You have a very good view of the garden from here. Was Alan Fairburn the only person you saw on the morning Liam died?'

'He was the only person I noticed,' she corrected. 'I probably didn't register more familiar faces. And besides, I don't spend my time when I'm in here looking through the windows.'

'So you didn't notice Jenny Shipman? She wasn't such a familiar face.'

'Familiar enough. She's around quite a lot, coming to see Gavin. In fact she was here the night before last. I saw her from the window of my room which overlooks the old stables when I was dressing for dinner. She drove up in her mini. And coincidentally, so was Alan Fairburn here. He had come over to offer condolences to Helen.' She gave Simon a conscious smile, as if she were fully aware of the implications of this for the police. Opportunities to poison Ben had been wide open not just to people who lived at Clifford's Place.

He turned to the window again. The sprinklers were suddenly turned off and he could see the gardens more clearly. He spotted Stephen Orchard wheeling a barrow along the path beyond the large herbaceous borders.

'Did you see anyone who wouldn't normally be here actually inside the house that evening, Miss Meddick?'

'I'm afraid I can't help you there, Chief Inspector. We were all in the dining-room from eight till about eight forty-five. Lewis and I went to watch television after that. I went up to bed at about eleven.'

'Where did Ben go after the meal?'

She paused to think. 'He left the dining-room at the same time as we did. I've no idea where he went.'

'Vita was also here?'

'She said she was going to have an early night after we'd finished eating.'

'And there's nothing you can remember of that evening that might be relevant to Ben's or Liam's death?'

'I only wish there were. All this has broken Helen. It's enough to send her over the edge.' For the first time in this interview Barbara Meddick spoke with what sounded like genuine feeling.

'Where did Mrs Hartley go after that evening meal?' Simon asked, standing and preparing to leave.

'She went to bed early. She's been taking tranquillizers to help her since Liam's death and they make her sleepy.'

'Where are the bedrooms exactly?'

'Helen and Enright have their room at the far end of the east hallway on the first floor at the front of the house. Mine is a few doors away facing north, as I said. You know where Ben's is. Vita's old room, where she stayed last night, is a couple of doors further on from his.'

'So no one would usually be about in that part of the house after working hours, except Ben?'

'Precisely. Though the west hallway is directly in line with the east, where the rest of us sleep.'

'There must be another stairway, though, apart from the main one?' Large old houses like these always had servant staircases.

'At the far end of each hallway,' she confirmed. 'They come off the suite of old servants' workrooms which runs along the back of the house on the ground floor and of course include the kitchen.'

'Thank you, Miss Meddick.' It had been impossible today to call her Barbara, as she had once insisted.

Longman joined Simon at the doorway.

'I do hope you catch this person, Chief Inspector,' she said as they were leaving. 'Because if I get to them first you may have another, more bloody, case on your hands.'

It was said with her habitual coolness, but Simon didn't doubt her.

'She's a hard one to fathom,' Longman said as they made their way down the main staircase. 'Too controlled and yet you get the idea there are some deep feelings under it all. I think she might just be capable of sticking a knife into someone. It's Helen Hartley she seems to care about the most.'

'As you say, she's hard to read,' Simon agreed. 'You found the phone?'

Longman produced it from his pocket. 'It definitely looked as if it had been hidden. I can't imagine Liam stuffed it under some tea towels in a drawer.'

They walked across the wide front hallway towards the recessed front entrance. Simon told Longman what Barbara Meddick had said about Ben asking at dinner the day before he died whether anyone had seen his phone. 'He didn't say when he'd last seen it though.'

They stepped blinking into the heat of the day.

'Well, we'll be asking people about it,' Longman said. 'But I don't fancy a search for it in a place as big as this.'

'And anyway, its significance is in its absence rather than its presence,' Simon said. 'Any prints would be wiped.'

'There might be calls on it, though, that could be of interest,' Longman said, screwing up his eyes and shading them with his hand.

Simon led them to a seat shaded by a glossy laurel on the far side of the conservatory.

'I've got to attend the autopsy with Dr Starkey, but I'll come back later. I want you to check with Liam's phone account-holder and get a record of his calls.'

'But if there was anything incriminating, surely the killer would have got rid of the phone properly?' Longman said.

'No. We'd be bound to check it at some point even if the phone itself didn't turn up.' Simon stretched his long legs in front of him. 'Ask Liam's service provider whether they had Ben's account as well. He always followed where his older brother led, so it might yield something.' He stood up, looking across the gardens.

'Otherwise,' he turned and looked down at Longman, 'the paperwork, phone accounts, should be at the cottage somewhere.'

'Right.' Longman got up, collecting his jacket from the seat. 'You could try phoning Ben's number,' Simon said. 'On the off-chance that his phone was left switched on. It just might locate where it's been hidden.'

'When are we going to speak to Enright?' Longman asked as they parted company at the corner of the house.

'When I get back. Arrange it with him. Savage and Tremaine should have something for us by then.'

CHAPTER 23

Fumitory – Spleen

Simon parked in the public car park on his return to Clifford's Place and entered via the wicket gate near Liam and Ben's cottage. The press had gathered again in even greater numbers around the main entrance gates and scarcely seemed to have noticed him drive in behind them. He refastened the police tape over the gate and took a detour through the gardens, passing the Arcadian plot where Liam had died. All was utterly still and quiet in the afternoon heat, sounds from the outside world locked out. The whole place felt abandoned and eerie, even the bees stilled as if hidden from threatened disaster. He felt himself an interloper, the garden an overpowering presence watching him and guarding its own. Roses hung their heads in a miasma of heady perfume, plumed grasses shivered as he passed and clipped hedges pressed close as he hurried towards the open section of lawns and herbaceous borders at the front of the house.

The figure of Clive Ashby loomed suddenly from behind one of the hedges, giving him an unpleasant shock. The man gave a slow grin, the deep lines in his weathered face intensifying when he saw Simon's startled expression. He held out a large hand, its back marked with numerous scars. For a moment Simon thought he was trying to shake hands with him.

'You were looking for this, your people said.' He turned over his hand and displayed a cellphone. He went on, his rural accent slow and deliberate, 'I suppose it's Ben's, anyway.'

'Thank you.' Simon slipped it into his pocket. 'Where did you find it?'

'I wouldn't have, only it was ringing. Mind you, it had stopped by the time I got my hands on it.' He pushed a hand through his thick grey curls. 'It was shoved in the wood pile over in the service area. I was getting some stakes to repair some fencing at the time or I'd never have heard it ring. And wouldn't have found it, not for a good long while.'

Simon thanked him again. 'It's fortunate you were there at the time.'

'Is it important?' Ashby screwed up his eyes questioningly. He was wearing a heavy grey work-shirt and cords and seemed unaffected by the heat that Simon was finding unbearable, standing in full sun as they were. Probably he wore the same work-clothes summer and winter, Simon thought, and had a countryman's indifference to any vagaries of weather.

'It may be,' Simon answered.

'Someone took it from him so he wouldn't be able to call when he fell ill.' Ashby nodded. 'Terrible thing. I liked young Ben.'

'You found it just now, did you?'

'About five minutes ago.'

Simon wondered why Ashby had taken a rather roundabout route only to chance on him on the opposite side of the garden, but realized he himself had decided on an indirect path. Perhaps Ashby had seen him park and merely cut through on a more diagonal route.

Ashby half-turned to go. 'I hope you find out what's been going on around here, Chief Inspector. Nothing is ever going to be the same again, that's for sure. I wonder if Mrs Hartley will have the heart to go on.'

He took a dignified leave, his tall lean frame moving quietly off though the adjacent inner garden.

Simon walked along by the water-rill towards the house and saw Longman emerge from the recessed door, raising a hand in salute. They met at the large ornate seat they had used earlier.

'Too early for anything useful from the post mortem, I suppose?' Longman said.

Simon gave a brief nod. 'Consistent with poison. But we may get an early confirmation of what it was, if it was the oleander.' He thought, as he often had before, that the requirement for officers to attend the autopsies of their 'victims' was some horrible form of penance. It seemed designed to increase any outrage they might already be feeling and focus their determination to bring their murderers to justice.

'I did what you asked. Lewis Enright will see us in the study in,' Longman consulted his watch, 'about ten minutes.'

Simon produced the cellphone from his pocket.

'Clive Ashby just handed it to me.' He explained where and how it had been found.

'I've been ringing it regularly,' Longman said. 'I got the number from Mrs Taylor.'

'Did you ask her if Ben had been looking for his phone?'

Longman nodded. 'She said he hadn't mentioned it but he'd had it with him at breakfast the day before he died.'

'So it could have been taken any time between then and that evening when he asked about it at the meal the family had together. Any information from the phone company?'

'They're ringing back. I found the paperwork at the cottage. You were right. They both had the same service provider.' Longman took the phone from Simon's hand and pressed a few buttons through the plastic bag that covered it. 'No messages left on it. There was none on Liam's, either. I suppose the killer would have wiped off anything that might be useful to us.'

Simon squinted in the intense light. The sun was now in the west, directly opposite, and the glare made it impossible to see across the garden.

'As we were saying before, there was no point in the killer getting rid of the phones so that we wouldn't find them, because we could check the calls Ben and Liam had made through them. But this way,' Simon said slowly, thinking as he spoke, "it was a message to us that Liam and Ben couldn't phone for help because the killer determined it should be so. It was a power thing, playing with us again, like the taunts with the flowers.'

Longman wiped his brow with a crumpled handkerchief.

'We'd know that, anyway, if the phones had simply disappeared.'

'This way it underlines it more.'

Longman shifted along the seat to where there was deeper shade.

'Did you hear from Savage and Tremaine? I thought we

weren't going to speak to Enright until they'd reported back.'

'No, I haven't heard. But we're likely to fairly soon. I thought we might as well get on with it.' Simon got to his feet abruptly.

'It should be a bit cooler in the study, anyway.' Longman said.

'About the only positive thing about our interview with Mr Enright.' Simon pulled a face at Longman as he held the house door open.

Enright was waiting for them hands clasped behind, his back to the dead fireplace, the Dutch girl smiling serenely over his shoulder. He lifted his chin at them in acknowledgement, as if scenting prey. Longman took a chair by the central table, Simon sank into one of the club chairs by the fireplace. After a moment Enright followed suit with the matching chair.

'Well? Your sergeant here said you had some questions you wanted to ask me.' Enright reached up to the mantelpiece and grasped a half-full whisky glass.

'How is Mrs Hartley?' Simon asked.

'Out of it. What would you expect?' Enright took a mouthful of whisky and smacked his lips. It was not a display of compassion. Simon paused, Enright's dark eyes fixed on his face.

'I wanted to ask you again about your talk with Liam on the morning he died,' Simon said neutrally.

'I told your officers all there was to say on that subject.'

'You said that Liam had been asking for a new vehicle, is that right?'

'That's what I said.' Enright compressed his lips into a thin line.

'We understand that he was asking you for money.'

'Same thing.' Enright tossed back some more whisky. It did not seem to be affecting him, his eyes still fixed brightly on Simon.

'Perhaps I should have said he was threatening you and demanding money, rather than asking for money.' Simon returned Enright's fixed gaze.

'Who says so?'

'I don't need to tell you that.'

'So someone can make accusations and I am not allowed any proper defence?' Enright's voice was cold and measured.

'We can make things more formal if you like. Would you prefer to have a legal representative?'

'I don't have to speak to you at all.' Enright emptied his glass.

'Unless we arrest you, if that's what you prefer. And even then you have the right, as you know, to remain silent. It's just that the police tend to draw their own conclusions when witnesses prove uncooperative.' Simon continued to stare back impassively at Enright. He had come here expecting to be intimidated, but instead felt only a mild irritation. It must be all that sun, he thought.

Enright made an impatient gesture, banging his glass down on the tiled hearth so hard Simon thought it must splinter.

'All right, the little sod was threatening me. He was always threatening someone. I was just getting in my car to drive off when he crept up on me like some villain in a pantomime.' Spittle had formed around his mouth and Enright pulled out a snowy handkerchief to wipe his lips.

'What was he threatening you with?' Simon asked.

'It wasn't true, you understand, what he was making out. It was just the fact that it would cause unpleasantness,' Enright growled, eyebrows lowered further over his watchful eyes.

Simon waited, his own brows slightly raised. Bars of sunlight streamed through the window casting the rest of the room into deep shadow.

'He was claiming I was fiddling with the trust funds his father left for the children,' Enright said at last, distaste curling his lips. 'But it is easily proved that I have not been doing any such thing.'

'We can check,' Simon agreed.

'Do that,' Enright said savagely. 'But you'll be wasting your time. Not an unusual occurrence, I should think.'

'Did he say what he wanted the money for?'

Enright hesitated. 'He wanted enough money to set up independently in his own garden-design business. He was much too young for such a venture and I told him so.'

'So he wanted a lot of money,' Simon stated.

'As you say.' Enright wiped his mouth with the back of his hand. He suddenly straightened in his chair. 'I don't know why you're pursuing me over this. I wasn't here and couldn't have done anything to harm Liam that morning.'

Simon's phone bleeped. He flipped it open and listened: Savage and Tremaine on cue. After a few moments he thanked them and rang off, his eyes and Enright's still locked.

'It seems you weren't where you said you were for a significant period of time the morning Liam died, Mr Enright,' he said, replacing his phone in a jacket pocket. 'Acording to our interview with the man you met that day.'

Enright was silent for a moment.

'Your people have spoken to Maurice Derringham, have they?'

'Did you think we wouldn't?'

'What a horrible intrusion the police are,' he said disgustedly. 'God knows what Maurice will be thinking.'

'It's a highly publicized case. I'm sure he'll understand it's routine,' Simon said unsympathetically. If this was Enright's only discomfort in the whole affair, a little embarrassment with a business contact, he could be considered fortunate. 'So what were you doing in the hour that you didn't need to drive to London that morning?'

'There were a lot of traffic hold-ups. And I stopped for a coffee on the way, at a service station.' Enright thrust out his chin.

Simon looked pained. 'The row with Liam on that Saturday morning wasn't the only altercation you'd had with him recently, was it? You also had a falling out a week before Liam died, on the Friday evening.' It was a shot in the dark but it happily made its mark.

Enright's colour darkened and for the first time he looked away.

'He had made the demands before, yes.'

'Mr Enright, we can check the traffic flow and motorway cameras for last Saturday morning. We can also check CCTV at the service areas. If you have nothing to hide, I'd be glad if you would save us the trouble.'

'The country's turning into a police state,' Enright muttered.

Simon personally had reservations about the prevalence of big-brother cameras. As a policeman he wasn't going to admit to them.

'Liam also threatened you about Vita,' he stated. 'Did you perhaps go to see her in that missing time?'

He had intended his words to unsettle the man, and he succeeded. Enright's fists bunched and he inadvertently kicked the glass on the hearth so that it fell over and shattered. 'Shit', he said under his breath.

'How was Liam threatening you over Vita?' Simon persisted.

Enright looked up from his contemplation of the shards of glass.

'How do you think the foul-mouthed little bastard was threatening?' he said sourly.

'That you had some sort of inappropriate relationship with her?'

'And that was as true as the other accusation he made!' Enright's anger raised his voice to almost a shout.

'But you did go to see her that morning after you had spoken to Liam?'

For the moment, Enright seemed to capitulate. His shoulders slumped forward and he leaned with his hands hanging between his knees. 'Yes, I did.'

'Why was that?'

'Why do you think?' Enright said wearily. 'I had to warn her what Liam was saying.'

'Had you not done so after the previous row with Liam?'

'Yes, of course I had.'

'So why bother a second time if Vita already knew what Liam was threatening? He was saying he would tell your wife, I assume?' Simon could almost feel sorry for the man. Even if what Liam had charged him with was not true, it would have caused a significant upset had Liam carried out his threats.

'I just thought she ought to know. I wanted her to keep away from Liam, avoid him and any unpleasantness from him. And yes, of course he was threatening to tell Helen. Helen had no idea what a poisonous little shit Liam could be. If he had gone to her with such stories it would have distressed her a great deal.'

'All of which gives you a significant motive for wishing Liam dead,' Simon said quietly.

'I did wish him dead,' Enright said harshly, jerking back in his chair. 'But I would have strangled him if I were to do the deed. Do you seriously imagine that I tiptoed around making him sandwiches and leaving bunches of flowers?'

'Someone did.'

'Well, it wasn't me,' Enright glared. 'And why on earth would I kill Ben?'

Perhaps, Simon thought, because you have indeed fiddled with the funds and this would come into the open before long, anyway, when the boys came of age. Vita would be more pliant. Or perhaps for the reason they had been thinking, because Ben had had some knowledge of Liam's death. He put forward the latter idea to Enright.

'This is ridiculous!' Enright threw himself out of his chair and went over to a drinks tray. He splashed neat whisky into a fresh glass, half-filling it. 'If that's what you believe, Chief Inspector, go ahead and arrest me. Then I'll sue you for it afterwards.' He glanced at Longman sitting mute at the table, his notebook open in front of him, pen poised. 'I'd have you for slander if it weren't for the fact that our only witness is a biased one.'

'I'd willingly stand witness,' Longman said softly. 'Trouble is, the case would soon turn into the sort of trial where a lot of things might come out.'

Enright eyed him as if he were an obedient spaniel suddenly turned into a mastiff. He drank back some whisky, his eyes fixed warily on Longman.

Simon unwound his legs and stood up, finding his limbs had become stiff.

'Thank you for clarifying a few things, Mr Enright. We'll let you know if there's anything else we need to ask.'

'I don't doubt it,' Enright said, still standing by the drinks tray as if in imminent need of a refill. 'But, if you will take my advice, which I doubt, you won't waste more time on enquiring into my affairs and look instead for the person who really did these terrible things. I admit I had no time for Liam, but Ben was a decent lad and would have been more decent without his older brother around. And what's more, I could never have done such a thing to hurt Helen in the way that all this has. And,' he added emphatically, 'pointing the finger at me won't make it any easier for her.' He punctuated his speech by tossing off the remainder of his whisky.

'You're not the single focus of our investigations, Mr Enright,' Simon said, holding the door open for Longman to pass through.

'I should bloody hope not!' Enright barked after them as they left.

'You didn't press him about his relationship with Vita,' Longman objected as they made their way to the old games room.

'I mean, he didn't exactly spend much time denying the allegations about him and Vita. I'd have thought he'd have protested how much he loved her as the daughter he never had and all that sort of stuff.'

'I've usually found that the more people protest the more they have to hide. Anyway, Enright would flatly deny it, as he already has. Liam's accusations and Mrs Taylor's suspicions don't amount to proof. In fact, there's precious little sign of proof of anything in this case,' Simon said flatly. 'Plenty of means and opportunity and even possible motives but little sign of anything more tangible.'

'Vita would crack if we pressed her about it,' Longman said, pausing to steady a vase on a stand that he had inadvertently set wobbling.

'Cracking would mean dissolving into incoherent tears, I suspect.'

'Enright had means, motive and opportunity for the deaths of both of the boys. And he was here that Saturday morning and he lied about it.' Longman sounded a touch exasperated.

'Lying was understandable in the circumstances. I think he's at least telling some of the truth now. But we need evidence, proof. If it comes to it we'll look into the trust fund.'

In the games room Rhiannon Jones and Monkton were seated as far from each other as was physically possible, diligently and silently doing their reports. Simon perched himself on the front table and brought them up to date on the events of his day.

'So Enright is still a main suspect,' Monkton stated.

'With no actual proof we'll keep an open mind. But you can look into Gerald Hartley's will tomorrow. Find out who the trustees are and so on,' Simon said. 'How did you both get on?'

'I think maybe Ben's death is making them open up a bit,' Monkton said, apparently mollified by his assignment for the next day. 'On the other hand, what we gleaned is no more than you found out by a different route. Mara Kennedy also saw Alan Fairburn arriving at around seven the evening before Ben died and Stephen Orchard spoke briefly to Jenny Shipman when she arrived a little later.'

'Is that all of it?? Simon asked, glancing between the two of them. Rhiannom was one of those unfortunate people whose colour altered dramatically when under stress. Simon focused his gaze on her. 'DC Jones?'

She cleared her throat. 'Not much else, sir. But Clive Ashby did say that Lewis Enright's car was parked in the service area, where he keeps all his stores and equipment, at about eight o'clock on Saturday morning.' She looked up, pink-faced and self-conscious.

Simon frowned. 'You knew I was seeing Enright today. Why wasn't I told about this?'

Rhiannon looked down again. 'Sorry, sir,' she said faintly.

Simon fixed his gaze on Monkton. 'Well?' he asked, knowing any obstructiveness had surely come from this source. Rhiannon would have failed to pass on this information only after a direct order to do so from a senior officer.

'Thought you'd have already have spoken to Enright by then,' Monkton said easily.

'I've just come from him now,' Simon said between his teeth, unable to disguise his anger.

Monkton shrugged. 'No harm done. You seem to have got the admission out of him anyway.'

'Don't let anything like that happen again,' Simon said coldly. He was not going to give the DI a dressing-down in front of others, it would wait for later.

'I thought Ashby wasn't in on Saturday,' Longman said.

'He said he'd forgotten some of his tools,' Rhiannon said, gratefully turning to the sergeant. 'He was here for only a few minutes.'

It was all enough for today. Simon wanted the information from the phone company before they did any more, and besides, it was getting late. After a few comments on what would be happening the following day he let them go. As Longman left again with Rhiannon he called back Monkton. The DI approached lingeringly and kept his distance.

'Finish writing up the rest of your notes tomorrow morning,' Simon said. 'And then you can report to Detective Superintendent Munro. You're off the case.'

Monkton's sullen expression turned to one of anger.

'You can't do that,' he said.

'I most certainly can,' Simon said folding his arms.

'You've got a small enough team as it is,' Monkton sneered.

'Exactly. Too small to survive the sort of attitude that you bring to it. What you did was obstructive and completely unaccept-able.' It was not the first time that Simon had had this sort of confrontation with Monkton but he hoped it would be the last – though the DI's general attitude was proving a distinct bar to promotion elsewhere. He outstared Monkton. What with Enright and the inspector he was getting quite practised in it.

Monkton picked up his black leather jacket along with his notes and flung out of the room. Simon watched him go. It was the only small satisfaction in an otherwise unpleasant day.

CHAPTER 24

Lemon Geranium –
Unexpected meeting

Next day Simon called at his office in Westwich police head-quarters before walking to the coroner's court for the inquest on the death of Liam Hartley. The court was housed in an ancient stone building near the law courts and pressed close to the old city walls, a narrow courtyard at its front. What space there was was filled with members of the press and media. So far Detective Superintendent Munro had, along with Katherine Solland, the press relations officer, dealt with these and Simon was conscious that a personal call on Detective Superintendent Munro from him was a little overdue.

He was surprised nevertheless to find her waiting in the bliss-fully cool entrance hall, dressed immaculately as always, today in a pearl-grey coat and skirt with a sparkling white undervest. Unconsciously he smoothed his crumpled jacket as he approached her and she smiled a smile as dazzling as her shirt.

'I knew I could catch you here at least,' she said.

Simon mumbled an incoherent apology while she ran her eyes over his usual sartorial shortcomings. His uncertainties in the presence of this woman had less to do with any feared percep-tions of his lamentable style of dress than her assessment of the inner man beneath the often unprepossessing exterior.

'I gather from your reports that you're not making much progress,' she said, the smile disappearing.

He looked up at the splendid high wood ceiling.

'It's often hard to tell how much progress as been made until you can see the view clearly,' he said, aware at once that such a philosophical comment would merely annoy her.

'Well, I hope the clouds evaporate rather quickly,' she said tartly. 'DI Monkton came to see me this morning.'

Simon waited, wondering what further sabotage Monkton might have achieved.

'I'm beginning to wonder if DI Monkton's particular talents might not be put to better use in Traffic Division,' she said. Simon glanced at her, unable to keep the amusement from his eyes. Monkton's character might well be better satisfied by the opportunities for swift retribution offered in that uniformed division.

'Meanwhile,' she went on, an answering smile on her lips, 'I've read your latest reports and I gather you are waiting on information from the phone company before you pursue any further suspects. Have you really no idea who is responsible for these terrible poisonings?'

'Not specifically,' he said. 'There are a few possibilities but we're lacking anything like proof in any of them.'

'I would have appreciated a personal visit from you after what happened to Ben Hartley. I assume you are aware how bad it looks for another death to have occurred during an investigation?'

'Yes, I'm more than aware of that.' Simon stared at his scuffed shoes.

'I realize it was very early days in the investigation but I hope you've tried to ensure that there's no repetition, no further death.' Detective Superintendent Munro was speaking in a low voice, glancing at others in the crowd and nodding to a face here and there.

'I think people are perfectly aware that they have to watch what they eat. They hardly need me to tell them that after what's happened. But I think Ben was killed because of what he knew. Not because some mad serial poisoner is on the loose.' He wasn't sure of any such thing, but it sounded better.

'So you said in your report.' She eyed him unblinkingly. 'I hope you're right. Whatever, I would appreciate a little more of such possibilities from you rather than the bald iteration of facts that

I get in your reports. Could you perhaps manage to come in and see me, or at least telephone and give me the less expurgated version of the pattern of your thoughts?' She suddenly put out a hand and straightened Simon's tie.

'Sorry,' she said with an apologetic smile. 'Couldn't resist.'

Simon felt his blood pressure rise another notch. It had been a small insignificant action, but such was his awareness of this woman, on all levels, that he felt for the first time the disadvantages of having a woman boss. No, not *a* woman boss, *this* woman boss. And he couldn't dismiss his response as mere knee-jerk testosterone, because, stunning as she was to look at, she had more powerful qualities of mind and character that affected him uncomfortably. She was not unlike Jessie in her challenging intelligence, and God knew how difficult at times he found it to sustain any element of tranquillity with *her*, but Munro had a level of female power that left him feeling almost emasculated.

His colour, of which he was acutely and painfully conscious, subsided slowly. Detective Superintendent Munro was again focused on the crowd around them.

'Will you do that?' she said, her eyes swiftly moving to his face.

His mind was blank for a moment.

'Yes, of course I'll do that,' he said quickly.

'Time to go in, I think,' she said, moving ahead of him. The crowded hall was indeed emptying, people filing slowly into the small courtroom through the wide oak doors. He took a seat next to Detective Superintendent Munro at the front and looked around the already almost full room. He was startled to see Jessie sitting a few rows behind him. She raised her eyebrows and gave him a wry smile. He immediately wondered if she had been in the crowded hall and seen that small intimate gesture of Detective Superintendent Munro's. Feeling foolishly guilty he returned the eyebrow signal and quickly turned back. He was dismayed that she might have been there in the hall while he had remained unconscious of it. The sense of guilt was new to him: he had always felt himself to be the vulnerable one in his relationship with Jessie.

'Is that Lewis Enright?' Detective Superintendent Munro said in a low voice, with a slight jerk of her head.

He glanced to his left where seats were set at a right angle to the central rows. Enright was there with Barbara Meddick by his side. They were speaking together with their heads lowered. As if aware of Simon's look, she lifted her head and stared across at him without the faintest glimmer of recognition or acknowledgement. He felt absurdly rebuffed.

The court was ordered to rise and the coroner, a tall thin man with white hair and a heronlike stoop approached his table and sat down. The proceedings began, medical evidence being given first. Simon, called on shortly afterwards, gave evidence of his discovery of Liam Hartley, and spoke as the officer dealing with the investigations, acutely conscious of Jessie's eyes on him.

It was a relatively brief hearing, the evidence being considered sufficient to bring in the expected verdict of unlawful killing. The coroner referred to the death of Benedict Hartley and expressed his sympathies to Mrs Helen Hartley and to their stepfather Lewis Enright, who kept his eyes fixed on the floor between his shining black shoes.

After the court had risen the coroner called Simon over for a few questions. By the time he returned to the hallway Jessie was deep in conversation with Detective Superintendent Munro. He watched them for a moment before joining them, faintly and illogically disturbed at seeing them together. They were of a height and both slender, Jessie, tanned from a hot summer spent toiling outdoors, was almost as bronze-skinned as Detective Superintendent Munro. But there superficial similarities ended. Jessie's brown hair, as wild and undisciplined as ever, tumbled in sun-bleached curls down her back, Munro's head was sharply outlined against the light in its neat black chignon. Their clothes, too, were in total contrast, Jessie in an ethnic cotton dress which reached almost to her feet but bared her freckled shoulders. As they turned to him, though, their smiles were equally warm.

'You didn't say you were coming today,' he said to Jessie, planting a brief kiss on her cheek. His words had sounded unwelcoming and he regretted them immediately.

'I felt a certain interest,' she said, slightly defensively. 'I was there, too, remember.'

He had perhaps disregarded her understandable interest in the case the night before when she had tried to get him to talk to her about it. This had been after they had gone to bed and had made love quietly and gently, Simon inhibited by his mother's presence in the small cottage. His mother had earlier declared that she wanted neither to think about nor talk about the case as she was finding it all horribly upsetting thinking about Helen and what she must be feeling. They had silently watched a documentary about a South American Indian tribe, which had unfortunately included vivid details of the poisons that they used and their effects.

He had not answered Jessie and had soon gone to sleep, leaving in the morning with a brief cup of coffee before either of the women had apparently stirred.

Detective Superintendent Munro said, 'I've just been telling Professor Thurrow that my daughter attends her lectures whenever she can. She was uncertain whether to study English or psychology and now she's on the English course she can't get enough of psychology.' Detective Superintendent Munro's daughter had just finished her first year at the University of Westwich.

Jessie said, 'She could change courses if she's really not happy with English. But it could create some complications, I suppose.'

'I've suggested she finishes the English course and then decides if she wants to go on with another degree in psychology,' Detective Superintendent Munro said enquiringly to Jessie.

'She could do that,' Jessie said. 'The two courses do have things in common – the exploration and interpretation of human experience.' She looked expressionlessly at Simon. 'I'm always trying to persuade Chris that my insights could be useful in some of his cases.'

Simon stood rigidly between the two women, unwilling to comment.

'He's fortunate if so,' Detective Superintendent Munro said, glancing with what looked like amusement at Simon's face. 'Free insights from a professional psychologist should not be lightly turned away. I hope you don't spurn Professor Thurrow's help, Chris?' she asked her voice raised in surprise.

'Call me Jessie,' Jessie said, also looking amused.

'I'm Sonia,' Detective Superintendent Munro smiled.

Jessie had neatly achieved a level of familiarity that Simon doubted he would ever reach. Feeling mildly irritated, he made a move to go.

'I suppose you'll be returning to Clifford's Place?' Jessie said to him. 'Will you have coffee with me first?'

His main impulse was to seek the undemanding presence of Longman but Detective Superintendent Munro answered for him. 'Why don't you, Chris? Jessie may be able to give you some helpful suggestions.'

Simon shrugged with little grace and held out a hand pointing the way.

'I'll try sending you some more people now that they've been freed up,' Detective Superintendent Munro said, following close behind them. 'And don't fail to keep in touch.'

For a moment Simon was unsure whether she was speaking to Jessie or to himself, but her eyes met his as he looked back.

'I'll do that. Super,' he said with his usual ambiguity.

CHAPTER 25

Canary Grass – Perseverance

On his way back to Clifford's Place, Simon was conscious that the time he had spent with Jessie should more properly have been spent with Detective Superintendent Munro. It was likely that she would instead be turning up at Clifford's Place in the not too distant future.

The morning hour being late, coffee with Jessie had turned into lunch at the cafeteria in the cathedral precinct. She had, surprisingly, kept off the subject of Clifford's Place and the murders there. He had found himself wondering if in future he would have to appeal for her professional and intuitive insights rather than have them offered, now that they had the official approval of Detective Superintendent Munro. Perversely he had wanted to talk, had been ready to share what had been going on at Clifford's Place, but she had turned away his hesitant starts on the subject and spoken instead of the garden, of his mother, of her sister and her family.

After negotiating stone-faced the press at the main gates he parked in the usual place and took the side path to the games room. Longman was there alone, Rhiannon having taken on the job of looking into Gerald Hartley's will. Savage and Tremaine were continuing with interviews, including asking Alan Fairburn and Jenny Shipman about their visits to Clifford's Place the evening before Ben's death.

'I've got the fax from the phone company,' Longman said, pouring himself some water and offering some to Simon.

'Thanks.' Simon took it and drank it down quickly. Even with the car windows open it had been a hot drive. 'Well?' he said, wiping his mouth with the back of his hand.

Longman went over to one of the tables and picked up some papers. 'The morning of the day before he died, Ben made a call to a garden suppliers at ten.' He looked across at Simon. 'I've checked the numbers, who they belonged to.'

Simon nodded. 'Any others before he lost the phone?'

'A few later in the day. One was to a plant-supply nursery at just after eleven thirty that morning, the next was at five past two to Mara's mobile phone number and the third was to the telephone in Mrs Taylor's flat at just before three in the afternoon. None of the calls was long and the last one was quite brief.' Longman lifted his bushy eyebrows and waited for Simon's comments.

'So whoever took his phone did so some time after three.' Simon helped himself to some more water from the big jug. There were ice cubes in it, an improvement on the semi-warm stuff they'd had to drink so far. 'Mrs Taylor?' he asked, rattling the jug.

Longman nodded. 'If it disappeared after three it was still in the right time-scale to prevent his calling for help if he took the poisoned capsules that night after supper, or, as was the case, after breakfast the next day.'

'It's Monday afternoon we're talking about, isn't it? The time Vita did a disappearing act.'

'Is that relevant?' Longman frowned.

'I shouldn't think so. Just trying to relate times and so on.'

'I've arranged for us to speak to Mara Kennedy, to find out if Ben said anything of interest when he called her that afternoon,' Longman said.

'She didn't mention it, did she, to Monkton and DC Jones when they questioned her?' Simon drank down his second glass of water.

'There's nothing in their reports. I checked. And they certainly didn't mention it in the meeting.'

Simon pulled a face. 'It's quite likely Monkton stuck to the main point and only asked who was seen about the place at the time relevant to Ben's death. I think Mara was the one who saw Alan Fairburn arrive here. Have you asked Mrs Taylor as well, about the call Ben made to her flat?'

'She says he didn't.'

'Oh? The call must have connected or it wouldn't be itemized. What time did you say he phoned her?'

'Just before three.'

'Why would he phone her—?'

'Or Gavin.'

'Or Gavin, as you say, at the flat. Couldn't he find her in the house? And surely he wouldn't expect Gavin to be in the flat at that time?' Simon propped himself on the windowsill, the open window wafting the scent of roses into the room.

'She doesn't work in the afternoon, from about three till seven. She has an early start getting breakfasts, she does lunch and then she's back in again for the evening meal.' Longman grasped the back of a chair.

'I hope she gets at least some evenings off. It's a bit of a tie, her job.'

'She seems happy enough in it.' Longman shrugged. 'At least, she did do, until all this happened.'

'I wonder why Ben used the phone. Presumably it was because she wasn't in the kitchen and he didn't like to intrude on her privacy at the flat. But if she wasn't there either, where was she? Did she say?'

Longman splayed his hands. 'I didn't press her,' he admitted.

Simon grinned, imagining Longman's struggles with the formidable Mrs Taylor. 'Even so, someone must have answered the phone.'

'Answerphone, I expect we'll find. It was a brief call, perhaps just enough to connect, find there was nobody answering personally and ring off. He might not have left any message.'

'Didn't Mrs Taylor offer that as an explanation herself?' Simon shifted from his position by the window, the heat on his back had become intense.

'We didn't really get into any detail,' Longman said awkwardly. 'I thought it best we, or you, speak to her later.'

'Was there anything of interest in Ben's calls in the previous week?' Simon asked, pulling up a chair and resting his long legs on one of the tables.

Longman sank on to the seat he had been leaning on. 'There's no particular pattern, no regular calls to the same number or anything. But I haven't checked them all yet.'

'What about Liam's phone calls. Anything there?'

Longman picked up the papers again. 'I haven't completed these, either, but in the week before he died he made at least four calls to Lewis Enright, both his mobile and office numbers He phoned Mara Kennedy a couple of times and he made three calls to Jenny Shipman, or at least to Colin Wheatley's number.'

'I'd have thought Jenny would have her own mobile phone in her job looking after the Wheatley's children,' Simon commented.

Longman grunted. 'Perhaps she didn't give him her number.'

'Quite likely. Anything else?'

'Apart from what look like business calls, he also called the number at the Taylor flat a couple of times.'

'I wonder why.' Simon mused. 'I mean as with Ben, it wasn't as if they didn't have enough access to speak to them personally around the place.'

'Privacy, I should think,' Longman said.

'Exactly. So what would be so private?'

'Perhaps we'd better ask them. Maybe Mara Kennedy will know something about it.' Longman looked at his watch. 'I said we'd see her in a few minutes at her cottage.'

The water-sprinklers were on again on the front lawns, making another display of crystal rainbows. The immediate horizons were misted into a strange blurred landscape and the air felt wonderfully cool. Simon was strongly tempted to avail himself of a cool shower, the heat making his mind as well as his body feel sluggish. But they kept dutifully to the furthest edges of the water sprays and found shelter by taking the long route round by the hedged walks.

Mara Kennedy quickly answered to their knock at her door. She was dressed, barely dressed, in an obviously bra-less brief top showing firm tanned arms and shoulders, and equally brief khaki shorts exposing similarly tanned legs. She looked as if she had just showered, her cropped dark hair lying sleek against her head like an animal pelt.

'Tea?' she asked as she showed them from the small hallway into her sitting-room.

Longman immediately agreed and Simon followed suit, less from any desire for it than for the opportunity to examine the room unobserved. And this was a total contrast to the girly conventionality of Vita's living room. There was no fitted carpet here, only bleached floorboards with scattered ethnic rugs. The furniture was cheap and cheerful: a chest of drawers painted grey-green with a set of shelves and interesting bits of crockery above; a table against the wall, its legs a matching colour and with a scrubbed pine top and individually painted chairs with tie cushions; a comfortable old sofa with an ethnic throw to one side of the fireplace, opposite an ancient brocade winged chair in faded green. There were bookshelves stacked with a variety of subjects ranging from gardening to astronomy and several detective novels. Simon could see no concession to modern technology in the form of TV or music centre until he investigated a tall cabinet with reeded doors which neatly hid them from view. The effect was individual and yet there was nothing in the room that revealed anything much of Mara's personal life – no silver-framed photographs such as Vita displayed.

Mara returned with a tray as he was examining the cabinet.

'Modern things are so ugly, don't you think? I mean they suit a minimalist style but they don't really fit into any other sort of room. They look so alien.' She put the tray on the table and turned to face him.

'It's a good idea,' he agreed, never having thought about it before. In Jessie's sitting-room there was a television set and a music system but they were on the floor somewhere and generally had to be uncovered from beneath books and papers before they were put into use.

'Do you have any family?' he asked, his mind still half on the absence of photographs. Not that everyone displayed such mementoes. There were none at his own flat and Jessie certainly had none in evidence. He was merely curious.

'A mother and two younger brothers,' she said. 'In London. My father left us a few years ago.' She picked up the teapot. 'Milk, sugar?'

When she had settled them on the low sofa with their mugs of tea she sat opposite.

'Your sergeant didn't say what you wanted to speak to me about. Though I'm glad of the break. It's far too hot to be working. I'm planning to do my work more in the evenings while the hot weather lasts.' Her expression saddened. 'I haven't been able to ask Mrs Hartley about it, though, for obvious reasons. She must be utterly devastated. I still can't believe it. It was difficult enough to believe what happened to Liam. But poor Ben!' She seemed suddenly aware that she was talking too much and subsided into the cushioned chair, folding bare feet and legs under her.

Simon observed her for a moment before beginning. People were often different in their home surroundings from the way they behaved on more neutral territory. Usually they showed greater confidence in the former and more uncertainty elsewhere. Mara Kennedy seemed oddly more vulnerable today than she had seemed when he had last spoken to her at the Clifford Arms and he wondered why. Perhaps she was one of those drawn to promoting an image of a public confidence she did not in reality feel. Or, more charitably, the death of Ben had affected and upset her. She, like most others, had seemed fond of him.

Conscious of his attention, her eyes had lowered, focused on some bright paper poppies in the dead hearth.

'Miss Kennedy, Ben phoned you on his mobile phone on the afternoon before he died. Can you tell us what it was about?'

She glanced up at him. 'He asked if he could come and see me here at the cottage.'

'And did he?'

She nodded, rocking her body slightly. 'He came over more or less straight away.'

'You didn't mention this to Detective Inspector Monkton when he questioned you yesterday?'

'He didn't ask.' Green eyes stared across at him expession- lessly. 'He just asked if I'd seen anyone about the evening before Ben died and I told him that I had seen Alan Fairburn.'

'So what was it that Ben needed to talk to you about?'

Her eyes seemed suddenly to fill with tears. She made no attempt to wipe them away, instead blinking rapidly and looking upwards in an effort to dispel them. She swallowed.

'Poor Ben, He was so worried about who had poisoned Liam. He said he needed to talk it over with someone and there was no one else he could talk to.'

'You were obviously fond of Ben. He was fond of you, too,

wasn't he?' Simon said gently, remembering the scene at the station when he had first seen the trio of Liam, Ben and Mara.

She sniffed and nodded. 'He was. But he was so much younger than me. Five years is a big gap at our age.'

Liam, then, had been four years her junior and certainly had not seemed it. But then, Mara looked much younger than she was. People of small build often did.

'Was Ben not close to his sister, then? Could he not have talked to Vita?' he asked.

She ran a knuckle under her eyes in a childlike gesture.

'Vita's a strange girl. She's a bit remote, if you know what I mean. Lives in a world of her own over there with her plants and propagating and her greenhouses. And she's younger than Ben. I suppose he needed someone older and his mother was too close to it all and Barbara isn't the type you go confiding to.'

Simon balked slightly at this slip of a girl referring to herself as someone older. And Ben had talked to Mrs Taylor during the last week. He remarked on this.

She gave a knowing look. 'That was part of the problem. Ben seemed to have got it into his head that Mrs Taylor or Gavin might have been responsible for Liam's death.' Mara shifted her position, bringing her legs in front of her body and clasping them with her arms. 'I told him it was a ridiculous idea.'

Simon took a moment to absorb this. It seemed perhaps unlikely, but not ridiculous. And Ben had tried to call Mrs Taylor not long after his talk with Mara.

'Did Ben give you his reasons for thinking this?'

She rubbed at a knee with a hand too perfectly manicured to be that of a gardener. The nails, painted deep purple, were, though, clipped quite short.

'He was very distressed, you understand. Said he couldn't get Liam out of his mind and nobody seemed willing to talk about it – as if they were all avoiding the subject so it would go away.'

'Are you saying he wasn't particularly coherent?'

She gave a quick frown. 'No, it wasn't quite that, just that he was so upset.' She looked across at Simon. 'He was grieving still, after all.'

'So what were the reasons he gave for thinking that the Taylors were somehow involved in Liam's death?'

Mara hesitated, as if unwilling or unable to put it into words.

'From what I could gather,' she said slowly, resting her chin on a knee, 'he thought Liam had been threatening the Taylors in some way and was afraid that one or both of them might have wanted him out of the way.'

'He didn't say what he thought the threat was?'

She shook her head. 'He said he had heard Liam having a rowing with Gavin the day before Liam died.'

'Was that perhaps to do with Liam's interest in Gavin's girl-friend Jenny, do you think?'

'It's quite possible', she said, colouring slightly and turning her head away.

'Is that what Ben thought?'

'I don't know.' She shrugged. 'He was talking about him rowing with Gavin before he saw him in the pub though. Anyway, I think he just wanted to know what I thought of his ideas. Talking it over with a friend can sometimes clarify your thoughts, can't it?' She glanced green-eyed at him from under her lashes, catlike. Yet her body language was too tense for the feline anal-ogy. Perhaps a watchful cat though, he thought.

'Was that all he discussed with you that afternoon? He didn't speculate about anyone else perhaps being responsible?' Simon finished his tea and placed the mug on the floor. The tea had been overly strong for him and his mouth felt dry with the metallic taste of tannin. Longman continued to sip slowly and watch on placidly.

She gave a brief laugh. 'He did say he could understand it if Lewis had done it. That Liam had been pushing him a bit too much lately.'

'But he didn't take the idea seriously?'

'I don't think so. He said he could imagine Lewis strangling Liam but not pussyfooting around with poisoned sandwiches,'

Very much Enright's own assessment, Simon remembered.

'And what advice did you offer to Ben after he'd put all these thoughts to you?'

She raised her eyebrows, her small brow crinkling in what looked like amusement.

'I'm not sure I gave him any. I just let him get it off his chest and did a bit of soothing back-patting.'

'You didn't make any comment at all?' Simon looked mildly sceptical.

Mara shifted uncomfortably, hugging her knees tighter to her chest. At last she glanced up.

'Actually, I did suggest he talked to Mrs Taylor. Not,' she said emphatically, 'to accuse her or Gavin. Just so that he could ask a few questions to get some idea of whether his thoughts had any substance.'

'Despite the fact that you thought his idea was ridiculous?'

'Exactly because I thought so. I thought it would put his mind at rest as he wouldn't let go of that particular fear.' She sounded defiant.

'And it didn't occur to you to suggest that Ben should bring his ideas to me, or any one of us? It didn't occur to you that if Ben started questioning possible murderers, it might have been very dangerous for Ben to hint of his suspicions?' Simon said, keeping his voice as even as he could.

'I told you. I thought the whole idea was ridiculous. It would have been a waste of police time,' she said, unrepentant.

'Hardly for you to judge. And the next day Ben was dead.'

She pushed her feet forward and placed them on the floor, grasping the arms of the chair.

'Well, I hope you're not blaming me for that! It's been your job to deal with this case and it's not my fault that we've got another dead body on our hands since you arrived.'

There was silence for a moment, in which Simon absorbed the startling venom of her attack and she subsided back into the deep chair.

Longman cleared his throat and carefully placed his mug on the small table beside him.

'How was Ben when he left you? Did he say what he planned to do?'

She glared across at him. 'He seemed relieved at my idea that he should ask Mrs Taylor a few questions, just to put his mind at rest. He was a bit happier than when he arrived, anyway.'

'And what are your own thoughts, Miss Kennedy?' Longman asked comfortably. 'You seem not to believe the Taylors could have beem involved in these deaths. The idea of Enright's guilt seems to amuse you. It doesn't leave so very many other possibilities. Surely you must have had some thoughts yourself on the subject of who did the poisonings?'

'That's just it! I haven't. How can you expect me to seriously suspect people I've lived and worked with happily of doing such dreadful things.' She put her hands up to her face. 'I suppose I've just been in a sort state of denial. I've just kept working and trying not to think about it. Though now that it's happened to Ben, I admit I've been afraid that the Taylors, one or both of them, might have done it.' She looked at Simon. 'You're right. I should have told Ben to speak to you. I shouldn't have said what I did just now. I'm sorry.' She blinked away more tears.

'I understand,' Simon said quietly. 'It's a terrible situation that everyone is in. But if you do come across anything, or think of anything you think might be relevant to the case, I hope you will feel able to come and see me.'

'I promise I will,' she said contritely and stood up ruffling her hands in a boyish gesture through her now almost dry hair.

Simon got to his feet, inevitably standing close to her in small space, but towering above her. She smelled of flowers with an underlying musklike smell that was very attractive. As Longman stood up she moved away.

'Well, good luck,' she said awkwardly, walking over to the door leading to the hallway.

They passed her, Simon feeling clumsy and male, and went out into the shaded hedge-lined pathway.

'I hope you realize the Taylors aren't such a daft idea,' Longman said.

CHAPTER 26

Sage – Domestic virtue

Nothing more was said until they found a seat in deep shade under a cedar-tree. The grass there was a brittle brown from the heat and drought and spread in brighter patches of green to specimen trees and the old brick walls of the vegetable parterre. They were perfectly private.

'We'll have to speak to the Taylors,' Longman insisted, sinking down beside Simon.

Simon continued to stare out across the dappled lawns. At last he said, 'Do you remember what Linda Carver said, about Liam getting people the sack?'

'She did, didn't she?' Longman agreed eagerly. 'I'd forgotten about it. You think Liam was threatening the same with Mrs Taylor, or both of them?' Longman leaned forward, his elbows on his knees. 'Don't forget, Gavin had his own motives for killing Liam after what happened with Jenny.'

'They both stood to lose their home as well as their living if Liam was making trouble,' Simon commented.

'Is it likely they both did it together?'

Simon stretched out his long legs and linked his hands behind his head.

'It has to be possible. Mrs Taylor was busy at the house, though, the morning Liam died, in the presence of Linda Carver. They were preparing food for the open day in the garden. It's conceivable she could have slipped out and gone to Liam's cottage. Or she could have made up the sandwiches beforehand and Gavin could have put them in the place of the ones Liam had made.'

'She'd need to know what sandwiches he'd made first, before she could fake a second lot,' Longman said.

'Gavin could have checked, and then let her know.'

'Easy, really.' Longman rubbed his knees. 'And no one knew better than Mrs Taylor what Ben's habits were with taking his supplements. She could easily have got hold of them and substituted some.'

'Means, motive and opportunity,' Simon said. 'Neatly solved.'

His tone made Longman glance across. 'You don't sound convinced.'

'It doesn't amount to proof. And I can't quite believe that Mrs Taylor cold-bloodedly poisoned Ben. She was obviously so fond of him. And Ben had breakfast with her as usual the day after he's supposed to have confronted her about having poisoned his brother. You'd think he might be a bit wary of eating food that she'd prepared.'

'Have you got anyone's word but hers for that?' Longman said derisively.

No, he hadn't, Simon admitted to himself. But then, in this case they had precious little but words all around. June Taylor could have been lying about the time she spent with Ben the morning of the day he died.

'But her grief for Ben was genuine, I'm sure,' he said to Longman.

'Well it might have been. She might have regretted the necessity of getting him out of the way when he faced her with questions about how and why Liam died. But if it was a toss-up between her own son, his and her livelihoods and home, and Ben Hartley, I don't have much trouble guessing who'd come out on top.'

Simon gave a sardonic laugh. 'If it is the cook behind all this, we'd better try and find out. Otherwise we could find ourselves with mass murder taking place.'

'She should still be at the flat on her afternoon break,' Longman said, checking his watch.

Simon stood up. 'Let's get it over with, then.'

They saw no one as they crossed the gardens to the east side of the house. There was still an atmosphere about the place, as if the human dimension had been discarded and only nature ruled. The sprinklers were off again and the grass at the front of the house sparkled in the sunlight. There was a scent of strong warm earth and sweet-smelling grass. Simon glanced up at the face of the house, almost anxious for some sign of humanity about the place: he thought he caught a glimpse of Barbara Meddick's face momentarily at the office window, but it could have been a trick of light.

Access to the flat above the old stables was via a door inside the far end of the building. Simon rang the bell. After a few moments they heard heavy steps descending on what sounded like an uncovered wooden staircase. June Taylor looked surprised to see them, brushing her frizzy fringe back with a floured hand.

'Do you want to come up?' she asked.

'If you wouldn't mind.'

'I was just making a pie for our dinner,' she said over her shoulder as they followed her upstairs. Simon's eyes were on a level with her ankles and he saw that they were swollen and that she had quite bad varicose veins. The glimpse of frailty made him even less happy with the confrontation to come.

'Do you mind if I just finish this off?' she asked, backing towards the open door of the small kitchen and wiping her hands in her apron. 'I won't be a minute. Just take a seat.'

Simon's first impression was that the flat was very clean. All the surfaces were polished ones, he noticed. The floor was covered with green vinyl and the sofa and chairs were old brown leather, a narrow strip of Axminster rug in front of them. A dark oak dresser displayed what looked like fine quality china plates and cups and a polished oak table and chairs were placed against another wall. It was unimaginative, old-fashioned and a complete contrast with the room they had lately come from.

'Do you want me to put the kettle on?' she called, following the question by leaning through the door. 'Do sit down both of you.'

Simon and Longman declined the offer of a drink, Longman sinking on to the sofa in front of a large television set. Simon continued to wander around the room. The only window faced south, overlooking the cobbled yard and the big house, so the room was not well lit.

June Taylor was obviously not a woman who favoured bric-à-brac or ornaments, apart from the prized china service. One photograph was displayed on the dresser, of a young Gavin sitting proudly on a pony, his parents standing each side of him, all of them laughing to the camera, the background a neat farm-yard. The only other photograph, over the fireplace, was a wedding picture of a slim and happy-looking June Taylor, her hair done up in a fashionable bouffant style and in traditional white dress and veil. Her husband, clinging to her arm, looked anxious, a half-smile on his face. He was a big man with a strong-boned face and a mop of dark wavy hair. The likeness to Gavin was evident.

'He died. Eleven years ago next week,' June Taylor said from the doorway.

'I'm sorry.' Simon turned back to her. 'What happened?'

'We had a small farm, tenant farmers we were. One day the tractor Jim was driving overturned on him. His injuries were terrible. He died a few days later in hospital.' She came into the room and sat down on one of the old leather chairs. 'Because it was only a tenant farm we had to leave. Gavin was heartbroken, he was going to take over from his dad one day, but he was still much too young.' She spoke matter-of-factly but it was likely the event and its consequences had been heartbreaking not only for Gavin.

'So you came here?' Simon asked, sitting opposite her.

'We had nowhere to live,' she said simply. 'And I couldn't have gone to work in a town. Gavin had always been used to being outdoors, so this seemed a good solution. He was allowed the run of the gardens except on special days.' She smiled. 'And he had the boys to play with when they were home from school, though they were just a few years younger.'

Simon was conscious that this woman would have fought fiercely against losing yet another home.

'The boys all got on well in those days, then?'

She looked troubled. 'There was no falling out between Gavin and Ben. It was Liam who started at playing the lord and master and bossing my Gavin around.' She looked down at her apron and began twisting it in her fingers. 'What is it you want to see me about?' she asked quietly.

Once again, Simon was struck by how different people could seem in their home environment. And yet again this was someone who seemed infinitely more vulnerable here than when he had talked to her in her place of work. Perhaps it was the greater wholeness of their character that appeared, without the carapace of work which perhaps gave a false image of strength. And in June Taylor's case her home was a particular source of vulnerability.

'I think Sergeant Longman here asked you something about a call Ben made to you on the day before his death?' he said.

'Yes.' She glanced at Longman who had his eyes on his notebook. 'And I told him that Ben didn't phone me. That there wasn't any call. Why? What's this all about?' She looked troubled.

'We've realized that the call that was made to you was probably picked up by your answerphone and, if Ben merely rang off without speaking, you wouldn't of course have registered who had called. You do have an answerphone, I suppose?' Simon asked.

'Yes, yes we do. It's over there in the hall,' she said anxiously, shifting forward slightly in her seat. 'And of course it quite often happens that someone rings but doesn't want to just leave a message. Quite often people just don't like answerphones. I admit I don't like them myself.'

'That's no doubt what happened then, Mrs Taylor. Ben called you at around three o'clock that afternoon. I imagine he would have looked in at the kitchen first to see if you were there and then phoned the flat to speak to you or ask if he could come and see you. Or maybe he wanted to speak to you in private rather than at the house. You weren't here to answer the phone, so where were you at that time?'

She looked bewildered. 'Which day are we talking about?'

'Monday. It was the afternoon that Vita disappeared, if you remember. You said, correctly, that she would be safe enough.' And if their suspicions were right, June Taylor was in a better position than anyone to give that prediction.

'Well, I didn't join in the search for her, that's for sure,' she said more confidently, her face clearing. 'I would have come back to the flat here at three, I'm sure. Maybe I was on my way from the house to the flat when he rang.'

That was perfectly possible, given the tight timing.

'So did Ben call to see you after you arrived here that afternoon?' Simon asked.

'No, no he didn't,' she said, her voice rising slightly. 'What is this all about, anyway?'

'You're quite sure about that, Mrs Taylor,' Longman intervened. 'Because we have good reason to suppose that he did come here to see you.'

'Well, I'm telling you he didn't,' she said, rounding on Longman with a touch of her old belligerence. The broken veins in her cheeks stood out vividly.

'What about Liam, Mrs Taylor? He phoned you too in the week before he died,' Longman persisted.

'What if he did! He might have been ringing Gavin about something to do with the garden. I'm sure I can't remember.' She spoke firmly but Simon noticed that her hands were now clenched in her lap and trembling slightly.

'Are you accusing me?' she asked, her voice strained, turning to Simon. 'Are you suspecting that I've got something to do with the terrible things that are going on here? Who says so?'

'No, Mrs Taylor, we're not accusing you,' Simon said quietly. Longman shifted noisily on the polished surface of the sofa. 'But we do need to ask you questions and clear up a few matters.'

'It's because I'm the cook, isn't it? Is that it? Because I make the food for them? Which of them has been suggesting such a thing?' Her voice was high, her face now a dull red.

'Please,' Simon said, alarmed at her colour. 'Calm down, Mrs Taylor. Get some water, would you please, sergeant?'

Longman slid to his feet and came back moments later with a mug full of water.

'Sorry, couldn't see a glass,' he said handing it to her. She took it from him without comment and obediently sipped.

'We don't mean to distress you, Mrs Taylor, but you must understand that we have to question people very thoroughly if we are to find out who killed Liam and Ben,' Simon said quietly.

'Well, I didn't do it, and neither did my Gavin,' she said with a touch of her former spirit returning.

'Unfortunately, the person who did do it would say exactly the same,' he said drily. 'You see our problem.'

'What a terrible time,' she said dully. 'As if the deaths and poor Mrs Hartley's grief weren't enough, the police have to turn our lives inside out. Oh, I understand all right,' she said, holding the palm of her hand towards him. 'I understand you've got to do your job, but why pick on us?'

'That also is what other people say, Mrs Taylor.'

'I see.' She put her mug of water on the floor and straightened up. 'Well you'd better ask away, then.' Her colour was more normal and she seemed resigned.

'Ben seemed to believe that Liam had been threatening you and Gavin in some way. Did Liam perhaps make threats about your job, or Gavin's, or both?'

Her mouth tightened. 'I could deny it but I won't. Yes, he did do that, to both of us, even before the fight in the Clifford Arms. I don't know what he'd got against Gavin and Jenny being together, but he'd been having a go at Gavin even before that particular row, telling him he could get rid of him any time he chose.' She bit her lip, close to tears. 'Gavin's a good worker and doesn't deserve that sort of treatment.'

Simon waited, anxious not to push her too hard.

'He'd done it before, you know! We weren't the only ones. Anyone who crossed Liam got the same kind of treatment – you could be sure he'd make trouble for them. He even tried to get rid of Barbara Meddick at one time, making out she was carrying on with Mr Enright. And Stephen Orchard, just because he interfered when Liam was teasing some poor animal, a mole or something.' She shook her head. 'And he did get his way over some people. There was Mara Kennedy's predecessor, an inoffensive young woman who slapped his face over something he said, and I don't doubt he deserved it. She had to go.' She sank back in her chair, folding her arms.

'So what did you do to cross him, Mrs Taylor?' Simon said, not unsympathetically.

She didn't answer at once. Simon became aware of the ticking of the carved-oak clock on the mantelpiece, the scratch of Longman's pencil as he scribbled or doodled in his notebook, the shadows lengthening on the roof of Clifford's Place.

Unexpectedly she laughed, shortly and bitterly.

'Wouldn't it just delight that young man to think that I was going to be accused of murdering him! He'd be happier about that than about you catching the real killer.'

'You really didn't get along, then,' Simon said in something of an understatement.

'Never did like him,' she said, 'even from when he was a boy. Too much of a tell-tale even then. Then, after he'd started working here properly we had a few fallings-out. I used to tell him I took my orders from Mrs Hartley. He used to expect me to prepare meals for him to suit his time and tastes, and even after he'd moved out to the cottage he'd got a habit of coming in the kitchen and criticizing what I was doing. White sugar and white flour! You'd think it was poison.' She seemed to be aware of what she had said and gave another bitter laugh. 'It's quite true, there were times when I could have poisoned him. But,' she said sharply, looking at Longman as he continued to scribble in his book, 'I did not.'

'And what happened more recently to give rise to his latest threats towards you, Mrs Taylor?' Simon asked.

Her colour rose again and she tightened her folded arms. 'He accused me of stealing food from the house, the little liar.' Her cheeks were pink with embarrassment or indignation, or both.

'I imagine there is a certain amount of laxity allowed for a cook,' Simon said, 'particularly with left-overs and so on. One of the perks of the job, perhaps?'

'Well, I've always been very scrupulous about that sort of thing,' she said emphatically. 'You can't be too careful in this sort of work. It's a matter of not abusing trust. Yes, if there was anything that would otherwise go to waste, I would ask Mrs Hartley if it would be all right for us to use it up. But that doesn't happen very often if you're careful in your work like I am. I'm a properly trained cook. It's too easy to slip into lax ways and persuade yourself that a little bit of this or that wouldn't be missed, and I've never been one to let myself slide into that sort of behaviour.'

She leaned forward and picked up the mug of water. 'I can tell you that I've never even had vegetables from the garden for us unless there's been an excess and it's been offered. Or, more often than not, Mrs Hartley has suggested it. She's been a good employer and a decent one.' She drank from the mug.

'It's evidently a point of pride with you,' Simon agreed. 'So what was Liam saying you'd done?'

'I told you, he said I'd stolen food,' she said heatedly.

'What, specifically?'

She took a breath. 'You have to understand that although Liam made a big song and dance about being independent and being vegetarian, he still used to come into the kitchen and see what he could take back to the cottage – and he wasn't always that strict about his so-called vegetarianism, either. He liked to sound off about principles and all that but he didn't always stick to them.' She replaced the mug on the floor.

'Well, in the week before he died, I made a particular favourite of the family's, a fish pie.' Seeing Simon's expression, she added, 'Yes I know it doesn't sound like much but it's a special recipe with a lot of flavourings and ingredients and a crisp cheese-pastry topping. It was one that Liam in particular liked in earlier days. I always made a big one exactly because they all loved it and had second helpings and so on. Liam had seen I was making it when he came in that day, in fact he remarked on it. Well, to cut a long story short, he came into the kitchen later on that evening when I was just finishing clearing up and looked into the pantry. "Where's the remains of the fish pie"? he asked. "All eaten", I said to him and carried on with my work. "You've taken it home for that hulking great son of yours, haven't you"? he said, getting angry.

'Well, I got angry back and then he started accusing me of always stealing food and so on.' She pressed her lips together and frowned. 'You're quite vulnerable in a job like this, to that sort of accusation, and I got upset and told him a few home truths about himself and said he should get his mother here because she could confirm that the four of them had eaten it between them. Of course he backed off from doing that, but he said he was going to get me for something and he'd see me and my stupid son sent packing.'

She pulled out a handkerchief from a pocket in her apron and blew her nose fiercely. 'Well, there you have it, Chief Inspector.' She wiped her nose again and pushed the hanky back, apparently all passion spent.

Simon could only imagine the resentment and bitterness this woman, who had been left a homeless widow to struggle as she could to raise and provide for her only son, must have felt towards a cocky young man who had never really had to strive for anything in his life, and who was intent on making her life as hard as he could. But sympathy with any motive she had made no difference.

'Just how real, or serious, did you think Liam's threat was, Mrs Taylor? I mean, were you genuinely afraid that he might cause Mrs Hartley to make you leave?'

'I was afraid,' she admitted. 'Of course I was afraid. This is our home as well as our jobs we're talking about. But when you say did I think Mrs Hartley would make us go, I'm not sure. That is, I don't think for a minute that she would have listened to Liam just complaining. What I was afraid of was that Liam might do something to make it look as if we had done something wrong so that she might feel she had no choice. I wouldn't have put it past him. And things had been coming to a head lately, what with the rows he'd been having with Gavin.'

Longman stirred on the sofa. 'You mean you thought he might frame you in some way?'

'Yes, that's right, I suppose,' she agreed.

Simon, who had been leaning back in his chair, straightened up.

'Thank you for being so frank with us, Mrs Taylor,' he said. 'I can quite understand why you might have wanted to poison Liam Hartley. Perhaps you can help me in proving that you didn't?'

'You can't prove a negative,' she said sardonically. 'Isn't that what they say?'

'How about proving innocence, then? Is that positive enough?' He smiled. His efforts at professional detachment were failing. He really didn't want this woman to be in any way involved in these crimes.

She gave a helpless gesture. 'I've told you I was with Linda Carver all morning on the day Liam died. I couldn't have gone out to the cottage. Why don't you ask her?'

'We'll do that. She has certainly told us she was with you that morning helping with the baking and sandwich-making. But did Gavin come in to see you during that time?'

She put her hands over her mouth in thought. 'He quite often does come in for a cup of tea about mid-morning. I can't remember whether he did that day. You'll have to ask Linda. What if he did? Oh,' she said, understanding dawning, 'you think I got Gavin to take some sandwiches over to the cottage, is that it?' Her hands were shaking again. She clutched them in her lap, tightening them until their reddened knuckles were white.

'You really believe I would involve my son in something so wicked? And hurt Ben,' she went on, her voice shrunken. 'It would have been easy with him, wouldn't it? I told you all about how he'd take his supplements after his breakfast with me.' She stared across at Simon, a mixture of fear and despair on her face.

'Mum! Sorry I'm late.' Footsteps thundered up the stairs and Gavin Taylor rushed into the room, hanging on to the door as he saw who was present.

'Oh, no, the pie!' his mother exclaimed and rushed to the kitchen. There was indeed a faint smell of burning in the air.

'What's going on?' Gavin demanded, looking from Simon to Longman. He was wearing a grey T-shirt and jeans and the smell of earth and sweat emanated from him. His face, too, was sweat-smudged and there were a few white petals caught in his unruly hair. He didn't wait for an answer, moving on to the kitchen, saying: 'Don't forget Jenny and me are going out tonight and I've got to have a shower straight away.' They heard his voice alter. 'What's the matter, Mum?' In a sharper voice he said, 'What have they been saying to you?'

They could hear no response from June Taylor. In a gentler voice they heard her son say, 'Sit down, Mum. Have some brandy.' They heard a cupboard door open and close and the clink of glass. When Gavin came back into the sitting-room, both Simon and Longman were standing.

'What have you been doing to her?' he said angrily, 'to get her all upset like that? She's in tears and it's not just because the pie's burnt.'

A touch of farce was essential in all good tragedies, Simon thought. But he still wasn't certain there was any tragedy in this small home, not of recent origin anyway.

'There was no intention to upset your mother,' he said quietly. 'Please convey our apologies. We just have to ask certain questions of people – it can't be avoided, and it's better done in people's own homes than in a police station.' He was excusing himself and was uncomfortably aware of it.

'And why Mum?' Gavin squared up to him aggressively, his jaw thrust out.

'Not just your mum, Gavin. Plenty of other people are being questioned.'

'But she says you think she did it!'

'That wasn't what I said.' Simon kept his voice low, hoping to calm him but Gavin edged a little closer. There was no point in wasting more words, they would probably serve only to inflame him more.

Simon moved back to the door.

'Try to help your mother to calm down, Gavin. Perhaps it would be better to stay with her tonight.'

'You've got a nerve!' Gavin followed after him.

Longman came up behind, saying sharply: 'Young man, you're not doing your mother or yourself any good, behaving like this. Now do as the Chief Inspector says and go and see to your mother. And make your mind up that we'll be wanting to speak to you soon, as well.'

Gavin swung round, his fist held high. He lowered it when he met Longman's steely glare, and moved away.

'Pigs!' he muttered.

Simon and Longman clattered down the wooden staircase and out into the late western sunlight.

'Well? What do you think?' Longman demanded.

'Dead of a disagreement over a fish pie?' Simon gave a half-smile. 'Somehow I'm not convinced.'

'You're too soft,' Longman muttered. 'You feel sorry for her, don't you? Well I hope you realize you're in no position to mess about with this one. We can't afford another death on our hands.'

CHAPTER 27

Belvedere – I declare against you

Though it was still early, the day was already uncomfortably hot. Simon waited for his small team to settle down with their various drinks and glanced out of the window. The sky had a brassy metallic cast and there was a heavy humid feel to the air. Perhaps his mother's prediction was right and there would be thunderstorms today.

The evening with his mother and Jessie had been peaceful and mundane. Neither had referred to Clifford's Place and he had been encouraged to mow the grass, 'but be careful the blades aren't set too low, with all this drought, though I think we'll get plenty of rain tomorrow.' The activity – there was a lot of grass – had eased him physically and mentally and he had slept well. Now, though, he surveyed the room gloomily, he was back in the thick of it and had no clear idea what his direction was going to be.

He nodded at Rogers and Tremaine to begin.

'Alan Fairburn said he turned up here on Monday evening and spoke to Enright briefly,' Tremaine reported. 'Enright said Helen was far too distressed to see anyone so he left straight away. He said he had come only to offer some personal condolences to Mrs Hartley about Liam.'

'Did he have anything to say about Ben's death?' Simon asked.

'Just that he was appalled and supposed Helen would be in an even worse way and that he'd write her a letter.'

'And he didn't see anything relevant?'

Savage loosened his shirt collar. 'He seemed a bit jumpy when he realized that we were interested in his activities that evening in relation to Ben's death. But he said he had spoken only to Enright and left straight away. This was at about seven that evening.'

'Any corroboration of this from the Wheatleys?'

'They'd gone into town when we were there so we didn't have a chance to check,' Tremaine said. 'But we questioned Jenny Shipman.'

'And?'

Tremaine shrugged dismissively. 'I don't think there's anything useful there, either. She says she turned up here at about half past seven and had a meal with Gavin which his mother had left for them to eat while she was on duty at the house. She says they watched television together afterwards until Mrs Taylor came back at about nine and then she and Gavin went over to the Clifford Arms for a short drink. She dropped him back here at ten thirty and then drove home to the Wheatleys.'

And while the family were eating the meal she had cooked at the house, Simon thought, June Taylor had had ample opportunity to go to Ben's room and find his box of supplements. And the morning following Ben's death the oleander flowers had been found in Mrs Taylor's very own kitchen. But it was precisely that artistic flourish of leaving the deadly flowers that stuck in his throat as far as June Taylor was concerned. It didn't fit.

On the other hand, while she was busy in the house kitchen, Jenny and Gavin had only each other for alibis, and both had had their own motives for revenge on Liam Hartley. But once again, the only subsequent discernible motive for killing Ben was what he might have known about the first murder.

They were waiting for him to say something.

'Anything else from your interviews?'

They shook their heads in unison.

'Nothing of any use came up.'

Simon turned to Rhiannon Jones. 'What did you find out, DC Jones?'

They all looked up, startled momentarily. It was as if someone had switched off the lights, except that there were no lights on, or needed. But after days of unrelenting fierceness, the sun had finally disappeared behind a bank of cloud. A faint cheer went up and some smiled, united in relief.

Rhiannon said unhappily, 'It's going to thunder, isn't it?'

'You're not scared of thunder, are you?' Savage teased her.

'No, I'm not actually,' she retorted, her Welsh accent very pronounced, 'But I am scared of lightning.'

Simon gave her an amused smile. 'You'll be safe enough in here, you know.'

She glanced nervously at the huge ballroom mirrors on the wall opposite the windows. 'My gran always used to cover the mirrors when there was a thunderstorm. She'd have a job covering those.'

There was general laughter. 'Take your mind off it by answering my question,' Simon suggested.

Rhiannon opened her notebook but began speaking without reference to it.

'Gerald Hartley left five million one hundred and fifteen thousand pounds in his will, plus this property. One million along with Clifford's Place was left to his wife Helen and three million divided equally between his three children, held in trust until their twenty-fifth birthdays. The residue went to friends, including Barbara Meddick who received fifty thousand pounds, and some charitable donations. There were a few other bequests to employees in his company and Linda Carver got five thousand, as did June Taylor.'

The first crash of thunder began, loud but not immediately overhead. Rhiannon looked over her shoulder.

'We should open the door,' she said nervously. 'Then any thunderbolts can get out if they come through the windows.'

Tremaine was jeering as the door did indeed open, admitting Detective Superintendent Munro.

'I feel like a witch in a pantomime,' she said. 'What an entrance!'

'There's a definite smell of sulphur in the air,' Simon agreed.

She gave an amused smile and pulled out a chair behind the others. 'Carry on,' she said, folding her arms.

Perhaps the presence of another woman inhibiting her,

Rhiannon swiftly continued: 'I looked into the trust fund,' she said. 'There are four trustees: Lewis Enright, Helen Hartley, Barbara Meddick and Maurice Derringham.'

'Derringham was the one Enright was using as an alibi, for Saturday morning, wasn't he?' Simon said.

Longman spoke for the first time. 'Why was he meeting him on a Saturday morning, anyway? What was so urgent that it could- n't wait for the working week?'

'I imagine you've got your own answer to that?' Simon raised his eyebrows.

'Just wondered if it had anything to do with the pressure Liam was putting on him, and his accusations about the trust fund and Enright misusing it. It's likely he and Derringham are the active members of the trustees after all.' Longman jutted out his chin and scratched it.

'It's certainly something we need to check on,' Simon agreed. 'If there has been misuse of funds it adds to any motive Enright had for killing Liam, and Ben as well. His closeness to Vita meant that she was unlikely to accuse him.' He looked at Savage and Tremaine. 'Perhaps you could both follow that up.

'Meanwhile,' he continued, 'I'll bring you up to date. I had a fax from toxicology this morning confirming that the poison used on Ben Hartley was indeed from toxins, including,' he glanced at his notebook, 'cardiac glycosides, nerioside and oldendrin derived from oleander and present in the capsules. So no surprises there.

'Yesterday Geoff received the accounts for Liam's and Ben's mobile phones and followed up some of the calls.'

A flash of light seared the room followed by a pause, during which everyone looked up and waited. As the thunder crashed Rhiannon jumped. The room had grown darker. Detective Superintendent Munro got up and went over to fiddle with the light switches. They flickered and steadied.

Simon continued his report on the interviews with Enright, Mara Kennedy and June Taylor. When he had finished and before anyone had time to respond, Munro's chair scraped back and she came to join Simon at the front table, her high heels tapping loudly on the wooden floor.

She stood tall, folding her hands in front of her, composed and immaculate today in peacock-blue. Simon slowly straightened himself from his habitual slouch.

'It seems to me,' she said in her clear contralto, 'that you have a number of potential suspects in this case. But no evidence to speak of. You are long on possibilities and short on probabilities – partly because you haven't yet completed finding out all you need to know.

'I know,' she held up a hand to Savage, 'you've been appallingly short-staffed on this investigation, but I shall be supplying you with some more officers tomorrow.

'So, to summarize, you have means, motive and opportunity with each subject: Lewis Enright has the motive of his ongoing conflict with Liam, Liam's accusations over the trust fund and his assertion that Enright had been having an illicit affair with his sister Vita. He was here at the time that the sandwiches were doctored and also in the house when access must have been gained to Ben's supplements. He had the same access to the poisonous plants used as anyone else.

'Then we have the Taylors. They have the motive of protecting themselves from Liam's threats to get them dismissed. Gavin had the additional motive of revenge for Liam's imputations about his girlfriend Jenny Shipman. Mrs Taylor's alibi for Liam's death depends on Linda Carver being able to assert that June Taylor did not leave the kitchen on that Saturday morning. And that should be thoroughly checked. If she were found to have remained at the house all morning, then to make up identical sandwiches to Liam's, she would need the ingredients to hand if Gavin were to deliver them. Gavin could have collected them from the cottage, supplied them to his mother and then taken them back to replace the ones Liam had made.

'All a bit convoluted, but possible. But it depends heavily on whether Linda Carver can give evidence that Gavin Taylor did come to the kitchen that morning for more than a cup of tea, or that Mrs Taylor left it.

'Then we have other possibilities: Jenny Shipman was very angry with Liam, and she was near the cottage, actually in it on her own admission, before Liam died. She also had motive and opportunity and the means of killing: the poisonous plants were as available to her as to anyone else.'

Lightning flashed and thunder banged very loudly immediately overhead. The lights went out briefly. Simon watched Rhiannon tighten her jaw and keep her eyes fixed on Munro. A sudden wind got up, lifting the papers on the tables. Then, with palpable physical release, the rain began, rattling on the leaves outside, hitting the panes of glass in the upper windows with the sharpness of rapid machinegun-fire. The room suddenly felt chilled.

Munro gestured to Tremaine and Savage to close the windows. Rain was already splattering the tables on that side of the room. Everyone waited while they struggled with the hockey stick and other implements jamming the sashes. Another bang and flash came simultaneously as they worked, making them flinch. By common accord they all watched the storm as the spectacular flashes and bangs continued.

Munro recalled them to her during a brief lull in the noises off by briefly clearing her throat.

'As I said, these are so far your most likely suspects. In each case the motive for killing Liam has been revenge or response to a perceived threat. Your only motive for Ben's death in any of these cases is that he might have known something of the killer and so was killed to silence him. Or that he was a threat to Enright because of the trust fund.'

She walked over to the window and leaned against the rain-streaked glass. 'The question no one seems so far to have raised is the most obvious and traditional one of *cui bono*. Who benefits?'

Longman said frowning, 'Well, they all do if they get Liam out of the way. Enright carries on with his own wicked ways, the Taylors keep their job, Jenny's honour is satisfied—'

'But who benefits financially?' she interrupted.

'Vita,' Simon said flatly into the silence.

Munro turned to face him. 'I gather from the reports I've read that Vita had as much opportunity as anyone else to carry out these poisonings. She certainly has motive for both of the deaths. With her brothers dead she will inherit not one but three million pounds or whatever the trust fund is now worth. And, if her relationship with Enright is as illicit as has been suggested, she has the extra motive of protecting that from Liam's accusations.'

Simon stared at his feet, thinking. Whether or not Munro's theory proved to be true, he was aware that it was something he should have considered himself. It had not occurred to him that the two boys might have been killed by their sister. His mind still resisted the idea. He looked up. The others were quietly talking among themselves. Munro's eyes were still fixed on him.

He said: 'Vita Hartley was in the vicinity of Liam and Ben's cottage on that Saturday morning, working in the plant-sales area and coming to and fro with plants. She could easily have slipped into the cottage and made up the fatal sandwiches. She was also in the house on the evening that we think Ben's supplements must have been interfered with. And, as you say, she had real motives for the murders.' He straightened up. 'I have difficulty in believing that she is the killer though.'

'Don't forget,' Longman said, 'she'd just had Lewis Enright turn up that morning telling her what Liam was threatening once again,' Longman said.

'I seem to remember that yesterday evening you were convinced it was June Taylor who was responsible for the murders,' Simon said a little acidly.

Longman said easily, 'I was convinced we ought to take the idea seriously. I also think we ought to look into this one.'

'Why do you have a problem with this?' Munro asked Simon, moving back from the window where the rain continued to rattle the panes.

He lifted his jacket from the table and shrugged it on, conscious of more than a physical chill in the room.

'I don't have any problem with looking into it,' he said. After all, what was one more distressed female left in his wake?

'But you think it unlikely that Vita Hartley could have been responsible. Did she strike you as being particularly close to her brothers?' Munro leaned beside him against the table.

He couldn't claim that Vita had come across as a doting or adoring sister. Between the three of them, any sibling closeness had seemed to reside only in Ben's faithfulness to Liam. Vita had been distressed on the day she disappeared, but that could just as readily be explained by a reaction to having murdered her brother, or tension over the complications of her relationship with Enright.

No, he had to admit that Munro's theory fitted quite neatly, providing clear motive for both deaths. And, after all, the only other motive they had been able to come up with for Ben's murder had been the slightly insubstantial theory that he had had to be killed because he knew something about who had murdered Liam – or, if it had been Enright responsible, Enright's fears over the trust fund. And that was highly speculative too, since they had no idea yet how the trust fund stood.

He admitted to Munro that he had not noticed any particular evidence of closeness between Vita and her brothers. And Ben had certainly not been a concerned searcher on the afternoon of Vita's disappearance. At the time, while others had been anxiously looking for Vita, it seemed he had been asking Mara's advice about his suspicions of the Taylors. Perhaps he had just not been aware of what was happening with his sister.

'So you'll look into it?' Munro said.

'I'll speak to her right away,' he agreed.

She lifted the cuff of her jacket and consulted an expensive gold watch.

'I thought we might have lunch at the Clifford Arms I've heard so much about. And you're more likely to find Vita available after the lunch period.'

A bang of thunder overhead shook the house: the storm was not moving on. Rhiannon was rigid in her seat. Simon suggested to the team that they make sure all their reports were up to date and take a meal-break until he returned.

'Savage and Tremaine, you can be on your way as soon as possible and see what you can glean about that trust fund.' He was not yet letting go of other strands of the investigation.

CHAPTER 29

Dragonswort – Horror

The rain continued to fall with the same intensity as the sun had shone so relentlessly for so many days. Rumblings of thunder prowled around the house like some wild beast balked of its prey and jagged streaks of light cut the dark sky in pieces. Simon stared through the streaming window panes at the sad bedraggled garden, wondering inconsequentially what the gardeners were finding to do in this pitiless weather. The roses that had scented the room so sweetly had been torn from their stems and lay flattened in the muddy earth.

He turned away from the scene. Only Longman and Rhiannon Jones were left in the room, Rogers and Tremaine having gone about their business. Munro, before she had returned to headquarters, had suggested that, if her idea about Vita proved to be right, his need of more staff had diminished. Feeling dispirited, he had not protested.

Most of the meal had been spent with her asking for details of every aspect of the investigation, at each step apparently savouring her theory and seeming to find that it still tasted good. She had also asked him if he had discussed the case in any depth with Jessie, as she had suggested.

'I seem to remember you cautioning me at one time to never mix the professional and personal in my life,' he had retorted.

She hadn't blinked. 'But I'm suggesting you mix professional and professional,' she replied.

Well, perhaps he would. But he thought that Jessie might now make him ask for her advice and the idea irked him. If Munro's theory was correct, though, he might not have any need to.

'What now?' Longman asked. 'Are you going to speak to Vita?'

'I'll take Rhiannon,' Simon said decisively. 'See if you can get hold of Linda Carver, Geoff. Don't make the interview confrontational, she's a bit of a nervous sort. Just talk her through her memories of last Saturday as gently as you can. And see if you can get any other thoughts or insights from her. She's a quiet type whom others tend not to notice but who picks up on things as a consequence.'

'I'll treat her like a baby,' Longman assured him.

As Simon and Rhiannon crossed the tiled hall at the front of the house they saw Helen Hartley descending the main staircase. It was the first time Simon had seen her since the day Ben had died and the loss of a second son had dramatically reinforced the damage done to her by that first death. She had been a woman full of health and vigour when he had first met her. Now all the light had gone out of her, her eyes dark and shadowed, her skin, previously glowing, looked thin and dry. She held tightly to the banister rail as she descended as if concentrating on the steadiness of her feet. Simon waited until she reached them.

'I'm just going to see Vita,' she said distantly, without any preliminary greeting or acknowledgement.

Her hair was limp, dragged through anyhow with a comb by the look of it, and she was dressed in a thin summer frock; poignantly, some of the buttons at the front were wrongly fastened. Simon glanced through the hall window at the tearing rain.

'Shouldn't you have a coat,' he asked her gently.

She looked vaguely around. 'The umbrellas are here somewhere.' With a small smile she spotted an umbrella stand, walked over to it and pulled out one in rainbow stripes.

'Would you like one?' she asked.

Simon gladly accepted a large black umbrella for himself and Rhiannon. They had both come to work that day ill-equipped for the weather and he was still damp from his short journeys to and from the car.

'The plants will be so grateful for all this rain,' Helen said, making for the recessed door. 'They've suffered so in all that heat.'

Simon wondered if he should call Barbara Meddick but decided to follow on. In the circumstances it would not now be possible to question Vita as planned – he could hardly do so with Helen looking on and in her present state. For the first time he considered the implications of Vita's guilt as they would affect her mother: Helen's already fragile grip on things would be totally shattered.

In the doorway they crowded together, awkwardly opening umbrellas. Simon felt Rhiannon tense beside him as another flash of lightning cut through the sky. He placed an arm around her and held her close under the umbrella as the following thunder crashed overhead. She smiled up at him gratefully.

Helen set off immediately, oblivious of another heavy rain squall, with nothing on her bare feet, he noticed, but a pair of thin sandals.

'I've been neglecting my daughter,' she said over her shoulder to them in an odd, flat voice. 'I haven't seen her for ages. I have to put that right.' She trudged on purposefully.

Simon wondered if Helen had not yet begun joining the others for meals again.

Suddenly she stopped, the water pouring from her umbrella.

'Are you coming to see Vita as well?' she asked with a small frown.

'We'll keep you company,' Simon said after a moment's hesitation.

It seemed to satisfy her. She turned and strode on through the rain. Simon's eyes were fixed on the sad sight of Helen's bare feet getting splattered with mud.

'What are we going to do, sir?' Rhiannon asked in a low voice. 'We can't question Vita with her mother there. She'd go to pieces if she knew what we were up to.'

'We'll just stay with her for now,' Simon said. 'I'll contact Barbara Meddick from the cottage and get her to come and fetch Helen.'

'Don't you think we ought to leave her with her daughter for now? I mean, if the super is right about Vita, she's not going to be seeing much of her daughter for a while.'

As it turned out, these concerns were academic.

Helen, rushing ahead, entered the cottage first, calling in a high voice of pathetic bravado:

'Vita darling, are you there?'

They followed into the hall but were met by Helen returning.

'She must be in one of the greenhouses,' she said, pushing past them.

Raising their umbrella again they hurried to keep up with Helen's dash across the twenty yards or so to the first green-house. She had not bothered with her own umbrella and her hair was quickly plastered to her head, clinging in dripping tendrils around her face. There was no sign of Vita through the stream-ing glass but even so Helen opened the door of the first building and called out again. Then she turned and moved on to the next. The first two buildings were large by domestic standards with two alleyways between three lots of staging. Having looked into both, Helen moved on to a large lean-to greenhouse, its panes white-washed, and went inside, Simon and Rhiannon close behind.

They looked over Helen's shoulders. It was evidently the place where most of Vita's current work was going on: much of the staging was taken up with pots of various sizes filled with what looked like cuttings. Flowering climbing plants took up the back border fronted by a gap and a central set of staging. Another wide border at the front contained a well-cultivated vine. Probably the shading had made the temperature inside the glass tolerable for working in. Towards the far end of the stag-ing bits of greenery were lying on the surface, some pushed inside clear plastic bags, rows of pots filled with compost lined up nearby.

They all stood looking around, the rattling of the rain on the roof adding a cosy feel to the warm earthy smell inside.

'She's not here, either,' Helen said fractiously, her eyes wide and dark. 'It looks as if she's been taking shrub cuttings.'

Simon, with the advantage of height, could see beyond the pieces of plant material to a tall drinking-glass placed beside the pots, evidence that Vita had indeed been here recently. With her habitual tidiness, he doubted that she would have failed to return the glass to the cottage if she had left. He moved gently past Helen and approached the path behind the staging with a sudden sense of foreboding.

For a moment, horrified disbelief rooted him to immobility. Vita's body was sprawled behind the staging, half on her side. He cast a warning glance at Rhiannon and moved forward, his limbs stiff.

'What is it?' Helen's high cry came as he knelt beside the body. There was a stream of saliva hanging from Vita's mouth and her face and neck showed glaring red patches. But her eyes were closed, not wide open as Ben's had been. He put his fingers to the side of her throat. There was a faint, very faint, slow pulse, though her skin was cold and clammy.

He moved her gently into the recovery position, careful that she should not choke on any residual vomit.

'She's still alive,' he said, standing up and sounding calmer than he felt. 'An ambulance will take too long. Rhiannon, go and get Barbara. Get your car out and running and I'll contact emergency services to meet you on the way.'

Rhiannon was out of the door while Helen was still stumbling towards him, gripping the staging as she came and making a low moaning sound. He looked at her with dismay. Coping with two collapsed women was beyond him at this moment.

'Helen!' he said sharply. 'You've got to be strong now and help me if we're going to save Vita.'

She halted the keening sound and stood staring transfixed at Vita's body. He knelt and lifted the girl into his arms.

'Now, get the door open for me,' he said forcefully to Helen.

She turned and blindly made her way to the door, pushing it wide, gripping it as the rain poured down on her and Simon eased himself through with his burden.

Later, Simon had no recollection of his breathless run through the storm to the stables where Rhiannon's car stood waiting. Helen scrambled into the back and he laid Vita on her side across her lap. She silently began smoothing the blonde hair from her daughter's brow.

Barbara got into the passenger seat.

'Drive fast, but carefully,' Simon said to Rhiannon at the wheel. 'Look out for the ambulance. I'll get them to keep the siren on. Put Vita and the others into the ambulance then follow on in your car. I'll be in later.'

Rhiannon gave a brief nod and was away in a stream of spray as Simon got on to the emergency services.

After all the drama he stood there in the rain, oblivious of the fact that he was soaked to the skin, conscious only of a deep and burning rage. As he slowly became aware of the chill penetrating his body he walked into the shelter of the old stables and, tight-lipped, put through a call to Detective Superintendent Munro.

After he had filled her in on events he demanded, heedless of political correctness, 'I want more manpower. I want everyone questioned closely. Absolutely everyone!'

She made no attempt to argue, nor did she waste time on expressions of shock or concern. Simon switched her off abruptly and went to find Longman.

'Bloody hell!' was all Longman said when Simon found him with Linda Carver in the incident room and blurted out details of the latest poisoning. For poisoning it surely was.

Linda Carver rose uncertainly from her chair, a look of dismay on her face.

'Thank you, Mrs Carver,' Simon said abstractedly. 'We'll talk to you again later.'

As she left the room Longman asked, 'Has the usual calling card been left?'

'I haven't had a chance to look,' Simon said tautly, making for the door. 'We'll go and check, shall we?'

He plunged grimly into the rain again, already so drenched that he was uncaring. Longman followed with an equally unhappy expression, his collar held tight around his neck.

It was probably Simon's imagination, but Vita's cottage already felt lifeless and abandoned. The gloom cast by the heavy cloud-cover added to the mournful atmosphere. They moved quietly into the sitting-room, as if afraid of disturbing someone who was no longer present.

'There!' Simon said immediately, his eyes on the table by the window. A vase filled with lily of the valley, innocent white bell-flowers with a delicate perfume that filled the air, stood on the polished surface.

'She grows them in pots,' he said, gesturing to the display on the windowsill. 'They're her mother's favourite flower. None of them liked cut flowers. And why cut them when you've got a pot full growing in the room. It's got to be what the killer left for us to find.'

He got out his phone and called Dr Starkey, quickly giving he details of the latest happenings.

'What do you know about the toxicity of lily of the valley?' he asked.

'It's highly toxic,' she said decisively. 'If that's what it looks like being, you'd better get straight on to the hospital. They'll need to do a stomach lavage. I'll check additional details and ring you back.'

He called Westwich City General and warned them of the imminent arrival of a suspected poisoning case, probably lily of the valley, telling them he'd be giving them more information soon.

'I should think it's more than just 'probably',' Longman said wiping the rain from his face.

'I'm not taking anything for granted,' Simon snapped. 'We're being manipulated, played with. Suppose the killer's used some-thing else and we caused the wrong treatment?'

'True enough.' Longman spread his hands placatingly. 'But how the hell did they get her to take it? After what's happened, nobody around here is going to be too casual about what they're eating.'

Simon went through to the kitchen and opened the gleaming fridge door. It was empty of food apart from an unopened packet of butter and some sealed cartons of yoghurt. The only other items present were a half-empty bottle of spring water, some lemon squash and an unopened carton of milk in the fridge door.

Longman looked into the waste bin. 'Empty,' he said. 'But I understood Vita was having her meals at the house, anyway.'

Simon's phone sounded.

'I've phoned Westwich General myself,' Dr Starkey said. 'They'll need to be quick. The poison is a convallatoxin. It's a glycoside similar to digitalis.'

Simon interrupted. 'Suppose it's some evil red herring and the killer has used something other than lily of the valley.

Would the treatment for this toxin be a problem?'

Dr Starkey paused before answering. 'The difficulty is, several plant poisons can present with similar symptoms. Was she salivating, red patches on her skin?'

'Yes,' Simon said.

'It fits,' she said decisively. 'Anyway, they haven't got time to mess about. They'll have to proceed on the assumption that it's what we think. I'm leaving them with that. I'll speak later.' She rang off.

Simon sank on to a kitchen chair. 'I'm sure the only sources of lily of the valley were either here in Vita's cottage or in her mother's room at the house. She said something about chilling plants to delay flowering, but she grew them for her mother rather than the garden.'

'There might be other pots then, in the greenhouses perhaps, coming into bloom?' Longman said.

'I suppose it doesn't much matter,' Simon said bitterly. 'There's plenty here in this cottage for the killer to cut for his usual taunting display.'

'He'd have to know that Vita had already taken the poison in some form before he did that.' Longman peered through the kitchen windows and turned back. 'We'd better check what she had for breakfast.'

'She doesn't seem to have eaten here and I doubt she had anything different from the others this morning.'

'Mrs Taylor would know,' Longman said pointedly.

'What?' Simon's voice was harsh. 'Are you suggesting that the mad June Taylor, after being questioned by us, set about killing off the remaining child of the family? Because Vita suspected that Ben was killed because he suspected who killed Liam, I suppose?'

Longman pursed his lips and lowered his shaggy eyebrows.

'Unlikely, I agree,' he said consideringly, unfazed by Simon's obvious ire. 'But I can't begin to think of any other motive for Vita's murder. Can you?'

'Not off the top of my head, no.' Simon flipped impatiently at a dripping lock of hair.

'Well, if it wasn't something she ate at the house, we'd better find out if she's been anywhere else to have her food.'

Simon shivered, the chill of his sodden clothing eating into him.

'You'd better get those wet clothes off before we do anything else,' Longman said.

Simon looked up at him. 'There was a tall glass. On the staging next to where Vita was working. The poison could have been in what she was drinking.' He quickly made for the door, Longman following.

There were dregs in the glass. Simon put on gloves and lifted it to his nose.

'Lemony?' he suggested, holding the glass out for Longman to sniff. 'There was lemon squash in the fridge. It was really hot earlier on today. She probably made some up to have while she was working.' He replaced the glass carefully in its original position and took out his phone again.

'Dr Starkey? Detective Inspector Simon once more. Do you know if it's possible that this particular plant poison could be easily transferred to liquid form in some way?'

'Certainly.' Her strong voice could be heard clearly by Longman, standing nearby. 'Children, in particular, have been known to be fatally poisoned by drinking the water that the cut flowers have been standing in. Why? Have you found something?'

'There was a drinking-glass next to where we found her. It looks as if she'd had some lemon squash. She had some in the fridge.'

'That could be it then. Get the glass sent in for analysis. And the lemon-squash bottle.' The bottle of spring water as well, Simon thought.

He rang off, telling Longman what she had said. 'SOC should be here soon,' he said to Longman. 'I'll get them to see to it.'

Now that he had done all that he could immediately, Simon's physical discomfort was beginning to displace even his rage. He shivered again as the chill hit him anew. There was no likelihood of begging a change of clothing from Lewis Enright even if he were present because they wouldn't fit, and it was unthinkable to make the long journey into his flat at Westwich and back. Besides, almost all of his clothes were at Jessie's cottage. Reluctantly he got out his phone again and called her.

She made no bother.

'Too wet for gardening. We're just lying about watching an old Fred Astaire and Ginger Rogers video,' she said, asking no questions. 'I'll be straight over.'

'I'll be sitting on the Aga in the kitchen,' he told her.

CHAPTER 30

Christmas Rose – Tranquillize my anxiety

As far as he knew Vita was still alive, and as he drove into the car park of the brutal-looking Westwich City General Hospital that evening Simon prayed fervently that she would stay that way. He took the lift to intensive care on the fourth floor, the anger he had been feeling overlaid by anxiety and guilt and fear.

He found them in a corner of the large room, Vita smothered in a face-mask and tubes and white as the sheets she lay in. A machine bleeped at her side and Helen was holding fast to one of her hands. Enright sat opposite Helen, mirroring her, clutching at the fingers of Vita's other hand from which trailed plastic lines. Barbara sat beside Helen and was the first to look up as he approached.

'She's stable,' she whispered to him.

Helen dragged her eyes from Vita's face. She looked as pale as her daughter but was composed, that awful vacant look having left her.

'Thank you, Christopher,' she said quietly. It was the first time since the investigation had begun that she had acknowledged any personal connection with him. He was touched, but the feelings of guilt twisted anew. Perhaps he had done something to help save Vita's life, but he had done nothing to save her from the risk of losing it. Thank God nothing had been said of their suspicions about Vita, he thought.

Enright kept his eyes on Vita and said nothing. Barbara stood up and leaned over Helen, planting a kiss on her brow. She gestured to Simon and they walked to the corridor outside where she moved several paces beyond the policeman on duty before turning to him.

'As I said, she's stable at the moment, but they don't know how much damage has been done. We have to wait and see. We should know better by morning.'

She looked tired, her immaculateness somehow smudged at the edges, her face softer. In all the accumulation of disaster that had begun with Liam's death she had kept her icy cool. Now that was gone, showing a gentler, more vulnerable underside.

'The medical staff said they were treating her for poisoning. That it seemed likely the poison was from lily of the valley. Is that right?'

He explained to her what they had found.

'But how could she have eaten anything that was poisoned? She had breakfast with us as usual and we warned her against eating anything that wasn't sealed.'

'She had lemon squash – took it with her to the greenhouse to drink while she worked. The poison from the plant is easily transferred to water.'

Barbara leaned back against the corridor wall, her expression bleak.

'She always used bottled water. Or perhaps it was added to the lemon drink itself. How easy. I wonder, is any of us safe? How do we protect ourselves against someone so determined?' She examined Simon's face. 'But why? Why is all this happening? Are you any closer to finding out?'

He couldn't lie at this moment.

'If I had had any idea, this wouldn't have happened to Vita. I can only promise that I intend to find out. And quickly. Meanwhile, no one should eat or drink anything at all that isn't from an impeccable source, or doesn't come fully sealed.'

The corridor was suddenly filled with the arrival of a patient on a bed surrounded by nurses, doctors and technological apparatus. Barbara and he pressed themselves against the wall as the bed was rushed into the room behind them. Silence prevailed again, that hushed noiseless space filled with hospital smells and human suffering and tears.

'It's the family, not anyone else who's in danger, surely?'

Barbara said, pushing herself from the wall and slowly walking towards the window at the end of the corridor.

'We can't be sure of that,' Simon said beside her. 'Poisoners often seem not to know when to stop.' He sounded calm yet inside his head hurt with ideas and speculations that ran into cul de sacs in his brain. At the moment all he could forsee was unending questionings of both people and ideas, until some light broke, some true pattern emerged, some lies were exposed.

They stood looking out of the window to the car park below. The rain had stopped, the storm had moved on, and lakes of puddles reflected the washed blues and pinks of the evening sky. People emerged from their vehicles clutching bunches of flowers and bags of supplies and gifts, others came out from the hospital entrance below them, arms around each other leaning one to another for comfort. From the silent distance ambulances arrived bringing more damaged lives, and paramedics efficiently went about their business, bringing a kind of order to the chaos of suffering.

'It's a whole world in its way, isn't it?' Barbara mused, her forehead against the glass, dark hair falling across her cheeks. 'You forget, when your own life goes smoothly onwards, that elsewhere lives are disrupted and changed dramatically. It's a bit like a war zone,' she said, turning away.

Her own life could hardly have been termed smooth in the last week or so, Simon thought. Perhaps that was the reason for her sudden empathy.

'How is Helen coping?' he asked. 'I thought she seemed near breaking-point earlier on today.'

'I think she was,' Barbara agreed. She glanced at Simon. 'I had no idea she had gone out. She's been so heavily tranquillized and spending most of her time in her room since Ben died. I'd been keeping an eye on her but trying to occupy myself in the office. She slipped out without my realizing it. Thank God she met you when she went to find Vita. I can't imagine what would have happened if she had been on her own.'

No one seemed to have questioned what Simon had been about at the time, or guessed that he was on his way to see Vita for his own reasons.

'Helen was in a bad way,' he agreed. 'But she seems more alert now.'

Barbara nodded. 'Her fright over Vita seems to have woken her up. But she's been blaming herself for neglecting her while she was in such a state over Ben and Liam. She seems full of guilt, poor love.' She sighed. 'It's grotesquely unfair that she's taking so much on herself. As if she hasn't enough to bear.'

They had reached the door of the ICU again.

'I'd better get back,' Barbara said.

'How's Enright taking it?' Simon asked.

She kept her eyes on Simon's as she spoke, her words deliberate.

'About the same as Helen, I'd say. He's devastated, of course. Vita is the only child they shared as if she were their own.' She gave Simon an odd half-smile. 'I imagine this might lay to rest your suspicions of him at last?'

Simon wondered how much Enright had imparted to Barbara, how close the two of them were. He had tended to think of Barbara in connection only with Helen.

He didn't respond to Barbara's challenge, just rested a hand on her shoulder for a moment before turning to leave.

On the drive to Oxton his earlier feelings of anger and misery resurged. He felt further than ever from any clear direction. The shape and pattern of the investigation shifted like a kaleidoscope with each new death, or attempted murder. And that was all it did, offering no clear image, just another and different broken picture. Barbara's remarks about Enright and Vita at the hospital put yet a different perspective on things. Had they been entirely wrong in going along with June Taylor's insinuations about Enright and his stepdaughter? And, if so, how many other false assumptions had they made about people in this investigation that was so long on words and short on facts?

He felt exhausted, mentally and physically, and was already resenting the reproach he expected to find in his mother's eyes. Jessie, having delivered his change of clothes and been told what had happened to Vita, had said nothing, given him a quick hug and departed, so the news would have gone before him.

Lights were on in the cottage signalling a refuge he didn't feel entitled to. It was getting dark, sullen heavy clouds depressing the efforts of a golden sunset. He went in by the back door to the kitchen.

'We thought we'd wait for you,' his mother said, coming into

the room and planting a rare kiss on his cheek. She handed him
a glass of red wine as Jessie joined them and began taking things
out of the oven.

'Are you ready?' she asked.

He recognized a hunger he hadn't known was there.

'Ready,' he said and took a mouthful of wine.

The meal was comfortable and relaxed. Neither his mother nor
Jessie made any reference to Clifford's Place, but the conversation showed no signs of strain, of things felt but not expressed. It
was obvious to him that between the two of them they had
decided to treat him gently. What came next? he wondered.

When they had finished eating, Elizabeth announced: 'You two
go and relax while I do the washing-up. Then, if you don't mind,
I'm going to bed. There is nothing more exhausting than being
forced to do nothing all day.'

He could have disputed that, but didn't bother: his mother was
merely making an effort at being tactful in leaving them alone
together.

They idly discussed the storm and its effects until Elizabeth put
her head around the door, offering them coffee.

'I'll do that. Thanks, Elizabeth,' Jessie said.

'Goodnight then,' Elizabeth said and closed the door.

'Let's have a fire,' Jessie suggested. 'It feels chilly with all that
dampness in the air. Do it while I make the coffee.'

He was glad enough to obey, to carry out the mundane and
reassuring task of twisting paper and laying kindling, coaxing the
fire to burn in the cold chimney.

When Jessie came back with the coffee, along with some
brandy-balloons, the fire was crackling and flames licking the
logs. Jessie lit some candles and put out the lights so that they sat
in a warm womb, isolated from the night.

For a while they sipped brandy side by side on the sofa and
stared into the flames, Simon feeling warmed and relaxed. Then
Jessie spoke.

'Tell me about it,' she said quietly.

And it was easy to do so, his resistance vanquished by the ease
of his surroundings and an exhaustion that had changed to a
languid passivity helped on by alcohol.

He talked for some time, covering things she already knew

about for the sake of chronological accuracy. He told of suspects, of motives, of unsatisfactory possibilities, of twists and turns and dead ends, and finally ran out of words.

She allowed the silence to continue for a little while, feeding more logs to the flames and sipping her brandy and coffee. Then she moved to sit on the floor and leaned against the sofa, her back to him.

'A murder case puts a lot of pressure on you. And an investigation like this, with a series of attacks and when you can't be sure where and when the next attempt might come, makes for intolerable pressure.'

He waited, hoping that she was not merely about to offer him counselling, a little psychotherapy for an overworked copper.

She said, tentatively, 'I wonder if all that pressure doesn't force you too close to things.'

'Meaning?' he said as neutrally as possible.

She shifted a little and glanced over her shoulder at him.

'I mean that you have followed the logical path, looking at the usual issues of means, motive and opportunity, but you haven't paid much attention to the more unusual aspects of the case.'

'It's fairly unusual in itself to have a series of people poisoned,' he said, keeping his tone reasonable. He didn't want her to stop, but he didn't want this to be a walkover.

'Granted.' He saw her move her head in agreement. 'But can you think of a few things that have puzzled you but that you haven't had time to stop and consider properly?'

'You mean the bunches of flowers left after each murder, for example?' he said.

'Absolutely. Have you asked yourself why they were left?'

He felt resentfully like a rather dimwitted schoolboy being led through an impenetrable piece of comprehension.

'Look, Jess, why don't you just have your say? I'm sure any comment of mine will fall short of your more penetrating interpretations.'

He saw her stiffen and thought for a moment that he had blown it. 'Sorry,' he said hurriedly. 'I'm feeling stupid and bewildered in this investigation and it's making me irritable. I'm also feeling guilty and responsible because two more people have been poisoned, who might not have been if I were better at my job.

And one of them is dead and the other may soon be. And I'm terrified that someone else may die if I don't sort this out soon. You don't need to try and save my pride because it's already lost for the time being. I'll be glad of anything you can say that will throw some light on all this.' He felt rather better for having hit bottom, and got up to fetch the bottle.

'Please,' he said, adding brandy to her glass, 'carry on.' He topped up his own glass and sat down beside her.

'I don't have any solutions, Chris,' she warned him. 'Really, I have only questions. But they are perhaps different ones.'

'Fine,' he said, his eyes on the flickering flames.

'Well, as I said, first there's the question of why the flowers left after each poisoning? There are two aspects to this: first, the killer meant there to be no doubt that the poisoning was deliberate. This of course was more relevant with the first murder – Liam's – because it might have seemed possible that he made a mistake over what he put in his sandwiches, and death by misadventure might have been the coroner's verdict. To underline the fact that the poisoning was deliberate, the killer left Liam's original sandwiches for you to find.

'Which brings me on to the second aspect – which is that the killer wants it known that he or she is glorying in these murders and is stating that he or she is the one in control.'

'And the question is, why? in both cases,' Simon said. 'Why did the killer want me in no doubt that Liam and the others were killed deliberately?'

'Not only that. It tells you something about the character of the murderer. Can you truly believe, for example, that Mrs Taylor, killing out of fear, would embellish her actions in the way that this killer has?

'So one answer to your question is that the poisonous flowers were a taunt.' She paused to sip some brandy. 'But the taunt was not necessarily aimed at you personally, nor the police symbolically. Though that may well be a part of the satisfaction the killer has gained.'

'Then who is it aimed at?' he demanded, unclear of her drift.

'How many victims are there in this case, Chris?' she asked, her eyes on the fire.

'Three. And don't play the schoolteacher with me, Jess. Don't lead me on like a dense pupil.'

She seemed to consider that response for a moment.

'Fair enough,' she said at last. 'But I need to know that you can see things the way I'm seeing them. Isn't there another victim?'

Of course there was.

'Helen.'

Jessie was silent, letting him think about it. Eventually he turned to her, seeing the flickering fire reflected in her dark eyes.

'Are you suggesting that Helen is the intended victim and that her children, or rather her dead children, are the weapons being used to destroy her?' He found it hard to keep the scepticism from his voice.

'I couldn't have put it better myself,' Jessie said.

'But that's obscene and outrageous and . . .' he hesitated, 'impossible.' He reached for his brandy-glass, wishing he still smoked.

'Is it?' Jessie turned to him, her voice more animated. 'Think about it a bit more. You could come up with several motives for people who might want Liam dead. But in any of those cases, wouldn't they have wished to hide the fact that he was murdered, rather than advertise it? Surely, with the motives you have, they would just have wanted him quietly out of the way, with the strong possibility that his death might be considered one of misadventure?

'And aren't all the motives you have for Ben's death based solely on the assumption, without much foundation as far as I can see, that Ben knew, or suspected, who Liam's murderer was and was killed to silence him?

'And why all the palaver with the poisonous plants anyway? Why did Helen's children all have to be poisoned? Wouldn't there have been convenient or alternative methods? *But instead, each of them was poisoned using plants from Helen's garden.* Another thrust at Helen, that her beloved garden, her other great love, should be used as an instrument to kill her children. And if it had to be poison, the murderer could have used wild plants or could much more easily and effectively have used a chemical poison, but instead chose Helen's plants.' She sank back against the sofa and raised her hands, letting them fall to her lap. 'Doesn't all that mean anything to you?'

'It's certainly a point,' he said feebly. It sounded good, he admitted to himself. But the facts that Jessie had homed in on were not the kind of facts that he wanted. He wanted good solid facts of evidence that provided proof. What she was offering was more akin to the subtle shadings of a painting, rather than the clearly drawn picture. The kaleidoscope had shifted again. He didn't know what he thought.

'Chris, these were not killings of fear. They were not carried out because the murderer was afraid of what Liam might do, or say, nor of what Ben knew or might tell you. And surely not what Vita as well might have to hold over the killer. They were not murders of expedience. Can't you see that?' Jessie leaned to put another log on the fire, her movements impatient.

He had to admit to himself that, strange and horrible as Jessie's theory might be, it held a clear rationality. It was the only theory so far that did fit the facts that he had.

'What you say makes sense,' he said slowly. 'I just find it unbelievable at the moment. I can't believe that anyone would hate Helen so much that they would destroy her in such a way.'

' "Whom the gods seek to destroy, they first make mad",' Jessie quoted.

'And it was succeeding,' Simon said. 'She seemed to be going out of her mind. But she's sane again now. As long as Vita stays alive.'

'So you're beginning to see the possibilities in what I've said?'

'Yes. But I'm not sure where it's leading me. I need to look at everything quite differently.' He knew he must sound obtuse, even perverse, but he had nevertheless to hang on to the integrity of his own perceptions.

'There's another thing,' Jessie said, shifting again so that she faced him more squarely. 'The matter of the phones, particularly Ben's phone. By the way, has the same thing happened with Vita's phone?'

He had forgotten to check. Or, more charitably, had had little chance to, what with everything else that had gone on.

'I don't know yet,' he said. 'Anyway, what's your point?'

'Why were they left in such a way that it would be obvious they had been taken from Liam and Ben deliberately; in Ben's case, still switched on?'

'I've already thought about that. Another gibe, I suppose. Another taunt, a statement that the killer had taken their phones from them so that they couldn't call anyone when they were taken violently ill. It would have been too modest of the killer to simply steal the phones and put them where it might look as if Ben or Liam might have mislaid them. The way it was done meant that once again the murderer underlined his or her power or cleverness or whatever.'

'There's certainly that,' Jessie said, her voice less approving than her words.

'You mean there's something more?' he said a touch irritably. 'Well, what?'

Jessie shrugged. 'Maybe nothing. I'll leave it with you.'

CHAPTER 31

Arbor Vitae – Unchanging friendship

Imperceptibly, by mid-morning of the next day Jessie's suggestions had woven their way into Simon's consciousness. By then he seemed unable to view the case from any other perpective and the current strands of the investigation now seemed hopelessly pedestrian. With Vita's attempted murder the perspective had anyway had to change. As Jessie had said, was he to believe that every murder attempt after Liam was merely consequent on something that Liam had done or said? The fact was, he had no useful way of looking at the case other than the one Jessie had suggested. He could not believe that each of the children had supplied individual motives for their murders, so the motives had to be somehow consequent upon who they were. If it was just an insane serial poisoner they were dealing with here, his or her targets were not random enough – which brought him back to the original proposition.

He had listened with only half an ear to Savage and Tremaine report on their enquiries into the trust fund and heard without surprise that Derringham, no doubt on Enright's advice, had allowed them access to the latest, apparently irreproachable figures. So Enright, apparently the only person with any motive to kill all three of Helen's children, was found to have no motive after all.

Longman's latest interview had been equally infertile. Linda Carver had reported that Gavin Taylor had indeed come into the kitchen on the morning of Liam's death, but only for his usual cup of tea. No unusual activity had been noted and June Taylor had remained there for the duration of the period in question. It was still feasible that Gavin Taylor could have gone into Liam and Ben's cottage that morning and changed Liam's sandwiches. But there had been equal opportunity for others as well. Simon continued to discount the Taylors as possible suspects if for no other reason, as he told the team, than that the floral flourishes left as a trademark after each murder were just not in keeping with the unimaginative Taylors.

The team, joined by two additional detective constables sent with Superintendent Munro's blessing, were dispirited enough after the attempted murder of Vita: the apparent dead ends of these latest enquiries produced an atmosphere of intense gloom. He had said nothing to them of Professor Thurrow's insights into the case. Routine work still had to be done, thoroughly and efficiently done. He set them to questioning everyone asssociated with the case – except Barbara Meddick and Alan Fairburn, whom he reserved for himself – particularly with regard to anyone seen in the vicinity of Vita's cottage on the morning before and also the evening before that.

As Rhiannon Jones had pointed out, these would be enquiries of ambiguous merit, since, given the location of Vita's cottage, several people had good cause to be near there, both to collect plants from the nursery and to work in the vegetable parterre close by. Not to mention access to the supplies in the service area. Nevertheless he wanted clear accounts of times and activities, of people seen or not seen. And everyone was to be reminded once more to take care of what they imbibed or ate. In addition, Vita's phone needed to be located. It had certainly not been with her when she was found in the greenhouse, and an earlier enquiry had established that she did possess one.

Now, as Simon drove back to the hospital in Westwich, he could only wonder what Helen Hartley might have done in her life to arouse such bitter hatred that someone needed to destroy her children and her sanity. From what he had seen and knew of Helen he found it hard to imagine that she was the sort of woman to have deliberately set out to hurt or damage anyone. But he could talk to people who knew something of her past.

The latest reports on Vita had been positive, so he travelled to Westwich with a somewhat lighter heart than he had the day before, a lighter heart but a brain perhaps more fogged than ever by the almost blank image of Helen's earlier life. And he could be wrong in assuming that this bitter rage in someone had been aroused by something Helen had done in the distant past. What if it were more recent in origin? Barbara Meddick should know, and Alan Fairburn might be aware of anything further back in time. And either of these could be a potential suspect. And however carefully he questioned them, if guilt were present then so too would be a self-protective wariness of his probings.

He recalled something June Taylor had said about Barbara Meddick and Lewis Enright – that while Gerald Hartley had still been alive the two of them had apparently been in a relationship. This would presumably have been after Barbara had started working for Helen, since she had joined Helen after Helen had married Gerald. So it would have been when Enright had visited as a friend of Gerald – as well as of Barbara. It was more than possible, then, that some bitter resentment lingered in Barbara if, after Gerald's death, Helen had coolly taken Lewis Enright from her. Barbara had been Gerald's secretary when he had met Helen. Perhaps Helen had shattered even earlier hopes that Barbara might have cherished in relation to her boss, so that Helen had destroyed Barbara's relationships more than once.

It was perfectly possible. But, Simon's favourite question in a murder inquiry was, why now? All this had happened years ago, so why would any repressed rage have resurged so recently?

Unless – the idea uncoiled like a snake – Enright and Barbara had resumed their earlier relationship and Barbara had, not long since, once again been cast aside, leaving her rival Helen yet again the triumphant possessor of everything she, Barbara, lacked: husband, children, successful career. That may have been how it was, but he had to concede that the idea lacked any real substance. Barbara appeared to be genuinely fond of Helen. Though that could be a deceptive performance. After all, until yesterday he had been convinced that Lewis Enright was having an illicit relationship with his stepdaughter. That might still be the case, though Simon was beginning to doubt it.

He turned off the Cotswold byway on to the long straight road that ran into Westwich and was forced by the speed of traffic and the spray flying from surface water to pay greater attention to his driving. British summer had returned and it was raining undramatically and persistently.

The ugly concrete hospital building was streaked unbeautifully with wet patches that bled from every windowsill, and he had trouble parking. Vita was still in intensive care and only Helen and Barbara remained with her. Her colour was less ghastly and her mother too looked less ill, though excessively tired, with dark shadows under her eyes. Both women looked up at him and gave faint smiles.

'She's going to be all right,' Barbara said firmly, as much, it seemed, to Helen as to himself.

'They're moving her to a private room later today,' Helen said. 'That's good, isn't it? It will be easier to look after her there. She'll be safe.' She studied his face as if for reassurance.

'She'll be safe,' he agreed. 'And the constable will stay.' One constable or another would stay anyway. The young one from the evening before had been replaced by a solid middle-aged presence.

'I'll be able to share her room and be with her.' Helen turned to her daughter again and clasped her hand. 'She feels warmer now.'

'Do they have any idea when Vita will regain consciousness?' Simon asked Barbara.

'She did surface briefly, but she wasn't really aware of what was going on. They think she'll wake up today some time.' Barbara sounded calm and satisfied, a voice of welcome normality. Helen seemed in part to have retreated to a fragile facsimile of herself. But she had probably been awake all night, afraid to sleep.

'I'm so very glad,' Simon said quietly to Helen.

She smiled sweetly and fleetingly at him.

'Would you care to go for a coffee in the cafeteria?' Barbara asked him.

Simon looked questioningly at Helen, who was once again absorbed by her daughter's face.

Barbara raised her voice slightly. 'You wouldn't mind, would you, Helen, if I go with Chris for a coffee? Unless you would like to come too? You could do with a break for a little while.'

'No, Barbara, please go yourself. You deserve to get out for a little while. You've been here all night too.' She tore her eyes away from Vita. 'But you can bring me some tea when you come back, if you wouldn't mind.'

'I'll do that. If you're sure?' Barbara stood up and, as she had the evening before, planted a kiss on Helen's brow.

She led the way into the corridor and they waited for the lift. Simon asked if they had managed to have any meals.

'Helen didn't eat much last night, but I persuaded her to swallow some toast this morning with some tea. It was a ghastly night, trying to sleep in those chairs. But I couldn't leave Helen.'

'Enright didn't stay, then?' he asked as the lift pinged.

'Not all night.' They stepped into the lift and she pressed one of the buttons. 'He stayed until they said they thought Vita would be all right. That was in the early hours. He went home to get a little sleep and brought us in some clothes and things early this morning.' She looked down at the fabric of the rich brown trouser suit she was wearing, a cream undervest beneath. 'It's hard to believe that the hot weather has broken at last. Still, it's warm enough in a hospital. Too warm if you ask me.'

Simon found the idea of Lewis Enright scurrying around selecting items of women's clothing and toiletries mildly cheering and humanizing.

The cafeteria on the ground floor was busy with refugees from the wards in their dressing-gowns and dressings accompanied by their visitors. Outside in a small courtyard, pressed against the shelter of the building, were the recalcitrant smokers, several in wheelchairs or on crutches. Simon collected coffee and biscuits and joined Barbara in a quiet corner sheltered by a plastic palm-tree. The coffee was strong and bitter but Barbara seemed indifferent to the fact, sipping it quickly and gratefully.

'Nothing new to report?' she asked.

A lot had happened since he had last seen her, but it had been inside his head rather than of the nature she was asking for, and nothing he could reveal to her.

'Not yet" he said

She twirled a spoon in her cup, looking remarkably composed and restored to her former elegance despite a less than restful night.

'Poor Helen,' she said. 'I hope to God she can recover from all this.'

'You've known her a long time,' he said. It seemed an age since he had first had that talk with Barbara in the rose arbour on a hot summer's day at Clifford's Place. She had been a bit of a mystery to him then and in many ways was an even greater one now. Why had this attractive elegant woman buried herself in the remote country to work for another woman in a situation where she would remain a mere appendage to her friend's successful career? Why had she apparently forgone any independent life of her own? He was enough Jessie's man not to demand why she had not made a marriage of her own with a family to go with it, but the question did hover about his thoughts.

'You think I'm a bit of a puzzle, don't you?' she said, a slight smile about her mouth.

'You're very perceptive,' he said drily.

'You don't have enough of a poker face for a policeman. It's a very sensitive face, yours, but a bit of a handicap at times, I imagine.'

Annoyed with himself, he felt his colour rising and took a mouthful of coffee.

'Your looks, too,' she went on, 'probably make for difficulties. I've seen the way that young female detective constable can't keep her eyes off you.' Her smile broadened into one of amusement.

'I think she wants to take me home and iron my shirts,' he said.

'Oh, I think she'd like to do rather more than that.'

'Is this attack as a form of defence?' he asked.

'Do I need to defend myself?' She raised one of her perfectly shaped eyebrows.

'From the thoughts I was having about you, as you so acutely perceived.'

'No defence needed. But why do I puzzle you?' She calmly sipped her coffee.

It was a difficult question to answer without in some way seeming to demean her, but he made an effort.

'I suppose I wonder why a woman of your calibre devotes her life to the needs of another woman and appears to have comparatively little life of her own.'

'But I have an extremely pleasant life,' she said, leaning back in her chair and eyeing him quizzically. 'Or is this male chauvinist dismay that an eligible female seems to be happy enough without a man?'

'You were in a relationship with Lewis Enright at one time, weren't you?' he asked casually.

'Now where did you hear that?' she asked, apparently unmoved. 'Mrs Taylor, no doubt. She's excellent at her job but a bit of a gossip with an imagination to go with it, which can make for difficulties at times.'

'Is she wrong?' Simon didn't bother to deny it. The maelstrom that was Clifford's Place could hardly be made much worse.

'No, she's not wrong.' Her long fingers played with the spoon in her saucer, tapping it gently, rhythmically.

'What happened?' he asked.

'You mean, I imagine, why is Lewis now with Helen rather than with me?'

He nodded and drained his coffee-cup, grimacing slightly at the bitter dregs. At least it was real coffee, if a bit overcooked.

'We were more friends than lovers, Lewis and I. The heat had gone out of any passion that had been there some time before Gerald died and Lewis turned his attentions to Helen. We were company for each other in the big lonely city, going to the theatre, for meals, to fill an empty evening for each other now and again.' She dropped the spoon into the saucer and looked up at Simon. 'I'm not the type that Lewis falls for. He is an old-fashioned male who likes to have a woman he can feel protective towards. I'm far too emotionally independent for him.'

She hadn't said whether Lewis was the type for her, though.

'But did he suit you, even if you didn't suit him?' Simon asked.

'I didn't want to marry him,' she said a bit disdainfully.

He propped his chin in his hand, studying her face.

'Have you ever felt that way about anyone?'

'Passion doesn't last,' she said lightly. 'And marriage becomes routine in almost every case. I might wish sometimes that I had been someone, like Helen, who had really wanted marriage, but I'm afraid I'm not.'

He felt a sudden rush of depression, reminded of Jessie. Was this how she felt? he wondered.

'We understand that Liam had been implying that Enright's relationship with Vita wasn't quite what it should be,' he said. 'I assume that was a lie, as with other things he accused Enright of?'

She gave a quick amused laugh. 'Lewis told me he'd been forced to admit to Liam's slander. Liam did the same thing with Lewis and me, suggesting we were having an affair. Fortunately I got to the little toe-rag before he upset Helen with his accusations. He could be a really nasty little beast if anyone thwarted him.'

'So you managed to persuade him to shut up? How did you do that?'

'I called his bluff. Told him I would report to his mother what he had been saying, along with details of his unsavoury behaviour towards other people and make a strong recommendation that he should get some more experience in another garden, preferably some distance away. He backed off,' she said.

He realized that she hadn't actually denied the accusations against Enright and Vita.

'So what he was saying about his sister and stepfather was a complete fabrication? I ask, because when I interviewed Vita she seemed very conscious around the subject of Enright – as if there was something going on.'

Barbara gave Simon a look of amused condescension.

'She would, wouldn't she? She was thoroughly embarrassed and upset that her relationship with Lewis should be seen as anything other than innocent. Lewis felt he had to warn her what Liam was saying and by the time you talked to her she was afraid of it all coming out again. I don't suppose for a moment that even Liam believed what he was saying about them. It was just another nasty way of trying to manipulate his stepfather into giving him money.'

Simon wished he had spoken about it to Barbara before. It had been embarrassed consciousness in Vita that had lookd like guilt. So much of this case had been dogged by speculation and innuendo – most of it deriving from Liam himself.

'Tell me about Gerald Hartley,' he said.

She had been gazing out of the window. Now her eyes flashed quickly to his face and a spot of colour appeared on her cheeks.

'Why?' she demanded.

He had evidently touched a nerve, but if he pressed on it too hard she might clam up.

'I'd like to know a little more about Helen's background. How did he and Helen come to meet?'

'An after-show party. Gerald had helped fund a theatre production and Helen had a small part in the play. He was smitten with her rather quickly and they married only a couple of months later.'

'What did you think of her when you first met her?'

'I thought she was beautiful but that she couldn't quite believe her luck,' Barbara said with a wry smile. 'I think she'd been having rather a lean time. She wasn't very sure of herself. I thought she seemed a bit depressed even – rather low, anyway. I met her first when Gerald had her call at the office not long after they got to know each other. I certainly didn't feel she was throwing herself at Gerald, in fact she seemed a bit unsure about it all. She always had that rather diffident quality that people find so attractive.' Barbara picked up her cup and slowly sipped. 'She seemed to come round rather suddenly in the end and Gerald didn't want to wait.'

'Was Gerald a similar man to Lewis?'

'Is this idle curiosity?'

'Of course not. You'll just have to trust that I have some purpose in asking.'

'How mysterious,' she said with a trace of sarcasm. 'Yours is a strange job. So much perpetual sitting in judgement of people, watching their words, their every gesture. It must require a quite different kind of consciousness from the rest of us.'

She was right that people's subtleties of behaviour were the material that he worked with, that constantly assessing them became as natural as breathing. It was a form of applied psychology.

'The difficulties come when one starts experiencing that sort of consciousness of one's own behaviour,' he said, smiling.

'I imagine so. Does it follow inevitably from the other?'

'Not always.'

'I imagine that having a stringent partner encourages it,' Barbara remarked drily. 'Professor of psychology, Helen told me.'

'Can we get back to where we were?' Simon asked. 'I was

asking you if Gerald was a similar man to Lewis.'

She leaned away, gazing through the window as if her interests were disengaged.

'No,' Gerald wasn't very like Lewis. He was physically very different for a start, taller, leaner, less the intense dynamo that Lewis is. But his children were very important to him. He'd always wanted a family of his own.' She laughed briefly. 'I think he had dynastic leanings. So he bought Clifford's Place for Helen and his descendants. While Liam was still a baby Helen had already started on the gardens and found her real vocation. It pleased Gerald. He was very proud of her. By the time she had started running her gardening-classes it was obvious she would be needing more help on the administrative side, which was where I came in. As I told you before, Gerald was all for me coming to work with Helen even though it meant him getting used to a new PA. He was a generous man, nicer, better-natured than Lewis – just fiercely protective of his family.'

'Was he more your type?'

She wrinkled her nose as if a bad smell had emerged.

'You're being very crass,' she said.

'I'm sorry. I believe it goes with the job. I'm not entirely insensitive, I just behave that way sometimes.' He gave an apologetic smile.

'I wonder what you're getting at,' she said, narrowing her eyes and studying his face in turn. 'I'm not entirely stupid, you know. Am I perhaps on your list of suspects now?'

Simon picked up a biscuit and toyed with it, breaking crumbs on the table.

'But what possible motive could you imagine I would have for killing Helen's children?' she breathed. She made a sudden movement and the spoon clattered from her saucer. 'Let me think. It could only be some kind of attack on Helen, couldn't it? Do you imagine that I'm wreaking a horrible revenge on Helen for some unimaginable reason? Ah,' she slapped the table with her palm, 'you think maybe that I have a deep burning jealousy of Helen for taking Lewis from me, is that it? Perhaps you even imagine I was cheated out of Gerald and have been nursing a wicked desire for revenge all these years.' Her scorn could not have been more obvious.

There was an ambiguous kind of relief in having the nature of the motive acknowledged even while she derided its interpretation. But he kept his expression bland.

'What an extraordinary idea,' he said. 'And have you?'

He expected her to react angrily, to walk out on him.

Instead she said simply, 'I love Helen.' She waved a manicured hand at him. 'Oh, I'm not a lesbian. But I have a friend in Helen, and it is a friendship that has counted more for me than any relationship I have had with a man. Perhaps it's something about Helen, that she arouses everyone's protective instinct. But it's a two-way thing with her because she is gentle, generous and kind.' Barbara gave a quick frown. 'There is an underlying sadness in her of some sort that I think people try to heal her of.' She shook her head. 'Whatever it is, I have been far happier working with Helen and living with her than I was working in testosterone city.'

Barbara clasped her hands and studied them. 'It's a peaceful existence. At least it was until all this happened. And now Helen needs me more than ever. Perhaps that's what she gives me that no one else has done, the feeling that I'm really needed.'

Simon couldn't doubt her. She who appeared to need no one needed someone who needed her. This didn't seem to be any act. It was true what she said about Helen, she did have a special quality that drew sympathy and warmth from others. She had that elusive quality called charm – something that could not be taught, despite the old-fashioned charm schools that used to try. In a world where people seemed to grow ever more assertive, Helen, despite her success, had an attractively self-effacing quality. It probably had a lot to do with her success in her career and particularly in her television presentations, where she allowed the flowers and plants to be the stars. She exuded a gentle sympathy that worked well in the world of horticulture. That world, as his mother had complained, had become flashier and more dynamic, but the mainstream of gardeners still had a reverence for their work that Helen managed to convey perfectly.

'Thank you,' he said quietly.

She was frowning again. 'Is that the way your thoughts are going? That the children have been murdered because of Helen?'

He hesitated. 'I think it's a possibility,' he said carefully.

'How utterly evil.' She looked at him, eyes wide. 'But who? Surely not?'

He splayed his hands. 'As I said, it's just a possibility. Have you any idea of anyone who might have some nasty grudge against Helen?'

'No, I haven't,' she said emphatically. 'Not Helen. She's not the kind that has ever trodden on others to get to the top. I've never known her do or say an unkind thing. And she is always decent in her dealings with people, whether they work for her, or she is working for them.'

He sighed. 'Maybe not, then.'

'I haven't known Helen all her life,' Barbara said less certainly. 'I suppose there may be something in her past. But who? Who could it be that's done this? We all know one another well enough. Except . . .' she chewed her lower lip. 'I wonder if Alan Fairburn might be able to help? He's the only person who knew Helen before any of the rest of us did.'

'Yes, I've arranged to speak to him today.'

'I can't imagine what Helen could have done,' she said thoughtfully. 'Though she did seem a bit uneasy about Alan's arrival. She wasn't exactly comfortable with him. Even so, I hope Alan can shed some light.' She pushed back her chair. 'I must get back to Helen.'

CHAPTER 32

Narcissus – Egotism

In the early afternoon Rhiannon Jones accompanied Simon for their interview with Alan Fairburn. Drizzle misted the fields and leaves seeped water, splattering the windscreen.

'Depressing, isn't it.' Rhiannon said.

'Are you referring to the weather or the investigation?'

'Both, I think. I mean, do we know where we're going with this case any more, sir? We seem to have suspects but they don't turn out to be satisfactory. It's a whole week now since Liam was killed and the first week is the make or break time in a murder investigation.' She sighed. 'Sorry sir. I think we're all a bit depressed after what's happened to Vita. We feel we've failed.'

'Well, at least don't let the weather get you down,' Simon said sardonically.

Rhiannon, ever ready to please Simon, made an effort to infuse a little brightness into her manner.

'Why are we interviewing Alan Fairburn? Do you think he's involved in some way?'

Simon, who had a reprehensible tendency to reticence when it came to Jessie's contributions to his ideas, debated whether to tell her of the direction his thoughts were now taking. He decided there was no reason not to, especially as the drift of his questions to Alan Fairburn would be fairly obvious. Besides, he would be interested in Rhiannon's reaction.

'I'm looking at the case from a different perspective. All our enquiries have been based on the assumption that it was Liam who prompted the poisonings because of something he did or threatened to do. The only motive we could think of for Ben's murder was that he knew something about Liam's murderer and was killed to keep him quiet. With Vita attacked in the same way it seems to be stretching the theory too far to imagine the same motive applies. I admit that Enright might have had a separate motive for all three of them if he really had been plundering the trust fund. But it seems he hasn't.

'Then there's also the peculiar behaviour of the murderer in first blatantly advertising the fact that Liam's death was no accident and then underlining all the poisonings by leaving an indication of the poison used in the form of a display of flowers from the poisonous plants. Not the behaviour of a killer who wants his victim's deaths to be as mysterious as possible.'

Simon glanced at Rhiannon to see how she was taking it so far. Her eyes were on his face, her expression absorbed. Remembering Barbara Meddick's mocking comments about Rhiannon's attitude to himself, he didn't allow himself to feel encouraged that it was merely his reasoning that was fascinating her.

'So,' he went on, 'we have a killer who is flaunting these murders, and who is not acting out of the kind of fear that drives many people to murder. The murderer wants there to be no doubt that the deaths are deliberate and, significantly perhaps, uses plants from Helen Hartley's garden as the weapon of choice.

'All this suggests we have a killer whose business is not just to kill but to be seen to glory in it. It raises the question of whether it is the other victim in this case who is the main object of the murder's intention to destroy.'

There was a moment's silence. Then Rhiannon's eyes widened.

'You mean Helen Hartley?'

'Yes. I'm considering the possibility that Helen Hartley's children have been killed as a deliberate act of revenge or attack against her. That they've been used as the murder weapons.'

'That's terrible,' Rhiannon breathed, staring ahead of her.

'But feasible.' He tried not to make it a question.

'Oh, yes,' her eyes came back to him. 'Quite feasible. It fits, doesn't it? And it's not such an unusual thing either. Although I suppose it is nowadays in modern Britain.'

'How do you mean?' he asked. They were entering Chairford and he slowed to enter the speed limit.

'I'm a bit of a fan of historical fiction,' Rhiannon confessed. 'It's the kind of thing that went on years ago, isn't it. Part of breaking your enemy's morale, or just wreaking revenge. And in this case the killer has certainly been succeeding with Helen Hartley. She was right on the edge of cracking up yesterday.'

'She seems better today,' Simon said, turning into the lane leading to The Forge. 'She's focused on Vita's recovery.'

'Ben was very worried about Vita, you know. It makes me wonder if he had an inkling of what was going on. That day we were searching for her he was really quite frightened that something had happened to her, didn't seem to think that she'd just gone off to be on her own for a while.'

Simon parked carefully beside Jenny Shipman as she fastened her charges into the back of her car. She turned as he got out to stand beside her.

'They're being impossible. It's being shut in from the rain after so much freedom in the sunshine. So I'm taking them to the Play House and they can work off their energies there. I hope.' Squeals came from the back seat.

'It should work,' Rhiannon said. 'I took my nephews there recently. They loved it – all bouncy castles and feet deep in plastic balls so they can't hurt themselves.'

'Huh!' Jenny said, opening the driver door. 'It's the other kids I worry about.' She paused. 'How is Vita?'

Simon gave her the latest medical bulletin.

'I'm glad,' she said. 'It would have been too terrible for poor Helen if she had lost Vita too.' She made a gesture of farewell, slid into the driving-seat and started the engine.

Alan Fairburn was already waiting for them at the open front door. He showed them into the sitting-room, and this time Simon selected the chair with its back to the window. In the meagre light offered by this grey day he had no wish to miss any nuance of Fairburn's responses to his questions.

'I was appalled to hear that Vita had been poisoned too,' Fairburn said, sinking into the huge sofa. 'Is she going to be all right?'

Rhiannon settled herself at a side table while Simon gave him the same reply he had given Jenny.

'I'm so relieved,' Fairburn said. 'It would have been more than

Helen could bear. And I do know a small part of what she has been going through, having so recently lost my son.'

'I'm sure,' Simon said quietly.

Fairburn leaned forward, resting his elbows on his knees.

'But why do you need to speak to me again, Chief Inspector? I don't know any more about what's been going on than the last time you spoke to me. Or have you come to question my alibi in relation to what happened to Vita?'

'It's routine. We could get that out of the way, if you like,' Simon said.

'I don't even know what time-period I need an alibi for,' Fairburn said, his injured tone suggesting this was alibi enough.

'Yesterday morning, Friday, and the evening before that, if you wouldn't mind.'

'Now let me see.' Fairburn rested his chin on his fist in a poor imitation of Rodin's Thinker.

Did the man never stop acting? Simon wondered. He had known Simon was coming to see him and must have been aware that the subject of an alibi was likely to come up and more or less what timenscale it would be needed for.

'Yes,' Fairburn said, as if having found the answer to some supreme intellectual challenge. 'On Thursday I went to London to see my wife Gina and got back here around midnight. Yesterday morning, like everyone else, I imagine, I was locked in with the others by the storm.'

'The rain didn't start until mid-morning,' Simon pointed out.

'I'm a late riser,' Fairburn said smoothly.

As an alibi it didn't amount to much. Fairburn could feasibly have prowled around Clifford's Place on Thursday night, perhaps when Vita was out of the way, having her evening meal at the house. They could check with Fairburn's wife what time he left London. Though she was likely to have been told to endorse her husband's account. As for the late rising next day, The Forge was a big enough house for Fairburn to have slipped away unnoticed and walked to Clifford's Place early on Friday, again while Vita was having a meal in the main building.

But any motive for such activity on Fairburn's part was as seemingly remote now as before. Though he did fit with one of Simon's questions – the 'why now?' He was something that had 'happened' recently, someone new on the scene. Could Fairburn's recent appearance possibly have been a factor in provoking the murders at this particular time?

'Perhaps you would give Detective Constable Jones details of how we might contact your wife,' Simon said.

Obligingly Fairburn quoted address and telephone numbers. 'What else?' he asked wearily, sinking back into the sofa.

'I'd like to know what you can tell me about Helen Hartley's earlier life.' Simon said.

Fairburn arched his eyebrows. 'Whatever for? You surely don't think that Helen has been poisoning her brood, do you?'

'A strange leap of thought,' Simon said. 'Why would you think that? Is there something in Mrs Hartley's background to make anyone jump to such a conclusion?'

'Of course not,' Fairburn frowned. 'I just don't understand why you think Helen's early life has anything to do with what's been happening to her children.'

'You don't need to,' Simon said.

'All right,' Fairburn agreed, with a theatrical shrug. 'I think I told you that I met Helen at drama school. She was the only child of parents who were dead and she was brought up by a doting and elderly aunt, now also deceased, Helen told me recently.

'As I told you before, Helen was a good actor but neither of us had a lot of luck with getting work. We lived together.' He hesitated.

'For how long?' Simon asked.

'Just over two years.'

'Did anything dramatic happen in the time you were with Helen?'

'Dramatic? That's an apposite choice of word.' Fairburn gave a short laugh. Simon waited.

'Helen got pregnant.' Fairburn leaned forward, his hands clasped between his knees. 'There was no question of my deserting her, you understand,' he said.

Yet the fact that Fairburn had even referred to the possibility managed to convey both insensitivity and self-congratulation.

'She had the child?'

'Oh yes, there was no thought of anything else. But times were difficult for us and it was especially hard on Helen.' Fairburn stopped, a pained expression on his face.

'What happened?'

'You have to understand it was a very sickly child. Helen had not eaten very well during the pregnancy because we were so short of money, and that may have been why. Anyway, after the birth, Helen became very depressed, post-natal depression I expect, and she couldn't cope with the baby, who really was very weak.' The pained look intensified, his eyebrows knitting with sincerity of feeling. 'She decided to put the baby into a home. The terrible thing was that the baby died shortly afterwards and that put Helen into an even worse pit of despair. She felt so guilty, you see.'

Simon didn't ask why it was that Fairburn had not taken over responsibility for the child. In all charitableness, perhaps he had been unable to cope with both of them, and in straitened circumstances.

'How long did your relationship last after that?' he asked.

Fairburn hung his head. 'Not long. While I was away in the States following up the hope of some work, Helen met Gerald Hartley. He would have offered her the security and support that she needed at that time.' He looked up. 'So I didn't come back. There was nothing to come back for.'

He had implied that he was the victim of the situation, Simon thought. Poor Helen. It was becoming a refrain, but one that he should have paid attention to sooner.

Helen had lost three children altogether. Was it because of this first child whom she had lost that, irrationally, she seemed to be feeling such guilt over her dead sons and Vita, as Barbara had reported?

'Nothing else happened to Helen during the time you knew her?' Simon asked.

'It was enough, wasn't it?' Fairburn said, his mid-Atlantic drawl pronounced.

'Were you greatly affected by all this?'

'Sure I was. I loved Helen very much.'

Fairburn had not included the baby in his answer. Had he blamed Helen for the fact that it had died? Had the recent death of his latest child unbalanced his mind enough for him to want to punish Helen with the loss of her own children? The gestures with the flowers left after the murders were a theatrical enough touch to have come from Fairburn.

A pale watery sunshine broke through, unkindly illuminating the lines on Fairburn's face.

'I don't seem to have much luck with parenthood, do I?' His hazel eyes were bright with what might be emotion.

'No. Nor Helen,' Simon agreed evenly. He was feeling a stir of interest, nonetheless. Was it possible, though, that someone as egotistical as Fairburn would risk his precious freedom in such dangerous acts of revenge? Was it even possible that anyone as self-centred as Fairburn could care that much about the loss of a child? But psychopaths were, of course, supreme egotists.

'You didn't meet Helen again until you came to stay with the Wheatleys, is that right?'

'We lost touch completely,' Fairburn agreed. 'Though even in America I couldn't fail to hear of her fame. She's designed gardens for film stars and rock stars over there.'

There was nothing more Simon could think of to ask him for the moment. It seemed worth thoroughly checking his alibi, though. He pulled himself with some effort from the soft chair.

'Thank you Mr Fairburn. We'll see ourselves out.'

Fairburn followed them to the front door and stood watching them walk back to the car. As she opened the passenger door Rhiannon said meaningfully:

'What do you think, sir?'

'What are you thinking, Rhiannon?'

'He fits, doesn't he?' she said as they buckled their seat belts.

She could hardly have chosen an expression less agreeable to Simon. 'Fitting suspects to our theories and scenarios is what leads to some of the most notorious miscarriages of justice,' he said. He was hypocritically aware that he had done exactly as she had done – it was having it articulated that caused him to recoil.

She looked dismayed. 'I know that sir. But not always. And we have to have some idea in our minds of what might have been going on as a motive. What you said earlier made sense. And I just wondered if Alan Fairburn might have flipped or something after his little boy died recently. And if maybe he blamed Mrs Hartley for the death of that first child and seeing her so nicely set up with a family of her own he decided to get back at her.' It came out all of a rush, as if Rhiannon was determined to have her say come what might.

Now that his own thoughts had been so swiftly summarized, Simon could only feel that it did indeed all seem a bit too pat.

Rhiannon, pink-faced, was looking at him anxiously as he started the car.

'It could be that you're right,' Simon said, relenting. 'I had the same thoughts. But I'm not so sure that Fairburn himself is the type to behave in the way we're thinking. I just can't believe he's capable of the depth of feeling that would be needed. It would take a deep rage in someone to carry out these murders as a form of revenge and I don't think Fairburn has it in him.'

He turned slowly on to the main road. 'But we'll check his alibi.'

'Well, if not him, who else?' Rhiannon said, settling back and folding her arms.

Simon's phone bleeped and he handed it to Rhiannon.

She put it to her ear. 'It's Sergeant Longman for you, sir.' Simon pulled over to the side of Chairford's wide high street and switched off the engine.

'We've found Vita's phone,' Longman said. 'It was in the oven in the kitchen. Very amusing. With all the worry about what people were eating and with her having meals at the house, it wasn't likely she'd be looking in there.'

'Had she mentioned to anyone that she had mislaid her phone?' Simon asked. 'After what happened in the case of Liam and Ben we warned people that if their phone disappeared they should take extra care.'

'I contacted Lewis Enright to ask if Vita had said anything at breakfast about it. He said she hadn't.'

'I suspect that the killer would have left it to the last minute this time before taking the phone,' Simon said, 'precisely because he or she wouldn't want to sound any alarm bells.'

'Very likely,' Longman agreed. 'Anyway, I'll get on and do the usual checks on the phone, shall I? Find out if there's anything interesting there?'

'Go ahead,' Simon said and switched off. Jessie's last words on the evening of their talk together came back to him. What was it she thought he had missed where the phones were concerned? He stared through the windscreen unseeing, Rhiannon silent at his side.

He thought about all that he knew with regard to the phones: what calls had been made, where the phones had been found, and started over again, going in circles. Then something clicked. It was something he should have questioned. Because, if things were not as they had accepted they were, if what they believed to be so were not so, then it changed everything. The phones had been stolen to stop the victims from calling for help; he was still sure enough that that must have been a motive for their removal.

But what if they had been stolen for this other reason too? And, if they had, how could he prove it?

It was the timing. He cast his mind back. So many things had gone on, so many overlapping and running into one another.

Obviously there had been no investigation prior to Liam's death, but what about the day before Ben died? He cast his mind back. 'Rhiannon. You were saying something when we pulled up at The Forge. Something about Ben.'

She stirred beside him. 'I was saying how worried he was about Vita when she disappeared,'

'He helped you search for her.'

'Yes, he came with me straight away. We looked in all the outbuildings. He said he knew all the places that we might not know about.' She was looking at him expectantly.

'But he didn't think of the oaktree,' Simon said, starting the car. This was it. There could surely only be one answer now to who the killer was. All because arrogance had overreached itself and a mistake had been made.

How had they missed it, though? Why had Rhiannon not noticed the discrepancy? He thought back to the meeting following Longman's receipt of the information from the phone company, the one Detective Superintendent Munro had attended. He realized that he had reported on the interviews subsequent to the reciept of that information, rather than the details themselves. It was all in his reports, though. Rhiannon had just not read them, or, if she had, she had not made the connection. Or had he failed to read hers?

'Rhiannon, remind me to advise everyone in future to read all reports made by others in the team.'

She gave him a worried look. 'Yes, sir.'

But he still needed the motive. Where was the link? He thought afterwards that it was fortuitous that his interview with Alan Fairburn, and his suspicions of him had been so recently in his mind. An answer to the question of motive arose as a direct result of these. He was still wondering 'what if?' when he arrived at Clifford's Place.

Longman was alone in the old games room, speaking on the telephone. Simon sat down at one of the tables, pulled a sheet of paper towards him and picked up a pen. Then he rang Alan Fairburn.

'Mr Fairburn, were you actually in England when the baby died, yours and Helen's?'

'Was it a boy or a girl?'

'And what year was this?'

'And you say you didn't come back, is that right?'

'What was the address you and Helen lived at?'

'What was Helen's maiden name?' Simon asked finally.

'Richmond. Thank you. Yes I'll explain later. I'll be in touch.' He finished writing then grabbed another piece of paper and wrote out some instructions. He passed them to Rhiannon who had been standing close by, a look of intense concentration on her face. As she read what he had written her face cleared slowly.

'My God,' she said, and reached for the phone.

Longman finished his own call at that moment. 'They'll fax the information about Vita's mobile as soon as possible.'

'I imagine there'll be little of interest, except a possible call to the Taylors,' Simon said.

'What's been happening? You're not back on the Taylors again, are you?' Longman's bushy eyebrows twitched.

Simon couldn't suppress a smile of triumph.

'Far from it,' he said. 'Come and buy me a pint while Rhiannon does her stuff and I'll tell you what it's all about.' He didn't have the final proof yet, but this time he knew it in his bones.

278

CHAPTER 33

Coltsfoot – Justice shall be done

She was weeding in one of the large herbaceous borders when they went to arrest her. He looked at her bent head before she glanced up, aware of their presence, and noticed again the light roots of her cropped dark hair. Had the change of colour been an attempt to shield herself from possible identification with Helen, or a rejection of her natural genes, he wondered. Perhaps something of both.

As Longman began to speak the formal opening lines of the arrest Simon studied her expression. The first flash of shock quickly changed to cold defiance. But she made no protest of innocence. She said nothing at all as they led her away, the small child that Helen Hartley had given into care so many years ago.

She continued to keep an inimical silence, her solicitor at her side, for almost two hours, during which time Simon explained to her that they could prove that only she could have used Ben's phone to make the calls on the afternoon before his death. That only she could have subsequently hidden it, switched on so that they would locate it and be led to question the Taylors. That they knew that Ben had neither visited her that day, nor phoned her.

'And we know your identity,' he told her. They had finally managed to extract the information from the adoption authorities. Juliet Richmond, as Mara had been then, had not died in the home as her mother had told her father while he was still in America, she had been adopted by a childless couple.

'Did your new parents have sons after they adopted you?' he asked her. 'Or was that all part of the fiction, like you being a year or so older than you actually are?'

She looked at him with scorn.

The silences were long.

He decided finally to try to provoke her.

'How could you do such terrible things to your own siblings, your own mother?' he asked, putting disgust into his voice.

'Mother!' she spat. 'Does a mother abandon a child? That's not what a mother does.'

'Mothers are human beings, with their own problems,' he said. 'There are good reasons why these things happen.'

'Oh, you think so, do you? You think giving away your child to be abused sexually and physically can be excused!'

Shocked, he said quietly, 'Is that what happened?'

'That's what happened to me. And all because my precious biological mother had better things to do with her life than to care for her child. Me!' Mara caught her breath and gulped. 'She even lied to my father about it. She told my own father that I was dead!'

And she had, in a manner of speaking, died, the child that Helen had left behind.

'How did you find out?'

She looked very small and defenceless, despite the fury of her words. Simon's virtuous taste of triumph had turned to ashes in his mouth.

'I heard them, the first day Alan came to see Helen, when she was filming one of her so successful television series. I was working outside the room they were in. They called me "it". They never once used my name.' Her eyes filled and she bit her lip, but they were tears of rage, not self-pity.

'She'd let him believe, all these years, that I was dead. But if he'd been half a father he would have come back for my supposed funeral, wouldn't he? He was as selfish as she was.'

Simon wanted to say that Helen had been ill, that Mara's parents had had no money, that Mara, or Juliet, had been too ill for a woman who was herself sick to cope with. But he said nothing of this. There would be time for Mara to find her peace, somehow, in the coming years.

'Tell me what happened to you,' he said. At least he could allow her some verbal expression of a rage that must have been growing since she was quite a young child.

The story she told was one of depravity, enough to make even an experienced police officer wince.

'I can't remember when it began,' she ended. 'But when I was twelve I ran away.' Her eyes flashed. 'I thought it was my fault! Can you believe that? I thought it must be something in me that made it happen to me.' She pressed her hands to her pinched face. 'I got picked up by the police and put in a children's home. It was bad, but not as bad as where I'd come from. I was covered in bruises. There was plenty of evidence of the things they'd done to me. The people who had adopted me were prosecuted. They went to jail. By the time they came out I had changed my name. Ironically I had started training in gardening.' She gave a bitter smile. 'I like to think that had more to do with the sanity and peace of it than any genetic tendency.'

'Wasn't any of your anger aimed at the two who had harmed you so much?'

'They fell under a train at Oxford Circus,' she said.

Simon closed his eyes.

'Then I set about finding out who my real parents were. And the gardening experience came in useful.'

Her solicitor, a young woman in a blue business-suit, touched Mara's arm and leaned to speak quietly in her ear. Mara shrugged her off.

'So I came to Clifford's Place, just after my spoilt brat of a half-brother Liam had managed to get rid of my predecessor.' She leaned forward across the table. 'I wanted to find out all I could about my bitch of a mother. I had always hated her for allowing what had happened to me. And when I came here and saw what a perfect life she had with her spoilt children who were given everything, children she adored so much, I hated her to the bottom of my being.' She leaned back and smiled narrowly at Simon. 'How I hated them all.'

How well she must have concealed it. He remembered the first time he had seen her, with Liam and Ben at Westwich station. Perhaps she had inherited her mother's acting skills as well as her horticultural ones.

'You've been at Clifford's Place for well over a year,' Simon said. 'Did you always intend to do what you have done? Why wait until now?'

'I wasn't sure exactly what I was going to do,' she admitted matter-of-factly. 'Part of the pleasure was biding my time, thinking of ways and means to make my mother suffer for what she had done to me. It gives you a wonderful feeling of power to look at people and know they are at your mercy.' She smiled another catlike smile.

'It was hearing what Alan Fairburn said that made me decide not to waste any more time. I thought I'd known what rage felt like before. But when I heard what they were saying . . .' She paused. 'I wouldn't have thought I could be hurt any more. But I was. It happened that I was going away that weekend. I needed to get a break from them all now and again.'

She stopped speaking again. 'Of course. That was when we first met, Chief Inspector, wasn't it? At the railway station when I was being seen off by Liam and Ben. Liam and all his posturings!' she scoffed. 'The way he flirted with me, thinking every female must fall at his feet. If only he'd known.'

Her solicitor again spoke, more sharply this time, and again Mara pushed her away, saying:

'Don't worry. This is a clear case of diminished responsibility, wouldn't you say?'

The solicitor sank back, a look of despair on her face.

She seemed to have been relatively indifferent to her father's complicity on the whole, variously referring to him as her father and by his name. Though, given the chance, Alan Fairburn might himself have died of some poisonous cocktail.

'But it was Helen you were really trying to hurt, wasn't it?' Simon said.

'The others were just icing on the cake, and incidental to the main purpose,' she agreed. 'Pity Vita survived. I had hoped my dear mother would have cracked up completely by now. Has she?' she enquired brightly.

'The flowers were a nice touch,' Simon said, mirroring her manner.

'You mean the fact that I poisoned them, in a manner of speaking, with her beloved garden, do you mean? Used one great love of hers to kill the other things she loved? Or the little floral displays I left so that there wouldn't be any doubt that they were all killed deliberately?'

'That wasn't really necessary after Liam's death,' Simon said. 'But I suppose it helped make it all more horrific for Helen.'

'Yes. And poison was so appropriate. My own life was poisoned, you see.' She stared at him coldly.

They took a break there. Simon's own stomach had taken as much as it could for the time being.

The rest would be mostly the tedious routine of going over the same ground to get down a clear statement. When they met again after the break he asked her why she had pointed suspicion at the Taylors.

'You had to suspect someone,' Mara said reasonably. 'The Taylors did have a motive for wanting Liam out of the way. He was itching to get rid of them. And I didn't like Mrs Taylor. She had rather a sharp tongue.'

'Hard on Gavin, though,' he said.

She smiled with her lips only. 'A good way of upsetting Jenny, I thought. He wouldn't be much use to a pregnant woman if he was in custody.'

The Taylors had come close to being taken in for questioning, if not arrest. Perhaps, he thought wryly, if Longman hadn't been so keen on the idea as to arouse his own perverse objections, it would have happened.

'What had Jenny done to you, that you should want to hurt her?'

'She was patronizing. She was always implying that I was suffering from jealousy of her and Liam. It annoyed me that I couldn't tell her just how wrong she was.' Mara folded her arms. 'Well, she'll know now, won't she?' she said with satisfaction. 'But more importantly, does Helen Hartley know that it was her little reject who caused all this mayhem?'

Simon studied Mara's face, seeking for any resemblance to the mother who had borne her. The facial proportions and shape were not dissimilar, but the mouth was tight, smaller than Helen's, whose mouth had generous curves. Perhaps experience had shaped a face even so young as Mara's. Her eyes were, like her father's, green, and large in her small face. There was little else that would have identified her to her real parents.

'No,' he replied briefly before getting up to leave. Helen must be allowed as much time as possible to grow stronger before she learned the inevitable truth about this lost child of hers.

He himself could acknowledge the full horror of what had happened to Mara in her childhood but he had no stomach for its consequences. He had had enough for today.

He had made sure that Longman and Rhiannon were present at the interview. Apart from the occasional sudden intake of breath, they had been silent. They remained so, allowing him to leave for the night with no more than a few words.

He had of course already spoken to Detective Superintendent Munro. He told her how Jessie had helped bring the case to its conclusion but she had, as always, been generous in her praise. Honest too:

'I'm afraid I led you astray with my insistence on looking for a more traditional motive, Chris,' she had said, offering him a small brandy in her office.

He had sunk gratefully into one of her comfortable chairs and opened one eye at her.

'If you hadn't, it's quite possible that Vita Hartley would not be alive.'

'God moves in mysterious ways,' she said solemnly.

'She does,' he agreed.

When he got home it was obvious he was exhausted. Jessie and his mother allowed him to eat his meal and go to bed after only a brief account to them of the conclusion of the investigation.

Jessie had had at least one helpful thing to say.

'Research has shown that sexual abuse in childhood can cause significant brain damage. This can affect areas of the brain where it can give rise to violent outbursts and uncontrolled rage.'

It might offer some hope of a useful defence for Mara when she came to trial, but as Longman had remarked, the nature of the killings was too premeditated to offer much room for manoevre. For the moment however, Mara's plan to plead not guilty – on the grounds of diminished responsibiity – might work, given the nature of her history. She could even retract much of what she had already said to him.

But after all of it, after all her extreme efforts, Mara's rage and bitterness were not assuaged.

For now, while Helen was shut away with Vita in the hospital, she was protected from the knowledge of what her first daughter had done. Simon had taken Barbara aside and told her about the conclusion of the investigation. And he had been unable to do that without an account of Helen's history.

Barbara had been silent for some moments before she said: 'I suppose it explains the guilt that Helen keeps expressing. I think she believed on some level that it was all a punishment.' She closed her eyes. 'How is she ever going to bear knowing that it's real. That it was a child of her own that did all this?' She took his arm and walked him further along the hospital corridor. 'Tell me how you found out it was Mara.'

When he had finished his account Barbara said quietly: 'Poor child. And poor Helen.' She looked bright-eyed at Simon. 'We're told to let go of our past, leave it behind, not dwell on it. But sometimes our past won't let go of us.'

A significant portion of Simon's past was taking its leave the day after the arrest. His mother, now that she knew the full story, had not had the heart to continue with Jessie's garden.

'I've been here longer than I intended, anyway, and the weather is not amenable.' Brief sunshine had again been superseded by steady rain. 'We've broken the back of it anyway, my dear,' she said to Jessie.

She insisted on taking in some very expensive flowers for Helen and Vita at the hospital. Helen seemed genuinely pleased to see Elizabeth and even went with her for a quick cup of tea in the cafeteria.

'Poor soul,' Elizabeth said afterwards. 'She is trying so hard to keep going for Vita's sake. The shock of finding out about Mara may prove too much after all that has happened.'

She examined Simon's and Jessie's faces as they stood waiting for her in the hospital entrance hall.

'You know my opinion on the irresponsibility of sexual relationships outside of marriage, and all the sorrow that can come from it. I never imagined such consequences could be as bad as this.'

'I don't think it would have made any difference if Helen had been married to Alan Fairburn, do you?' Simon asked mildly. 'The children of marriages sometimes get taken into care as well.'

'If they had been married,' Elizabeth said emphatically, 'the responsibility of a possible child would have been one they would have discussed and taken steps to cater for. Then, maybe, none of this would have happened.'

Simon and Jessie glanced at each other and didn't attempt to argue.